When I Was Invisible

Please note: This book contains a storyline
that some may find triggering.

Sounds like Dorothy Koomson . . .

Dorothy Koomson is the author of eleven novels including *That Girl From Nowhere*, *The Chocolate Run*, *The Woman He Loved Before* and *The Flavours of Love*. She's been making up stories since she was thirteen when she used to share her stories with her convent school friends.

Dorothy's first novel, *The Cupid Effect*, was published in 2003 (when she was quite a bit older than thirteen). Her third book, *My Best Friend's Girl*, was selected for the Richard & Judy Summer Reads of 2006, and her novels *The Ice Cream Girls* and *The Rose Petal Beach* were both shortlisted for the popular-fiction category of the British Book Awards in 2010 and 2013, respectively.

Dorothy's novels have been translated into over 30 languages, and a TV adaptation loosely based on *The Ice Cream Girls* was first shown on ITV1 in 2013. After briefly living in Australia, Dorothy now lives in Brighton. Well, Hove, actually.

While writing *When I Was Invisible*, Dorothy rediscovered her love for music – especially 80s tunes – and has been asking everyone she sees nowadays, 'What's the one song you're embarrassed about loving?' So, what's yours?

For more information on Dorothy Koomson and her novels, including When I Was Invisible *(and to answer that burning question), visit www.dorothykoomson.co.uk*

When I Was Invisible

Dorothy KOOMSON

CENTURY

1 3 5 7 9 10 8 6 4 2

Century
20 Vauxhall Bridge Road
London SW1V 2SA

Century is part of the Penguin Random House group of companies
whose addresses can be found at global.penguinrandomhouse.com

First published in Great Britain by Century in 2016

www.randomhouse.co.uk

A CIP catalogue record for this book is
available from the British Library.

ISBN 9781780893365 (Hardback)
ISBN 9781780893372 (Trade paperback)

Typeset in India by Thomson Digital Pvt Ltd, Noida, Delhi
Printed and bound in Great Britain by Clays Ltd, St Ives plc

Penguin Random House is committed to a sustainable future for
our business, our readers and our planet. This book is made from
Forest Stewardship Council® certified paper.

For
everyone who has helped me to create a place called 'home'.

Thank you

to my gorgeous family and friends;
to Ant and James, my amazing agents;
to all the brilliant people at my publishers, Cornerstone (especially
Susan, Jenny G, Jen D, Emma, Kate, Charlotte, Rose, Rebecca &
Aslan);
to Emma D, Hayley and Sophie, my fabulous publicists.

A special thank you goes to those who were kind enough to help me
with my research for this book.

And to M, E & G thank you for always being who you are. I love
you.

As always, I would also like to say thank you to you, the reader, for
buying this book.

Prologue

'Class, we have a new girl joining us today.' Everyone was sitting in rows, at their wooden desks, in their blue school uniforms. They were probably looking at me, but I was looking at my teacher. She had one ear bigger than the other (I wondered if she knew that) and her hair was so long it reached her chest. 'Class, meet Veronica Harper.'

Lots of the children gasped, others said 'Wow' really loudly. I looked at the other children then. Why was my name so strange to them that they were behaving like that? Some of them were turning round in their seats to look at a girl who was staring right at me with her eyes really wide.

'That's right,' my new teacher said, 'this is the second Veronica Harper we have in this class. Except they are spelt differently. Our Veronika Harper has a k instead of a c, new Veronica Harper has a c instead of a k. Isn't that fascinating? Two names that sound exactly the same but are spelt differently and two girls who are both eight years old, called the same thing but who look very different.'

I grinned at Veronika Harper with a k. I thought she was the prettiest girl I had ever seen.

'Fascinating as this is, though, it's going to become very confusing very quickly,' my new teacher said. 'Do they call you anything else, Veronica with a c?'

I nodded. 'They call me Roni,' I said very quietly.

'Brilliant. They call Veronika with a k Nika, so that's settled. Now, if you'd like to take your seat next to Nika, we can begin the class.' My legs were wobbly as I walked towards the other Veronica Harper and everyone stared at me. 'Nika, I take it you won't mind showing our new pupil around?' the teacher said. Nika didn't even have a chance to say anything or nod and the teacher said: 'Good, good.' She stood up and went to the blackboard.

'Nice to meet you, Veronica Harper,' Nika whispered when I sat down at the free desk next to her.

'Nice to meet you, too, Veronika Harper,' I whispered back.

'Veronika and Veronica!' the teacher snapped without turning away from the blackboard. It was like she had super-hearing or something. 'I hope you're not talking. I don't want to have to separate you both on Roni's first day.'

'No, Miss,' Nika said.

'No, Miss,' I said.

It wasn't possible, anyway. It wasn't possible to separate us now because we were going to be the very best of friends.

1

Nika

I've been here for hours.

It's probably not been *that* long, but it feels like it. It seems like I've been sitting on this uncomfortable plastic bench with my head on my knees, my arms curled around myself, the sounds of this police station going on around me for long enough for me to feel like my life is draining away. People come and go, the officers behind the bulletproof glass of the reception desk have conversations that are a touch too far out of range for me to understand or hook myself into. Every time the door opens I am treated to a blast of the noise of the outside world, and it, like everything else, is a reminder that I probably shouldn't do this.

If I have to wait to speak to someone, then maybe it's a sign that this is not meant to be. Maybe I need to unfurl myself, stand up, walk out of here. Slip back into the world outside and disappear again – become as faceless and invisible as everyone else out there.

Maybe, because I have to wait – and the second thoughts I didn't have before I walked in here are now arriving, settling in my mind like roosting pigeons on a roof – I should admit to the absolute stupidity of this. Maybe I should be more brutally realistic with myself about what the repercussions will be, how doing this will touch the lives of everyone I know. Maybe I should stop thinking of justice

3

and start thinking of real life and what honestly happens to people like me.

A voice calls out my name.

Too late to run now, too late to change your mind, I think. Slowly, I raise my head, lower my legs, place my feet on the floor, my gaze seeking out the person who called my name.

I stumble a little when I am upright, but catch myself before I fall, curl my fingers into the palms of my hands, trying to hide the trembling. *No escape, no retreat. I have to go through with this now.*

'How can I help you?' the police officer asks. Plain clothes, some kind of detective, as I requested. He comes closer to me, but not too close. He doesn't want to get too close to someone like me. Despite his slightly bored, uninterested expression, when he continues to speak, he sounds neutral and polite: 'The desk officer said you wanted to talk to a detective, but you were reluctant to say exactly what it was about?'

I take a step closer, try to narrow the distance between us, so I can speak without being overheard. There is no one here now except the person behind the desk, but I still want to be careful. Quiet. *I can't do this,* I realise. *I need to, but I can't. I can't open my mouth and say another word.*

The detective's face quickly slides from 'slightly bored' and 'uninterested' into 'perturbed', teetering on the edge of 'annoyed'. I am wasting his time and he does not like that.

I take a deep breath, inhale to see if I can shake off the second thoughts and recapture the certainty that brought me here. 'I . . . I . . .' My voice fails. *I really can't do this.*

Unbidden, the sound, the one I first heard less than a week ago, streaks through my head, as sudden and loud and clear as the first time I heard it. It ignites every memory cell in my body with horror and I almost slam my hands over my ears again, try to shut it out.

Determined now, I firm up my fists, I strengthen the way I stand and I look the detective straight in the eye as I say: 'I . . . I need to report an attempted murder.'

Nika

'Sorry to keep you waiting,' the police officer, DS Brennan, says.

I lift my head from the table. I must have dozed off. Everything was so quiet and still, almost peaceful, while I sat in the interview room and waited for him to come back, that I had closed my eyes for just a few seconds, determined simply to rest my tired, red eyes. The eye rest must have segued into a nap. Or – I stretch my back, feel the taste at the back of my throat, the heaviness of my eyes and limbs – into a sleep.

I blink heavily a few times, moisten my lips and stare at him, concentrate on what he's about to say to me.

Before he left the room, I'd talked and talked at him, answered his very few questions, and then spoke some more. With every word I felt lighter, freer. I was reliving it all, sure, but it was liberating, too. When he left to 'go and check on a few things', I'd been able to unclench then. My body had almost melted into my seat.

When the police officer sits down opposite me, I notice that he's different. He left here almost sympathetic, slightly buoyed that I was willing to talk about someone they've obviously had their eyes on for many, many years. Now, it is as if he has gone out of the room and changed his attitude. He is holding himself a little more reservedly, his cerulean eyes are a little colder, his expression a little more stern. He hadn't exactly been overfriendly before – why would he be? I'm

5

not your average witness – but I could see him softening as I spoke to him. As I explained what had happened, what I had seen, why I'd made the decision to come here, *who* I was actually grassing up, he'd seemed slightly warmer. Now that's all gone, replaced by the cold barrier of someone who doesn't like to be lied to. 'Who are you?' he asks. Direct, to the point. 'I mean, who are you really? Because you are not Grace Carter.'

I sit back in my seat, stare at the table that separates us as he continues to talk.

'I went to verify your story and everything is as you say, every single detail, apart from your name and who you are. In fact, none of that checks out. I made some other calls and yes, people do know you as Grace Carter, or simply "Ace", but I can't find a birth certificate that matches your age, your fingerprints aren't in the system and there's nothing on any of our computer systems with a person of your description linked to the name Grace Carter. You are, what, thirty-five, thirty-six? And yet there isn't a single credit card, bank account or financial record in your name. I'll bet if I asked you to empty your pockets I would maybe find cash, but not one thing with your name on. I'd go as far as to say that you don't actually exist. Except you obviously do and you're a witness to a very serious crime committed by a very dangerous man.' He leans his elbows on the table, closes his hands together as if in desperate prayer and then leans his chin on his clasped hands. After a few seconds of silence, he says: 'So, who are you? Really?'

My name is Grace Carter. It has been for more than ten years. I do not have a bank account; I do not have a credit card, a library card or passport in my name. I avoid anything that means I have to use identification and when I can get work, it is often cash in hand. Or it's paid into a friend's bank account and they draw it out to give to me. My name *is* Grace Carter. I used to be called something else, I used to share my name with another girl who was once my best friend at school and in ballet class, but not any more. She's not my friend any more, and that name is no longer mine.

I *am* Grace Carter.

And I should not have come into this place and told the truth. Telling the truth, doing the right thing, has never worked for me. Not ever. And now it is going to go wrong again. But that sound, that inhuman sound made by someone I desperately love... I couldn't let that go.

Time crawls by and I accept that the detective is going to wait it out. He, after all, has all the time in the world. I don't. I can barely keep my eyes open, let alone sit here and wait for him to speak again. 'Does my name and who I may or may not be have any bearing on what I told you?' I eventually ask. I need to open a dialogue and see where it leads us.

'Not to me, no,' he says. 'Like I said, everything you say you witnessed has checked out so far, and because of who this is we're talking about, I have to hand all of this over to my colleagues in organised crime. After this, you probably won't see me again.'

I sit up straighter in my seat, force my eyes not to widen and reflect the momentary panic him telling me that has sent spiralling through me. He is easy to talk to – not nice or anything silly like that, but easy to communicate with.

What do I do next? Do I get up and run for it? Do I just get up and walk out of here? He hasn't arrested me or suggested he's going to arrest me. I haven't done anything he knows about, so I am a free woman who can come and go as she pleases.

Or do I tell him everything? Explain about my name, about who I am, who I was, why I had to leave my former name, Veronika Harper, behind and become Grace Carter instead? I swallow a laugh at *that* idea. Tell the truth? All of it? Where would I even start? Where would I stop?

Leaving without another word is probably my safest option here.

He suddenly speaks again, when I thought he was going to leave me spinning in silence. 'My colleagues, to speak out of turn for a moment or two, will be very pleased that you are not who you say you are. To them, it will probably mean that you know far, far

7

more than you originally meant to tell them. If that's the case, when they find out who you are – and they *will* find out who you really are – they will use that knowledge to compel you to appear as a witness.'

'Are you trying to scare me?' I ask him. This is how I ended up here, after all: someone using fear to make sure I always do what they want.

DS Brennan unclenches his hands from the tight, giant fist they have formed under his chin and sits back. A modicum of shame plays in his eyes. 'No, no,' he says, shaking his head. 'Honest is what I'm being with you.' *Now I want honesty from you*, he adds without actually saying the words.

I nod, my gaze fixed on the table.

'You must have been very frightened once upon a time to have changed your name, to have so completely removed yourself from society,' he states. 'What happened? And can we help you with it?'

I continue to stare at the table and at my music player that I took out of my pocket before I went to sleep. I had meant to put some music on while I waited but I didn't get any further than taking it out of my pocket. I stare at it, its thin black noodle-like earphone wires wrapped around its body, its earbuds like full stops that begin and end the existence of the player. When I was eleven I had a fantasy. When I was twelve I had the same fantasy. When I was thirteen the fantasy continued. When I was fourteen and fifteen the fantasy became more desperate, necessary. When I was sixteen and a half it wasn't necessary any more but I still had it. The fantasy. *My* fantasy. It pirouettes now through my head: 'rescue'. That is the word I have always used to describe those fantasies. *My Rescue Fantasies*. Someone would swoop in, rescue me. Everything bad from all of before would be swept away by those big powerful wings and I would be lifted up, cradled, loved better. In every fantasy I am rescued and I am safe. Slowly I raise my line of sight to the policeman opposite me.

He's only a little older than me in physical, countable years, but maybe he is older on the inside. He must have seen so much, doing this job; he has probably seen every crime it is possible to commit. He has probably had every excuse for that crime thrown at him at some point in his working life. Nothing I say will shock or upset him. He may be The One. He may be the rescuer I have longed for all of these years. He may listen, hear it all, and then he may tell me those three words I long to hear and confirm that he is The One, he *can* save me. He will make sure everything is going to be all right.

I focus on the table, my music player again. 'My name is Grace Carter,' I say. 'And I am here to report an attempted murder. I will speak to whoever I need to, but that is who I am and what I am here to do.' Rescues never happen to people like me. You can, after all, only rescue the people you can see are in trouble. And, if you're like me, and you are invisible to everyone, especially the people who might carry out the rescue, then you have no chance at all, have you?

DS Brennan's shoulders fall, his mouth lets out a small sigh of disappointment and frustration as he shakes his head. Carefully he stands. 'Have it your way,' he says. 'My aforementioned colleagues will be here soon to talk to you.' At the door he stops and turns back to me. 'Good luck, Grace Carter, whoever you really are.'

I dip my head further. I can't let him see the tears that have sprung to my eyes, I can't give away that a treacle-like emotion has coated my throat. No rescues today, but kindness, concern. They are so very alien to me.

London, 1999

I stood by the bins, hidden as much as I could be from the back of the theatre, slowly enjoying my last ever cigarette. It'd been a short but meaningful relationship with those tiny white devils, I'd enjoyed every moment of every one, but I'd promised myself the opening night of my first professional play where I was a stagehand, I would stop. I would have one last cigarette and never go there again. I was good at keeping promises to myself.

'Ah, a fellow deviant and pariah,' a smooth voice said.

9

My heart, my heart. It was as if someone had squeezed it, stopped it from beating, and instantly my body was on edge, on guard, ready for trouble. I didn't look at his face straight away, I wanted to get the measure of him first, to see what I would be dealing with. I kept my head lowered and checked him over from the corner of my eye.

Tall, handsome, fit. Expensively dressed, polished. He reminded me of someone, a celebrity; he was a looky-likey who probably dined out on the similarity even if, like me, most people couldn't quite place him. He wasn't overtly threatening, I didn't feel as if I was in imminent danger, but danger comes in all sorts of shapes and sizes, and I knew that. So, I turned towards him but I didn't drop my guard, and I reassured myself that in five quick steps I'd be back at the stage door, which I'd wedged slightly open when I came out here.

His smile was smooth and easy when I looked at him. 'Are you in this play, because I didn't see you?' He moved his hands when he spoke, an unlit cigarette was clamped between the forefinger and middle finger of his left hand. 'I certainly would have noticed you, if you were.'

I didn't know what to say to that so smiled at him. I'd 'run away' from home two years ago, when I was seventeen, and no one had said anything that nice to me in that time. I'd been felt up on public transport, I'd been propositioned with vile terms and words, I often had to sleep with a chair propped under the handle of my bedroom door because one of my housemates liked to 'sleepwalk' into the women's rooms at night, but no one had ever said anything as nice as that to me.

'I'm sorry, does that sound a bit creepy?' he asked. 'I imagine you hear things like that all the time.'

'No, I don't hear things like that ever, actually. I'm one of the stagehands and I shouldn't be out here – I should be in there running around with everyone else – but I wanted to have a quick cigarette.'

'Really?' he asked, astonished. The more I looked at him, the more he reminded me of that celeb I couldn't quite remember. His name was on the tip of my tongue, what he was famous for was teetering on the edge of my memory, but neither of those things would fall into place, let me recognise him properly.

'I'm really surprised by that. You deserve to be told that every day for the rest of your life. You're very, very noticeable.'

I smiled a little wider, then caught myself. I knew nothing about him and he could be saying all that to get me to relax my guard. Even the nicest guys could be dangerous. 'Thanks,' I mumbled. I stared at my cigarette for a moment: it was two-thirds gone, but I had to stop now. Get back inside, go back to my job that it'd been so dream-fulfilling to land.

'I also like that you're a secret smoker, too,' he said, raising his cigarette. 'Every day I promise myself no more, but every day I seem to find a reason to break that promise.' Another grin, this time conspiratorial, trying to bring me into his world. 'My manager and coach would kill me if they knew.'

'I see,' I said.

'Don't say much, do you,' he stated.

'No, not really,' I said.

'I'm Todd,' he said. He held out his hand for me to shake.

I hesitated. What exactly would I be doing if I took his hand? Would I be promising myself that I would stay out here, just a little bit too long, become a little too involved with this man instead of simply going inside and going back to work? Would I be telling myself that maybe I was ready for this, and I could maybe be someone other than Veronika the runaway whose sister forwarded her mail but who no one in her family spoke to even now, two years later?

'I'm Nika,' I said.

'Nika, like Nikky or Nicola?' he asked.

'No, short for Veronika, actually. Veronika with a k.'

'I think Nikky suits you better.' He smiled at me, so sweetly I thought I would burn up with embarrassment. 'I'm only going to call you Nikky from now on. That's if you let me see you again?'

'You want to see me again?' I asked. I probably had a frown on my face. '*Why?*' I wasn't exactly dressed up, I had *no* make-up on – why the hell would he be interested in me after a few minutes of conversation?

He laughed. 'Why do you think? I'd like to take you out. Like on a date?'

'Oh,' I said.

From his jacket inside pocket he produced a small white card. 'This is my agent's number. Call him, tell him who you are and he'll pass on the message.'

I took the card without looking at it.

'Go on, Nikky, take a chance and call me,' he said.

After the last few years, after everything, maybe I was due. Maybe this man was going to help me change my life. Make me be the Nika I was meant to be. He had noticed me, after all. After years and years of being unseen by most people, this nice-looking man had seen me and *liked* me. I smiled. 'OK, I'll call you.'

Roni

London, 1988

In our little town, on the south-east side of London, a new dance school opened. They were offering a free session to all local children and teen-agers who were interested in dance and Mum didn't need much persuading to let me go. I had got there late because Mum was taking her time as always and in the end Dad had got really cross and said, 'Come on, Veronica, I'll take you,' and we'd had to run to the car and I had to almost run into this large room with mirrors around every wall, a long wooden barre running around the middle of the mirrored walls.

There were lots and lots of other children sitting in there but the beautiful teacher was talking so I couldn't look around to see if there was anyone I knew. I sat down and listened to her. And after I listened to her speak, I knew I was going to be a dancer.

I was eight years old and I was going to be a dancer. Not any type of dancer: a ballet dancer.

I wanted to be like the pretty lady in front of me. I loved her leotard and her floaty skirt, her tights and her shoes. Her shoes were the loveliest things I had *ever* seen. She was wearing black, but her shoes were as pink as candyfloss with shiny ribbons that tied up around her ankles and nearly up to her knees. She said they were *pointe* shoes and that you only ever wear them for exams or for dancing in shows. She had them on today to show us what we could wear if we decided to become ballet dancers, too.

I was going to be a dancer. I wanted to look like her, so I was going to grow my hair long and wind it up on top of my head into a bun, and I wanted to be able to do what she had shown us she could do. A few minutes ago, she'd stood on the toes of both feet, and then she'd stood on the toes of one foot – *en pointe*, she'd called it. *Then* she'd spun until she was a blur, her leg going up and up and up. She was amazing. *Amazing.* I wanted to be like that. I was going to be like that.

'Some of you are going to make it as ballet dancers,' she said, smiling at all of us sitting in front of her. We could see ourselves in the mirror wall behind her, we could see what she saw. 'Some of you are special, and I – we,' she pointed to the tall man standing by the piano who was holding a long black stick, 'we will be able to bring that out in you, help you to become dancers who will dance on stages across the world, and will appear in films and on television. Others of you won't be able to become professional dancers, and that is OK because we can help you to dance, to nurture and grow a true love of dancing. You might not become a professional dancer, but you will be able to dance much, much better than most people and, most importantly, you will love it.' She smiled at us. Her face was bright and shiny, she looked excited to be here in the room with us, to be talking to us. 'You need to decide now if you want to be a dancer. And when you've decided, don't tell anyone else, don't share your dream, don't dilute your dream by telling anyone else, just decide and let it be your little secret. We'll know, of course, so you don't need to tell us. But it's important to know what it is you want. And then, we will help you to get it.' She grinned at us again.

I'm going to be a dancer, I thought to myself. *I want nothing else more in this world than to be a dancer.*

I looked around to see if I could see what the others were thinking. If anyone else had made the same decision as me and I'd have someone to do this thing with. I saw *her* then. We both stared at each other at exactly the same time, and she had the exact same expression as me, and she was sitting upright like I was, and I could see the decision to be a dancer made her as happy as it made me. It was the other Veronika – Nika.

We kept on staring at each other. It was like we were made to be best friends. We sat next to each other at school, we had the same name and now we were both going to be ballet dancers. Suddenly she smiled at me and she looked so happy to see me and to know that I was going to be a ballet dancer like her. I smiled right back at her, just as happy as she was.

Nika

Birmingham, 2016

I'm still staring at my music player, working out if I can get my hands to reach out and make contact, when the door opens again. Two new officers enter the room. They have notepads, they have files, they have the exact same look on their faces: 'Don't mess with us.' Anyone would think I was a criminal they'd dragged in to torture information out of, instead of someone who had voluntarily walked in with vital information.

DS Brennan had been trying to warn me, I think, that things were going to get tougher the moment he left the room. He had no idea, of course, what I know about 'tough' and what usually comes with telling the truth.

'Right, "Miss Carter", we've heard much of what you told our colleague, shall we start again from the top?' The officer who hasn't spoken reaches out and presses the record button on his machine. I look at both their faces, slowly moving my gaze from one to the other.

'What do you want to know?' I ask.

London, 1999

'I don't want you to go home,' Todd said. He grabbed me back from opening his front door, and pulled me into his arms.

Todd wasn't a celebrity looky-likey, he *was* a celebrity. Not in the Hollywood megastar sense, but in the being paid a lot of money to play football sense, in the having a wonderful flat that had fancy gadgets and an amazing view over the River Thames sense. And me having to sneak out of his flat in the middle of the night and get a cab home from around the corner so no photographers would connect him and me sense.

I'd been doing that for four months. Sometimes, to throw people off the scent that I might be dating him and not any of the other mega-rich people in the building, he'd go out and I would arrive after the show and let myself in and sit in the dark so people would think he was still out. Then he would come back at least half an hour later, and turn the lights on, and we'd spend time together until I sneaked out in the small hours. We never had got around to going out on a proper date and I didn't really mind.

Todd had transformed my life. He made me fizz with excitement. He told me all the time how much he wanted me, how much he liked being with me; he even gave me a mobile phone so he wouldn't have to leave messages for me at the theatre, at the café I worked at or at my shared house. Now he was saying he didn't want me to leave. The excitement inside fizzed up so much I could hardly breathe. I never thought it'd be possible to feel like this. If he put his arms around me, my flinch would be momentary, my innate panic at having someone so close would last for seconds. Todd was incredible and he thought I was incredible, too.

'What do you mean?' I asked him about him not wanting me to leave. Did he want me to stay all night? I held my breath, waited for him to say one day soon I'd be allowed to stay all night. *All* night.

He unhooked my bag from my shoulder, dropped it on to the ground by the front door. Then slowly tugged my leather jacket – another present from him I'd taken weeks to actually accept, and then a few more weeks to actually wear – off my shoulders. He moved closer to me, smiled before he pressed his lips against mine. 'I mean.' He pressed another kiss against my lips. 'I want.' Kiss. 'You to.' Kiss. 'Stay.' Long kiss. 'For ever.'

For ever? He really wanted me for ever? Not only one night – *for ever.* He, who could have anyone, looked at me and thought about for ever? 'You really mean that?' I asked. That fizzing inside was bubbling up and up. If he meant it, I would be with him any time I wanted. We would be together. We would have so much time together, we'd have a home together. No more sneaking around, no more sharing the bathroom with four other people (Todd's flat had three loos, and two bathrooms) and no more labelling my food in the fridge. Todd and I could recline on the sofa together and watch television. Recline. On. The. Sofa. *Together.* Simply reclining on the sofa would be novel – since I'd stopped smoking, there seemed very little reason to leave my room nowadays. When I did venture into the shared living room, I would sit tensed up, trying to work out from the way conversations were going who had fallen out with who because they'd moved someone's yoghurt in the fridge, or had left hairs in the shower for the third time that week. All of that would be smooshed aside if Todd meant it.

Since I'd met him, since we'd started this thing between us, I hadn't been homesick, not once. I hadn't wanted to go home, fix things with my parents, tell them that I'd do better, I'd appreciate all the sacrifices they'd made for me if they'd just listen to me. *Believe me.* Since Todd, all I did was look forwards. The past was easier to walk away from, not run and run away from. Sometimes, when I was with Todd, I didn't feel like a runaway at all.

'For ages I've been wanting to say that you can keep that key you've got. Murray keeps telling me that I shouldn't rush into this thing with you, especially since you're younger than me and no one in the press knows about you yet, and it's coming up to transfer time soon so I need to keep a low profile off the pitch while at the same time really up my game on the pitch. Murray's thinking I could make it into the Premier League if I box clever and I shouldn't let anything get in the way of that.'

My stomach did a little spin – I thought Murray, Todd's agent, liked me. He'd certainly been really nice to me every time I'd spoken to him on the phone.

'But then, in the next breath, he's telling me not to let you go because since you've been around, happiness has made me play like a demon. No one can touch me when I'm playing and that's cos I'm so happy with you.'

I didn't understand. Was he saying to stay or not? I'd be happy either way, but I didn't know which way it was. I would happily put my 'Recline. On. The. Sofa. *Together*' dreams on hold if it meant I was still with him.

'I don't understand,' I confessed. I needed him to explain, to tell me outright what he wanted.

Todd hooked the tips of his fingers under my chin and raised my face a little to look at him. 'I love you, Nikky Harper. Please move in with me.'

Who's Nikky? I wondered. Then I remembered: me, I was Nikky to Todd. 'Even if Murray doesn't approve?' I asked.

'Murray will approve. Murray always approves of the things that make me happy.' He stared intently into my eyes, and I was lost for a moment in the depth of his, how green they were, how beautiful they were when they were focused on me. 'What do you say? Are you going to stay?' Another sleepy, sexy smile. 'For ever?'

My chest swelled with the huge breath that had filled me. I was so full at that moment. My heart, my head, my everything was full of Todd, full of the man who loved me and who I loved. At one time, my chest had been paralysed, incapable of letting love in or letting love out; at one time, my chest was barely able even to take in or let out air.

Before Todd, my life had seemed flat, one-dimensional; a bland peach that blanked everything out and made it indistinguishable from everything else in the world. In the four months we'd been together everything had changed. I had someone again to share things with, to talk to, who wanted to be with me all the time. When we weren't together he would call me and ask when we'd be together. He told me all the time how much he liked being with me. I'd never had so much attention in all my life. No one had ever taken so much interest in me – ever. I loved it. I loved him. Under the fizziness and excitement, there was the knowledge that my heart belonged to Todd.

'Yes,' I said. 'Yes, I'll stay for ever.' I knew when I said that, that I'd taken a step closer to being part of the wonderful, multi-coloured world we lived in.

Nika

Birmingham, 2016

I stand at the bottom of the stone steps that lead into and out of the police station. There are marked and unmarked police cars parked on either side of the entrance and ahead of me there is a low, concrete wall with a wide gap for the pavement and the road in and out for cars.

From my place at the bottom of the steps, I slowly unwind the wires of my player, carefully push each little bud into their corresponding 'R' and 'L' ears.

It's a silky, black night, the sky is dusted with stars, a late-winter/early-spring coolness teasing the air. When I walked into the police station darkness was rolling in, inking the sky as it moved. I had walked here from the hospital, thinking about what I was about to do with every step, allowing myself the permission to not go in if I had changed my mind by the time I arrived at my destination. I'd needed that walking time to think and had used every step to remind myself what it would mean for my life, where it would lead to for 'Grace Carter'.

I have spent so many hours in that building, talking and answering and listening, then talking again. They offered me coffee, they offered me food, they offered me water and I had turned it all down. The only thing I had done was go to the toilet to take some time out, to centre myself and remind myself how to be Grace. I have talked so much

I have begun to hate the sound of my own voice, to cringe at its intonations and phrasings and crazy, jumbled accent. I have told all that I know and now it's their turn to check things out, to join up dots, to make connections in all the right places. And to find out who I really am, of course. Who came before Grace 'Ace' Carter, as everyone in Birmingham knows me.

With all my concentration, I scrawl through my music player's screen, searching for the right song. It's there, I know it is. My fingers work quickly; my brain works slowly as it mentally plays the songs, waiting for the right chords, for the correct words, for exactly what I need to hear right now. There it is. 'Paris Nights/New York Mornings', Corinne Bailey Rae. My thumb hits the play button, and the intro begins. In my ears she sings about *breakfast at her favourite greasy spoon, wearing her make-up from the night before*; through my brain she croons to me with thoughts of: *dreaming of the night before in Paris, this morning in New York, remembering the fun she'd had.*

Her voice starts to smooth over the raw edges of the last few hours. DS Brennan's 'colleagues' seemed to believe I am Grace Carter. No one asked me about it again, although they must have known she was only born ten or so years ago instead of the thirty-six I am. They were just interested in what I had to say, or so they led me to believe. I'm not stupid. I bet they were allowing me to relax, to talk, hoping I'd give away information about myself while I told them everything I knew.

Nothing is going to happen immediately, which is why I am standing here, with my headphones in, listening to Corinne, allowing myself to believe I could be the woman she is singing about. I could walk down towards Birmingham New Street, to Bernie's, the greasy spoon that stays open all night, sit in there and pretend I'm the woman from the song – that I've just had an amazing night in one city, an excellent day in another, and now I'm kicking back with a coffee and a cigarette.

I'm sure Lou (who runs the place for Bernie) would spot me a cigarette, I've enough money in my pocket for a coffee and I've enough energy left to get me there. I can rest for a few hours before I crawl home.

All the while I've been listening and living out my woman-from-the-song fantasy, I've been watching the policeman from earlier, DS Brennan, stare at me from the driver's seat of his blue Volvo. He is sitting next to someone I assume is another police officer, and they have been studying me since I walked out of the station's doors. Now he lowers the driver's window and mouths at me as he leans his head and torso out.

I don't remove my earbuds right away because I don't want to know what he's saying. I'm enjoying being the woman in the song. I'm enjoying being able to forget everything for these precious seconds.

He continues to speak to me, and I can make out a few of the words from the shapes they form on his lips: '*Drive*'. '*Waiting*'. '*Treat*'. I squint at him. '*Home*'. Did he say 'home'?

Reluctantly I take out my earphones and wait for him to repeat himself. 'Get in, we'll drive you home,' DS Brennan says.

I shake my head. I'm going to come back tomorrow. I've started down this road, there is no way for me to back out now, so it isn't necessary for him to take me home and impress upon me the importance of following through. 'I'm fine,' I say. 'I don't need a lift. I just want to sleep. I will come back tomorrow – I've said I would and I will.'

He opens his car door and climbs out. He then opens his back door. 'We insist,' he says.

'Right,' I say quietly. 'Course you do.'

London, 2000
I arrived home to Todd's flat from one of the technical rehearsals at the theatre up in the West End to low lighting and candles flickering from around various points of the room. The blinds were rolled back and the buildings dotted along the opposite riverbank were twinkling at me. There was the glug of champagne filling and foaming in a glass before he handed it to me. It was a familiar romantic scene, one that Todd liked to set for when I'd been out at work till that bit later, but this time it was different.

The music was different from normal. I recognised it straight away, which ballet it was from. Soft and gentle, it flowed through the room, wrapping itself around the scene he had set like a giant bow. I stood immobile in the doorway. I knew how I should be feeling; I knew I should be grinning, and fizzing inside and longing to slip onto the sofa with him, rest my head on his chest, listen as he told me about his day, about his practice, about what the plans for the team were.

I should have been feeling that but inside I was tangled. Snarled up by dread. This was a scene from one of my recurring nightmares, and not only that, any second now, Todd was going to put himself in my past. He wouldn't mean to, he wouldn't even know he was doing it, but that was what he'd do the moment he touched me. There were needles in my veins, pricking holes in the life I'd built for myself away from Chiselwick, the town where I grew up.

'Do you like it, baby?' Todd asked, handing me the glass of vintage fizz he had poured for me. He'd taught me a lot about life on the finer side in the past year, and now I'd learnt the smell of the expensive stuff. Our fingers brushed as I took my glass and the needles in my veins, under my skin, ignited themselves.

Smile, I told myself. *Smile for the man you love.* 'I love it,' I lied. I tried not to lie, but to protect him, I had to. 'Thank you so much.'

Before I'd even had more than two sips of champagne he was taking it away again, grinning at me in that goofy, playful way he had when I had first met him. His hands were all over me, shedding my coat, removing my T-shirt, unbuttoning my trousers. I let him do it, he preferred it that way. Todd liked to be in complete control at times like this and I didn't know how to tell him I absolutely hated it. That being controlled, especially at times like this, was one of my nightmares. The music seemed to swell, seeping deeper into my skin and fanning the flames of the burning needles.

I can't do this, I thought as he pushed me gently onto the sofa. *I can't do this, to this music, in this way.* 'I hate you working and coming back so late,' Todd said as he slowly took his clothes off. 'I miss you when you're not here.'

24

I tried to focus on him, on being in the moment, on not noticing the music morph into the 'Danse des Petits Cygnes' from *Swan Lake*. I used to love this type of music, it would thrill through me, move my body as though it had been written for me, was floating through every cell in me. Slowly, slowly, this type of music stopped being about freedom, and instead, I began to search for ways to curl up inside the notes and hide.

'I wish you were here all the time, waiting for me,' Todd said as he finally climbed on top of me. 'Instead of the other way around.'

I love him, I love him, I love him, I love him, I love him, I love him, IlovehimIlovehimIlovehimIlovehimIlovehim. The words ran together. A ticker tape of intention and a spur to carry on with this. I'd done this, had sex, like this, so many times over the last year. Even when I didn't particularly enjoy it, didn't particularly want to, I'd done it because the look on his face, the hurt in his eyes when I said no, was far too upsetting. *IlovehimIlovehimIlovehimIlovehimIlovehim.*

The memories the music dragged up fought and foamed, desperate to come out of my throat, spew themselves out into the open. *IlovehimIlovehimIlovehimIlovehim. IlovehimIlovehimIlovehim. Ilovehim-IlovehimIlovehim. IlovehimIlovehimIlovehimIlovehimIlovehim.*

The bouncy, jolly opening of the 'Dance of the Sugar Plum Fairy' from *The Nutcracker* began and I couldn't pretend any more. I couldn't go elsewhere and let my body carry on as I usually did. 'Stop,' I heard myself say. 'Stop, please, stop.'

'Not right now, baby,' Todd murmured with his eyes closed and carried on, pushing himself inside me, starting to move. 'Not right now.'

'Please, stop,' I said again, a little louder.

'Shhh,' Todd hushed, covering my mouth with a kiss. 'Shhhhhh.' He kept moving, taking his time, being gentle, trying hard not to hurt me, but I wanted him to stop. In my ears the music was so loud, so present, it had set fire to my skin, was burning me up from the inside out.

'Todd,' I said loudly, even though my throat felt closed over and closed up. 'Please! I need you to stop. I need you to stop.'

Todd pulled himself up on to his hands, away from me. I'd had my eyes closed and now they were open, staring up at him. His face was full of upset. He used to look like that when I would say I wasn't in the mood, and that look would break my heart. I'd feel so horribly guilty I'd pretend to be in the mood, would go through with it, so his expression would go away.

'I'm sorry, sorry,' he said quickly. 'I didn't realise you were serious. I'm sorry, I'm so sorry.' He climbed off me, sat back and stared at me. 'I love you, I'd never want to hurt you.' I was in his arms, but this time he was holding me, not trying to have sex with me. 'Baby, tell me what the matter is. Tell me and I'll make it all better.'

You can't make it better, I almost whispered. 'I just need to tell you something. Something about me and why I need you to stop when I ask you to,' I confessed instead.

'What is it?' he asked.

I looked into his eyes for a second or two, then had to glance away. I couldn't look at him and tell him. I couldn't see his face as I tore apart the ideas he had about me. With my gaze firmly fixed on the wall of glass opposite, the night cityscape beyond, I told Todd as much as I could.

I couldn't tell him the whole tale, not even half of it could come tumbling out, but some of it. A bit of it. *Enough* of it. Todd listened and listened, and at the end of it, he thanked me for doing him the honour of telling him. He assured me he understood every single word. And he promised he would never ignore my wishes again.

Birmingham, 2016

'You don't need to drop me right at my door,' I say to DS Brennan from the back seat as we get closer to home. I know they have my address, could turn up at any time, but I have to be careful. Yes, I am doing this thing but that doesn't mean being reckless. 'A couple of streets away should be fine... Anywhere from here, actually. I can walk the rest.'

DS Brennan's gaze flicks briefly towards me in the rear-view mirror and then he slows down as though he is about to stop. But doesn't.

He drives on, excruciatingly slowly, this time as though deliberately trying to make sure everyone who is on the streets at this time will see me in the back of a police car. Will start to wonder if I've done something completely stupid and dangerous, especially after what had happened less than a week ago.

I lower my gaze to my lap, wondering why he is determined to get me killed.

London, 2001

'Baby, I just need you to do this one thing for me.'

Pale and shaking, Todd was on his knees in front of me. After a night out like last night (a new nightclub opening), dark, hollowed-out shadows would be scored under Todd's eyes, his skin would be a mottled beige that would periodically fill up with red, his hair would stand on end from where he'd constantly run his fingers through it. The morning after a night before, he would be sullen and snappy, prickly and pale, and I would do well to keep out of his way. Normally there'd be no way on Earth that he'd be on his knees in front of me asking for help.

He'd been up half the night, pacing the living room floor, keeping me awake with his banging about, snarling at me to go back to sleep if I asked what was wrong. All morning he'd been on the phone, with Murray, I assumed, swinging wildly between snarling and shouting, then weeping and begging. I knew I'd cop the end of it, that he'd hurl his phone at some point and I would be the next target for his upset.

I'd sat on the corner seat of his new sofa, reading as quietly as I could (when he was stressed even reading would be too noisy and would cause him to scream at me), waiting for my share of the rage.

Truly, I hadn't expected to have him prostrate in front of me, trembling, close to tears. This must have been to do with how quickly Todd had bundled me out of the club last night. As always on these nights out, Todd had 'worked the room', talking to all the important people – celebrities and business people – while hissing at me to keep drinking rather than standing there not saying anything. At some point, which was usually when I was too drunk to do much but sit in a corner by myself, he would disappear off as usual, returning some time later with a cigar, a grin and a fuzzy look in his eye. Last night, he'd been gone less than five minutes before he came thundering through the crowd, virtually scooped me out of my seat and practically dragged me out. I was drunk, tired, my feet hurt from the new designer shoes he'd bought me for that night out, so I didn't really understand what was going on. Usually when he acted like this, he'd accuse me of flirting with another man, but I hadn't been, I'd been on my own, nursing a double vodka and cola. I'd stumbled on the way out of the club on those shoes, had grabbed his forearm to steady myself on the way out. The sudden flare of camera bulbs had stunned me for a moment and I'd stumbled again, igniting his temper – his hand was painfully tight around mine as he dragged me towards the black car we'd arrived in and then virtually threw me into the back.

The whole way home I'd felt sick. Not only from too much booze, but knowing I would be in for it, for being too drunk, and for showing him up in front of the cameras. But nothing. We'd got in, the door had slammed loudly behind us, and he hadn't even looked in my direction. I'd waited by the door, expecting him to say something, to sneer his derision at what I had done wrong that night, decide which room to go into while we 'talked' out the night. Instead, with barely a look in my direction, he'd pressed a few buttons on his phone and headed off in the direction of the bathroom. I'd stood waiting. This was new. Scary. What was he going to do? Ignore me this time? Punish me with silence? I'd waited and waited and waited until it was clear he wasn't coming back. I'd listened to his voice in the bathroom, loud and wild. *Something huge must have happened*, I'd decided. Something so big he didn't want to talk about it in front of me.

Now he was about to tell me what had happened, and how I could help him by doing this one thing for him. He held on to my hands, gently rubbing his thumbs over their veiny backs. 'Nikky, I need you right now, more than I've ever needed anyone in my life,' he said. 'Thing is, baby, I did something really stupid last night. It was a one-off, but it could ruin everything. We could lose all this.' He moved his head around to encompass the room. 'I was about to do a couple of lines of charlie at the club last night,' he continued, 'but as it was an opening night, there were lots of reporters and photographers there. Before I knew it, someone had snapped me getting it out of my pocket. Baby, I can't be caught with that stuff.'

'Oh, God, that's awful,' I said. What he wanted me to do about it, I had no idea.

'Baby, I need you to say they were your drugs,' he said, staring right into my eyes, pinning me to the spot with his pleading, green-eyed gaze. 'I know it's a lot to ask, but if we play it right, we can say that I took them off you, put them in my pocket and forgot they were there and when I got a light out, they came out too.'

'But they weren't my drugs,' I said.

'I know, I know, and it's not fair but if I get found out... Greenbay Park Rangers have a decency clause so they can terminate my contract at any time. If they find out that I made a mistake this one time, it'll be the end of me. The end of everything I've worked so hard for. They could ask for all their money back. We'd have to move out of here, sell the car, no more car service or quality booze.'

I went to say, 'It doesn't matter', that we'd be together so it wouldn't matter that we didn't have any money and I would be able to get a job to help support us, but stopped myself. He wouldn't agree with that, not in a million years. I looked at him properly and could see the suffering on his face. He was scared. Really scared. I had known fear and I didn't want to wish it on anyone, let alone leave it sitting on the shoulders of someone I loved so deeply. 'I don't think anyone will believe that story, though,' I suggested gently.

'Look, once they know they weren't my drugs, the whole thing will blow over and no one will mention it again. Tomorrow's chip paper, honestly, baby. It'll be fine, no one will remember you did drugs one time in a club. Especially when we say you'll be going into rehab. We'll make a sizeable donation to a drug education foundation and then everyone will forget about you and the coke.'

It sounded like *he'd* forgotten about me and the coke – i.e. that it was a lie, that I hadn't actually been involved with any drugs, ever, let alone last night, let alone so I would need my boyfriend to confiscate them from me. But that was silly, how could he have forgotten? He loved me, and he knew the truth and I knew the truth. Nothing would change the truth. Nothing would change the reality.

Birmingham, 2016

'Give us a minute,' DS Brennan says to his colleague. It's been an odd drive home, almost as though we've been travelling alone since none of us have spoken to or even acknowledged each other. The other passenger doesn't even glance in my direction before he unclips his seatbelt, climbs out of the car and shuts the door behind him. He walks a little way down the street before stopping, taking out a cigarette and lighting it. Outside my home some lads are loitering. They're a lot younger than me, but they have left their teenage years behind. This part of town is hardly ever still; it is very rarely emptied of people and sounds and traffic. At night, the garish street lighting creates islands around which people collect to communicate with each other because they do not want to be properly illuminated. That's part of the price you pay when you live somewhere where they don't need very much ID to rent you a room and share a bathroom. The lads clock the policeman standing near the lamp post, slowly smoking and openly watching them, and decide to leave. They don't want trouble, don't want to be in the right place at the right time to fit the description of suspects in a new crime. A couple of the cannier lads hang on a little longer, peer into the back of the car to see who's in there, who's turned grass, before they wander off, probably calculating how much they will get for such info as they scarper.

I rub my fingers across my eyes, wait for the policeman to release me back into the wild. He sits still in the front seat, watching me in the rearview mirror. I wonder if he's really seeing me, or if I'm irrelevant now he's done his duty and made sure I have no choice but to go through with testifying given that he's outed me to all my neighbours.

'Are you going to tell me who you really are, Grace Carter?' he asks, his gaze still on me via the reflection in the mirror.

I say nothing. What does he expect me to say? To throw myself on his mercies and tell him whatever came before?

DS Brennan sighs when he doesn't get an answer. 'All right, are you going to go through with this, "Grace Carter"? Are you going to testify if this goes to court?'

'Yes,' I reply.

I look down at my hands. I'm shaking. I'm sitting in the back seat of this blue car with this police officer in the driver's seat and I'm trembling. Scared of what I've done, terrified of what is to come next.

London, 2001

Maybe I should call Mum and Dad. I thought that every time I saw myself – barely able to stand, glassy-eyed, slightly dishevelled – on the front of those papers, those magazines, those websites. I thought it every time a new photo surfaced of the inside of my bag with a little white packet. (It was odd that I never actually remembered leaving my bag long enough to have it photographed by the people I was with, nor did I remember putting any such packet in there.) I thought it whenever there were more photos of Todd looking cross and upset with me, as though my drug habit was ruining his life and reputation. *Maybe I should call Mum and Dad. Maybe I should call them and tell them the truth.* Tell them that this was all meant to be yesterday's chip paper, that it hadn't been intentional that the whole thing – where my noble, clean-living boyfriend stood by me while I worked out my personal demons by sniffing white powder at every given opportunity – would suddenly make me interesting. Would suddenly have a situation where people I'd never met were being anonymous sources for the press and who had seen me snorting the stuff and rowing with my noble, clean-living boyfriend about it. Todd had, apparently, threatened to ditch me so many times if I didn't stop, and I had promised so many times that I would. I wondered after every one of those pictures appeared of me, usually in sunglasses now (Todd's idea to hide me better), if I should write Mr and Mrs Harper a note explaining that I would never touch illegal drugs, had never touched illegal drugs ever, and none of it was true. But I couldn't put the record straight, not even with my parents and siblings, because, even if Todd wouldn't be absolutely *furious* with me that I had told someone and had upped our chances of the actual truth coming out, it wouldn't do any good. It wouldn't change anything. They'd never believe me.

I stood in front of the newspapers and magazines in the corner shop, staring at the woman who had been snapped months and months ago – before drugs and an (allegedly) stormy relationship had made her interesting – with her white knickers, prominent against the dark brown skin of her legs, on show to the world. She'd been about to get out of the back of the chauffer-driven car and had missed a step, her legs had opened for the briefest of moments, and someone had taken that photo. Had probably not been intending to keep it, but now she was infamous, this was a perfect example of how 'out of it' the woman was; it was an example of how that woman was probably drug-addled and unsteady on her feet before most nights out and how much her clean-living boyfriend was suffering.

Maybe I should call Mum and Dad, I thought to myself. I hadn't even properly read the headline accompanying the photo, I just saw that woman who looked like I would look if I wasn't the real me I was in my head. *Maybe I should call Mum and Dad, tell them everything.* But then, what was the point of calling them? They'd never believe me.

Birmingham, 2016

'Do you know what I think, "Grace Carter"?' DS Brennan asks me in the silence of the car.

No, I don't. I almost say that, but decide not to. I decide to wait for him to enlighten me since I am shaking so much and I am so very, very tired. Right now, I may be able to sleep for the whole night through.

Slowly, he turns in his seat until his whole upper body is facing me and he leans forward slightly until he fills the space between the seats and he can't be seen by his friend, who is still smoking, the street light causing him to look mean and irritated. (I don't blame him: it's not warm enough to be standing outside smoking and waiting for your colleague to be done threatening a witness.)

My gaze moves from the outside policeman to the one who is sitting in front of me. '*I* think, "Grace Carter", that a long time ago someone hurt you very, very badly but no one believed you. So you felt the only choice you had was to run away and become a different person. And *I* think that because of that, you're risking your life now so that you can feel like justice is being done and someone will be punished for a crime they commit instead of getting away with it.' He stares at me again. 'That's what *I* think, "Grace Carter".'

'You don't think justice should be done? That's a pretty odd stance for a police officer.'

'I think justice should be done, but I don't think a person who has gone to such extraordinary lengths to conceal her identity should be a part of it,' he replies.

'Well, it's too late for that now, I've done it and I'm going to go through with it.'

'I understand you feel guilty—'

'No, you don't,' I cut in. 'You have no idea at all. If you did, we wouldn't even be having this conversation. You'd let me out of this car and let me go inside to get some sleep so I can go back to the police station tomorrow and answer any other questions your colleagues may have.'

'Grace,' he says quietly, as though for the first time he believes it is my real name. He's humouring me, playing along so I will listen to what he has to say, and because of that, Grace doesn't feel like my name any more. It feels all wrong, like a jumper put through the hottest setting on a tumble dryer – I need to wriggle and wriggle to fit into it again. I move in my seat, trying to make the name fit me again. 'Grace,' he repeats, to get my attention, 'don't do this.'

'Why not? What have I got to lose? You've just driven me through the neighbourhood at a snail's pace, everyone's going to know soon enough what I've done. Why wouldn't I go through with it now?'

'Is this really the life you saw for yourself when you were little, Grace? When you were called what you were originally called, is this the life you imagined?' He points out of the window at the building I live in. 'Is this the place you see yourself living out your days? Are those the clothes you'll be wearing for the rest of your life? Is this truly the life you should be living?'

Of course it is.

Certainly it isn't.

'My life is what it is. And I do all right.'

He is silent now, his turn to contemplate what I have said. I know enough about human behaviour, about people like him, to guess that he is wondering what he has to say, which button he has to press to get me to change my mind.

He stares at me for a while longer, stares and thinks and then he starts to speak. As he speaks the noise that drove me to the police station rips through me again, and I have to brace myself, hold myself tight to not start screaming to drown it out. With my shoulders hunched up, my face tensed against the noise repeating itself, I listen to the policeman. I listen to his words, his reasonings, what he tells me will happen next and I know he's right: if I go through with this, everyone I know will be hurt, damaged, hospitalised or worse to get me to shut up. At the end of it, they'll probably do the same to me. The trembling is suddenly more severe, maybe not to anyone outside of my body, but it feels like all of my organs are vibrating due to the words he's uttered, the chords he has struck.

'It's too late now,' I say to the policeman when he stops talking. 'I've started on this thing and I need to see it through.'

'No, it's not too late,' he says. 'Just go.'

'What do you mean?'

He lowers his voice, as though now, having said all that other stuff, he thinks someone will hear him and it will be the undoing of him and his career and therefore his life. 'I will volunteer to come and pick you up tomorrow morning,' he murmurs. 'Don't be here when we arrive.'

'Where should I be?' I ask, confused.

'Anywhere but here. I doubt you'll be able to leave the country by then, but leave the city.'

'But won't your lot come looking for me?'

'Yes, and I'll probably be the one who has to look hardest for you since I'll be the one who lost you, but that is exactly why you must leave and why you must not come back. Cut all ties to this city and start again somewhere else.'

'I can't just—'

'Yes, you can. You did it before. Do it again now.'

'But what—'

'I'll take care of all of that. I'll take care of everyone and everything. But you have to go now.'

'OK,' I mumble, even though it goes against all I believe in. 'OK, I'll go.'

Without another word, he gets out then opens my door like a gentleman does for a lady. I remember a time in my life when I was regularly getting out of cars opened by professional, expensive-suited drivers, all of them polite, all of them being paid to not see what had been going on in the back seat. My high-heeled feet would step onto red carpet, a sea of cameras would click and flash, voices would shout my name, trying to grab my attention. And I would ignore them all, try to ignore the boiling mass of nausea inside, hating every second of being noticed like that. Todd would clutch my hand with one of his hands, while the other would be raised self-effacingly to wave to his adoring public; he, Todd, would enjoy every spotlit millisecond in the limelight.

'Remember what I said, "Grace Carter",' DS Brennan says as I climb out of the car. 'We'll be back to pick you up at ten o'clock tomorrow morning. Be ready.' His voice, his face, his whole demeanour is back to the cold, emotionless police officer who looked me up and down and groaned inside when I told him I wanted to report an attempted murder. Is he that good an actor, or is he playing me?

Does he want me to run so he can pursue me and make sure I pay for whatever crime he thinks I might have committed? Or, my blood slows for a moment in my veins, have I just been played in a shockingly ostentatious way?

My gaze goes to the man who has smoked three cigarettes in quick succession during his time outside the car and has brought the sweet nicotine fog of them with him as he approaches us. He couldn't care less if I fall off the face of the world. I return my attention to DS Brennan. He gives nothing away, just stares at me with hard eyes and a fixed, stern mouth. 'Yes, officer,' I mumble, then fumble through my pockets for my key to the outer front door. My fingers locate the piece of brass-coloured metal – bare and alone with no keyring fob to give away anything about me – in my right pocket.

I walk away from the two men and know this: whatever that police officer's motivation, he has catapulted me towards this road. The road where the next major stop is the one where I end my life as Grace Carter and become Veronika 'Nika' Harper all over again.

Roni

Coventry, 2016

It is loudest at night, when the Great Silence begins.

We are as silent as we can be during the day, and at Divine Office, the official prayers of the Church, I push out as much of the noise inside, coating every word I utter in the sound of chaos that lives inside me. I do this to prepare for the Great Silence, the hours between last prayers and morning prayers where there is no speaking, no noise, absolutely no unnecessary sound.

When the Great Silence begins, the noise in my head becomes unbearable. The voices, the memories, the music, the words, the flashes of my life ill-lived are there, screaming to be heard, shouting to be let out. I often have to push my hands over my ears, trying to drown out the racket inside.

It wasn't always like this. When I came here, the first time and now this second time, it wasn't like this. I used to be able to hook into the silence, I had peace in my head, tranquillity in my heart, and I was free for a time. My community accepted me for who I was *at that moment in time,* they didn't care about the me who walked in through those gates, covered in shame and guilt. They only saw the person they renamed Grace because what I had been, what I had done was a lifetime ago, another person ago. I became this person and I could revel in the near silence that brought to my mind.

Now, the Great Silence is when I am most scared. When there is silence all around me, the noise inside starts as a hush, slowly building, swelling and growing until I cannot hear, I cannot think, I cannot even entertain sleep.

Tomorrow night it will be different. I will be in a different bed, in a different city. I will be in a different life. And I will no longer have the Great Silence to worry about.

The fear flutters up inside again. *Is this what you want?* I ask myself again. *Truly, is this what you want to do?*

It isn't what I want to do, it is what I have to do. I can't become a part of the Great Silence any longer – the quietness here scares rather than energises me. I cannot live with this inner life of noise and chaos any longer, not when I know what I can do about it.

The other ones who have left in recent years, who have stepped outside the convent walls to never return, wanted a husband, children, a life lived within their control. There's none of that for me. I have to leave because I have finally admitted that I *am* like Judas. I have done a terrible thing and I have to put it right.

Tomorrow, I am going to stop being Sister Grace and I will become Veronica 'Roni' Harper again.

Father, forgive me, is the only prayer I can manage tonight. The noise in my head is too much to think anything else except: *Father, forgive me.*

2

Roni

London, 2016

The house seems so small. It isn't, and I never felt like it was when I lived here, either. When I was little, this house seemed large, *was* large, *is* large. But I suppose it's like trying to put on clothes from your childhood – they don't fit any more because you have outgrown them. Not that I'm saying I've outgrown my parents' house. I would never be so rude.

'Your bedroom isn't quite how you left it,' Mum says. She's still all smiles and nerves, never quite looking at me enough to meet my eye. This is how she used to act when the priest came over for tea, how she would act, I suspect, if the Queen were to drop over for a cuppa. I want to reach out, rest my hands on her shoulders and tell her to relax a bit, to remember it's just me.

Every step through the house, on the stairs, peels back a layer of time, changes the wallpaper, the carpet, the furnishings, the very atmosphere, I suspect, and I can almost see how it used to be, I can feel the house become what it once was when I lived here, when it was what I called my home.

'It's not really my room any more, though,' I say gently.

'Well, no, but I was simply warning you in case you were expecting everything to be the same as it was. It isn't.'

'Thank you for letting me know,' I eventually say. It's good of them to take me in, especially at such short notice, so I don't want to upset her equilibrium within minutes of walking through the door.

The stairs still creak just before and just after the turn, the carpet – a deep, soft royal blue – is different, not surprising since it was virtually threadbare the last time I came down these stairs to be driven to the station. I look at all the doors at the top of the first-floor landing, all painted a glossy white, all with brass, push-down handles, all closed, as if determined to keep their secrets hidden from the merest glimpse from the most casual of prying eyes.

My bedroom was at the end of the hall, next to the bathroom. I am eleven again, suddenly. My body is small, flat-chested, my stomach a smooth round closing bracket in shape. My legs are thick and strong, my toes are gnarled and ugly out of ballet shoes, my arms want to constantly reach up – into position, into a gesture of wanting someone to lift me out of the life I am living.

'We redecorated,' my mother says.

I used to have so much crammed in here: furniture and clothes, shoes and books, make-up and jewellery, notepads and pens. Stuff; I used to have so much stuff. I place my suitcase – the same red one I left with – on the floor beside me and stand in the middle of the room that was once mine and turn slowly. The bed was there, by the wall, my pillow against the wooden footboard so I could stare out of the window at the houses over the back, instead of watching and waiting to see who would come into my room with or without knocking first. My dark-wood wardrobe with its brass flower-shaped handles was there, by the door. My rickety white desk with its uncomfortable white chair was there, by the window, beneath the huge poster of Mikhail Baryshnikov and Gregory Hines in *White Nights*. At the window, I can see the full-length blue velvet curtain drawn to one side, while the white net curtain, strung halfway up the window, hooked on each side of the frame by a white-covered wire on nails, moves gently from the breeze of the not-quite-airtight window. The top part of the window is bare so full daylight enters the room. I turn back to my bed from all those years ago: my pink duvet cover with darker pink spots, and don't forget the matching pillows. Above the bed, my nearly life-size poster of Sylvie Guillem, pressed into place first with Blu-tack, then taped over each corner and the exact middle of each side to make sure it stayed in place, where I could see it from every part of the room. A smile moves up my face as I look at that poster, gone, of course, but forever there to me. I was going to *be* Sylvie. She had started at the Paris Opera Ballet at age eleven – so three years after I had started dancing – but she was everything I wanted to be. Her poise, her body, the almost perfect straight line she managed to achieve *en pointe*.

I was going to dance in *Swan Lake*, and I was going to be famous, so famous Sylvie would come and see me dance. She would come to me after the performance, would open her arms to me, tears in her eyes—

'Do you like it?' Mum asks and inadvertently shakes me out of my eleven-year-old self. *Silly girl that I am, silly girl that I was. Fantasy and silliness*, that was what I was all about.

'It's lovely,' I tell my mother about her rose-pink walls with their tiny rose band around the room's middle and cream Roman-blind-covered window, pale beige carpet, circular pink rug, and chest of drawers in the corner where the wardrobe used to be. There is a metal-framed fold-out bed (possibly borrowed, possibly reclaimed from the attic), and the duvet is too big for its tiny metal frame. 'You've obviously spent so much care and attention making it a calming space to be.'

'We weren't sure how long you would be staying with us,' she says. 'If it's more than a couple of weeks we'll maybe think about getting you a proper bed instead of this one. Although it's perfectly good to sleep on. Not one person who has slept on it has complained.'

'I'm sure it's wonderful,' I say with a smile.

My mother returns what is probably a mirror image of my smile without actually looking at me. She's very good at that still: directing attention at me without making any kind of eye contact. 'I'll give you a few minutes to settle in. Dinner is at six-thirty. If that is all right for you?'

'It's perfect.'

A cross between a smile and a frown flitters repeatedly across Mum's face as she hovers uncertainly by the door for a few seconds, her right hand moving between the handle and her left hand, not sure what to do with itself – whether to open the door, or clasp itself with its mirror twin.

Ask her, just ask her, she's probably telling herself. *Just ask her how long she's staying. It's* your *house*, your *home*, your *sewing room that she's moved into, ask her how long you'll have to be on your best behaviour and mind everything you say. Ask her, just ask her.*

She opens her mouth and I prepare myself. 'It's nice to see you,' she says.

'You too,' I say, and I mean it. It is nice to see her after all these years. The last time I physically saw her was when I had special dispensation to attend my eldest brother's wedding about five years ago.

She nods, fixes the smile on her face and leaves, shutting the door firmly behind her.

The tension escapes my body in one heavy sigh as she exits and I fall heavily on the bed. It creaks menacingly under my weight, promising me a night of torture I can't even begin to imagine, but I'm glad to have something semi solid under me.

I should have known she wouldn't ask. That could result in a fuss being made, and that would never do. If she had broken with tradition and asked, *'Veronica, why did you leave your convent and decide to stop being a nun?'*

'At this moment in time, I don't know, Mum, I honestly do not know,' I would have had to say. I wouldn't have added: *'I think it had something to do with finding and making things right with the other Veronika Harper.'*

Nika

The whole way down here, in between attempts to sleep on the overnight coach with my rucksack as a pillow and my coat as a cover, I have been turning over what the policeman said to me while he tried to get me to leave. Not the stuff about me testifying being dangerous to everyone I knew, the other things he said: the other stuff about the life I was meant to live. That is what has been swirling through my mind since I hastily packed my rucksack, small cloth bag I'd got free at a book festival, and my battered black guitar case. Have I lived the life I was meant to? The path to how I got to this part of my life is clear, I can look back and see every turn, every step, every decision that has led to here. What has been strung across my mind like intricate worry beads are these thoughts about whether this was the path I was meant to have taken. Was there another option for me? And am I too far along this path to make a change, and relive my life?

London, 2002

I know there are photographers somewhere in this restaurant, I think for the umpteenth time.

I couldn't completely relax because of it: out there somewhere, there was someone behind a lens waiting for me to mess up so they could press the button, capture my slip with one treacherous click.

45

They'd stopped following us as much now that I refused to go out to clubs and very often I didn't leave the flat unless necessary. With nothing new to take photos of, I was literally yesterday's news story. Other people were taking over the front covers, other people were having more public rows, break-ups and reunions.

There were still photographers out there, though. I could feel them.

Todd still went out, but never touched anything more illicit than booze in public. At home, every couple of weeks, when he wanted to properly chill out, he would invite only a trusted handful of his friends over. (They were trusted because they had as much to lose as he did if anyone found out what they got up to.) They would spend their time alternating between downing shots of expensive whisky, drawing deep on real Cuban cigars, sniffing up white line after white line after white line. Sometimes they'd throw speed into the mix, and would become wild-eyed, talkative and dangerous – dangling off the edge of the balcony, trying knife tricks, arm-wrestling and often full wrestling if they lost. Then they'd collapse on to the sofas in the small hours to skin up and then smoke copious amounts of skunk to calm themselves down. By the end of the night the flat would be heavy with the smell of skunk, booze and sweat; when I left the bedroom in the morning, everything would smell stale and rancid, all of them would be sullen, pale and rude.

I hated those parties. Apart from the drugs and the out-of-control drinking, the disrespect shown by his friends to me... it constantly made my stomach churn. Todd would think it funny when one of his friends would run his hand over my bum, or another would tweak my breast, or would 'beg' me to get down on my knees to '*sort me out, real quick*'. He thought it was hilarious – and a compliment – that his friends treated me like a sex object because it meant they thought I was hot.

Todd had had one of his parties last week, and to make up for it (one of his friends had gone too far with his groping), he brought me out to this lovely restaurant for dinner. And I couldn't relax because I knew there was a photographer out there somewhere.

'You look incredible,' Todd said to me. The restaurant had sedate music, lighting set up to emulate candlelight, black leather booths that gave instant privacy, crystal glassware, fine bone china crockery, heavy silver cutlery. Everything about this place was classy.

'Thank you,' I replied. I stared down at my manicured fingers, a metallic grey that matched my long silver dress Todd had bought me for the occasion. I was fluttery inside – not in the way I used to be when I saw him, talked to him. This was about the photographers, about the waiting staff and what snippets of our conversation would be passed on, about perfect strangers recognising me and judging me for things I hadn't done.

Even when I was at home, I worried. Yes, I worried less, but I often had the blinds closed, shutting out the views of the river and the city skyline, in case someone used a long-range lens to take snaps of me. *'Don't be ridiculous,' Todd had said when I'd confessed that was what I did. 'No one cares any more that you used to take drugs. You're not that important.'*

'I didn't used to take drugs, Todd,' I'd said, 'I've never taken drugs in my life. I let you tell people I did to protect you.'

'You know what I mean,' he'd said dismissively. He'd seen the hurt on my face and had pulled me into his arms. 'I'm sorry, baby, it was an amazing thing you did for me. But don't let it make you into one of those paranoid freaks who sits around in a foil hat cos they think people can read their thoughts. If they were going to use long lenses to watch you, it'd only be when I was here. You mean the world to me but no one else really cares. Just live your life, OK?'

'We've been through a hard time lately,' Todd told me. He leant forwards, lowered his voice to a whisper – obviously the paranoia wasn't only mine. 'You've really stuck by me and helped me out when I needed you most.'

I smiled at him, but kept my eyes lowered to make it harder for anyone to take a photo of me. I hadn't wanted to wear sunglasses when Todd first mentioned it, but now, I felt naked and exposed without them. As it was, I was only half listening to Todd since I knew from the way he'd lowered his voice that he had concerns that information about us would be leaked somehow.

'You're so beautiful and loyal, and I can't imagine my life without you.'

I couldn't imagine my life without him, either. Some days, he felt like my whole world; some days, he was the only person I saw in real life if I hadn't left the flat in a few days. My life wasn't meant to be like that, I knew that, but it was a good life, and I had a great guy. How many other twenty-two-year-olds lived in a flat overlooking the River Thames and had a boyfriend who bought her things, took her to places and, most importantly, knew some of her most disturbing secrets but loved her anyway? My life was about Todd, and there was nothing wrong with that.

I was aware that he was moving, and raised my head. *Are we leaving?* I wondered. Todd tugged slightly on his right trouser leg before he got down on that knee. The music lowered, and a group of wait staff appeared around our table. One holding a mist-covered champagne bucket with a bottle of champagne on ice, another holding an armful of roses, another still with a white cloth over his arm, obviously ready to pour. I looked back at my boyfriend, and he slowly uncurled his hand and showed me a pink velvet box.

I gasped, drew my hands up to my lips and gasped again.

'Nikky Harper, will you marry me,' he said. It wasn't a real question. Why would he even need to ask? Of course I would marry him. I would have married him three years ago when we met, I would have married him yesterday, I would marry him tomorrow. He was the love of my life. I loved him so much – the thought that he felt the same, he wanted to always be with me, was so amazing. SO AMAZING. I could have jumped up and screamed! Yelled to the world that he was my man and I loved him so much.

I nodded, my fingers still covering my lips.

'I'm going to need a proper reply,' he said with a laugh.

'Yes! Of course, yes,' I said. I leapt up and threw my arms around his neck.

One of his arms wrapped itself around my waist as he held me close and laughed happily into my hair. Around us the air erupted with the sound of other diners clapping their approval. And over my happiness, his laughter, and the loud clapping, I could still hear the click-click-click of someone taking photographs.

Roni

London, 2016

There's a knock on my bedroom door. I have been staring at my suitcase and trying to remember what it was that I packed. I don't actually have that much 'stuff', so I'm wondering what I folded inside and then shut the lid on because I'll be blessed if I can remember. I don't want to just open up the case, that would be cheating. That would be admitting that I was completely absent for the whole of the packing process and facing up to that would be like accepting defeat in the fight against the noise in my head. It would be saying to myself that I was so busy trying to find moments of silence I had completely checked out of reality. I did not like to admit to things like that.

Mum is on the other side of the door. She has a silver tray with a teapot, one cup and saucer, a milk jug, a sugar bowl, a large slice of Victoria sponge, and a silver cake fork resting on the plate.

'I thought you might like tea,' she says.

'Thank you,' I say and attempt to take the tray from her. She brushes me aside and walks into the room and places it on the surface of what is probably usually her sewing table. She didn't actually think I might like some tea – she wants to talk to me again before Dad comes back from work. She wants to know my plans, how long she has to put up with me for.

The thing about Mum is that more than anything in the world she hates 'a fuss'. She thinks we should put up with all sorts of things to stop a fuss being made. I don't know what her fear of 'fusses' is about, really, or what she thinks might happen if one was caused, but that's what my brothers – Damian (the eldest by five years), Brian (three years older) – and I grew up with: a mother who disengaged the second she saw anything that might cause upset in her world.

London, 1988

During the summer holidays when I was eight, our favourite uncle, Uncle Warren, would often come over and take one or both of my brothers out. He'd never take me out because he didn't know what to do with a girl, he kept saying. It didn't matter, really, I adored him. Whenever I saw him coming up the garden path I would fly to the door, ready to be scooped up by him and swung round and round until I felt sick and dizzy. When he wasn't taking the boys out, he would sit and read with me, do jigsaw puzzles, sit still while I drew him, and watch me pretend to be a ballerina.

This day was the kind of hot that made everything seem hazy and sleepy. I'd been lying on the living room floor, reading a book about famous ballerinas, and jumped when there was a loud banging on the front door. When Mum opened it, Damian came limping in.

'What happened?' Mum asked. Damian continued across the hallway, aiming for the stairs where I was standing, dragging his right foot along the floor as though it didn't work any more. Uncle Warren was right behind, trying to wheel Damian's bike. He couldn't move it very fast, though, because the frame was bent and twisted, as if someone very big (probably a giant) had picked it up and twisted it into a new shape.

I stared at the bicycle frame: its blue and red paint was scraped away in huge chunks, showing the silvery metal underneath. My mother opened her mouth in shock then slammed her hand over it when she saw the state of the bicycle. 'What happened?' she asked again.

Uncle Warren handed the bike to Mum and chuckled. 'Our boy here thinks he's a stuntman. Had a bit of an accident, didn't you, mate?' he explained. 'Don't know how, but he skidded and fell off, his bike went out from under him and under the wheels of a car.'

I went to my brother, took his hand and helped him limp towards the stairs so he could sit down. Mum was stunned by the state of the bike, more than by Damian's pain. His right jeans leg was almost shredded at the knee and dripping in blood. His right elbow and the top of his arm were also scraped, scored with lots of black marks, bits of gravel still sticking out of the chunks of red below where his T-shirt ended.

'You're all right, aren't you, mate?' Uncle Warren called at him.

Damian nodded, and didn't speak. He looked like he'd been crying but had been told to shut up and be a man, like Uncle Warren always said whenever one of my brothers fell over. He only ever said that when my dad wasn't around, I noticed. I was only eight, but that was one thing I noticed. When Dad was around, Uncle Warren didn't say half of the sometimes not very nice things he said.

'He'll be all right,' Uncle Warren said to my mother. She was worrying over the bike. She hadn't even looked at Damian – she was running her fingers over the scratches on the bicycle frame, her mouth still open with surprise and shock. Whenever we hurt ourselves, Mum would react like that – she'd stare and stare at whatever we'd hurt ourselves on, like it was her child and not one of us.

'Are you all right?' I whispered to Damian quietly. I didn't want to get him in trouble with Uncle Warren.

He sniffed. 'It really hurts,' he whispered back. 'I can't stand on my leg.'

'Nothing broken, is it, mate?' Uncle Warren called. 'He'll be all right. Just clean him up and get him up, he'll be fine. Soonest mended and all that.' He looked at his watch, which had a huge face that you could see from really far away. 'Aww, must dash. Mag-rat, see you soon. Damian, you were really brave, mate, really proud of you. And Roni, my little dynamo, see you soon.'

I stared at Uncle Warren. I couldn't believe this had happened and he wasn't even going to wait to see if Damian was all right. Up until then he'd been my favourite uncle, but right then, I wasn't sure I liked him at all. Sometimes he could be not nice but he'd always say sorry afterwards, but this was the not nicest thing he'd ever done. He was going to leave us like this, and Mum would take ages to notice that Damian needed help and probably to go to the doctor if not the hospital. Dad wouldn't be home from work for hours.

'But Uncle Warren,' I said. 'Can't you stay for a little bit longer and help look after Damian?'

'I wish I could, sweetheart, but I really have got to run. Damo will be all right, won't you? Your mum will look after him.'

I looked at my mum, who was still examining the bicycle – she was going to be no help at all. When the door shut behind Uncle Warren, Mum propped the bike up against the corridor wall, staring at it like she was confused and upset. 'We'll never be able to fix this, we'll have to get a new one,' she said. 'I suppose your father will be upset.'

'Mum, Damian's leg really hurts,' I said.

'Oh, poor love,' she said. 'Like your uncle Warren said, it'll be fine. Just walk it off.' She smiled at us.

'Mum, you really need to do something,' I said. Damian didn't look very well: he was pale and his eyes were like he was far away. Then he put his head on his arm and started crying. It was quiet at first, but it got louder and louder.

This seemed to shock Mum out of whatever weird mood she was in. 'Yes, yes, you're right, of course, Veronica. I don't know what I was thinking. Why don't you go and get him some new trousers? Then go into the bathroom and get a few plasters and the TCP.'

I ran up the stairs, went into my brothers' bedroom and got him some clean trousers. Then I went into the bathroom and opened the mirror cabinet and took out the TCP and the whole roll of sticky plasters. I got the scissors, too, so Mum could cut some off the roll. All the while I could hear Damian crying and I heard nothing at all from Mum. I stood at the top of the stairs with everything in my arms, ready to go down, but I decided not to straight away. Instead I went into my parents' bedroom. I wasn't allowed in there normally, but they had a phone in there. I wasn't allowed to use it, but Dad had taught us to call 999 in an emergency. This felt like a nearly emergency. I settled everything on the bed, then picked up the phone. Each button beeped when I pressed it.

Twenty minutes later, Dad came home. Mum was still trying to stop the bleeding from Damian's knee without taking his trousers off, and she kept sending me upstairs to get towels and cotton wool, and warm water in a bowl.

Mum was really surprised to see him. I hadn't told her I'd called him because this was a nearly emergency and I wasn't allowed to dial 999 unless it was a real emergency.

'He's fine, Geoffrey, really he is,' Mum said as Dad gently bundled up my brother and headed straight for the open front door.

'He is not fine. Look at him, Margaret, he's barely conscious. He could have concussion or anything. If Veronica hadn't called me, you'd have let your son sit here in pain until six o'clock tonight when I got home,' he said.

'Honestly, Geoffrey, you do make a fuss sometimes,' Mum said. 'You and Veronica, both. This sort of thing happened to me all the time in my day and I was fine.'

'This can't happen again, Margaret,' Dad said. He was so cross I could see all the muscles in his face bulging because he was trying not to shout. 'It can*not* happen again. Do you hear me?'

Once the door shut behind them, Mum turned to me and shook her head. 'He's going to look very silly when the doctor tells him it's a little sprain. Children are too coddled nowadays, everything is always the worst-case scenario. He'll be fine.'

I nodded at Mum, wishing that Dad had taken me with him. 'Come on, Veronica, let's start dinner before they come back and Brian comes back from his friend's house.'

Damian came home on crutches with a severely torn ligament and five stitches in one of his knee cuts. Mum apologised to Damian for not realising how bad he'd felt and she promised Dad she would take this sort of thing more seriously next time. Even as she was promising him, I could tell she couldn't understand what all the fuss was about and was only saying sorry so that Dad wouldn't cause more 'fuss' by still being angry with her about it.

London, 2016

'I hope you like the cake,' Mum says. She is moving the tray items on to the table to avoid having to look at me while she starts this conversation. I really would help her out if I knew anything about what next. When I asked to be released from my vows, I thought it would take months, as it had with other professed Sisters, but mine was granted in weeks. Was this divine intervention or had something Mother Superior said meant they'd expedited my release? I didn't have time to dwell on it, or to formulate a more robust, non-parents/ Chiselwick-involving plan. *This* was the plan; what next is a genuine mystery.

'I'm sure I will. I love Victoria sponge,' I say.

'Now, Veronica,' Mum begins. She rattles the cup and saucer and has to set them down quickly before she breaks something.

'Yes, Mum?'

'It's nice to see you and everything but...' Her voice peters out.

'Yes, Mum?' Is she going to break the habit of a lifetime and start a potentially difficult conversation that could result in even the slightest hint of unpleasantness?

'But don't forget that dinner is at six-thirty,' Mum states.

'That's perfect,' I say, disappointed in her. *I thought you could do it, Mum, I really thought you could.*

'We've got a guest for dinner, too,' she adds. 'I'm sure you'll be very happy to see him.'

'Is it Brian or Damian?' I ask.

As usual, Mum smiles at me without making eye contact. 'You'll just have to wait and see. Don't let your tea grow cold.'

'I won't,' I say to her. She closes the door and I know who it'll be coming for dinner: Uncle Warren. Mum won't have told Brian and

Damian I am back and asked them to come to dinner, because she won't take the risk of them explaining to her they aren't desperate enough to see me to see her, too. The only person, apart from Dad, who hasn't effectively washed their hands of Mum is Uncle Warren.

Oh well, I think to myself as I search for the positive in the situation, *at least if he comes to dinner tonight, that will get that part of being back in Chiselwick over and done with.*

Nika

London, 2016

Wasn't sure I'd see this place again. I didn't think I'd ever come back to Chiselwick, let alone this part of it, and let alone this road. The house I grew up in is near the middle of a terraced street and it stands out to me because I spent seventeen years going in and out of it. The door is the same colour – a sombre black – as when I shut it behind me over eighteen years ago, when I was seventeen, but it's newer paint. The whole of the outside has been repainted a few times and the windows look sort of new, like they've been updated in the last decade.

My plan, hastily formulated when I left Birmingham last night, is to fix things with my parents. I'm going to turn up, talk to them, be humble, be contrite, see if we can find a middle ground. See if they will let me stay with them for a couple of nights so I don't have to sleep on the streets. Their address was always my home address, because I could never be sure I'd get everything when I lived in a shared house. When I moved in with Todd, my sister used to package up my post and forward it to me at his address, even though she didn't still live at home. My parents never spoke to me but apparently they accumulated all my post. My sister, who would clean up for them, still, would send on the post with a little 'how are you?' note, but nothing more. I'd guessed it was because she didn't want to get in the middle of what had happened. I never explained to her the reasons for my exodus, and since we were never close – despite sharing a room – I didn't feel the need to make her choose a side. Besides, I'd rather have an arm's length relationship with her than one where she didn't believe me when I told her one of my secrets.

Our family had an odd dynamic: Sasha and I were never ones to share secrets or have each other's backs but we always seemed to be waging wars against the rules our parents imposed – she being the older girl, getting the brunt of their control, me being younger, getting the best of their disinterest if I was doing what they wanted. Our brother, Marlon, was the golden child: first born, most loved, the one who treated them with the most disdain but seemed adored for it.

I won't think about that now. I got off the coach at Victoria with a plan: I will fix things with my parents as much as I can to let me stay and then I will get a job and then I will find somewhere to live. Saying all of this, it's only really occurred to me now, standing in front of their door, that they might not live here any more. One or both of them might not be alive any more. I haven't been in touch for so many years, I don't know what fundamental and microscopic shifts have taken place in the Harper household.

I have thought about them over the years, I've even thought about sending Christmas cards, birthday cards, etc. but I never got around to it. I could never bring myself to send them when it would all be fake – fake sentiments from a fake woman, who stopped signing her name Veronika or even Nika a long time ago. Every time I had the urge to get in touch with my family I would remind myself that I was Grace Carter and Grace Carter had no past and no family. That was all there was to it.

Veronika Harper, on the other hand, raises her hand and presses the doorbell before she changes her mind and runs away, pulling on her Grace Carter protective armour as she runs.

Immediately, there are sounds of movement on the other side of the door, someone getting up, a woman's voice that doesn't sound like my mother's comes closer, and through the mottled glass in the door I watch the approach of a shape that is too tall and too slender, to be my mother. They don't live here any more. Maybe they are both dead and I will have to deal with that news, too. I take a step back, ready to run rather than hear that news from a stranger, but I don't move quickly enough because the door swings open.

The woman who opens the door frowns, the action scoring deep creases into her forehead. She frowns some more and then her mouth drops open, and her eyes are suddenly awash with tears.

'Who is it, Sasha?' my dad's voice calls from somewhere in the house and he sounds the same. Through the open doorway I see the ornate gilt mirror on the wall, the brown, flowery carpet, the coats hanging up beside the mirror, the neatly lined-up shoes below the coats. I see the square of window in the back room that overlooks the back garden. That is the room where I last spoke to them, the place where I made them choose me or denial. Denial won.

My sister clamps her hand over her mouth, blinking hard at me.

'Sasha? Who is it?' my dad calls again.

'Erm, erm, no one, Daddy. Just someone trying to sell something.' She shakes her head at me, presses her forefinger to her lips, holds her hand up for me not to speak.

'What are they selling?' Daddy calls.

'Nothing, nothing. Look, I'll get rid of them, OK? It's nothing for you to worry about.' She steps out of the house, comes right up to me. Her slender hands with beautifully shaped and varnished nails are on my face, holding me as though she can't believe I'm real. Tears are burgeoning in her eyes and she draws me close, hugs me, although I'm not sure I smell very pleasant after a night on the coach. 'The park,' she whispers to me. 'Twenty minutes, in the park by the swings. I'll see you there, OK?'

I nod.

She covers her mouth with her hand again and her face collapses into the beginnings of a cry. 'Twenty minutes,' she whispers. 'Twenty minutes.'

I nod again and stand waiting for her to shut the door before I leave. Seems like, from that reaction, my parents have still chosen denial.

London, 2003

The dark was approaching and the air was cooling as though the temperature and the light were keeping each other company, holding hands as they fell and lowered themselves into night-time.

I sat on a park bench, wearing the leather jacket my boyfriend had bought me when we first started dating, staring at the cemetery opposite the park. The headstones and statues, monuments and plaques took on different forms the longer I sat there, immobile and stuck. My parents lived not far from there, probably about a mile or so away, in Chiselwick. I'd got the Tube all the way across London and walked to this park and then my legs decided they'd had enough walking. Memory Lane was, as expected, no fun at all. I'd sat on this bench and hadn't moved since.

I wanted to go home. I wanted to see my folks and have them put their arms around me and tell me that they loved me, and everything that had gone before was forgotten. We didn't need to talk about it unless I wanted to, but if I did we would and they would listen, they would hear, they would believe. I wanted to be folded into the safety of my mother's arms, comforted with the pat of my father's hand on my shoulder, and told none of it was my fault. From a distance – even one this close to them – I could imagine the parents I wanted instead of remembering the parents I actually had.

My parents were only on my mind because I had finally seen Todd's true form earlier and it had terrified me.

I'd stepped out of the shower, caught a fleeting glimpse of the bruise – the perfect size and shape of his hand – around my left bicep, the colours so deep and severe that they had been prominent against my skin, and I had stopped and stared. And stared. And stared some more. While what had happened, what he had done three nights ago, had come stampeding into my mind on a crescendo

60

of loud hooves. The noise of the memory had been inside my head, and I hadn't been able to get it out. And while the memory had continued its violent journey across my mind, one of those hooves had caught the edge of the blinkers I had been wearing and kicked them clean off.

After everything I had told him, everything we had been through, Todd had... I'd put the palms of my hands over my eyes.

My eyes had been covered, but I'd been able to see, suddenly. Slowly, slowly, slowly, he'd been doing this thing to me for years. It had never been as clear, though, not like the other night. But slowly, slowly, slowly with the never stopping when I wanted him to, the underwear, the degrading positions, the wanting to take photos, the wanting to let others watch, he'd been doing it for years. I'd just never been able to admit it until the other night when I had said an outright no.

Slowly, slowly, slowly, he'd eroded my resistance, he'd persuaded me to go ahead with things when I hadn't wanted to, he'd keep on asking for my reasons for saying no until I stopped arguing that I hadn't 'wanted it really', he would carry on having sex on me to prove that I'd 'enjoy it once we got going'. Slowly, slowly, slowly he had become this monster that I only saw when he finally stopped pretending to take my wishes into account.

I loved him. He noticed me, he paid me attention, and I used to believe he wanted what was best for me. He loved me and I was always, *always* desperate to please him.

Seeing his hand mark on me, with the memories galloping wildly through my mind, I'd been able to see who Todd was. I'd had to *acknowledge* what he had been doing over the years, and then the tears had started to fall. I wasn't really a crier, so it had been shocking to feel them swell through me and fall from my eyes like a flood.

I wasn't really a crier, and I hadn't been crying for me. I hadn't been sobbing for the pain, for the sickness that had sat in my stomach since last Saturday night, for the bruised skin and painful muscles. I'd been crying for the fact I loved him so much. I loved him so much.

And now I'd seen the shape of him, his true form, I wasn't allowed to love him any more.

I'd pulled myself together, I'd managed to get dressed, but when he'd returned from his run, and I'd seen him, I'd broken down again, the tears faster this time, each breath a deep gasp of sorrow. He'd come straight to me, gathered me in his arms, hushed me, rocked me with his love. 'Oh baby, please stop crying,' he'd whispered. 'I didn't realise how much it'd upset you. Please stop crying, please.' He'd made me promises, told me I was the only one for him, all the while begging me to stop crying. Still I'd cried. I'd tried to stop: every breath I'd held, every sob I'd tried to swallow, every tear I'd tried to stem, but it hadn't worked. I hadn't been able to stop.

He'd kept saying the right words, more hushing, more explanations, more pleas for me to understand. More and more until 'STOP IT!' he'd screamed at me. He'd got to his feet, almost tossing me aside he'd been so desperate to get away from me. '*You're making me feel like a rapist*,' he'd snarled.

'I'm sorry,' I'd whimpered.

'Just stop it. Stop trying to make me feel guilty.'

'I'm not,' I'd gasped. 'I'm really not.'

'Then stop crying. *Stop crying!*'

'I can't,' I'd sobbed. 'I can't.'

I'd pushed the palms of my hands on to my eyes, doubled over, but nothing, *nothing* would stop it.

'I'm going for a shower,' he'd growled at me. 'Either you will have stopped this nonsense by the time I get back or don't be here.' Every word had been like a razor through the centre of my being, each syllable a sword that slashed another part of me and produced large, quiet tears.

He really hadn't understood why I was sobbing: I'd been crying because he had done this thing – I couldn't pretend it was anything other than what it was – which meant I wasn't allowed to love him. But I did. I loved him so much.

When I'd heard the shower spurt on, I had got up, grabbed my jacket and left the flat. Without really knowing where I'd been going, I had walked down to the river, still hiding behind huge sunglasses as the tears continued to stream down my face. This was the money shot the photographers would love to have: me leaving the house in tears, proof that all was still not well in the world of Todd and Nikky. At the river, I'd turned towards the Tube station, walking slowly with my head down. With every step, the tears had slowed, with every movement away from the flat, away from Todd, a real calmness had descended upon me. My phone had begun ringing in my pocket and I'd known it would be Todd. I had virtually no one else to call me.

By the time I had got to the Tube station my phone had rung at least twenty times; each time I had let it go to voicemail. Normally, there'd be hell to pay for not answering – he'd ask me and ask me and ask me what I was doing that meant I couldn't answer the phone; why did I disrespect him by ignoring him; who was I with, what was his name, how long had I been fucking him... On and on and on he would go until I'd be quivering, wondering if I *had* been doing something, if I *was* behaving in a way that was disrespectful. In the gaps between rings, I'd stood outside the Tube station entrance, taken the phone out of my pocket and switched it off to go underground. I hadn't switched it on again and I didn't really care what the consequences would be.

Once my trip down Memory Lane had halted at this park bench, I had felt totally calm. Totally calm, totally alone – just some girl, sitting on a bench, looking sad because she'd had a row with her fiancé. I closed my eyes, tried to call up a song that would play through my mind and take me away from it all. Run-DMC's 'It's Like That' began. Its heavy beat was like a balm, it dampened down all the raw edges of my nerves, helped me to think. Helped me to see the reality of the situation: I had nowhere to go.

I had nowhere else and it was getting dark. Eventually, when the dark and the cold had merged to create night, I got up and started the long journey back.

The moment the flat's front door shut behind me he was there, I was in his arms, he was holding me so close I could barely breathe. 'I didn't mean for you to leave, you big silly,' he said. 'Where the hell have you been? I didn't mean for you to actually go – I thought it would stop you crying. I didn't think you'd take me so literally. When have I ever meant anything like that? I've been calling you. I was so worried. Where the fuck have you been?'

He paused then, his monologue over, and I was meant to take up the loose end he had left for me.

'Just around,' I said quietly. I wanted him off me, away from me, but I couldn't say that. I had nowhere else to go, no parents to reach out to, so I had to accept all of this, didn't I? It wasn't like he was going to change, it wasn't like I had any other option.

He finally let me go, but took my hand instead and led me through to the living room and to the sofa. 'I've been thinking,' he said, 'that we should set the date for the wedding.'

Married? *Married?* After the past few days, after today, he thought that was a good idea?

'Nikky, I've been a dick to you recently. I'm under so much pressure at the club and I'm not dealing with it very well. I shouldn't take it out on you but I do. I'm sorry. I'm really, really sorry. I'm going to change, for you. I love you, and I'm willing to change. I don't want you to feel bad again, about anything. I'm going to change and having the wedding to focus on will be really helpful.'

I could feel the tears welling up again. But not the tears from before – these were tears of pure, unadulterated relief. I pushed them down, though, stopped them leaving my eyes in case he misunderstood. This was what I wanted. I just wanted him to admit it, to understand what he'd been doing, to acknowledge that he was taking things out on me and then try to change. If he changed, went back to being the lovely, perfect man I'd met years ago, we'd be all right. I could pretend the other night didn't happen, I could ignore all those things I'd been thinking about earlier, and we could go back to being happy.

'What do you say?' Todd asked.

'I think it'd be amazing if you could do that,' I said quietly.

Todd reached out to stroke a lock of my hair out of my face and I flinched. Shame flittered across his face and guilt spun inside my chest – he was trying his best. 'Baby, I love you,' he said softly. 'And I'm sorry for how things have been. I am going to do my absolute best to turn this around so we can get married as a new start.'

'OK,' I replied. 'That'd be great.'

He pulled me down on to his lap and reached around me for his diary, which was splayed open on the coffee table. 'I'm going to need a lot of help,' he added. 'I'm going to need you to let me know when I'm being out of order, don't just let it slide.' He was distracted as he talked because he was flipping pages, searching, I presumed, for a month that was free. 'And don't be too hard on me if I don't always get it right.' *Flip, flip, flip.* 'I'm going to try to stop being such a stress head.' *Flip, flip, flip.* 'And it'd be great if you would stop pushing my buttons so often.' *Flip, flip, flip.* 'It'd be great if you could reassure me more often, and let me know how well I'm doing.' *Flip, flip, flip.* 'How does that sound?'

He finally stopped flipping and looked at me. It sounded like I would be doing as much as him, if not more, to change.

'Fine. It sounds fine,' I said. What else was I going to say when I had nowhere to go and he had promised to change?

Todd leant in to kiss me and I flinched again. This time he didn't seem to notice, didn't experience any shame or regret. He had moved on from what had happened so I let him kiss me knowing I was expected to have moved on now, too.

Roni

'To be honest with you, Veronica, I thought you'd be back by the weekend after you left. Begging for your room back and wanting to get back to your studies,' my father reveals. He doesn't do big emotions, my dad. Taciturn is how I would describe him. He takes his time to consider things, to formulate how he feels.

I know, though, that he is pleased I am back. Gently teasing me is his way of telling me so. I was seventeen when I told my parents that I wouldn't be going to university after A levels but instead, I was going to start the process of becoming a nun, which meant speaking to many different convents and having visits with them, working up to a short stay and then eventually moving into a convent. They had both been stunned, enough for Mum to pause in her sewing, but not to actually look up at me, and enough for Dad to lower his paper and ask me what had brought that about. 'A book?' I said. *And the silence reading that book brought to my constantly noisy mind.* 'A nun gave me a book and it made me want to be a nun.'

'Right you are then,' Dad had said. Mum went back to her sewing.

It'd been a big deal to me at the time. I had thought they would have something to say about me admitting that I had found God; that the thought of being closer to God was the nearest I had come to finding the silence inside. This, though, was my parents' reaction.

66

It was pretty much their reaction to everything: Dad would ask a couple of questions, Mum would avoid looking me in the eye, then everything would go back to normal. I was the last of their children at home: my brothers Brian and Damian had both fled to university as soon as they were old enough, rarely to be seen back at home again – not even for Christmas, Easter or summer.

This evening, four of us are sitting around the dinner table and it feels small in the dining room. Small's the wrong word – probably more close, snug, almost like we're all sitting on top of each other.

'Your mother had far more faith in you,' says Uncle Warren of my leaving to join a convent one hundred miles away from home. 'I knew she believed you were gone for good when she celebrated by throwing a party for twenty of her closest friends to regale them all with the plans she had for your room.'

After the time Uncle Warren left after Damian's accident, I started to notice how mean-spirited he could be. He could be nice most of the time, but then he would see a small sliver of vulnerability and he would crack it open with a nasty remark. However, there's more than a droplet of honesty in his meanness this time. The briefest of glances at my pink-cheeked mother shows he is telling the truth – the moment she and Dad waved me off through the iron gates of the monastery in the Coventry suburbs, she came back home and threw an 'I'M FREE!' party.

'I'm really grateful you threw that party, Mum,' I say. 'Thank you for believing in me enough to do that. When I first left, even though I'd been working towards becoming a nun for all those years, I wasn't sure it was what I wanted, or if I could do it, but I must have known on some level that I wouldn't have a place to come back to and that helped me to stay focused.'

Across the table, my uncle seems uncomfortable with what I have said because I haven't risen to his baiting either by biting back or bursting into tears.

'I hope you didn't really think that, Veronica?' Dad says. His forehead is knitted in a frown, his fork is paused halfway between his mouth and plate. 'You will always have a home here. Won't she, Margaret?'

'Hmm-hmm,' Mum replies.

It's odd, being called Veronica again. I was Sister Grace for over eighteen years. And now I am Veronica again to these people. When I introduce myself to new people I automatically go to call myself Grace.

'At least you don't look like a nun,' my uncle says. 'Those big penguin suits you all wear, used to give me the heebie-jeebies.'

I've missed Vespers. For the first time in seventeen years, since I was a postulant (a nun-in-waiting), I have missed Vespers and I am unsettled. I said my final Mass this morning, I carried out Lauds, even though it meant rushing for the train down from Coventry, but I have missed having my mind and heart filled with the beautiful singing of Vespers and I do not feel right. This is what I have to look forward to, I know. Stretching out ahead of me is a long life without the order, the calming islands of prayer, contemplation and Mass in my day. I used to almost resent them, those obligations I had to fulfil no matter what I was doing, no matter where I was, but now, I miss them like the second skin they were to me. I miss them for the moments they drew me from here and left me there. Even though, if I am honest with myself, in the past year, there has been so much disquiet in my prayers, a constant nagging need to follow another path.

'What, are you praying or something like that?' Uncle Warren asks.

'No,' I reply.

'I was saying, at least you're not all dressed up in the garb like demented, giant penguins.'

'I wasn't aware you required an answer to that,' I say.

'I'm just making conversation,' he says, again rattled by lack of upset.

'I see.'

'That's what people do, isn't it? Someone says something, the other person replies. It's called conversation.'

I smile at my plate. 'I often spend great swathes of my day in silence, and only really speak if I absolutely have to. Conversation is often very much rationed.'

'You really did that? You honestly lived in silence? I always thought that was a load of cock and bull.' Mum and Uncle Warren are very different people. She is posh and middle class and always keen for people to know how posh and middle class and refined she is, and he is posh and middle class but always being the mockney, playing at the East End-boy-done-good role.

'Yes,' I reply.

'That'd drive me bananas,' he says. 'Wouldn't it drive you bananas, Margaret?'

'Quite possibly,' Mum replies.

'How about you, Geoffrey, wouldn't it drive you crackers?' Uncle Warren asks, wanting more backup than a wishy-washy 'possibly'.

'No, I don't think it would, actually. I think it's admirable that Veronica was able to do that.'

'Yeah, especially since we could never shut her up as a kid,' Uncle Warren says.

Veronica. I am Veronica now, not Grace. The other Veronika Harper's middle name was Grace and she told me once that if she ever got to go on the stage as a dancer she would use Grace instead of Veronika or Nika, like everyone called her, because it would make her a different person. She wouldn't be shackled to all the different expectations that came with her given, used name. When my first Mother Superior named me Grace (she had asked me to choose a name, but I wanted her, and therefore God, to find the right one for me), I knew I had done the right thing. It was a sign from above that I was meant to dedicate my life in service to others for what I had done to Veronika. It would be a daily reminder of why I was there. I needed to atone for what had gone before, do as much as I could to make up for my betrayal.

'I said, especially as we couldn't shut you up as a kid,' Uncle Warren repeats. I am supposed to laugh.

'I know what you said,' I reply.

Irritation radiates outwards from him, and with my eyes fixed on my food, I can still see him look first to my mother on his right and then to my father on his left, surprised that neither of them are laughing either. They both have small smiles of quasi-amusement playing around their lips, but none of us are laughing, nor tumbling into anecdotes about how much I used to talk. None of us have any because it didn't happen.

'You wanna watch her,' Uncle Warren declares. 'She'll have you down at that church in no time if you're not careful. Daily Mass and weekly confession, you mark my words.'

'I would never do that,' I say. 'Everyone has to find their own path to God, or their own path without God. I would never force anyone to choose.'

My mockney uncle looks at his watch, the same ostentatious, large gold Rolex he has had since I was a child. 'Phew! Who had twenty minutes before God was mentioned? Geoffrey? Margaret?' Uncle Warren throws his head back and laughs, his slender hand bashes on to the table – *bang, bang, bang* – to emphasise how funny he is.

'I'll make a start on the washing-up,' I state.

'Oh, no, no,' my mother says.

'It really is no bother at all. Once I've washed up, I'll make you a cup of tea or coffee.'

'Wow, this is like having maid service,' Uncle Warren chimes in.

'Yes, I suppose it is,' I reply.

That wave of irritation swells to tsunami proportions and may well engulf him. There was a time, even after I stopped liking him, that I would worry about pleasing him, would panic if I had upset him in any way. I don't feel that way any more. Maybe it's being thirty-six now. Possibly it's my time away. Most likely? It's the obsession I have with Veronika. I keep remembering the first time I saw her and knowing that we were going to be best friends for ever.

Nika

My sister runs across the park towards where I am sitting on the bench by the swings. She has a box in her arms, and it bounces as she runs, her straight black hair whipping into her face, the wind clawing at her long black coat. I stand to meet her and she virtually throws the box on to the bench beside my rucksack and guitar case, and barrels into me, clutching me to her.

Slowly, I slip my arms around her. I didn't expect this kind of welcome from her. We'd never been close and I didn't know she'd miss me. 'Nika, Nika,' she says with each sob, bringing me closer and closer to her. 'Nika, Nika, Nika. I thought you were dead. I really, really thought you were dead. I thought—' Her words disintegrate into the sobs that fill the tiny space between us. Her grief ... it seems huge, it seems unassailable. She clings to me as she cries, as though she has been waiting years to let go like this, years to accept that she may never see me again. I didn't even know. I didn't know anyone would miss me if I was gone.

London, 2004

I sat beside the quiet man in the expensive, well-fitting suit, watching a train gear up to speed off into the distance. I loved to do this on the days I went shopping or to the hairdresser or to the gym twenty minutes away. I loved to take a detour and come and sit here, by the

71

river, on the hood of this black car, watching the trains come and go from London Victoria.

'What do you think I should do, Frank?' I asked after the train horn had faded into the distance, and we watched another train come crawling towards the station.

Frank was my driver. Todd's last big new signing, which was for so much money it made my eyes water just thinking about it, had meant he was able to splash out a little more: get himself a newer, faster car, more designer clothes, pay off a huge chunk of the mortgage on his flat. And also have a car service on hand for me whenever I wanted to go anywhere. I'd wanted to learn to drive, had brought it up with him, but Todd had thought this would be better for me. Less dangerous, less stressful. The driver would be able to take me to places, look out for me, stop any photographers getting too close. Not that the photographers bothered with me any more. Hadn't since we'd announced the engagement. They bothered with him, were always showing photos of him chatting to various women, spinning the stories to never quite say he was cheating, but hinting at it.

The driver thing was kind of nice because I got to know the drivers: very often they'd let me ride up front with them and we'd have a chat about films, music and books. Frank was my favourite. He drove me the most regularly, and we liked the same books and films, he also *loved* music. We talked a lot about music – not only the albums and singles, the charts and types of music. We talked about the words, the way they were woven into the threads of the music, the way certain ones were chosen, placed here, omitted there. Words and sound were like a dance, we agreed, a duet that had to be carefully managed, always spinning and moving together in perfect motion with each other. He'd confessed, when I asked him, that the song he was embarrassed about listening to over and over was 'Pride (In the Name of Love)' by U2.

'About what, Miss Nikky?' he asked. He was a tall, gruff-looking man in his forties. He had shaved his head, he said, when he was younger because he thought it'd make him look tough. As he got older and worked in more respectable jobs, he'd thought about the idea of having hair and it made him look odd whenever he tried to grow it, like he was trying to hide who he was.

'My name's not Nikky,' I confessed to him.

'I'm sorry, Miss, have I been calling you the wrong name all this time? I'm ever so sorry.' He was well spoken even though he was wrapped up in that gruff, tough, hairless package.

'No. I suppose that's part of what I was asking you. See, when I first met Todd, I told him my name was Nika, as in short for Veronika, and he decided he preferred Nikky, so called me Nikky. I never really pushed it with asking him to call me by my name because I didn't want to hurt him. And that's never changed. Because I never want to hurt him, I don't make a big deal of it when things upset me, or when he's hurt me, and now we're here. I'm getting married in four weeks and I don't know what to do. If I don't marry him, then he'll be hurt. And if I marry him...'

Frank remained silent as I talked, but he was listening. I knew he was also listening to the words – how I'd woven them together, what they meant, how they danced through what I was telling him about my life.

'Do you think I should marry him, Frank?'

'With all due respect, Miss Nika, I don't know anything about your relationship except what I see when I drive you both in my car, and what you have just told me.'

'OK. Forget what I've just told you – from what you've seen, do you think I should marry him?'

'With all due respect, Miss Nika, I think people should marry for love or for money, but never to avoid hurting someone and never to make anyone, not even themselves, feel better.'

I heard what he said without saying the actual words, and I heard how he used my name twice without question. The conversation was like a song: all the words used were ones that danced around what I wanted to ask, what he thought I should do, how I was going to tell Todd I couldn't marry him.

I can't marry him. The acceptance of that was like a sudden bloom of relief in my chest. *I can't marry him.*

Todd hadn't changed in the last six months, he hadn't gone back to being the man I fell in love with, even though I had to think three times before I spoke so I didn't push his buttons, even though I told him every time I left the house where I'd been, who I'd seen and what we'd talked about. He still did it, as well. *Still* did it. We pretended it was no big deal most of the time because I didn't cry any more so he didn't need to scream at me to stop making him feel like a rapist.

Todd had tried, I knew he had, but he couldn't manage it. This was who he was, and it wouldn't be fair to keep on expecting him to be any different. He was who he was. I had to accept that and find a way to explain to him that I had to move on.

'Thanks for the chat, Frank,' I told him as he held open the back door for me to get out. We always stopped a little around the corner and I would get out and go into the back seat so outside the flat he would be opening the expected door for me. I didn't ever want to cause any trouble for the drivers by being inappropriate.

'You're welcome, Miss Nika. And remember, only ever marry for love or money.'

'I will.'

He carried the cardboard bags with long string handles, filled with five different pairs of potential wedding shoes from two expensive shops, to the front door of the flats, and left them on the metal mat.

'Goodbye, Miss Nika,' he said. 'And good luck, with whatever you decide to do.'

'So, which is it?' Todd asked while we ate dinner.

When I'd come in, he'd nipped out to the shops for some extra supplies and had come back to find me in the shower. I'd gone to the shower to think about what Frank had said. I'd turned it over and over in my head like I was moving a coin over and over in my hand. After the shower I'd gone to find him but he was in his office, wearing his thick, padded headphones, listening to music, so I'd gone back to the bedroom, had lain on the bed, thinking and staring at the ceiling.

Before I'd realised it, hours had passed and in that time he'd whipped up one of his amazing creations: spinach and ricotta ravioli with a delicious red meat ragù. He'd put on low lighting and he'd opened a really expensive bottle of red. He didn't have practice any time that week so he had time off, which meant he could cook, we could eat together and talk.

'Which is what?' I asked.

'Which is it that you're doing with me? Marrying for love or money? Isn't that what *"Frank"* told you?' he said, adding a sneer on the driver's name. 'He's fired, by the way, for being overfamiliar. I'd already told them he couldn't drive you any more after today, but then he was calling you Nika, like he knew you, and I realised he was probably in love with you. And I can't have that.'

'Sorry, I don't understand.' I moved my head up from staring at my food, snatched my mind away from what I was thinking about because it seemed important that I paid full attention to Todd and what he was saying. I had heard it and now I replayed it, I couldn't quite believe what he'd said and needed him to clarify it. 'What do you mean, Frank's fired?'

'What do you think fired means?'

'But why? And how do you know . . . ' My voice trailed away for a moment, not sure I should ask what I was about to ask: 'Have you been bugging the cars I use?' No one would *actually* do this unless they were on a TV show. Todd and I weren't on a TV show. Although parts of our life were unreal sometimes, and seeing myself on magazines was odd, seeing him play for England was surreal, but we didn't live *that* kind of unreal life.

'You haven't stuck to our agreement, have you?' he said insouciantly.

Todd was being so casual, so nonchalant, that I wanted to stand up and, in the same manner, upend his glass table. Maybe that would get him to take this a bit more seriously. 'What?' I asked.

75

'I asked you, practically begged you to help me. To not push my buttons, to not give me things to worry about, to reassure me that I was doing well, and you haven't been doing any of it. In fact, you've given me nothing but more worries that you're going to cheat on me. Because of that, because of what you have done, I had to be sure what was going on when I wasn't with you. And from what I heard, I've a right to be worried.'

'*You* have a right to be worried? *You?* I'm not the one being photographed with a different woman draped over me every night. With little digs from "anonymous sources" that these women have intimate knowledge of your tattoos and birthmarks. If anyone has the right to be worried, it's me.'

'Don't try and turn this on me. You're the one who's been having cosy little chats with the drivers.'

'I talk to people. That's what most normal human beings do. I talk to people. And you've had someone fired for it? You're sick. I can't believe you had me recorded. Who does that?' I stopped talking and moving. Slowly, the only things that moved about me were my eyes, darting around the room, trying to spot them, trying to see if they were there. 'Have you bugged this place as well so you can listen to me during the day? Is that why you're always listening to stuff on your headphones? Have you been recording me? You're *sick.*'

'What's sick is having to listen to you talking about music and love songs with another man.' In other words, yes – he had bugged the flat. 'You never talk to me like that.'

I couldn't believe what I was hearing. 'Todd, I never talk to you like that because you have no interest in talking to me. I try to chat to you and you always dismiss it, or tell me I'm frying your brain. You have no interest in me whatsoever. And you don't like me having friends – some of your friends' wives try to be friendly but you make such a big deal every time I talk to them or make arrangements to go out I don't bother. You don't like me calling people, you huff and puff every time I speak on the phone. You don't like me emailing – and have to check all the time who I'm messaging and what I'm saying. So, you know what, yes, when I get the chance to speak to real people, I do.' I shake my head at him. 'I can't believe you convinced those people to let you record me in the car.'

'It didn't take any convincing. The owner of the company understood my worries about what you might do given your drugs history.'

'I HAVEN'T GOT A DRUGS HISTORY!' I screamed at him. I was on my feet, my whole body burning with rage. '*You* are the drug taker, *you* are the drug user, I've never taken drugs in my life!'

The shock on his face was real. Partly because I'd never shouted at him before, and partly, too, because he'd genuinely forgotten that I never actually took drugs, that I only allowed him to say I did to save his reputation and his career.

'Look, let's forget all this, calm down.' He indicated to the chair behind me. 'Sit down. Talk about this rationally.'

'There is nothing rational about what you've done. No matter how long we talk about it, it will never be rational.'

'Come on, Nikky, I just need to be able to trust you. Surely you understand that. It'll be better when we're married. I'll feel more secure. Once you're properly mine, we'll be all right.'

Todd thought he owned me. Or rather, he thought that he partially owned me – when I married him the process of ownership would be complete and I would be stamped across the forehead as 'sold'.

'I am not marrying you,' I replied. 'There is no way on Earth I'm marrying you.'

His anger, which was always there, simmering and brooding just below his calm, charming surface, exploded and he swiped away the plates, the glasses and cutlery in front of him. 'YOU FUCKING WILL!' he roared at me. '*It's all planned, the guests have all replied, there are important people coming to it! You will do as you're told!*'

This moment, his final explosion, had an odd effect on me. Instead of being scared, or desperately trying to work out how to appease him while scrabbling around for excuses to make myself believe he didn't mean it, I stayed calm. I *was* calm. I stared at the fiery form of my fiancé and felt nothing but a certainty about what to do next. I slowly twisted the diamond ring off my finger, placed it on the table between us.

All his rage and fury fled, and he stared at the ring in shock. He didn't expect this, truly he didn't. 'Nikky—' he began.

'My name's Nika or Veronika. I am not called Nikky.'

'Nikky suits you better.'

'But it's not my name. Why can't you understand that? Why can't you use it? I told Frank my name *once* and he used it. I'm sure if I told anyone my name they'd use it. Why can't you?'

'Is that what this is all about? Frank? If he means so much to you, I'll get him his job back. But he'd better be grateful.'

'Grateful for getting back a job he never should have lost in the first place?' I ran my hands over my head, smoothing over the curls that had been put in three days ago. 'Can you not see how crazy that sounds?'

'Look, look, we can get over this. We can go back to working on our relationship, trying a bit harder.'

'No,' I said. 'I don't want to. Not any more. It's over, Todd.'

He smiled, then chuckled to himself, then laughed out loud. Disbelief, of course. 'It's not over. It can't be. I won't let it be. We can't break up.'

I said nothing. I was sure that it only took one person to break up a relationship, but Todd wouldn't accept that. He would argue and argue with anything I said, would try to engage me in justifying why I wanted to split up. And I knew, from all the times he'd done it to me about other things – mainly about sex – nothing I said would convince him I had the right to make my own decisions, including the right to end this.

'You, you're nothing without me. You do realise that, don't you?' he said. 'The clothes you wear, the shoes on your feet, the jewellery, make-up, hairstyle, all of it is from me. You were nothing and I made you who you are. And more than that, your phone, your computer, the money in your bank account, the credit cards are all mine. *All mine.* Without me, you're nothing.'

'I know,' I replied. 'You're right.' '*And that's why I have to leave. Maybe without you I'll be me again, not this Nikky person you created,*' I added silently.

'You'll be back,' he said as I walked towards the door. 'When you realise what life is like out there in the real world, you'll be back.'

'*I won't, you know,*' I said in my head. And I wouldn't. I knew no matter what happened, I would not be back.

Roni

London, 2016

'I was only joking earlier,' Uncle Warren informs me. He made a big deal of coming into my parents' kitchen from the dining room and helping me to wash up. He stands across the kitchen, arms across his chest, leaning against the fridge. This was his favourite room in the house at one point. He was often dragging me in here to show me something or other.

'I know,' I say. The pan my mother has used to cook the rice is proving tricky to clean. I should probably soak it, but I remember how much Mum hated seeing things soaking in the sink: *'It makes the place look like a junk yard,'* she would say. I have to clean it now.

'If you knew, why didn't you laugh then?' Uncle Warren asks.

'Did you need me to laugh?' I ask.

'Come on now, Roni, it was only a little banter.'

'I see.'

'You're really getting on my nerves with that holier-than-thou attitude,' he snarls. His voice is low so my parents can't hear, even though they are in the living room at the front of the house, and he is suddenly, I'm aware, a lot closer to me.

'I'm sorry to hear that.'

'If someone makes a joke, you laugh. That's the polite thing to do. I'd have thought you of all people would know that.'

'Me?'

'Yeah, a nun.'

The rubber gloves go right up to my elbows and I'm sure they're hindering rather than helping the process of removing seemingly welded-on pieces of rice from the bottom of Mum's pan. The rice is rock hard and web-like. I drop the sponge and instead pick at it, although the rubber gloves make that much more difficult. 'I'm not a nun any more.' I take off one glove and go at the piece of rice again. I concentrate on it until I hear him leave the room.

Once I am alone, I stop the frantic cleaning. 'I'm not an adoring seven-year-old any more, either,' I add under my breath.

Nika

'Sorry for all the cloak-and-dagger stuff,' Sasha says. She's aged in the eighteen years or so since I last saw her. Her face has filled out a little, but her eyes – large, brown and beautiful – are underscored by lines of sleep deprivation. Her forehead is pretty unlined, and her skin is dewy soft and blemish-free thanks to the make-up she has expertly applied, but she looks like she has lived every single second of her years the hard way. She looks younger than me, though, I'd imagine, because she hasn't lived as eventful a life as I have.

'Mummy and Daddy still think I'm the demon child, then?' My laugh gags me as it should. If they won't have me to stay for even the briefest of whiles, no one will, because it's impossible to do anything without ID today. Much as I didn't have much ID as Grace, I have even less as Veronika.

'No, no, not at all. It's your ex,' Sasha explains.

'My ex?' *Vinnie?* I haven't had anything to do with Vinnie in over five years and even then he only knew me as Grace or 'Ace'. Then I remember: the other ex, the one who started all this. 'You mean Todd?'

'Yeah, him. Mr Big I Am.'

'What's he got to do with anything?'

'He comes over here sometimes. In fact, he's due a visit any day now.'

'What?' I ask in despair. 'We finished over ten years ago. And he's still hanging around?' *I knew he wouldn't let me go. I knew it.*

'No, no, not exactly like that. It's complicated. A couple of months after they said in the papers that you'd split up and you'd just disappeared, he showed up at Mum and Dad's house. Caused a huge stir on our street in his posh car and everything. People were coming out to get his autograph and everything. Mummy called me and I went over with Ralph and he was there, with your stuff, saying you'd run away and he was so upset because he didn't understand why. How he'd always wanted to meet them but you'd done your best to keep them apart. All he'd ever tried to do was help you, especially with your drug problem. Mummy and Daddy were lapping it up like it was chocolate milk. Me and Ralph were like, "Yeah, right, Nika, drugs, don't think so." But you know what they're like, they listen to the person who sounds the most plausible, especially after all that stuff in the papers. Anyway, he said to them to call him if they saw you so he could come and talk some sense into you.'

'Yeah, but that was ten years ago.'

'Yeah, it began ten years ago, but for a while he started coming over once a month for Sunday lunch and Ralph told me a couple of months later that he was sure he saw him hanging about across the road from Mum and Dad's, just watching the house. Now we've moved back in, every now and then I'm sure I'll catch a glimpse of him. Different car, but I'm sure it's him. Then sure enough, a few days later, he'll drop by with an expensive bottle of something for Daddy, a bunch of flowers for Mummy, some line about just seeing how they're doing and feeling like they should have been his parents instead of his own.' My sister shakes her head, her onyx-black hair glistening in the light. 'Seriously, at one point I thought he'd murdered you and was trying to find out how much we knew cos he was trying so hard to be Mr Nice *all the time*. And when I never heard from you about where to send your post on to... I kept thinking... The worst, basically.'

I run my hands over my head, agitated, annoyed, highly irritated that after all this time he still hasn't let me go. 'I really thought he'd have given up by now. Especially since he's been married twice and is engaged again.' Is it because I was the one who ran away? With all the others he has had very public break-ups, copious amounts of mud-slinging on each side, some of it sticking in unpleasant clumps. He never had the chance to do that with me, so maybe that's why he can't let it go. Todd hated to lose more than anything: if you gave him the choice between winning something or being eternally happy, he wouldn't have to think carefully about it, he would choose winning any day of the week.

'You know all that about him?' she asks.

'Yes, I always try to make sure I know where he is.'

'Where've *you* been all this time?' she asks.

I stare at my older sister and suddenly I feel antiquated compared to her. I feel like an ancient being who has much knowledge and wisdom to impart to an unwilling pupil. She doesn't really want to know – she wants to hear a neat, nice story about what I've been doing and where I have been living. 'Birmingham, mainly,' I say. 'How come you moved in with Mummy and Daddy, then? Is one of them sick?'

'No, no... Ralph lost his job a while back. We tried to struggle on, but in the end we had to give up the house or declare bankruptcy. So about a year ago, all of us moved in with Mummy and Daddy. It's really generous that they've let us stay this long, really. We've nearly got enough saved so we can move out again soon.'

'That sounds like it was really hard. I'm really sorry to hear that.'

'It was hard; Ralph was so depressed, I almost lost him... But, you know, onwards and upwards.'

'What do you mean, all of us moved back in? Has Marlon come back, too?'

'No, I mean... Oh my God!' Sasha sits upright in her seat, claps her hands. 'You don't know, do you? I've got a daughter! You're an aunt!'

The world seems to slow right down, the people, the air, *everything* is barely moving. I'm an aunt. I've missed out on being an aunt. 'That's amazing!' I shriek and throw my arms around her like she's only just told me she is pregnant. I suppose she has only just told me – that she's pregnant, had a baby and has had a certain number of years with her. These are several bits of fantastic news all bundled together and delivered in one go – that deserves a shriek. 'How old is she?'

'She's six and she's called Tracy-Dee. And she's the light of my life.'

'Where is she?' I ask.

'Mummy's taken her out to some family day thing up at the library. You know what Mummy's like – loves a baby and a toddler, can't really deal with anyone above eight though. She dotes on Tracy-Dee.'

From the pocket of her jacket, Sasha produces her mobile phone and, after pressing a few buttons, hands it to me with a photo of the most gorgeous little girl I have ever seen filling the screen: her hair is in three neat sections, each plaited and tied at its base with yellow ribbons that have huge, bunny-ear loops. She smiles at her camera, with a glint of mischief in her eyes. 'She's beautiful, adorable,' I say. 'I love her and I haven't even met her.'

'You don't have any... ?' Sasha asks gently.

'Me? God, no, no.'

After a beat of silence, after watching me look at her daughter, she speaks again. Quietly determined this time, she asks again: 'Where've you been, Nika?'

'I told you, Birmingham.' I turn my attention to the box she brought with her. It is not big, but it is awkward to carry. The brown lid is folded together to form a cross that provides a flimsy security. 'What's in the box?'

'Your letters and some of the things your ex brought back. Your passport's in there, your birth certificate, National Insurance card, I think. Some of your old payslips. I hope you don't mind but even before we moved in I've been destroying all the really old bank statements and stuff because they were really piling up and Mummy and Daddy wouldn't do anything with them. You can always get new statements from the bank. And I think you got a new bank card recently, which should be in there, and the pin number, I think.'

A bank card, a pin number. That would mean I could get money from my old bank account. Yes, Todd was probably keeping an eye on it, but if I took all the money out in London, I could close it down, open up a new account wherever I moved to. Yes, I had planned to stay here, but if Todd is still around, it's probably best if I stay well away. But this is a lifeline: I have ID. Yes, it's in the form of an out-of-date passport, but I have cards and people rarely question cards. I have money and I have no need to beg my parents for forgiveness nor consider the 'sleeping rough' option.

'Where have you been, Nika?' Sasha asks again. She raises her hand. 'And don't say "Birmingham". I mean really, where have you been?'

I shake my head at her, try to find the words from all the millions out there that will make some sense of it all. When I can understand it, I will be able to explain to her. 'I can't talk about that, not right now,' I confess. 'Can you take my word for it when I promise you that I will tell you about it one day?'

'Suppose I'll have to, won't I?'

I reach out and rest my hand on my sister's shoulder. I'm overwhelmed by having the ability to touch her. Since her reaction to seeing me, I've been wondering why we weren't close, and why I didn't send her a card just to let her know I was still alive. Was it all the secrets I had, the ones I shared with the other Veronica Harper that I didn't dare share with her? Was it that she seemed so happy when we were growing up that I seemed insignificant to her? Or was it that our parents seemed to have pigeonholes for each of us to fit into: Golden Boy (who could do no wrong); Good Girl (who sometimes did as she was told); and The Other One (who told a secret that they didn't want to hear) and those pigeonholes meant we played our roles and we never tried to cross over into the other's place. Touching her now, feeling that she is real and human and someone who I could probably relate to, I am wishing myself back into the past. Back to the point where she is the person I turn to, I confide in, who I ask for help. I am wishing that I realised who my sister was, could be, all those years ago. 'Sash, please don't be angry with me for not telling you. It's not a simple story of I went to there and I did this and now I've decided to come back... I will tell you, everything, one day, but not today, not right now.' I'm still reeling from having to escape from a life where not only the police but a very dangerous criminal are both going to try to hunt me down.

My sister heaves a deep sigh and looks me over. It's not often people look me over, or really see me, and it's an odd sensation, someone checking me out. 'I like your hair,' she says after a bit.

'I like yours,' I tell her.

'Do you have somewhere to stay tonight?'

'Not right now, but I'll find somewhere.'

'Look, we can go back and wait for Mummy and I'll tell them not to call your ex. I'm sure they'll let you stay for a few nights.'

'You know, thanks, but I'll be fine. I thought I wanted to see them, but now I've seen you I've realised that I don't need to. You're enough. I'll come back and see them another time.'

Her face is suddenly fierce and hard. 'You're not going to disappear again, are you?' she asks sternly.

I shake my head. 'No, no, I'm not. I'm probably not going to stick around London, especially now I know Todd is still hanging around, but the last thing I'm going to do is disappear again. I can promise you that if nothing else.'

I'm going to do things differently this time. That policeman has put the kernel of the idea of living a different life into my head. I am going to do that. With my identity in the cardboard box, I am going to start again, properly. I am not going to disappear again.

London, 2004

The shock took a little while to wear off.

I sat on a bench in Victoria train station, the world whizzing around me at a breakneck speed. I did not know where I was going, I did not know what I was doing. I had virtually nothing with me because Todd was right: it was all his. He had bought almost everything for me. I had disappeared into the role he had carved out for me: I had become Nikky. Because he was nice to me, because he didn't seem as bad as what had gone before, I had let him lead me into being a person of his choosing.

The shock was wearing off, I was shaking and I didn't know what to do. When I had run away from home last time, I'd been seventeen and had planned how to get away from the life I was living for nearly two years. I had a rucksack and an old red suitcase I'd found in my parents' loft when I finally packed up to never come back to them. I had been through *Loot* every day until I'd found a house share and with the money I'd saved, I'd been able to move in. That was only seven years ago, but the world felt different now. I was different now. I hadn't worked in years because it had caused Todd such angst me not being there when he got home. I would need a job so I could get money, so I could find somewhere to stay.

I needed a place to stay.

I stared around me, at the people who rushed on by, all with somewhere to go, somewhere to be. I could be her – the woman in the grey skirt suit, her head down, her bag clutched to her shoulder, weaving in and out of the crowd, desperate to get somewhere. She had a purpose. I could be him – the man with the slow walk, a large rucksack on his back, no worries on his face, hood up, no sense of needing to be anywhere in a hurry, but still with somewhere to be. I could be that toddler, ambling along with bunches in her hair, trying to keep up with her adult, but wondering at the world of busyness around her. I could be them: all of them, any of them, except they were there for a reason, passing through – I was there because I had nowhere else to go.

I could go back to Todd's to grab some of the things there, but almost everything there belonged to him, had been paid for by him. If I went back, he would keep me there.

I knew what he'd be doing right then: he'd have called my mobile, only to find it was ringing and ringing itself out on the bedside table. Then he'd sit and go through my phone, looking for something, any clue that would *prove* that I was cheating on him, that I was contacting people without clearing it with him first. When he found nothing, absolutely nothing, he'd really panic. He'd call Murray, start screaming about how I'd betrayed him, stabbed him in the back, and how they had to find me. 'Murray, mate, she knows stuff, stuff that could hurt me, hurt you, too. We have to find her,' he'd be shouting. Because he knew what it could mean for him if I told anyone the truth about what he got up to. The things he sniffed and smoked, the stuff he got turned on by. He knew, too, that I wouldn't need proof. Just the hint of scandal, just the right words in a few ears, and he would be sunk. All those advertisers and sponsors who paid him huge money now he was in a team at the top of the Premier League, who had decency clauses in all their contracts, would desert him in an instant.

It was him, I realised. All along he had been the 'anonymous source' who fed the press those stories about me, who had given them photos of drugs in my handbags, who had started public rows so he'd be seen telling me off. Of course it was him. It had never occurred to me he would do that, because we were 'in it together', but there was no one else who would bother with that. It benefited him in so many ways, not only to deflect anything off him, but also to keep me isolated, paranoid, reliant on him. Every time I thought someone was talking about me behind my back, it made me cling to him tighter because it proved that I didn't have anyone else to go to.

He'll find me, I thought to myself. He has the money and the single-mindedness to do that.

The only things I had in my pockets were my keys and my purse. I didn't need to open my purse to know that I had £100 cash with four credit cards and two cash cards – one for my account and one for the account Todd had opened for me, the one that he put money into. He preferred me to use credit cards because he could see what I was spending money on – cash meant I could do something he couldn't control.

I was scared then. All these things coming into focus, all the big ways and little ways he controlled me, dressed up as love, painted as concern and care, were all ways to make me helpless and dependent. I wouldn't get far with the little cash in my purse. If I used credit cards he'd find me. If I used the cash cards for my accounts, he'd find me. Todd had shown me quite clearly when he got the car service to record my conversations that he had the means and determination to find someone willing to look the other way or do something completely unethical, to get what he wanted.

My eyes scanned the people moving around the station, the people I could be in another life, the people who had purpose and a place to be, and I realised that all of them were strangers. And I was safer with strangers than I was in the place called home. We're always taught to be scared of strangers: stranger danger, the person lurking in an alleyway, the person who will plan your demise. But what about the people you know? It'd only ever been the people who knew me who had hurt me. Even Todd had been nice to me when I was a stranger, when I didn't know him. And people like Frank, poor Frank who was essentially a stranger, who was now out of a job because he was kind to me.

I had to walk away from this life I had, where, once again, someone I knew was hurting me. I looked around the station, looking for a cashpoint. I spotted one, right across the concourse, right near where the trains went to Gatwick Airport, and the coast. Todd had taken me to Brighton a few times: he liked to stay in the big, posh hotels and go out clubbing. It was a smaller city, but there were fewer photographers, more people who wouldn't recognise us, and even more who would look the other way if he got his stash out as long as he shared. I'd loved it there, and fleetingly I thought of heading there, but I couldn't go there now. Far too likely to be spotted and remembered.

No, Brighton was out. I would get cash out now. I would sit and wait until after midnight, then I would get another lot of cash out to the limit from both accounts. Then I would use the credit cards to buy some things, ditch them all and then leave London. London would be too unsafe; I would be forever looking over my shoulder, always wondering when I would bump into someone who knew

Todd, knew me, knew us when we were a couple. It wouldn't take long for Todd to give up – a couple of months should do it. He'd realise that I wasn't going to say anything to anyone, he would find someone else and everyone would forget that I ever existed. Three months was all it would take, I was sure of it.

I handed the driver my brown leather rucksack, filled with three pairs of jeans, five jumpers, five vests, seven bras, seven pairs of knickers, socks and another pair of Converse trainers. All things I'd managed to find in the shops around Victoria station earlier that morning. It obviously hadn't occurred to Todd to come to the station. He'd be driving round to his friends' houses, begging their wives to tell him if they'd seen me because we'd had a huge row and he was so sorry.

I had walked the streets around Victoria most of the night. Each street was unique in how it felt. Some of the darker streets were not as threatening as the brighter, neon-cast ones; others were deathly quiet, the silence seeming to hide a thousand dangerous secrets. As I had walked, I'd suddenly started to see them: the people who were living on the streets, the ones I was like, who had nowhere to go. They curled up in doorways, grimy sleeping bags pulled up to their chins, hats pulled low over their ears, rucksacks used as pillows. I knew thousands of homeless people were out there, but I had never seen them so vividly before. It was like, before, they had been invisible but now I saw them. Clearly. I saw them and I knew that I could soon be like them.

I hated myself for that. For not seeing these people until it was a sudden possibility that I could be living like that. But if I left London, which I had to do anyway, went to a cheaper city, maybe I could make the money last a bit longer until I found a job and could maybe get a house share, maybe a long-term youth hostel. Anything but going back to Todd. Anything but going even further back to the world of my mum and dad. I had to move on.

I didn't bother to look around one last time as I boarded the coach. What was there to see? A city that I had loved, that I had believed in, that had let me down twice. London had been my one true love, it had so many wonderful parts to it, but at the end of it, when I analysed it, the city I loved had let me down. Let me get hurt. And I had to leave her behind. Maybe, one day, I'd be able to come back and stay here. Maybe we'd find each other again and we'd be happy together.

In the meantime, I walked the narrow walkway, head down, ignoring the other passengers, until I found a seat near the back of the coach, flopped myself into the seat by the window. I was on the slow coach so I'd have the chance, after the night I had just spent walking around, to sleep for a few hours. Before we even set off, I pulled my knees up to my chest, draped my jacket over myself and closed my eyes. I thought of poor Frank again just before I drifted off. I hoped Todd would do the right thing by Frank to sweeten the deal of me coming back if (probably *when*, in his mind) he found me. I wanted to help Frank, wanted to plead his case with his employers, possibly threaten them with exposure because them recording clients becoming public knowledge would be bad for business, but I couldn't. If this was going to work, if I was going to completely escape Todd and the life I had been living, I wouldn't be able to contact anyone from this life or my previous life again. In fact, I had to leave behind Nika Harper and become someone completely new by the time I arrived in Birmingham.

Roni

London, 2016

I am back in front of the suitcase, trying to guess what is in it rather than simply opening it and finding out. What if I'd gone rogue during my forgotten period of packing? What if I'd 'borrowed' the large wooden crucifix without the body of Christ from my wall? What if I'd decided to appropriate a hymn book or two so I could observe and sing Lauds, Vespers, Compline and other parts of the Divine Office, too? What if I had packed my habit? I am a little fearful that the stress of leaving, combined with the anxiety of returning to Chiselwick (and the unknown of who I might bump into), had turned me into a kleptomaniac who wanted to hang on to the important parts of convent life.

My suitcase is the same large red one that I took with me when I left for the convent in the first place. It had been stored for me and returned to me with every move I have made over the years, and there have been several. It was by far the largest of all the suitcases the other postulants brought with them, and I'd been worried that Mother Superior and all the other professed Sisters would look down on me, would find me too attached to earthly belongings to take me seriously, even though I had been to stay with them more than once as an aspirant so I would find out if convent life was for me.

They did not bat an eyelid, especially since it was virtually empty when I arrived. I'm sure they would have thought differently then if they'd known then there was even the possibility that I would take to stealing things when I left the Sisterhood, secreting them away in the suitcase's voluminous depths. Not that I have stolen anything. At least I don't think I have. I honestly don't remember packing. I do remember telling myself to hold it together, to not cry, to not throw myself on Superior's mercy and beg her to take me back. I do remember the earthquake that erupted in my chest when I was being driven away from all I have known. I had only lived in that convent a year this time around, but it had been the first one I had gone to when I'd left home. I was being driven away not only from my physical home, but also from the home that was my way of life. I had sobbed and sobbed in the back seat, trying to hang on to what Superior had whispered to me when she had hugged me goodbye. 'Have a drink for me, Sister Grace. That would be a fitting goodbye.'

Coventry, 2015
'Sister Grace, it is so lovely to see you.'

I smiled at Mother Superior. I had been around the world, it felt like, I'd had so many different experiences, many conflicts, many fears and many moments of joy, all thanks to her decision not to allow me to remain there back in 2000, when she sent me off to train as a teacher. I was grateful to her, although at the time, if I had been honest, as I had been in confession, I'd harboured some resentment that she thought she knew what was best for me. When I had applied to come back this time because I had decided I wanted to live the next few years in cloisters, away from the noise and chaos of the outside world, she had willingly welcomed me back.

Her office had not changed in the time I had been away: it was snug and warm. Old wood, incense and what I now knew was the smell of comfort and acceptance. From the smile on her face, I could tell she already knew why I was there.

'Superior, I have been thinking a lot about Judas,' I began. 'About his betrayal. Do you think, I mean, truly believe with all you have seen of the world, all that you have read in Scripture and prayed on, that Judas betrayed Jesus for money and money alone?'

'Do you believe that?' she replied.

Under the table, my left leg began to jiggle. I hadn't done that in years. I didn't know what Superior was going to say, though. How she was going to receive this news. I knew even less why I'd started the conversation this way. An attempt at honesty? 'I believe that sometimes, you can think you're doing something for one reason, but deep down you're doing it for another reason. I think to betray someone you love in such a fundamental way, there must be more to it than money. Maybe it was fear of what is being asked of you. Maybe Judas couldn't reconcile who Jesus was asking him to be and rather than take a chance on being that person, on making that personal sacrifice, he turned on our Lord instead.'

'Are you asking to be released from your vows, Sister Grace?'

Was I? I had walked in here asking to be released. Coming full circle, living here again with complete silence outside of my head, had reminded me of where I came from. The life I had had before was visiting me in the quiet times. In the moments of stillness and prayer, I had the tugging, the pull to be elsewhere. I would close my eyes, and I would try to will it away. Then the thoughts of Judas would settle. I would wonder about betrayal from the ultimate betrayer. Why had he done it? *Judas*. His name was synonymous with betrayal, with the act, with the most devastating thing anyone could do to someone they loved. *I am a Judas. I am a betrayer.* Those thoughts kept preying on my mind. I needed to make it right. Like the tug towards this life, the ache and yearning that had brought me to this place where I chased the silence, I needed to go back. Maybe for ever, maybe for a month or two. Maybe that was it. As I had sat down, I had thought that I would have to leave for ever, but maybe I needed to leave for a little while, to make things right, and then I would come back.

'Yes, Superior, I am. But only for a little while. Maybe I can have some time off to think about things and then return?'

Superior smiled at me, in that way she always did that said she knew what was in my heart even if I didn't. 'Sister Grace, I will apply for you to be released permanently.'

'I'm not sure I want to be released permanently.'

'I am. You surprised me. I thought you would not stay, you would not take final vows. I rejoiced when you did, but I was surprised. No one worked harder than you, but your calling was always driven by escape, and I believe you are now strong enough to face what you were running from, therefore it is time for you to leave.'

'I'm not sure I want to go, now.'

'Pray on it. When you have prayed on it a while longer, come back. My door is always open.'

'Do you feel I have wasted your time, Superior?'

'No, Sister Grace. I feel blessed to have had you amongst us. Have more faith in yourself, Sister, and your ability to do the right thing. I will make the application in five days if I have not heard from you in that time.'

London, 2016

My attention is still on the suitcase.

I hope I haven't stolen anything. Of course I haven't. I am being ridiculous. Why would I go against everything that I am and start stealing?

I don't feel like changing my clothes, though. In actual fact, I want to fall down on the creaky bed and sleep fully clothed, so I have no need to go near the suitcase. It can stay there unopened for a while longer. Kicking off my socks with the big toe of the opposite foot, I swing my legs off the ground and lie back. Then I turn off the lamp on the floor, plunge my former bedroom into darkness. The moonlight throws shadows from the oak tree in my parents' back garden against the wall. Menacing and beautiful at the same time. So much like a lot of life.

I close my eyes. When I first learnt to pray, I would lie in bed and close my eyes. I would think of all the things I wanted to say to

Nika – all the little happenings and challenges and victories in my day – and I would share them with God. I would try to empty some of the noise inside. It was like trying to empty the sea with a child's beach bucket, but I would still try. I would simply talk to God, like I was talking to Nika, and hope that God didn't mind too much.

When I answer his knock on my door, my uncle Warren puts his head to one side, and smiles at me with his mouth closed. He is mollified and altogether different from before.

'It was nice to see you again, Veronica,' my uncle says. 'I just wanted to say goodnight. I'll be leaving soon.'

'Goodnight,' I reply.

'About before,' he adds before I can step back to shut the door. 'I'm sorry, I was a little out of order.' He must see the scepticism on my face because he adds: 'All right, yes, I was a lot out of order. I forget, sometimes, that not everyone finds me funny.'

'I'm sure a lot of people find you funny,' I say. I am trying to be kind. My uncle has very little in his life. Over the course of the evening it's become clear that his life has stalled: he does not have a wife or significant partner, he doesn't have children and he holidays alone two or three times a year in Spain. He has friends, and he regaled us with tales of them tonight, but underneath it all, he has nothing, really.

He smiles at me again, even though I am keeping my gaze fixed over his left shoulder as I have been since he arrived in the house. 'You're a good girl.' He nods. 'I always thought you were a good girl. Like the daughter I never had.'

This was always the 'problem' with Uncle Warren overall. He could be mean, his tongue and phrasing exhibiting a vicious edge, then he would apologise, he would be nice. And it'd be particularly hard to hold those earlier things against him. After my brother's bike accident, he came over a few days later with a real leather football and a full England footie strip to say sorry for what had happened. Damian had loved that football so much that he'd forgotten how much pain he'd been in.

It always felt wrong to hold a grudge against Uncle Warren, but it feels even more wrong to hold a grudge after I have learnt about forgiveness and atonement. Especially since I have left my vocation to try to find Nika, to try to atone for what I did to her all those years ago. Everyone deserves a second chance. At least I hope they do.

'Goodnight,' I say to him.

'Goodnight, Roni,' he says.

I shut the door on my uncle. Another metallic groan fills the room as my full weight makes contact with the bed again. The noise in my head is filling up, when I thought it would be quieter tonight without the imposition of the Great Silence. Why did I think I could do this? I am supposed to know humility, and so why does it feel like this idea to find Nika and make everything right is one of the biggest exercises in conceit I have ever undertaken?

3

Nika

I strum my fingers over my guitar, sitting on a bench, facing the sea, watching the sun climb out of the water and into the sky. I have a place to stay, but for reasons I'm not too sure of myself, I wanted to sit out with my guitar and watch the day come alive.

I'm not as tired as I should be, since I grabbed half an hour's sleep on the coach journey from London Victoria to Brighton. I'd checked into a B&B but then had found myself walking along the front with my guitar and rucksack, needing to be outside for a while. When I sat on this bench, I started to think of Todd, and how I got involved with him. After those memories were all played out, used up and cast back into that unvisited area of my mind, I'd started to think about Veronica Harper. Roni. She had been my best friend back when best friend meant 'my whole life'. Our virtually identical names, and our absolutely identical love for ballet, had joined us early. I'd started to revisit that love we had for each other, the friendship that had defined my childhood, and then a big STOP sign had gone up in my head. There was no need to go back there again. What happened, happened. I really had to get over it. I *had* got over it. I would never understand why she did what she did and some things are best left in the past where they originally lived. What would be the use in dragging it all back out again?

I move my fingers over the taut strings again as the guitar's wooden body lies flat on my lap. The sound rises up and dissolves into my ears, the chords to signal the start of a new day. Of my new life in Brighton.

I've moved on, haven't I? From all of it. Everything that has gone before is in my history and I do not need to revisit it again.

Even if Roni did want to find me, if she did want to explain, what would she say that would make it all right? Nothing at all comes to mind. If I can't think what would rewrite the past and make it all right, then how can she?

I create another chord from my guitar, watch the sun shake off the drops of the sea that cover its body, making those drops into the orange that brightens the sky.

I am in Brighton and this new day is the start of a new life for me. I do not need to think of the past. I only need to face the front, tackle my future.

Roni

It is 5 a.m. I know that because my eyes snap open at 5 a.m. no matter where I am.

My body stays still as my mind scrabbles around for its bearings. The window, it is large and has a blind on it. There is a band of roses circling the middle of the room. My large wooden cross is missing. There is a large amount of furniture in here. *Where am I?* I ask myself.

At home of course, I reply. And I remember . . . I remember that I am not *home* any more, I am 'home' instead. I tug the duvet up until it is under my chin and I lie still, listening, settling, pushing myself outwards to become part of the fabric of this house again. This is my home. This is not my home.

The night before last I lay in my cell, taking in every inch of it, plain as it was, simple as it was, it was part of my home and I knew I would miss it. I tried to experience every part: the shadows, the shapes, the smell, the feel. I had tried to hold on to them, make them a part of my memory so I would not forget. Even though that was wrong: a nun has no possessions, she is bound by the vow of poverty and everything she has is to be shared with her community. I wondered what my Sisters would say if they knew that one of my last acts as a nun was to try to steal a permanent mental image of the way I lived?

*

103

5 a.m. I am awake. I am ready to start the day. I hear the final peals of the bells, the gentle nudge to begin the day. I close my eyes and see myself. I see myself in my last cell, opening my eyes, staring at the ceiling, sitting up to start the day. I move away the covers, I slip down on to my knees and I pray. I ask for a good day, for God to bless my family, my friends, my fellow Sisters (professed and aspiring). From my bed in my parents' house, I watch myself shower, get dressed, taking time and care to make sure my habit is neat and in place; everything I do is a service to God and I must do it properly, carefully.

It is 6.40 a.m. I am at Vigils, observing the first Office of the day, readings from the Scriptures, passages from the Psalms; they wash over me, wash into me; they bring me peace, they ease me closer to the silence I am always searching for. A line from a psalm, it touches me today, causes my heart to skip a beat. I understand it today. I have never understood it before. I heard its surface before, listened and thought I understood its meaning. Today, I can see how it fits over my experiences of the world.

It is 7 a.m. I am standing in the oratory, singing Lauds (our morning prayer) – the voices of my Sisters bring tears to my eyes every morning. The purity and the innocence rise up towards our Lord, and I feel a part of it. It is not silence, but I am a grateful, happy part of it.

It is 8.15 a.m. and I observe myself from my present as I listen to today's selection of readings as we eat breakfast. I am working in the kitchen today. I like to cook. I like to lose myself in the silence of working for my Sisters, making food that will fill their stomachs and lift their spirits.

It is 5 p.m. I have worked all day, and the silence imposed upon me is tiring now. I am always searching for silence, but today it seems hard, it seems a burden, not part of my vocation. I know I have to pray on that, to try to uncover why I am struggling. I watch myself hang my head in shame as I enter for Vespers, our Latin songs every bit as beautiful and moving as our Lauds in English. I watch myself sing our evening prayer and I know I am sad because I am struggling.

It is 7.30 p.m. And I am not reading my book, taking part in my free time as usual. I stare at the pages of the book, seeing nothing but alien squiggles that I cannot decipher today. Those few words I do manage to read fall out of my head again, unable to find purchase or rest in my mind. Inside my head is becoming loud. That is why I am struggling. The noise inside wants to come out.

It is 8.30 p.m. I am a little more careful with Compline (Night Prayer) tonight. I see myself enunciating every word, pushing the noise inside my head out by trying to coat every word we sing in it. I feel better as I enter the Great Silence for the night. I do not feel I will combust because I have let a little of what is inside out and I will not struggle to stay silent and extremely quiet until Lauds tomorrow.

I see you, Sister Grace, I think to myself. *I see you lying in bed, reading that book and seeing the words this time. I see you, Sister Grace, waiting for Lights Out at eleven so you can sleep until five. I see you, Sister Grace. I see you and I see that what is on the outside is not what you are feeling on the inside.*

In my parents' house, I roll over, I close my eyes again, shut out the visions I have of Sister Grace, the person I used to be, and try to be Veronica Harper. Roni. The girl who was so very often hungover from drink and drugs, for whom waking up at eight every morning was an issue, let alone waking at five. I tug the duvet right up over my head, feel the metallic groan of the fold-out bed in every part of my body. I can sleep as late as I want now. I can do whatever I want, whenever I want. I missed Vespers and Compline last night. Once I came to my room Uncle Warren ensured that the Great Silence didn't happen by coming to my bedroom door. I am no longer a nun, nor am I a Sister. I am Veronica Harper and sleeping in is what Veronica Harper does.

It takes me another minute of pretending before I slip back the cover, I get down on my knees and I start to pray.

4

Nika

'You seem to have a lot of long gaps in your CV, Miss Harper,' the interviewer, Mrs Nasir, says diplomatically.

'Yes, yes, I do,' I reply. I had thought of an explanation, something that would help gloss over the mess that is my CV. No college experience, A levels started but not finished, three years of waitressing and working as a stagehand in a London theatre. And then yawning years between then and now when I was Nikky Harper, then Grace Carter. My CV isn't so much like Swiss cheese as the crater-pocked side of the moon – big gaps everywhere. I did have an explanation polished up and ready to present to her with a clever flourish of diversionary prowess, but I can't quite recall it. Not when I'm sitting in front of a real-life person, and not when I know it would sound like a load of nonsense. It would be lying, anyway. Concealing, like I did when I was living as Grace Carter, I can do – I had to do – but out-and-out lying goes against my nature.

'Can you explain why?' Mrs Nasir asks. I think she was expecting me to jump in after her statement and I haven't.

In response, I sit up straight in my seat, pull back my shoulders, and tuck the strand of hair that has escaped from behind my left ear back where it belongs. From the waist-length dreadlocks that I've had these past few years, I have had my hair cropped to just above my ears, and straightened. Even now, nearly three weeks later, it's still a

109

mini shock when I move not to feel the comforting weight of my dreadlocks twisted into a low bun at the back of my head, or hanging down to the middle of my back when loosened to hide my face. (The Brighton-based hairdresser had asked for reassurances several times that I knew what I was doing with this extreme cut and I wouldn't come back and sue her when I realised what I had asked for.) But this is who I am now. Grace 'Ace' Carter had long dreadlocks grown over ten years; Nika Harper has short, straight hair, and she wears rectangular tortoiseshell glasses. When I had my eye examination, the optician didn't want to give me any sort of glasses, because the prescription was so weak it was hardly worth her time writing it up. I'd insisted; they were the perfect way to cover my face, they would allow me to hide and they would distinguish me from all the different names I've had. Now, they feel a part of my face whenever I leave my flat.

Slowly I push my glasses back up my nose, buying myself time. Nika Harper has a lot of explaining to do and I'm not sure how I do that. If I couldn't tell a police officer even the half of it, how am I going to tell this immaculate-looking woman who has a neat, orderly desk, flawless make-up, and wears a hijab that is the exact same colour as her suit? She is beautifully presented, has a gentle manner and runs the HR department of a large hotel – she won't be able to comprehend what the last ten years of my working life have entailed. Nor the five years before that when I was with Todd.

'The thing of it is…' I begin, and the shame of it, of what my life has been like, bubbles right up to my throat, it chokes the words and I am mute, suddenly, tearful, as well. I am scared, too. I'm not sure why, since danger is so many miles away and all I have to do is perform well in this interview and I may have a job and I can move on. But suddenly, I am scared. I want someone to come and hold my hand, help me through the hard bits. I think, then, of the other Veronica. She was always wanting to hold my hand, trying to connect us with that touch.

'I see,' Mrs Nasir says when my muteness extends beyond the acceptable time limit of starting a sentence, pausing, then finishing it. She sits forward in her seat, knits her fingers together over the papers on her desk. She sighs heavily, and fixes me with her large, maple-brown eyes. 'What were you convicted of and how long were you in for?'

That sweeps away my muteness. 'I'm sorry, pardon me?' I ask.

'We do have ex-offenders working here, but it is wise to be honest about these things and state them clearly on your CV. Most people will give you a chance if you are honest.'

'No, no,' I say, shaking my head. *Where's my hair?* I wonder for a few seconds before I speak again: 'I wasn't in prison. I've never been in trouble with the law. You can run all the checks on me you want and you'll find nothing. No, I fell on hard times and I had to do a lot of cash-in-hand work, mostly cleaning. I like cleaning, making things right again. I'm efficient at it; I can do things properly but quickly. I'm discreet, which I'd imagine is helpful for a hotel. I'm also available to work as many shifts as you need, especially unsociable hours because I'm new to the city and I don't know many people. Well, actually, I don't know anyone.' I stop speaking.

Mrs Nasir listens to me with a slightly puzzled expression – she clearly doesn't know what to make of me: am I a bit crazy or am I simply odd? Now that I have stopped talking, she opens her mouth to speak and I interject with: 'Sorry, and I meant to add that I'm a fast learner. If you give me a trial of one shift, after someone shows me the ropes, I'll prove to you that I can do the job and do it well. Sorry, sorry to interrupt you there. But I thought it was a good idea to mention that in case it in any way influenced what you were about to say next or whether you'd give me a chance or not.'

She doesn't speak this time, doesn't move to speak; instead she looks down at my sparse, one-page CV. Not even the most creative writing and rewriting could have made me sound desirable. I'd been tempted to use forty-eight point for the section heads and twenty-four point for everything else, just to fill the page a bit.

'Nika Harper,' she murmurs, staring hard at my name in capitals at the top of the page. I had written Veronika but told her when I sat down to call me Nika. That was probably a mistake since it is so very close to Nikky Harper, and now she is dragging through her memory, trying to remember where she has heard that name before. Wondering if I am telling the truth about not having been in prison, not having been in trouble with the law. Thinking that even if I am being honest about prison, maybe she's heard that name for another reason and not a good one, since anything good of note that I have done would surely be there on my flimsy-as-tissue-paper CV.

If I want this job, which I do, I can't risk her connecting me to that other life, that other time.

'Mrs Nasir?' I say gently, tugging her away from the words on the page. 'If you were possibly considering offering me the job, I could start straight away. I could even do the trial shift this afternoon if you want?'

'Hmmm?' She lifts her gaze to me. Frowns. 'No, no, that won't be necessary. I'm a little torn right now, Miss Harper, to be honest. It is not our policy to offer positions in our hotel to people without experience or references or who have been working – as you have admitted – cash in hand.'

My heart sinks. So much for being honest and from that people will give you a chance.

'However, if there's anything I know about jobs that are cash in hand, it's that there are so many people queuing up for that type of work, if you don't work hard enough you have no work. Which does tell me you're a hard worker. Can you see where I am conflicted?'

I nod. She seems a fair woman, not someone overly given to being nice or doing people favours, but not one to dismiss people out of hand, either.

'I suppose the best thing I can do, to be fair to my head of housekeeping, who is desperate for good cleaning staff, and to yourself, is to give you a one-week trial.'

Without meaning to, I gasp. I'm finally being given a break. Another one, actually, if I count having enough money in my semi-defunct bank account to find somewhere temporary to stay and get my hair cut properly and buy a decent second-hand interview suit and glasses. But this break is huge. This break could change everything.

'May I remind you, it is only a trial. If the head of housekeeping doesn't think you are up to the position, I will be forced to terminate your employment. Does that sound fair to you?'

'Yes,' I say. I have to stop myself reaching across the table and grabbing her hand to shake it vigorously, and I put my hands on the arms of my chair to physically stop myself climbing over the desk and throwing my arms around her. 'That sounds so fair, I can't even begin to tell you.'

'Very well. If you will kindly wait outside for a few minutes, I will contact the head of housekeeping to let her know to expect us and I will show you around the hotel and introduce you to her. Since you said you could start immediately, shall we say six o'clock tomorrow morning?'

'Yes, yes, that's brilliant. I can't even begin to tell you how much . . . Thank you. Just thank you.'

'This is your chance to show us what you're made of, Miss Harper. Please don't let us down.'

'I won't let you or myself down,' I say. *I promise.*

Roni

I am starting at the very beginning. And yes, that thought has triggered the song from *that* movie to play in my mind. I have tried to push it to one side, but it's there. **'Veronika Harper.'** I type the words into the Internet page on my parents' computer, hit the return button and pages and pages come up. Some have photos, some are links to the glossy magazines and a woman who spells her name the same way that Veronika did. I was supposed to start looking for a job today. I woke up at 5 a.m. like I do every morning, and when both my parents left the house, I came down to their computer to start my job search. Instead, I became distracted by the search for my former best friend.

Tomorrow I will look for a job. This is more important. I have to know where she is, what is going on with her. She left home at seventeen and as far as I know, she never came back.

London, 1989

Of the thirty-five children who had come to the taster sessions at Daneaux Dance Studios, a year ago, only fifteen of us were left, and Nika and I were the only ones who came every single week to the lessons.

This lesson, Monsieur Armand asked us to stay after class. Everyone looked at us like we had done something wrong, and Nika

114

seemed terrified. I was, too. We sat cross-legged on the floor by the mirrors while everyone else picked up their bags, coats and shoes from along the back wall, and then waited for their parents to come and collect them. They were all still watching us, feeling sorry for us, because we were probably going to be asked to leave the ballet school and then that would be the end of our dreams of being dancers.

It was all Nika and I talked about at school. We would discuss the different ways you could move from first position to third without going through second. We would talk about which ballets we would like to dance in. We would sometimes have everyone staring at us in the playground as we practised what we had learnt the week before. I loved to watch Nika dance, she was so good at holding herself upright, looking as professional as Madame Brigitte – like she was born to dance. She often told me that when she watched me dance she couldn't breathe because she thought I looked so beautiful, that I *was* Odette in *Swan Lake*.

Once we were alone with our dancing teachers, I took Nika's hand and found it was cold and sweaty. She was really scared. *I* was really scared. There were other ballet schools, of course, but we loved Monsieur Armand and Madame Brigitte. He seemed to know so much about dance – he had worked with so many famous ballet dancers, or *premiers danseurs*, as he called them. Some of them danced on stages all over the world and he said he had followed the career of Sylvie Guillem very closely and would one day tell any of us who were interested all about her. Madame Brigitte was the most beautiful dancer we had ever seen. She was my real-life Sylvie (apart from Nika) and I wanted to be like her in every way possible. I knew Nika felt the same. The thought that we wouldn't be allowed to come any more made me feel sick. I knew I was going to throw up right there and then if they made us leave.

'Do not look so worried,' Monsieur Armand said. He had a strong French accent, even though he had lived in London for several years, his wife had told us.

'Yes, this is a good thing,' Madame Brigitte said with a big smile and a really kind voice. She wasn't French. 'We have seen real talent and passion and drive in you two. More than anyone I think we've ever had in this school. And we would like to extend an invitation for you both to be taught individual lessons on Monday evenings by Monsieur Armand.'

Wow, I thought. I was holding my breath and couldn't quite believe what she was saying to me, to us. They thought we had shown the promise that they had talked about in the very first lesson. I looked at Nika to find she was looking at me. I wanted to do it, I so wanted to do it.

'For the first three months it would be free of charge,' Monsieur Armand said. 'That way we would be able to assess whether the individual lessons are of true benefit to you or not.'

'Would it be just the two of us?' Nika asked. I was glad she asked because I wasn't sure if it meant lessons just taught by him or if it meant one lesson each.

'*Non, non*, it would be me and you, Vero*nique*, and then me and the other *Ver*onique.' You could always tell which one of us he was talking about because he emphasised our names in different ways. 'Whoever went second would wait outside for the first to finish, that way you can walk here after school together and your parents will only need to make one trip. Simple, *non*? Your parents are outside, so we will talk to them and provide them with a form to sign, but we wanted to know if you were interested first?'

'Yes!' I blurted out.

'Yes!' Nika blurted out at the same time.

'*Bon.*'

'That's wonderful!' Madame Brigitte's grin made me smile even wider. I was going to be a ballet dancer. It was really going to happen.

London, 2016

'Veronika Harper' produces no results that are of any use to me. Which should I try next? 'Nika Harper' or 'Nikky Harper'? I suppose Nikky

Harper because that is the name she is most famous for. I often wondered, when I saw her on the front of the magazines and in the gossip columns in newspapers, why she hadn't used Grace, like she'd always planned to. **'Nikky Harper.'** I type. Press: enter.

London, 1991

I wanted to tell Nika. I knew she'd understand. She would hold my hand and tell me it would all be all right. I was waiting outside the ballet studio because Nika was second today, and I was sitting there, wishing she would come back. I missed her when she wasn't with me. Monsieur Armand had extended the lessons today for both of us. I was meant to be doing my homework, but I couldn't concentrate on it, I couldn't think about anything. I felt odd, in my body. Monsieur Armand said I was stiff and moving like an elephant riding a donkey, but I felt so strange. I wanted to tell Nika about it. Mum had said to Dad she thought it was growing pains that I was complaining about, that my body was growing much faster than the rest of me could keep up with. I knew it wasn't that, but I didn't tell Mum because she would think I was causing a fuss and I wasn't.

The door to the studio opened and Nika walked out. She had a funny look on her face. Sometimes Monsieur Armand would get cross with us. He would say he was frustrated because we weren't concentrating, we weren't being as good as he knew we could be. Nika and I would compare notes afterwards, we would ask each other if he had commented on our pirouettes, on our positioning, our landing. Sometimes he said the same things to us, sometimes it was completely different. He made us cry sometimes, and we would comfort each other. It was hard work, but both of us knew if we wanted to be professional dancers, it was necessary. Madame Brigitte had told us that. Nika was odd today, though. She came out, cradling her ballet shoes, with her chin on her chest. She sat down on the floor beside her school bag and pulled her knees up to her chest and stared at the floor in front of her.

117

'*Ve*ronique?' Monsieur Armand said. 'Why don't you come back in for a few minutes before your parents arrive?'

'Yes, sir,' I said and jumped to my feet. I kept looking at Nika but she wouldn't look at me. She wouldn't look at anything except the floor. Usually she'd give me a look to let me know what sort of a mood he was in, if I should brace myself for a telling off or if he would be over-brimming with compliments.

'Are you OK?' I asked Nika.

'She is fine,' Monsieur Armand replied for her. 'We covered new material and new ground today and she is unsure if she can do it. I know she will be fine.'

'Last night I asked my mum if I could give up ballet,' Nika told me.

'But you love ballet,' I reminded her.

'Yeah, yeah, I do,' she said sadly. 'But I don't want to do it any more. It doesn't matter anyway because Mummy said I wasn't allowed to give up. She said everyone knew I was doing it and they were all so impressed that only one other person – you – had been asked to have private lessons too, and I wasn't stopping on a whim.'

'Do you really want to stop ballet?' I asked her.

'Don't you?' she asked me.

I shook my head. I never wanted to stop ballet. It was my one escape. The only time I felt right was when I was dancing. I could never give up ballet, even if I wanted to.

Three weeks later, Monsieur Armand introduced me to the new material and the new moves. They weren't so hard, weren't so bad. But I understood why she wanted to give up ballet.

London, 2016

'Nikky Harper' is more fruitful, but not that much. There are a few articles from that time when she was everywhere, a few more where they mention Todd Chambers, the man she was with, some talking about her drugs problem. But all of them end the same way: she simply disappeared. One day she was with him, the next she was gone and no one had heard from her since.

'**Nika Harper**' next.

London, 1993

Monsieur Armand called us all to attention before the class began. He always wore all black – poloneck and tight trousers – and he always carried a long black stick with a brass top. He didn't need it for walking, he used it to correct you if you were in the wrong position. Sometimes, if you got it wrong too many times, he would bang it on the ground and shout at you. It was awful when he shouted. The sound of it would go right through you. I always felt bad, too, because you could tell he didn't like shouting. He seemed to shout more at Nika these days, I could hear it when I sat outside during her individual lessons.

'Ladies, we will soon be starting the audition process for our Christmas show. This is the first show we have ever held, but I feel so many of you are capable and talented enough to be able to handle the process. The ballet will be our version of *Le Nutcracker*. Everyone will have a role, but the lead role will be that of the Sugar Plum Fairy. She will have the longest solo dance and then a *pas de deux*. A duet. I have already decided that one of the Veroniques will dance this part. I am telling you all now so you are not disappointed. You will all work hard, I believe, no matter what your role.'

My heart started to dance in my chest. I adored *The Nutcracker*. After *Swan Lake*, it was my absolute favourite ballet ever. Dad had taken me to see it up in central London last year at Christmas. It had been magical, and I'd loved the Sugar Plum Fairy. Her solo had made everyone gasp, hold their breath and then give her a standing ovation right in the middle of the ballet. I wanted the role. More than anything I wanted the part. Nika would want it, too, I knew that. Monsieur Armand was staring at Nika and she was staring at the ground.

119

'OK, ladies, dance on. And remember, from now on, I will be watching you, assessing you. Every move you make will help me to decide which role you are assigned. Dance on, dance on.'

I leant towards Nika. 'I really want to be the Sugar Plum Fairy,' I whispered to her.

'I hope you get it,' she whispered back.

'Don't you want it?' I asked.

'No,' she said. 'No, I don't.'

'Does he ... ?' Nika asked me. She only said the first two words but I knew what the other two would be. We often knew what the other one was saying without actually saying everything. We were thirteen now, and it'd been like that since we became best friends at eight.

'Sometimes,' I admitted. 'Not all the time. I pretend it's not happening so I don't have to give up dancing.'

We sat side by side outside the studio, waiting for Monsieur Armand to be ready for us. We had one extra lesson a week now, as preparation for the Christmas show. He still hadn't told us who was going to be the Sugar Plum Fairy. Everyone else had their roles, their parts they could practise at home. Nika and I had to both learn the part as though it was ours. Whoever didn't have the role would be understudy, which meant she wouldn't dance at all in the show unless the other was ill.

Nika sighed. 'Same.' She was watching me then, staring me right in the eye. She said: 'Sometimes it's months between ... and I almost forget so I concentrate on the dancing.'

It wasn't as bad as it could have been, though. I knew it could be far, far worse ...

'I didn't know if he was doing it to you, too. When I asked you if you wanted to give up dancing you said no, so I thought it was just me,' Nika said.

'He wasn't at the time you asked.'

'I went to see Madame Brigitte the other day and I told her. I said that I wouldn't tell anyone and I wouldn't stop ballet if they didn't want me to, but I wanted it all to stop.'

Nika was so brave. I would never have told. If she hadn't asked me, I would never have told. 'What did she say? Was she cross?'

'No. She almost cried and she said she would talk to him, and she said she would make it stop.'

I held my breath for a few seconds; tears filled my eyes. It was going to stop, we'd be free and safe now. 'Do you think it will stop now? As in this lesson?'

Nika's leg started to jiggle as though she was trying to stop herself from sobbing by jiggling herself, like I saw mothers do to babies to stop them from crying. 'He came to my house yesterday. He told my parents that there'd been a misunderstanding, that he only touched me to help me find the right positions.'

I felt sick for her. He had sat in her house, lying.

'He said he had explained everything to his wife when she had asked and now he was explaining it to my parents so they would know not to be worried by the things I told them. And all my individual lessons are free now to make up for the misunderstanding. Last year, I told my mum everything, and she didn't believe me. Now they're never going to believe me because they think he's wonderful.'

Nika covered her face with her hands, ran them slowly over her face and up over her hair, which was pulled back into a fluffy pony-tail. 'I'm sorry, Roni. I know you wanted to be the Sugar Plum Fairy but last night he said the role was mine and he was looking—' Her voice broke, her face crumpled as if she was about to cry. Then she pulled herself together, became strong again. 'I'm sorry you won't get to be the Sugar Plum Fairy, Roni.'

I reached out for her hand. I didn't care about that. I cared about everything being OK for both of us. She had told her parents and they didn't believe her. And now Madame Brigitte didn't believe her. 'I don't care about that. I'm sorry they didn't believe you,' I added.

'After the show, I'm not going to dance any more. If you tell your parents they'll tell my parents and then we can both stop the lessons or he'll leave us alone,' she said.

I nodded. 'OK,' I said.

'Deal? You tell your parents and then we can end this?'

'Yes, deal.'

The door to the studio clicked open.

'*Ve*ronique and Vero*nique*,' Monsieur Armand said. 'What a true delight. Vero*nique* will be the Sugar Plum Fairy, and *Ve*ronique, you will be her understudy. Next time, you will be the star and she will be the understudy,' he said. 'Vero*nique*, come.' He held out his hand to her. She stood up slowly, and moved even more slowly towards the studio. She did not take his hand; she did not look at him. She kept her gaze straight ahead as she walked into the large room where all our dreams had begun.

Minutes passed and there was silence on the other side of the door. Without warning, the music of the Sugar Plum Fairy began. Loud. Louder than it had ever been before; so loud it was distorting on the longer notes. So loud, it set off the noise in my head.

I pressed the palms of my hands over my ears, tried to keep out the noise in my head, tried to shut out the music from the studio. It didn't work. I could still hear Nika's pain on the other side of the door.

London, 2016

'Grace Harper.'

The last name to try. I knew it wouldn't be easy to find her – I have no idea what she even looks like now – so I have to try every combination I can think of.

London, 1993

She was incredible. Not even Sylvie, the most amazing ballerina in the world, could have done better than Nika. Everyone was on their feet at the end of her solo, exactly like when I had been to Central London. She did not put a foot wrong, her body had been strong and steady the whole time. I had watched from the wings with eyes of wonder. Madame Brigitte had made her a pink dress covered in sparkles that reached her thighs, rather than a tutu. Her hair was

122

swept back into a high bun, with a tiara on top. Madame Brigitte had dusted her cheeks with gold and pink glitter and she had put on false eyelashes. When Nika was on the stage, she *was* the queen who welcomed children to the land of sweets.

Nika smiled all the way through her performances, she beamed at the end of the show, she even smiled when the local press took a picture of her with Monsieur Armand. I could see she was somewhere else, that she recoiled a fraction when *he* put his arm around her. We'd agreed. After this, we were going to stop. We were going to tell our parents that we wouldn't be dancing any more. We were going to tell them why. That was how we had both made it through the extra rehearsals – we knew after the last performance, in three days, there'd be no more. No more of any of it.

London, 2016

Before I shut down the computer, I begin one more search: **'Veronica Harper'** and **'December 1994'** and **'Chiselwick'**.

The picture, which looks like one of a series that have been scanned in from someone's newspaper cuttings, is one of the first to come up. There I am. Standing beside Monsieur Armand, my arms full of flowers, in my white swan costume, a beautiful tiara on my head. The caption reads: 'Odette/Odile, danced by Veronica Harper with her mentor, Armand Daneaux'. In the background, I can see Nika. Standing with the ensemble, smiling like a professional, putting on a show.

5

Nika

In situations like this, I would usually unwind the headphones of my music player, push them into my ears and find a song to listen to.

There are various songs that take me away, make me feel safe, hide me in moments of uncertainty and fear. This flat I am standing in is as big as Todd's and is set over the top floor of an iconic Brighton block of flats that sits two roads away from the seafront and everyone knows by name.

Once I had a job, I could rent a small one-bedroom place five floors below this one. This flat has panoramic views over Brighton, I'd imagine. Not that we'll get a chance to see it. The man who owns this flat, Sebastian, knocked on my door three days ago to invite me to this residents' meeting and went on and on until I said I'd be there. The living room is vast – as big as my whole flat and furnished by a couple who obviously have a lot of money: thick carpets line every floor, expensive flock wallpaper, dark wood furniture that looks antique. They have set out a long table with nibbles, red and white wine, juice and fizzy water.

I have chosen red wine and stationed myself by the table, so I can watch people arrive, and maybe find someone to talk to. I have not drunk red wine in so long I have forgotten what it tastes like. When I take a sip from the plastic wine glass I have carefully filled to the middle, I'm surprised. So surprised I look at it sitting like blood in its plastic vessel, then look again at the bottle. Red wine, even from a bottle, even from a bottle with a fancy label and a posh-sounding name, tastes remarkably like vinegar. To be sure, I take another sip. It washes out my mouth, leaves it clean and arid. In fact, this red wine tastes more like vinegar than most vinegar I have had drizzled on my chips.

I cast my gaze around my fellow guests: they stand in small groups, chatting to each other in quiet tones; it's almost funereal. They all seem to know each other, they are all connected to each other. Anxiety coats my tongue and mouth like the scratchy aftertaste of the wine. I have to do this. I have to stay here and become a part of something. I have to slip myself into this life if I want to hide in plain sight. People notice the loners and the non-joiners, they notice and talk about the people who don't want to share in their community. If you dip yourself in the right amount into the pool of other people, they overlook you most of the time, they don't notice you.

If this is going to work, I have to be normal, join in just enough, try not to draw attention to myself by being too friendly or too offish.

'I'm impressed,' a woman's voice says, just to the right of me. I didn't see her approach, didn't notice her at all because I've been too busy looking around, trying to blend in enough for people to speak to me. I turn in her direction, and notice how liberal she has been with her perfume, how heavy-handed she's been with her beige foundation and peachy-coloured powder. She is slightly taller than me, dressed conservatively in dark blue skirt and white shirt; her hair hangs like blonde curtains on either side of her face.

I smile at her. She grins back at me, obviously waiting for me to say something. 'Sorry, what are you impressed by or about?' I ask.

She leans in towards me, her perfume filling the space around us, and lowers her voice: 'I'm impressed that you're drinking *that*.' She nods her head slightly towards the glass in my hand, while pulling a grimace across her face. She leans closer, lowers her voice to nothing more than a whisper: 'Astrid and Sebastian always buy the cheapest wine they can find for these meetings. They are so tight I don't know why they bother. Everyone always offers to do a B.Y.O. but they always insist on "catering" for their neighbours. Wouldn't mind, but you should see the amount of pricey plonk they've stored up in their "pantry". It's almost like they assume we don't appreciate how generous they are to hold these meetings here so they punish us with cheap offerings. That, and obviously to have the home-field advantage and to control the meetings.' She smiles, stands back and then pulls a face at herself. 'Wow, wasn't that a classic case of bitter oversharing! Sorry.' Now she holds out her hand, wanting me to shake it. 'I'm Eliza,' she says. 'Please ignore everything I just said, it was a moment of madness. The fact you're still standing here talking to me *and* drinking the wine tells me you're new in the building?'

'Yes, yes, I am,' I say. I push my glasses up my nose and take her hand. 'I'm... I'm Nika.' I almost forgot which name I am meant to be using. 'I have just moved into the building.'

'Buying or renting?' asks a man who has joined us. He is taller than both of us, he has a pleasant smile on his face, and from the way Eliza has subtly but definitely shifted her body ever so slightly towards him, like a heater she wants to warm herself against, I'm guessing the tall man is also hers.

'Sorry?' I ask him.

'No, no, I'm sorry. How rude of me. I just heard you saying you were new in the building and I was wondering if you'd be sticking around for a while, in other words, had bought the place, or if you might be gone in six months because you were renting. And then, I realised that it was none of my damn business so I should probably shut up. I'm Marshall, by the way.' I can see why these two are together. I wonder if they have these sorts of conversations where they retract everything they've said all the time. It must be so tiring.

'As in the speaker system?' I say to the man. 'As in, you go all the way up to an eleven?'

'Hmmm, never heard that before,' he says without humour. 'Ever.'

'You seriously, honestly have issues with being namechecked via the most famous line in *Spinal Tap*?' I ask him.

'Only if people expect me to actually get a guitar out and play all the way up to eleven,' he replies. And I get it: he isn't offended, he was joking.

'Not a problem for me, personally, but hey, we all have our limitations.'

Marshall moves to speak but Eliza clears her throat, a small *aha-hem* sound that reminds us that she is there and I am skirting dangerously close to what could be mistaken for flirting with her man.

'I'm Nika, short for Veronika,' I say. I want to bring Eliza into a conversation, stop her thinking she has anything to worry about from me. 'How long have you two been together?'

They both immediately look at each other, shock lacing their very different faces. I look from one face to the other: his has slightly widened eyes, hers has a slight grimace at the mouth – that's not shock. True shock is momentarily expressed, this is more like mortification.

'We're...we're not together,' she stutters and her cheeks take on a deep flush that is visible even under her heavy make-up. She is mortified that it is obvious, even to a stranger, how she feels about him.

'We've known each other a long time,' he adds. 'Since our uni days, actually, and our paths keep crossing, so we've ended up working in the same building – for different companies, and living here – in different flats.' He is mortified because he does not feel that way about her, *at all*. From the way he looks as if he hopes the ground will swallow him up, I doubt he's ever had anything other than platonic feelings towards her. *Poor Eliza*, I think. *That must hurt. Seeing the object of your love every day, knowing he is not interested, must be a special kind of torture.*

'Sorry,' I mumble and take a huge mouthful of the wine as punishment. 'Sorry. I didn't... I just assumed... sorry. Sorry.'

'No, no,' Eliza says, 'don't apologise. It's fine, really. We don't mind if people make mistakes like that, do we, Marshall?' She laughs and lightly rests her hand on his forearm.

Marshall's smile is a little tighter, and he carefully moves his arm away from her. In fact, he has been carefully edging away from her. His black-brown eyes betray a little pain. This is so much worse than a case of unrequited love: at some point, Eliza has declared undying love to him, and he has been forced to turn her down gently. Marshall suddenly takes a big step away from her, using the excuse of reaching for a glass of juice to do it. *Urgh*. It's been more than once that he has had to tell her he doesn't see her that way.

I down the entire glass of wine – the vinegariness makes me gag, coats my mouth and tongue with a just-scrubbed sensation. I think: *Good, it's no more than you deserve. Next time, think before you speak.*

'Good evening, everyone,' our host says. 'If you'd like to take your seats, we can get on with the meeting and get that over with as soon as possible so we can get back to mingling and chatting.' There's a definite undertone to what he is saying. His glossy brown hair is combed with a perfectly straight side parting, he is tanned to the point where it gives him a bright, white smile that can probably be seen from space. He is presenting a pleasant façade, but there is a threatening edge to his words, a subtle hint that anyone who challenges him in his own home will be dealt with – severely. I understand what Eliza means: the meeting is in their home, but the virtually undrinkable wine, the welcome that is more menace than gesture of neighbourliness – all point to a seriously dysfunctional man with an odd way of viewing the world.

'And the final item on the agenda, not that this is a formal meeting or anything like that,' Sebastian says, laughing hollowly, 'is the issue of the "people" who hang around outside the building.' He has an impressive way with inserting 'air quotes' into ordinary speech without so much as raising a finger.

'To be fair,' Marshall says from the other side of the room, 'since that hostel opened up a few streets away, there haven't been as many transient people as there were previously.'

'Not as many, no, but still not zero "people", though, hmmm, *Marshall?*' Sebastian says. 'We want to get the figure of people who hang around near and outside our building down to zero, don't we. Hmmm?' He's telling us, not asking. Which is why he keeps talking before anyone can commit the same sin as Marshall by interrupting or being a bit too 'right on'. He continues: 'I've been researching the methods that seem to have worked to peacefully and non-confrontationally move these "people" on and it seems some of the more exclusive buildings in London, buildings that aren't too dissimilar to ours, I have to say, have had these deterrent measures installed outside their properties.' At this, Astrid, Sebastian's wife, comes into her own. She has the vaguest look of a 70s game-show hostess about her, and she is suddenly on her feet, handing out A5 sheets of paper with a picture of what could be a torture device from the 1600s: metal spikes, evenly spaced and welded into a metal sheet protruding from the entrance to a building.

The room becomes a hush of embarrassment as people stare intently at the paper they've been handed and studiously avoid eye contact with anyone else around them.

'Deterrent measures?' Marshall asks casually. He's the only one, it seems, brave enough to say something. 'Are these those so-called anti-homeless spikes people were up in arms about in London recently?'

'I give money to *Big Issue* sellers,' Sebastian suddenly declares. Colour rises to his cheeks, his eyes widen and his body becomes rigid, ready to defend against any and all sorts of attacks. 'I understand it can be hard to be out there in all weathers, when you've got a drink or a drug problem and you don't have a hope in hell of getting clean, but let's be honest, most of those "people" don't *want* help. They want to live out there, where they can drink wherever they want, take drugs whenever they want, and that's fine. I'm a liberal man. I can understand the need to be free and to live without rules. But why do they have to do it on my doorstep? Your doorstep?' He holds up his piece of paper, shakes it with conviction. 'I, for one, don't mind saying the things most of us can't say nowadays because of all this blessed political correctness. Something needs to be done. And because the police won't help us, we need to do it ourselves. These are just an idea. Something for those of us who care about our homes, who want to protect and preserve what is ours, to think on, to consider and to weigh up against those "people's" rights to be free and ours to live in nice properties.'

'Mate, all I asked was if these were those so-called anti-homeless spikes. That's all,' Marshall says. That isn't all, and he knows it. We all know it, apart from maybe Sebastian, who has spectacularly shot himself in the foot. Marshall's question has shown that Sebastian's first motivation is to satisfy his deep hatred for a group whose humanity he wants to 'air quote' away.

What Marshall has done is to show others in the building that yes, they may have concerns about homeless people hanging around near their building – as homeless people hang around most buildings, to be fair – and the residents are well within their rights to be pissed off about it and to call the police to see what can be done, but agreeing to things like anti-homeless spikes would be hanging very large question marks over their compassion and basic human decency.

'Look, no one has to decide anything right now,' Sebastian says quickly. He's unsettled by the lack of support for what he has said – no one is nodding, no one has applauded what he has said. They may agree, but his ranting has prevented anyone from showing the slightest bit of agreement. 'All I ask is that you think about it and let me know what you think. When we've reached a decision, I can always get some quotes on prices, just so you know what we may possibly, *possibly*, be signing up for.'

I glance around the room again, sketching in the expressions on people's faces from the overview I had earlier. As I take in all the people in the room, I wonder what they'd think, what they'd say if I stood up right now and said: 'For the last ten years of my life, I was homeless.'

Roni

I should really be going home, but I can't move.

Most school staffrooms seem to be the same: easy chairs that have seen better days, usually arranged in some kind of circular formation that always puts me in mind of group therapy. The walls are neutral, a noticeboard is crammed with pinned-up different-sized and different-coloured pieces of paper, and there are often teachers pacing around looking as though they could do with a fag and a drink.

It's the end of the day and I sit in my easy chair by the fridge watching the comings and goings of the teachers who belong here, who have a vested interest in keeping their jobs, who know and love the children, who are so wrapped up in the fabric of the school their whole lives revolve around the place. Everything is winding down, and even though I am a supply teacher, I cannot bring myself to leave this place yet. Teaching was never my idea, although I have grown to love it since I was assigned the role.

Coventry, 2000
'Novice Grace, we have decided that convent life is not for you,' Mother Superior told me. 'We have prayed on it for a long time, and we have come to see that your time would be better served elsewhere. As a teacher. We will enrol you in a university in Liverpool which you will attend for four years, with one year for teacher training. There is a

place for you in the Light of the Virgin Mary convent, which is attached to a school, so you will be able to work there. It will be a lot of work because you will also be studying for your final vows but I know you will be able to handle it. Our Sisters at the Light of the Virgin Mary are looking forward to welcoming you to their community.'

I had not been expecting this when I sat down in her office. I *had* been expecting to be told that I maybe needed to spend a bit longer on my duties, that it wasn't a race and that I didn't need to be in a constant rush. Instead, I was essentially being asked to leave.

'But Superior, I like this life.'

'That may be so, Novice Grace. We see, though, that you struggle with the silence of monastic life.'

I wasn't sure what she meant. God was in the silence. I was always searching for silence, for a way to dampen down and then erase the noise in my head. I knew in here, once I had found the silence that the noise put in there by what had been happening since I was young, would disappear I would find God.

Observing the no-speaking rule and constant prayer was a liberating chance to revel in the stillness of my mind that came from following the strict structure of the convent's day. I had not been expecting the languid stretches of peace I had experienced when I had finally been allowed to begin my training as a novice. Now it was being taken away from me. 'I do not struggle with not speaking, Superior,' I said. 'Not at all.'

She smiled at me, serene and understanding; she regularly smiled at me like she could see deep into my heart and know what I was really thinking whenever I spoke. It was unsettling, as though she had a power given to her by God to know the truth about most things. 'Silence is not simply the absence of speech. Silence is also a time to think and reflect and pray, to feel closer to God. Is that how you experience silence, Novice Grace? Or is silence a means of escape for you?'

'I feel closer to God when there is silence,' I explained to her. 'I feel Him when I am praying, when I am working, when I am carrying out my chores. This is the life I have chosen, this is the life for me.'

'Monastic life is not an escape, Novice Grace. This is why we believe you struggle – you are not here purely because the simple life is something you are committed to – we believe you are trying to escape, to hide,' she explained. 'You are dedicated, we can see how much you have devoted yourself to God, to the life of praying for the world, and you would make an excellent Sister, but not a nun. Not when you are hiding.'

'I'm not so sure I would make a good teacher,' I replied. 'I'm not sure I'm cut out for that.'

'Obedience, Novice Grace, is one of the most important tenets of choosing to dedicate your life to the Lord. I have told you that several times, have I not?'

'Yes, Superior.'

'It is very difficult for novices to understand why we require obedience, but somehow you seem to have particular trouble embracing it fully. Do you know why that is?'

I stared at Superior and wondered if that was a trick question. I was not good at answering questions correctly, trick or otherwise. I had this knack for entirely missing the point in these sorts of conversations. I also suspected that Superior was, having told me that she knew that I had been trying to hide by coming here, questioning my commitment to this life. She knew as well as I did that I was not someone who had seen *The Sound of Music* too many times (I couldn't stand the singing in it, for one, which kind of negated the whole point of the film), because I had worked so hard for over two years to be accepted. I was dedicated, I did want to be here and I knew I would get there with the silence, that I would not be searching for God in the silence – at some point, I would go to Him in silence.

'Fear,' I confessed in answer to her question about my struggles with obedience. 'I am scared to simply trust what I am told is what is for the best.'

Superior beamed at me. 'That is a remarkable moment of self-insight and reflection. Do you know why you were able to show that at that moment?' she asked.

'Because I said the first thing that came into my head?' I replied. 'I mean, apart from momentarily thinking about Maria from *The Sound of Music*.'

Mother smiled at me again, her lips showing her perfect white teeth. 'Contrary to what you may believe, I do not want to dampen the natural exuberance you have, Novice Grace, simply direct it. Obedience in a novice, in us all, is about trust. To have trust, you must have faith. I have faith in you to find the right way along this path that God has chosen for you. The path needs to deviate slightly from the one you thought you were on, but we believe this next section of the path is the right one for you.'

'To be a teacher?'

'To be a teacher,' she confirmed.

But what if you do not know what it is to trust any more? What if your ability to have faith, to let go and simply be, doesn't work? Are you supposed to go against everything you feel to simply obey and trust God's will be done?

'Yes,' Superior said.

'Did I say that out loud?' I asked.

'Your face did,' she said. 'You have a very expressive face – it's a good thing you don't gamble. Novice Grace, relax. You will make mistakes, we all of us make mistakes, but that is what growing is all about. Will you be a good Sister? I firmly believe so. Will you be able to continue until you take your final vows in seven years? I am not sure. But I have faith that you will be the best you can be. You are a natural Sister, if not a nun, and through that you will offer the world of teaching so much. I suspect, also, that you will always find a way to resolve your somewhat liberal approach to obedience, and that may not be a negative thing.'

'Yes, Superior.'

I did not tell her, as I got up to leave, how terrified I was of leaving the silence of life behind the convent walls, and re-entering the world where everything was noisy, chaotic and a reminder of where I had come from.

London, 2016

It feels odd to be interacting with people and to be dressed like everyone else. I feel underdressed, slightly vulnerable. At the time, when I would dress as a Sister in my skirt, blouse and veil, it had never felt like armour, like a protective shell that stopped the outside world encroaching on who I was. If anything, it made me stick out but in an invisible way. People never saw me, they saw the veil, the crucifix and not much else. A lot of Sisters dress quite casually, nowadays, some don't even wear veils, but I enjoyed the anonymity of the veil, of the sober clothes, the way people would look at me and then look through me because I wasn't anyone of note.

The man who has just dropped himself into the seat beside my chair has on a navy-blue V-neck cricket jumper with a logo on its right breast. His black hair is slicked back, and his trousers of choice are brown cords. I'm assuming he has left his tweed jacket with its elbow patches in his locker. Most of the teachers dress smartly and could be mistaken for office workers, while this man seems to buck the trend by going retro.

'Hi, I'm Cliff,' he says. He leans over in his seat to stick out his hand.

'Pleased to meet you, Cliff.' I shake his hand. 'I'm Veronica, or Roni, as most people call me.'

'How are you finding it?' he asks.

'It's fine. I'm only here for a few more days, but it's been fine. Great, actually. The staff have been helpful and the children haven't been too trying. What do you teach?'

'I'm Head of Maths and Year Ten form tutor.'

'Head of Maths? I see. Is that why you dress like a teacher?' I say to him. To be fair to him, I do dress like a Sister – skirt, blouse, cardigan – because those are the only clothes I have. Even though I don't wear my larger cross outside of my clothes any more, I can't bring myself to take it off – it has been a part of me for half my life, I would be naked and vulnerable without it.

I'm pleased when Cliff grins at me, then I realise how rude that sounded. How much like Uncle Warren that was. 'I'm sorry, I'm sorry,' I say. 'That was actually quite rude and unnecessary. I simply noticed you don't dress like most people around here.'

'No, I don't. But it's fine,' he says with a laugh. 'It was only a little banter.'

'I dislike that word so much.'

'Really? Why?'

'It's simply a way for people to get away with being rude. And I was rude, and I don't even know you. I'm sorry.'

'You're the nun, aren't you?'

'I'm not a nun any more,' I say. I'm going to be saying that for a long while to come, I suspect.

'Does that mean if I ask you out for a drink you'll be able to say yes?'

I frown deeply. 'Are you asking me out on what the youngsters call a date?' I reply.

'Yes,' he says with an amused smile and a short nod of his head. 'Any time you fancy. But the sooner the better, if you're not going to be around much.'

I haven't been asked out on a date . . . ever, I don't think. When I made the decision to become a nun, I stopped drinking, I stopped taking drugs and I stopped going out clubbing. In fact, I had stopped most of that when I made the decision, but that was only because Nika wouldn't speak to me and I had no one to go out with. I'd tried apologising and she would act as though I wasn't there. Without her, I didn't seem to be able to do it alone. Once I had found my focus, I didn't notice boys, men or any of that. I was on my journey and I did not need my head turning, my attention diverting by anyone else.

'Erm, that would be lovely. I must warn you, though, I don't drink.'

'That's fine. When would you like to go out?'

Mum's face shimmers into view. Last night she smugly told me that Dad doesn't like shepherd's pie and was tight-lipped when he proceeded to eat it all; her mouth was practically concave by the time he asked for seconds. 'Tonight?'

'Excellent. If you give me your mobile number I'll text you the time and place.'

'I don't have a mobile,' I say.

'No need for it in the convent?'

'No, other Sisters had mobiles but I didn't feel the need. I saw a pub down on the high street, The Forbidden Grapes or something? I live over in Chiselwick so we'd need to meet there at eight so I've time to go home and change.'

'Sounds great. Meet you at eight… You wouldn't think I was a maths teacher with such rhyming skills, would you?'

'No, no, I wouldn't. I'd better get going if I'm going to get back to you in time. I'll see you later at eight.'

'Yes, see you later.'

Nika

Birmingham, 2004

Carefully, I wrapped up the slick bar of soap in a small clear sandwich bag and placed it back into the gaping hole of the large clear sandwich bag on the sink of the toilets in Birmingham Library. Next, I carefully wrapped up my damp blue flannel in another sandwich bag and placed it beside the soap. Hopefully I'd get a chance to dry out the flannel later so it didn't become slimy and mouldy, but for now, I had to keep it in a plastic bag so the other things in my bag stayed as dry as possible.

I felt a little better now that I'd had the chance to brush my teeth and have a wash, change my underwear and generally 'freshen up' after another night spent walking the streets. When I'd got off the coach, I had followed the crowd as much as possible, assuming they were heading for the city centre. I had passed over a canal and had paused to watch the waterway disappear in both directions. Like the trains at Victoria station, I loved watching rivers and canals, seas and oceans. I loved the idea of them bringing people near and taking them far away.

I'd continued down, walking quickly to try to catch up with the people who had got off the coach. The numbers had dwindled, people branching off in different directions, heading somewhere they needed to be, seeing people they wanted to see, pressing on with the plan they'd had when they'd got on the coach. My plan had consisted of getting away from London before Todd could track me down, and that was it.

The first time I'd run away from home I had planned it meticulously and I'd known where I would be going. I had saved so hard for nearly two years, every single penny that I'd earned, I'd saved. I had walked to school instead of buying a bus pass, I'd delivered papers before school, worked lots of shifts in cafés at the weekend, got a supermarket job for evenings I didn't have ballet class or individual lessons. I had been organised, focused only on escape.

This time, I'd had no plan, no idea where I was. I'd chosen Birmingham because it was a big city and in all the time I'd been with Todd, we'd never gone there. Brighton, Liverpool, Leeds, Manchester, Glasgow, Aberdeen, York, we'd been and stayed there, had gone out with friends there. But Birmingham, we'd never so much as gone through, so I'd known that was the place to be. He was less likely to know people there and I was less likely to bump into anyone either of us knew. That was my hope, anyway.

Once I'd hit Birmingham city centre and all the people from the coach station had dispersed, I'd wandered around a bit, trying to take in the area, trying to physically learn the lay of the land – which streets were narrow and awkward, which were cobblestoned, which had beautiful old buildings that rose up into the sky like gentle giants, watching over the city. I'd had no idea where I was going, but I'd walked. As I'd walked, the sky had rubbed out its blue colour with black as night had approached, and I'd seen more and more of the previously invisible people. In the archways of buildings, in the doorways of shops, beside cashpoints, in or near the park. I'd walked and watched, knowing that I had to stay awake, find out where things were, see what the city was like before I found myself somewhere to stay. *Where are all the women?* I had asked myself more than once as I'd continued my walking vigil around Birmingham city centre. *Why can't I see any women sleeping out on the streets? Is it too dangerous for them out here? Or are they doing what I had to do: weighing up which is more deadly – sleeping on the street or sleeping in a bed with the man you are supposed to love?*

Part of me knew I was being ridiculous when I thought about Todd like that; after all, there was nothing he could do. Yet, most of me was terrified of him. Of what he could convince other people of. I knew from past experience that even the people closest to you wouldn't necessarily believe you when you asked them for help, so why on Earth would the police believe me? And seriously, what was I going to tell them he'd done to me which meant I needed their protection? That he'd bought me clothes that he wanted me to wear? He'd paid for me to be driven everywhere? That'd he'd recorded me? That he would control how much of his money I had access to? That he made it difficult for me to get a job or to have friends? The only thing that could possibly be taken seriously by them, would maybe cast him in a bad light, was that he regularly had sex with me whether I wanted him to or not. Even then, I knew they would blame me. They wouldn't boldly say it, but would ask me questions that would tell me they blamed me, they held me more responsible for what he did than him. They wouldn't outright say it, but there would be questions: *'Why didn't you walk away?' 'If it was so awful, with the money, the clothes, the expensive gym membership, the car service and staying in luxury hotels, why didn't you just leave?' 'He's not a mind reader, so why didn't you just tell him that you didn't want to have sex?' 'He didn't physically trap you in the house, did he? So why didn't you just leave?'*

How did you explain to people who only dealt in things that were legal and illegal, people who had no idea what it was like living with him, that I didn't know how to leave? That I was scared to. That he had made me so convinced that it was all down to me, I kept thinking that there would be some way to change myself that would stop him treating me how he treated me. In the eyes of the law, all he did was provide me a lovely, easy life, and *quid pro quo*, he should get something in return – even if that 'something' was sex that I didn't want, sex that was breaking little pieces of my soul every time it was forced on me.

Who would understand that?

And who would understand if I verbalised that for the last year or so, at the back of my head, I'd had a feeling, an uneasy, unformed sense that Todd was going to kill me. If I said that, though, to the police – to anyone – they would laugh in my face and tell me I was being silly. But the way he had worked so hard to make my life extremely small, the way he had managed to twist the changes *he* was meant to make into changes *I* had to make, the way he'd been able to control what I did and who I saw without ever shouting at or hitting me, had made me think he would annihilate me before he let me walk away from him. That feeling, of being in danger, had settled at the back of my mind like a contented cat settled on a fleece rug beside a roaring fire. It had been there, mostly sleeping and mostly undisturbed, but the fire had been constantly stoked by the things Todd did, the quiet little violences he'd committed against me, and the cat would be roused, would stretch itself out and would prowl around for a little while to remind me how precarious my situation was.

After my wash, I sat in the main part of the library in front of a computer. I was trying to find homeless shelters, somewhere I could sleep at night, and then I would be able to look for a job during the day. I was so tired, my feet were sore from walking and walking, I had no idea where anything was even though I had bought a guide-book and an *A–Z* and I had walked so far in the last few hours.

The library was warm, full of books, which for some reason made me feel secure, and there was a music section where I could go to listen to music once I'd done this. I was hoping I would be able to find a quiet corner, maybe get an hour's sleep. No one would bother me here. And then, find a shelter for the night, just somewhere to stay where I wouldn't have to pay. The money I had wouldn't last very long – I had to be very, very careful with it.

There were a few shelters, but none of the information was very clear about how you got in there, if you could just turn up, if they were closed during the day, if they had showers. I needed a shower: the wash downstairs had been refreshing, but not enough. My body wanted to be properly cleansed. Who knew that I should have appreciated every shower I had, especially one I could programme to my exact temperature requirements, because I wouldn't know when I'd get the next one? In the notebook I'd bought earlier along with the soap, flannel, toothpaste and pen, I noted down the addresses of the shelters. *If I can get to sleep tonight, even for a few hours, I'll be able to get up early in the morning, grab the local paper, walk around newsagents', see if there are any jobs vacant cards up, see if there is any way I can afford a house share.* I had looked at B&Bs: one night would eat into a huge chunk of my money. Under the list of shelters on my notepad, I listed youth hostels. Again, it was money, but not as expensive as B&Bs, and it'd be a place to have a shower, regroup. Maybe make a few friends. Todd had been keen for me to have no friends, so maybe that's what I needed. I'd been wary of people in the past; maybe I should start to trust them.

Once I finished on the computer, I got up and walked down the vast, red-carpeted walkway beside the desk space, heading for one of the upper levels. Upstairs, I was sure I would find a place to sit quietly. It was such a huge space, no one would notice me hanging around for a bit.

'Love, love, it's time to go.' The woman's voice was kind, lilted with a strong Birmingham accent, as she tried to wake me up. I sat up, suddenly, realising I'd fallen asleep in a public place. I checked my bag, cradled like a baby under my arm, first of all. Nothing had been disturbed, I didn't think. My money was safe.

'Sorry,' I said to her. I stood up and was immediately taller than her. She was a slight, small woman – only the oval of her friendly-but-concerned face was on show because of the black hijab she wore. 'Sorry,' I said again.

'No, it's all right, love,' she said. 'I'm sorry to have to wake you. The library's closing, though, so you have to go.'

'Thank you, sorry.' Closing time? I obviously hadn't woken up after an hour as planned; it'd probably be too late to find a youth hostel or shelter now.

'Do you have somewhere to go?' she asked. Her voice was kind, gentle, as though trying not to scare me.

Is it that obvious? I'd been homeless for two days, only one of them in this city – did it show that quickly that I was of no fixed abode? Or was it the sleeping in a library that gave me away? Or… horror of horrors,

145

did I smell? Did the lack of a shower for two days prove that I had nowhere to go? I quickly clamped my arms down to close up my armpits.

'Erm, I'm kind of new to the city,' I told her with a glance at her name badge: 'Nikki B', it read. The name I'd fled from. The first person to notice me, to see me, in Birmingham was a Nikki, but she was a real one.

'You know, I might be speaking out of turn here, but there are a couple of day centres not far from here. You can go there during the day, get tea or coffee, a couple of times a week they have hot food and you can often have a sit down and sleep if you need to. They also help you with CVs and finding a job and the like. You might not need a place like that, but if you do, there are a couple of leaflets downstairs you can pick up on the way out.'

She smiled at me and I wanted to throw my arms around her. To cry and tell her thank you, to sob and say that the fact she'd spoken to me, had noticed me, had actually seen that I was a human being, meant so much right now. I'd disappeared with Todd, I had to disappear again to make sure I got away from him, but it didn't seem such a hardship if nice people saw me, spoke to me.

'Thank you,' I said quietly.

'You can come back here any time you want to, though,' she said. 'The library's for everyone. No one's going to throw you out just for being here.'

'Thank you,' I said to her again. Mumbled it actually. I would probably cry if I said anything else.

'You're more than welcome. Like I said, you're welcome back any time.'

At the door, which she had to use a key to open to let me out, she told me good luck with everything and that she hoped to see me again. Then, she asked me my name.

'My name?' I replied. 'Grace. Grace Carter.'

'I'm sorry, without ID I can't let you stay here,' the lady at the desk of the latest youth hostel I had tried said.

'But I don't have any,' I pleaded with her. 'I lost it all.'

The woman had a badly done curly perm, and a face set in a permanent sneer. Actually, she probably didn't, but she seemed to be sneering at me. I wanted to guarantee a night where I didn't have to walk and walk and walk. I had blisters developing, my socks were rubbing at the edges of my toenails. I just wanted to sleep for the night. It would use up a bit of my money, but I didn't care. The real Nikki in the library had given me hope. Talking to her, being seen by her, made me realise that maybe I could try doing things the normal way, maybe I would be OK. It was completely magical thinking, as it turned out, because this was the third place that had turned me away because I didn't have anything to prove who I was. 'I'll pay in advance,' I said to her. 'Leave a deposit?'

'I'm sorry, I can't. It's not worth my job. I'm sorry.'

I sighed, my whole body suddenly heavy and tired. Weary. I'd used that word before but had never properly felt it. Never until then. 'I just want somewhere to sleep tonight,' I said to myself. I said it out loud so I could hear if it sounded like something ridiculous, something so outlandish that I shouldn't even hope to have that wish granted.

'I know.' The woman's whole demeanour softened a little. 'I can't let you in without any ID, though. Do you really have nothing? Not even a cash card?'

I shook my head. I had nothing. The credit cards, cash cards and key to Todd's flat were inside my expensive, designer-label purse, left sitting in a bin in London Victoria before I boarded the coach. This was a reminder, though, that I couldn't get anything without ID. I would find it hard to do anything without proper confirmation that I was now Grace Carter.

Not many people knew my proper name, Veronika Harper, but I couldn't be sure who was looking for me, what sorts of systems were going to be flagged up if I tried to use that name. It would only be for a few months, until Todd got bored and realised that I wasn't going to reveal all about him, until he found someone else to start over on, but it was going to be a hard few months if I needed ID.

'Look, the only thing I can suggest is you come back when you've got proper ID? Yes?'

'Yes, yes, of course,' I said. 'Of course.'

It was all very well calling myself Grace Carter, but if I couldn't prove it, it meant nothing, did it?

It never grew quiet in here. It was dark, not pitch black, but dark enough to sleep, dark enough to have to wait for your eyes to adjust every time you opened them so you could make out which shapes were human, which shapes were not. It was dark, but not quiet. People coughed, people grunted, snored, moved on creaky beds, talked in their sleep. The air was heavy with the breaths of the twenty or so sleeping people, all curled up or laid flat on fold-out beds that were positioned a few feet from neighbouring cots.

The man who had checked me into this homeless shelter hadn't been that keen to admit me, had told me there were no other women there that night so he couldn't put me near any other females. I'd been so tired by that point, the exhaustion permeating every part of me so extensively, I'd just wanted to walk around in tiny circles to make the tiredness stop. 'I don't mind,' I'd said to him. What I'd meant, of course, was that I didn't care. I wasn't there to socialise, to find my new best mate; right then, I'd just needed somewhere to sit down and think, to lie down and sleep, to not be disturbed and moved on for a few hours.

This shelter was in an old building, not far from where I'd stopped to look at the canal. It looked like a former religious building with its large stained-glass windows, but its outside shape was nothing church-like at all. Both sides of the building were flanked by other buildings under renovation, both of them covered in scaffolding and hoarding that was complicated and prominent, like braces on a teenager's teeth.

This place wasn't so bad. It was all right, actually. It was clean, no one seemed to bother with anyone else, it was somewhere inside and out of the cold and I had a blanket to cover me. I'd lain down fully clothed, with my jacket on top of me, the blanket on top of that, and the soft leather of my lumpy, bumpy rucksack under my head instead of the pillow. I would be finished if I lost my rucksack, so I had to keep it close.

Obviously for all the tiredness, now I couldn't sleep. Now I lay awake with my eyes open, listening to the never-quite-falling silence and trying to work out what to do next. I would check out what Nikki the librarian had said about the day centres tomorrow. I could do with drinking copious amounts of coffee, and starting a job search. I wasn't qualified for much: since leaving home I had worked back-stage at the theatre and waitressed and then had become the infamous girlfriend of a man who could kick a ball around a pitch. Not much for the CV.

I could do it, though. I knew I could. I just needed a chance. I just needed to meet the right person, hear of the right job, and I would have the chance to start over. I was owed a break, I knew that. I was owed the chance to turn it all around. I closed my eyes and kept them closed.

The sounds around me slowly spun themselves like thread on a spinning wheel into a melody, a backdrop that was unusual but oddly soothing as I let go and drifted off to sleep . . .

Suddenly, a hand – calloused and hard – clamped down tight on my mouth, shutting off air. My eyes flew open, my chest expanded to try to pull in air, but it was useless. Another hand, pushing aside the blanket, moving away my jacket. Then a weight on top of me, pinning me down, fixing me to the bed. I couldn't see a face, not in the dark, not from the way I was being held down, but the other hand was inside my clothes, inside my jeans, my knickers; rough fingers, ragged nails were clawing away at me. I struggled, but the hand on my mouth, the weight on my body, made it impossible. I knew what was going to happen. The sounds of the room were the same as before, all normal, all the sounds you'd expect from so many people sleeping in the same room, and this was going to happen. Surrounded by so many people, this was going to happen to me.

149

His breathing, loud and heavy, filled my ears, and no one else could hear it, no one else could hear the noise of him forcing his fingers inside me, nor the sound of my desperate struggle, nor the silent volume of my 'no' being shouted against his hand.

'Get off her, you bastard!' a voice said in the darkness, and I felt the weight being shoved off me before I heard him landing loudly on the floor.

I was on my feet before the attacker could react. I snatched up my rucksack, held it against my body as protection, then snatched up my jacket, clung on to that, too. It was hard to see in the dark; the shape of the man who had been on top of me stayed on the floor, a lumpy, almost curved mountain. He swayed a little – maybe he'd hurt himself when he fell, although the fall wasn't from any sort of height. Around us others seemed to be making waking-up noises.

'Come on, we'd better get out of here,' the man who had saved me said. 'I just kicked him in the head. When he comes round a bit, he's going to be *pissed off.*' Before I could protest or properly react, he grabbed my hand and began to lead me out of the room, weaving our way around the beds at speed. Without looking back, we left the building and ran a little way down the road until we could turn the corner and move out of sight of the front of the building, throwing ourselves into the false shelter created by the scaffolding on the neighbouring building.

We flattened ourselves against the wall, trying to disguise ourselves in the shadows in case the man came after us. It was ridiculous, really, especially when we were both breathing loudly, our bodies shaking instead of being silent and stationary if we were to blend properly into the darkness. When nothing happened, no shouts, no loud, angry footsteps hurtling down the street, we stopped holding ourselves against the wall and relaxed forwards. The wind swirled around us, rattling the scaffolding, an eerie soundtrack to what had almost just happened. *What had almost just happened.*

My legs went from underneath me at the thought of it, and I was on the ground, clutching my bag and jacket, shaking. 'He was going to…' I couldn't even say the word. I'd never been able to say the word. Every time I saw the word it took me to a different place, a different time, a different horror that I'd tried to forget. 'He was going to…' *Why? Why?* I buried my face in my jacket and rucksack, the full horror of it descending upon me.

'I'm sorry about that, mate,' the man beside me said. 'He's a bastard.'

'Why me?' I asked myself aloud. The man beside me couldn't give me an answer, obviously. In fact, I didn't even know him. He could be as bad as the man in the shelter; he could be worse. Maybe they worked together to get women alone, away from any source of help. I stumbled quickly upwards, steadying myself on my feet as I moved away from him, checking behind me all the while in case someone was going to jump me from behind. I didn't know this place well enough to know where to run and escape. Would I be fast enough? Would my exhausted legs be able to carry me fast enough and far enough?

'Nah, nah, I'm not working with him,' the man said when he saw what I was doing. 'I wouldn't do nothing like that. He's just a bastard. Every time there's a woman in there he tries it on. We tried to get him banned but they say there's nothing they can do, everyone's welcome and no one's ever pressed charges. Like that was ever going to happen. There's always one of us looking out for the girls – tonight it was me.' He stared at me with his open face. 'Felt good to give him that boot to the head.'

The man was only a fraction taller than me, with a wiry frame, his many layers of clothing hanging off him. He looked grimy; not dirty, just a bit grubby, his clothes coloured with the grey of city living, his shoes worn, and his surprisingly clean but yellow-stained fingers, peeking out of fingerless gloves.

'You just arrived?' he asked. He didn't try to close the gap between us, seemed to know that I needed space from him. I liked that. It showed a modicum of decency and understanding.

'I suppose so,' I said.

'Do you want me to show you round?' he asked.

'It's the middle of the night.'

'All the best things happen in the middle of the night,' he said. Then stopped. 'You know what I mean, sorry. That was thoughtless.' He didn't have a Birmingham accent, it was more cockney than anything, maybe a bit of south London, too. It was hard to place because it kept dipping in and out of various areas of London.

'It's not your fault,' I said. 'I just wanted somewhere to sleep. One night's sleep, that was all.'

'It's hard for girls on the street, I won't lie to you ... What's your name?'

'Grace.' It was easier that time – it tripped off my tongue like people had been calling me that all my life. Grace, my middle name. Carter, my mother's maiden name.

'I'm Reese. Well, that's what I call myself, it's not my real name. No one knows my real name, not even me, I don't think. I've changed it so many times to suit whichever situation. Right now, I've had Reese for three years. Saw it on a film once. Liked it, used it.' He paused for breath. 'What was I saying? Oh yeah, it's hard out on the streets for girls. The mixed night shelters aren't that safe, and there aren't any women-only ones round here. The best way to get some sleep is to hide. Find somewhere hidden and sleep there. That's where all the girls are. They sleep out, but they hide at night. It's the best way.'

I was going to have to do it, I realised that then. I was going to have to sleep on the streets, on the ground, until I could find a way to make money. *People walk on those streets with their dirty shoes. Dogs take dumps on the street, wee up against walls. The streets, the pavements, the ground that I've always thought of as dirty and disgusting, are my only option – unless I want to go back to Todd, or go back to my parents.*

'It ain't so bad, ya know?' Reese said. He had probably worked out what I was thinking. How need was going to have to trump disgust. 'There are some real bastards out there, but ya know, mostly, we look out for each other when we can.' He nodded to himself before hoisting up his once-green sleeping bag on to his shoulder. 'I can take you to a café that's open twenty-four hours if you want? The owner's sound as a pound, he don't mind us lot coming and going as long as we don't take the piss, like. No dealing on the premises or crap like that.'

'That sounds good,' I said.

'Come on then, Grace,' he said. 'And tomorrow, when the normals are awake, I'll find out about getting you some ID. A photo driving licence should do it.'

'What do you mean?'

'You'll see, Grace me old girl, you'll see.'

I had been wrong earlier when I'd thought I hadn't gone to the shelter to make friends: that night was the night I met one of my best friends.

Roni

I'm not sure how to dress for a date. Not that I have many clothes to choose from. I have visited the local charity shop and found myself a few non-dowdyish dresses, some flat, sensible shoes. I had to debate with myself over them, though. I wasn't sure if they were worth using the scant money I had to pay for them, nor whether they would suit me. I missed Mum so much at that moment. The mother I have is not the mother I have in my fantasies. The mother in my head would have come along shopping with me, would have told me what suited me, what I should simply put back on the rail and walk swiftly away from.

I stand in front of the hallway mirror, examining myself. I have chosen a pinstripe suit jacket, one of my usual blouses, and jeans. I'm not sure if I look like a nun in jeans or not. The chain of my crucifix is visible around my neck, but the actual cross is below the top button of my white blouse. My only other jewellery is the gold-plated watch my parents gave me for my eighteenth birthday. I'd left it behind because we were only allowed the absolute basics in the first convent I entered. It'd been one of the first things I'd put on when I got home. I stare at myself again: my brown hair's a bit plain, but there's not much to do with a cut like mine. It wasn't necessary to cut my hair short, but I liked it short and easy to manage. I suppose I could grow it out.

'I'll be off then,' I say to Mum, who is sitting in the living room with her needlepoint on her lap, one of her quiz shows on the TV. 'I don't think I'll be back too late. Say bye to Dad for me.'

Mum is openly horrified: her needle sticks upwards from her canvas, her glasses slip down to the end of her nose. This is her version of the scratch across a record when strangers enter a pub. 'You're going out? What about dinner?'

'I'll probably get something when I'm out,' I say.

'You're not cooking tonight?' Mum asks, clearly aghast.

'Sorry, I wasn't aware you wanted me to. You haven't been very happy that I've been cooking so I didn't think you'd mind.'

'I simply wasn't best pleased with the mess you left behind.'

I don't like to call my mother a liar, but: *'Liar!'* I wash up as I cook – it is second nature to make sure everything is as near pristine as possible when you sit down to eat in almost all the places where I have lived. 'Well, you won't have to clear up after me tonight,' I offer as a halfway house to ease her indignation.

'Really, you should have told me you weren't going to do what you committed yourself to. I would have made other arrangements. I wasn't aware that they taught you not to honour your commitments in that convent of yours. I'm very disappointed, to be honest. Very disappointed.'

'You look nice, love,' Dad says, coming up behind me. I step aside to let him pass and watch him settle into the dynamic of the room. His chair is nearer the window than Mum's and looks altogether more comfortable, too.

'Thanks, Dad.'

'Off out?'

'Yes. Look, I'm sorry about not making dinner. I didn't realise it would cause so many problems. Thing is, I don't have the number of the person I'm meeting so I can't call and cancel.'

'Cancel? Don't be ridiculous. We weren't expecting dinner, were we, Margaret?' Dad says. He sits heavily backwards, picks up his newspaper from where it is resting on the armchair and shakes it open between his hands.

'It simply would have been nice to have some notice if Veronica wasn't in for dinner and she wasn't going to cook as planned.'

'Have you had some sort of knock on the head?' Dad asks Mum. He holds his paper away from his face, which is corrugated with confusion. 'Since when was it a plan that Veronica cooks? It's been lovely of her to do it these past few weeks, but you're the one who won't usually let anyone into the kitchen. If I try to so much as boil water for pasta you're telling me off.' Dad shakes his paper out again with a stern look at my mother. 'Go on, Veronica, have a lovely evening.'

'Thanks, Dad. Thanks, Mum,' I say. I shouldn't laugh, but when I step out of the house, I can't help but have a little giggle. *Have you had some sort of knock on the head?* That makes me want to laugh and laugh and laugh.

The Forbidden Grape is a dark pub, lighting set to 'intimate'. I realise my mistake the moment I enter. *Cliff is going to think all sorts*, I tell myself.

He can think what he likes – doesn't mean he'll get anything out of me, I reply to myself.

I am here early because the pub is a bit of a walk from my parents' house. I choose a table near the bar, then decide a booth at the back might be better. Then I question what sort of message that might send. I do not want Cliff to think this is anything more than a drink or two. I have never been on a proper date, and if that becomes obvious to him, which it probably will, I do not want him to take advantage. Or think about taking advantage. Leaning over and kissing me without permission would certainly be seen as taking advantage. That is far more likely to happen, though, in a booth. I slide myself out, and move back to the table near the bar. It's got a distinctive wobble and a rickety frame; the backless stools aren't much better. I feel on display here, as if I am trying to make a

'NOTICE ME' statement. I move to a table near the toilets, but it is too near the toilets and there's a waft of tangy toilet cleaner every time the door opens, plus the table is too big for two. I move to the other side of the bar, near the exit to the beer garden. Smoke from the smokers' area is blown back inside, though. I go to move again, when I spot Cliff arrive. He's quite handsome away from school. He isn't much taller than me, and his hair is nicer when it's not slicked back, he has glasses on that seem to have been made to emphasise his bone structure, and he is no longer dressed like a teacher: jeans, white shirt and pinstripe suit jacket. No, he's not dressed like a teacher – he's dressed like me. The absolute blessed shame of it!

'Hi,' he says, and he colours up a little; obviously our twin-like dressing faux pas has mortified him as much as me.

'Hi.'

'What would you like to drink?' he asks. When I was younger and used to go to clubs, someone buying you a drink meant one thing and one thing alone. The world must have changed since then... although I'm not so sure sometimes. If I allow him to buy me a drink, expectations may arise...

'An orange juice and soda, please. In the same glass,' I say.

'Do you mind if I have a pint?' he asks.

'No? Unless you're expecting me to pay for it, which may change my answer slightly.'

He laughs gently. 'I mean with the...' He waves his hands around as though they are meant to speak for him but they don't, not effectively anyway. 'You know, the whole...'

'The whole...?'

'The whole... G. O. D. thing.' He whispers this. I'm certain God will hear him no matter how quietly he talks, but he seems tense enough so I don't tell him this.

'Are you thinking God will mind if you have a pint? Because I'm told that Jesus once turned water into wine. I mean, I wasn't there so I can't say what colour wine it was or if, indeed, it was something like

Prosecco or champagne, since it was at a wedding, but that's what I'm told. From that, I'm guessing God might overlook the odd pint or two.'

'You don't drink, so it's easy to assume that you might disapprove if I do.'

'I don't drink because I spent most of my teenage years falling down drunk every chance I got. I don't think I could drink any more even if I wanted to.'

The tension binding Cliff's shoulders and pinching his face melts away and he seems happier now to go to the bar.

London, 1994

'Why didn't you tell your parents, Roni? You said you would.' Nika wasn't cross with me, she was sad if anything. She was sad because if I had told my parents like I said I would, then they might have told her parents and maybe they would have believed her. They still didn't believe her and the thought of that happening to me made me feel sick. Nika was brave and strong. She could talk and say the truth and she kept saying the truth even when no one believed her.

It must have killed her soul every time when it happened, when she was sent back to him, and he probably said to her what he often reminded me: 'No one will believe you if you tell, everyone will think you're a dirty little liar.'

'I wanted to,' I said to her, 'but I was too scared.'

'I would have come with you.'

'Don't be angry with me,' I said to her. 'Please. I was just too scared.'

'I said to my parents I wasn't going back to the ballet lessons. They told me if I wanted to carry on living in their house, I had to do what I was told.'

'I don't think they mean that, do you?'

'My parents always mean what they say.'

I took her hand. 'Do you want to come out with me on Friday night?' I asked her. I hadn't told anyone about what I did at the weekends. It was my little secret, my chance to escape. Nika needed to escape, to let go of the noise and find silence like I needed to; she might find that in the way I did.

'Where are you going?'

'You'll see. Just tell your parents you're sleeping over at my house and then I'll show you a night you'll never forget. Honest.'

London, 2016

Cliff and I have managed to make some pretty pleasant small talk so far. Which means, so far, I like dating. If it entails this sort of thing, then I like dating very much.

'Did your superiors at the convent mind that you had such a colourful past?' Cliff asks. He's got *that* question there on his face, in his eyes, teetering on the edge of his tongue. I guess this is his way of working up to it.

'I didn't say my past was colourful, I was saying I used to drink a lot when I was younger.'

'Didn't they mind?'

'They at the convent, you mean? Not especially. I wasn't exactly going to be recreating it in the convent environment, and besides, you have to confess all before you can enter a convent. The confessional is binding so nothing could be mentioned again outside of it and once you say your Hail Marys, and complete your act of contrition, you can walk away with the means to atone for your sins.'

'Did you really believe you could do that?'

'Are you asking me as a former nun or a woman you are sitting in a pub with?'

'Both.'

'Why don't you ask me the real question you're dying to know the answer to, Cliff?'

Dipping his head, Cliff scratches a little at his ear, runs a hand through his hair. 'I'm not sure which question you're referring to.'

'Have it your way. But I won't be answering it unless you ask me outright. You won't be able to con me into it.'

'Wouldn't dream of it. If I knew what you were talking about. Drink?'

'Another orange juice and soda, please.'

'Sure thing.'

London, 1994

'Please don't do this. *Please*,' Nika shouted at me.

'It won't take long,' I said with a giggle.

Nika hadn't wanted to wear as much make-up as me, she'd refused to use the same dark kohl pencil on her eyes or my thick mascara on her lashes or my red lipstick on her mouth. In the end, I'd told her to at least put on some lip gloss and wear my heels because we wouldn't get into any of the clubs we were heading for.

We had been in the club about an hour when he approached me. He'd bought me two drinks – one had been for Nika but she'd refused to drink it. Spoilsport. He was a lot older, and a bit big around the middle, but he liked me, had kept patting my bum and telling me how sexy I looked. When he'd asked me if I wanted to go outside so we could be alone, I'd said yes. He wanted to and that meant I probably should. Nika had asked where I was going and I'd just pointed in the general direction of the exit. My hand had disappeared in his thick, meaty grip and he'd practically dragged me outside. Nika had been right behind us. 'We're coming back in,' I'd heard her tell the bouncer, who'd grunted in reply.

The meaty grip tightened around my hand and it hurt a little as he pulled me towards him. He slapped his spare hand on my bum and squeezed, hard. Probably hard enough to bruise. That made me laugh. How was I going to explain *that* to Mum? He laughed too, then he was pulling me along again, down the street, and then he was pushing me towards the cut by the club, not very far in.

I wasn't thinking very much, but I thought he might kiss me then, now he'd shoved me against the wall. I'd had too much to drink too quickly, I could barely stand. This probably wasn't a good idea. His meaty hands, which had been sweaty and a bit cold, were suddenly up my skirt, his fingers ripping at my knickers.

Whoa! I thought as I swayed again. *This really isn't a good idea.*

'Don't do this,' Nika called to me again. Nika. My lovely Nika. I turned my head towards her voice and saw she hadn't left me alone. She was standing there, waiting for me, telling me not to do it. This was a usual Friday night thing. It meant nothing.

He snarled at her, and I could tell by the look on her face that his eyes were probably threatening her to shut up. Go away.

'Don't, *please*. We can just get the bus home.' She was so brave. So strong. She didn't need to drink, she didn't need drugs, she didn't need to do this to stop the noise in her head.

He growled at Nika, showing her all his teeth, and she took a step back, scared suddenly of what he might do. I knew what he was going to do. It was always the same, they always did the same. 'It's OK,' I told her. But my words sounded all blurry. 'It doesn't mean anything. It never means anything.'

His hands had freed my knickers, his thighs were pushing mine open, he was doing something to himself, his meaty fingers bumping against me as he moved. I turned to look at Nika again and she was facing the other way, obviously didn't want to see what would happen next – how roughly he would enter me, how hard he would move. The guttural *gnnnrrrr-gnnnrrr-gnnnrrr* of his grunts mingled with the music spilling out of the club and pouring into my head.

Silence. There was silence.

Silence.

Silence.

Silence.

Silence.

'You really wanted that, didn't you?' My vision focused on him. *Who was he? Why was he talking to me? Why was he saying those awful words to me?*

I stood still while he tucked himself away, zipped himself up, buttoned at the top. He sniffed; his bulbous red nose seemed to glow in the dark of the alleyway. His small, piggy eyes were turned up like his lips were in a hideous, nauseating leer.

'I've never seen a girl want it as much as you.' His laugh, nasty and rancid, joined the noise in my swirly, blurry head. 'You coming back inside?'

I shook my head.

'Sound.' He left the cut after giving Nika a filthy look.

Nika averted her eyes while I pulled up my knickers, and then waited for me to join her on the pavement. She had her arms folded around herself against the cold and she had that look on her face. She'd had it the very first time at the ballet studio when Monsieur Armand had said he'd given her new material and new moves to try.

'Let's go home,' she said.

'No, no, I want a few more drinks,' I told her.

'Roni, no.'

'Nika, yes. I just want to have some fun.'

'That didn't look like fun,' she said.

It wasn't. Of course it wasn't. But for a moment, there was silence. I would do almost anything to get some more of that silence. To find time away from the loudness lodged permanently, maddeningly, in my head.

'Come on, Nika, come back in and have a drink. Everything is so much better with a drink.'

She didn't agree with me, she didn't drink with me, but she never, ever left me.

London, 2016

'Is it OK if I kiss you?' Cliff asks as we stand on the pavement. We've had a nice evening. Once he knew I wasn't going to answer his question unless he asked, he seemed to relax even more. All pressure and expectation to try and trip me up gone.

'I'd rather not, if you don't mind,' I say to him. He's nice, he's very good-looking, and I haven't been kissed in a million years, it feels like. But I'm not sure he's the one I want to kiss right now.

'Is it because I didn't have the courage to ask the question?' He's disappointed, but not overly so. He certainly will survive.

'No, it's because I met you for five minutes earlier today and three hours now. I don't want to rush anything.'

'Does that mean you might possibly think about seeing me again?'

'Yes, I might possibly. Let's talk about it at school tomorrow and set off lots of gossip about whether you managed to bag yourself a nun.'

Cliff laughs and I laugh. 'I'll see you tomorrow,' we say at the same time. Which reminds us that we're wearing the same clothes.

'Let's never speak of this,' I say to him before we wander off in different directions.

As I approach the top of the high street, the door to a wine bar opens and two people stumble out, giggling like they've taken some of the extra-good drugs. Slowly they stop giggling, they stand upright and he draws her to him, presses his lips against hers. I try not to stare at them, but it's difficult. Difficult because he is anywhere upwards of forty-five, maybe even pushing fifty, and she is about sixteen. It's obvious how young she is to anyone who is interested in knowing; obviously the man who has been drinking with her is not interested. I'm surprised they allowed her in that bar, let alone served her. I have shoes older than her and her age is very obvious. I try not to stare, but it's like a window to my past has opened and I am standing there, peering at my history. That is what I looked like: dressed up, but obviously still a child, being pawed at by someone three times my age.

I swerve myself away from the window to my history, ashamed at how often this played out, sick with sadness at the reasons *why* it played itself out like that for me. I leave the 2016 version of me, in the street, ashamed and disgusted at what I used to be.

Nika

Eliza, Marshall and I walk slowly down the corridor outside Sebastian and Astrid's flat towards the lift.

After the way Sebastian had ranted about the great unwashed homeless that live on our doorstep, any good humour or will to socialise in the room seemed to seep out like a slow but potent leak in a tyre, leaving a tense, nervous atmosphere. Several people made no excuses at all and got up to dash out of there as soon as the meeting was finished, almost all of them leaving the leaflets behind. Others stood in huddles of four and five, talking quietly, pausing to smile at Sebastian and Astrid, while shifting themselves closer and closer to the door as though they were being watched by men with rifles in gun towers and would be shot if they all made a sudden break for it. Eliza, Marshall and I went back to the snack table, none of us wanting to seem rude, especially since Marshall had been the one to set Sebastian off. We hung around, not talking to each other, sipped a bit of the vinegar wine and then waved goodbye on our way out.

'Well, that went a bit wrong for ol' Sebby, didn't it?' Eliza says quietly as we arrive in front of the metal lift door. I'm a little giddy and light-headed on the warm muskiness of her perfume, and after the excitement of the end of the meeting, I could sway where I stand.

'Hmmm,' I reply.

'And you,' Eliza says to Marshall, 'you were well out of order winding him up like that.'

'*I* was out of order?' he replies. 'Are you sure?'

'Well, no, but you know how he gets after someone – usually you – winds him up. He'll start issuing edicts because he's been through the rule book, and he'll stop us putting plants outside our flats, and keeping pets that can possibly escape.'

'Oh, right, so I'm supposed to sit there listening to that crap and say nothing?' Marshall turns his attentions to me, lowers his voice. 'What do you think? Do you think I was out of order, or do you think someone needed to call Sebastian out on that crap he was spouting?'

'Does it matter what I think? I'm only renting, after all.'

'Everyone's important, as far as I'm concerned,' Marshall says passionately. My gaze flicks to the door that we have just exited and then to him. 'It's why I had to say something about those spikes. You know, that's one step away from saying homeless people aren't human and I can't have that. No, even if it does mean Sebastian fights back by making all of us get rid of all the pets, and plants and off-white paint, I don't care. You don't keep silent about something like that. It's not on.'

'I suppose you're right,' Eliza says, mollified.

Marshall's impassioned gaze swings back in my direction after settling on Eliza, daring me to disagree. I hold my hands up in surrender. 'Don't look at me, I'm just waiting for the lift to the seventh floor where I'm going to go into my rented flat and think happy thoughts.'

'Sorry, but people like him make me so *angry*.'

'Don't worry,' I say, 'I couldn't tell at all. You've hidden it so well, right down to shouting about it outside his house – I really don't think anyone noticed.'

Marshall laughs, his face turning away from me for a second and then turning back to grin at me. I grin back at him. A spinning top of excitement rotates at the bottom of my chest and top of my stomach. He's handsome. Not good-looking or gorgeous, more handsome. Dignified. I like the shape of his face, his lack of hair, which allows you to see all the contours of his head. I like the warmth and depth of the colour of the dark brown of his skin. He is so handsome in a way I haven't noticed in a man in a long time.

'*Aha-hem!*' Eliza interjects quietly. 'Seventh floor, you said, didn't you, *Nika*?' She jabs at the lift's down button.

'Erm, yeah, yeah,' I say and drop my visual link to Marshall. I take a step away from him. I do not need to make an enemy of a woman who knows where I live. I did enough of that in Birmingham. Plus, I do not need to get in the middle of these two people, whatever the status of their non-relationship.

'I think I'll walk down, actually,' I say. 'Stretch my legs.' I move off before anyone decides they'll walk too. 'I'll see you both.'

'Oh, right, see you,' Marshall says.

'*Bye, then,*' Eliza says, snippily.

'Nika,' Marshall calls as I'm about to disappear around the bend in the ornate staircase.

'Yes?' I say. I've paused – only my head is visible to them, and they look like giants from this angle.

'It was nice to meet you,' he says. I grin at him, I can't help myself. 'I hope to see you again soon.'

I nod at him. Behind him, Eliza stares at me stony-faced and betrayed. *I'm sorry, Eliza,* I think and tuck away my smile, duck my head and pretend that I'm not incredibly flattered at the idea that someone as handsome as Marshall might possibly like me.

6

Roni

London, 2016

'Bless me, Father, for I have sinned. It has been six weeks since my last confession.'

Six weeks since I have done this and unburdened myself by talking to a priest about what has been playing on my mind. I have travelled almost to the diagonal opposite side of London to find this church. It is large and stands at the centre of a large Regency square surrounded immediately by grass and trees, then encircled and enclosed by a road, then a semi-circle of smart-looking houses. I crave anonymity to do this. My former childhood priest still serves in the church near where my parents live and I got to know him very well during the years of contemplation and prayer leading up to me becoming an aspirant. I do not want him to know what I am about to say; I do not want to have disappointed him by not staying as someone who officially serves the Lord.

'How can I help you, my child?' The man on the other side of the carved wooden grille, whose outline I can make out if I raise my head and stare hard enough, sounds nice. He has a hint of an Irish accent, and his words are gently delivered.

Inside this wooden box, with the door closed and the world on the other side, my life seems so simple. My heart feels stilled and rested. I am peaceful, fingers of silence are smoothing out the edges of my anxiety. This is what I felt when I first entered the monastery in

Coventry. The noise and chaos of the world had been shut away – I could pretend the same was happening on the inside, too.

'One of the things I need to confess, Father, is how long it has been since my last confession. I feel embarrassed and ashamed.'

'Why, my child?'

'I recently left my convent,' I tell him. 'I feel very odd about that. I feel bad, but I know, ultimately, it was the right thing to do. I thought at first I would observe the Divine Offices I had when I was a nun and a Sister, and then a nun again, but that hasn't happened. I am ashamed. It's been such a short time and I have let it all slip.'

My confessor is silent, probably a little shocked that a former nun is admitting these things to him.

'Are you experiencing a crisis of faith?' he asks.

'No, Father, I don't think I am.'

Coventry, 2000

'Novice Grace, will you come for a walk with me around the gardens?' Novice Maria Mary asked me. It was the start of recreation and the most sound-filled part of our day. There had been a tension over dinner, the silence between moments of speech loaded with something other than the usual thoughts we brought to the dinner table at night. I had noticed Novice Maria Mary seemed unsettled and had been constantly staring at the Novice Mistress but I did not dwell on those thoughts. Dwelling on those thoughts would always lead to thoughts that the professed Sisters would tell us were gossipy. Gossiping was an unkindness that fostered a meanness of spirit in thought and deed.

'Of course,' I replied. I was not going to speculate on what it was she wanted to discuss. For all I knew, she may want to check on the progress of the beans we had planted a few weeks ago. Novice Maria Mary and I spent a lot of our recreation together and we were quite close even though individual closeness was discouraged in general.

Once we entered the maze-like area of the gardens, its high leafy walls reassuring but equally a little overbearing (as the convent walls sometimes seemed), Novice Maria Mary relaxed. Her whole demeanour seemed to unclench and she grabbed my hand as we walked.

'I'm leaving,' she said in a whisper. 'Tomorrow. The Novice Mistress said I am allowed to tell one person and that person is you.'

'I don't understand.' I really didn't. Out of all of us, Novice Maria Mary was the one I knew would make it to final vows. She seemed so suited to this life, dedicated, certain. Whenever doubts would creep in for me, I would look at her, look at her example and know that if I behaved like her, stuck with it, I would find the silence and I would find God in that silence. 'How can you be leaving? You out of all of us?'

'This isn't the life for me,' she said. She covered my hand with her other hand. 'I thought it was, it's all I've ever wanted since I was a little girl. But I am not cut out for this life. I'm twenty-one like you, and I've realised I want a husband, I want a baby. Babies. I think I would be able to serve God so much better by becoming a wife and mother. Haven't you ever wanted that, Novice Grace?'

The question stumped me. I had never wanted those things. It had never occurred to me they might be possible. I had spent my early teenage years being wild, and never thought I would settle down with anyone then. I had spent my later teenage years in the search for silence and then in my dedication to becoming a nun. Husband and children hadn't even occurred to me. 'No, I haven't,' I told her honestly.

She nodded and smiled. 'That's why, out of all of us, I know you're the one who'll make final vows,' she said. 'You've never wanted anything else. I was always conflicted, but being a nun won over for a while.' She stepped forwards and hugged me. 'I'll miss you.' She released me from the hug. 'You won't be able to talk about me after tomorrow. If you do, that will be gossiping. But I hope you remember me? In your prayers, if not in everyday life?'

'Of course I'll remember you,' I told her. 'Every day, not only in my prayers. Every day.'

Novice Maria Mary was gone before morning Mass the next day. We remaining novices did not speak of her, but we all looked at each other, wondering who would be next. It wasn't going to be me, I knew that. I was here to find the silence. The only reason I would ever leave, I knew, would be for her. For Nika.

London, 2016

'You did not leave your monastery because of a crisis of faith?' the priest asks.

'It feels very simple inside my head, Father, but when I try to explain it, it goes a bit wrong. I let down a friend very, very badly once. I've never quite forgiven myself, Father.'

'Have you spoken of it in confessional before?'

I stay silent.

'I mean, have you given a confessor a chance to help absolve you from this burden?'

'I want to say yes,' I reply carefully. 'I want to say that I have confessed all my sins over the years and I nearly have, except this one. It feels too big to say out loud. I feel so disgusted every time I think about it, Father. I couldn't say it out loud.'

'Do you not have faith that the Lord will forgive you for it?'

I sigh and have to admit it to him: 'I'm not sure I want forgiveness for it, Father. Until I confess to her, the friend I let down, I don't see how I can allow myself to be forgiven. It would feel like an indulgence at her expense, if you see what I mean?'

'Yes, I see what you mean.'

'It's not so simple, though. I don't know how to find her. She could be anywhere; she could have died for all I know. I want to go round to her parents' house and ask them, but she left home twenty years ago under a cloud and I doubt they'll have patched things up. I suppose it felt that I had got too comfortable, that I was living a good life as a nun and I didn't deserve to. I'm not even sure what I'm confessing, Father.'

'I am. You are confessing to punishing a child of God for twenty years for a mistake she made when she was a child. You sound young, as though you have punished yourself for a long time. I can give you penance, you may undertake the act of contrition, and I can offer you absolution, but you will not believe it when it comes to this act. I am not talking only of the act which you feel guilty over, but also the sin you have committed in punishing yourself for so long.'

'I can't not punish myself, Father, until I've seen her and made things right.'

'I know.'

'I suppose I've completely wasted your time.'

'You haven't. Talking, seeking counsel when you are troubled, is never a waste of time.'

'Thank you. I do actually have a couple of other things to confess, though. Apart from not going to confession for such a long time and not observing the daily sacraments like I thought I would, I have been having some really, *really* uncharitable thoughts about my mother.'

The priest smiles a little – I can hear him through the wall between us. 'Tell me,' he says.

And for the next little while, I can unburden myself about the increasingly crazy situation brewing in my parents' house.

7

Nika

The woman in room 213 hides things.

I'm not sure exactly what, but I know she does it because the things that most hotel guests, especially ones like her, who've been in a hotel for a week, almost always have – toothbrush, toothpaste, face wash, make-up – are nowhere to be seen. Also, the various gadgets and businessperson's accoutrements that go with the various chargers she has plugged in around the room are missing. I'm sure she's hiding all this stuff from 'the cleaners'. Maybe she thinks I will use her toothbrush to clean out the toilet, possibly she thinks I will use the twelve minutes I have allotted to clean her room to sit down and use her iPad or laptop to surf the Web.

Oddly enough, I've noted that every day this week she leaves out the little blue and white contact lens case on the frosted glass shelf in the bathroom, beside the bottle of cleaning fluid. I wonder, as I've done every day this week, why she's more concerned about her teeth than her eyes. If I was the sort to use her toothbrush down the loo, would I not be as likely to pour bleach into her lens case? Every day she leaves a tide mark around the white enamel interior of the claw-foot bath, she leaves reddish-brown pubic hairs along the tray of the shower, and every day her towels are left in the bath so she can have fresh ones – she clearly doesn't care about the planet. I've made up a story about her, like I make up stories about all the guests whose

177

rooms I clean. I think she is a corporate spy. I saw a programme the other night where people were getting caught for being corporate spies and I reckon the way she leaves her room, hides her essentials, probably doesn't need her contact lenses, points to her being one.

Or not. Maybe she's an ordinary businessperson who has a deep mistrust of cleaners and hotel staff, who forgets to hide her contact lens case and promises herself every night to remember to do it before she leaves. Once I have sprayed the bath, I get on my knees to scrub the shower tray, remove all the soap scum, pubic hairs and other stuff that sticks out of the plughole. After that, I spray and polish the shower screen. I clean the sink, I bleach the toilet. I mop the white, brick-shaped tiles.

In my ears, while I clean, Bobby Brown sings about his prerogative.

I am happy. That is what is odd about this. I am happy being a cleaner, having a small flat, living in a city where very few people know me.

I am happy. I'd almost forgotten that is what life is meant to feel like.

Birmingham, 2004

Reese was right, this did feel better, safer. There was the smell of rotten food that clung to the air because I was behind the bins of a super-market car park, which had been emptied earlier, and that smell was undercut with the stench of constantly wet earth, and leaked car oil, but it was better than the shelter. I was out of sight, no one knew I was there, and I could bed down wrapped up in my newly bought blanket, and zip myself up in my also-new sleeping bag, with my rucksack as a pillow. Being hidden meant I could pretend that I was back in Todd's flat in London, sleeping with the blinds open so I could see the lights of London, I could watch the journey of the stars. Because I'd wanted to do that, Todd had always refused. I was free of him, so I could do it now. I could lie back and fall asleep after watching the stars.

This was one of those nights that was clear, the sky a dark royal blue, the stars so bright it felt like I could reach out and pluck them out of the air, hold them in the palm of my hand. I loved the stars, loved how they reached all the way back to the beginning of time. I could look up and see all the way back to the point, that pinprick of light, where I began; where my future was being written out for me. I could look up and see right to the end of time, where how I would end was marked on the eternal timeline of life.

I watched the stars, each one probably holding the answer to where I began and also where I would end. I knew my end wouldn't be out here on the street. I knew that. I didn't know why, I just did. I felt safer out here, safer than I had in all the time I had lived with Todd. It was scary how those realisations kept coming to me. The longer I was away from him, the more I had space, the more I realised how uneasy I had felt around Todd, even in the early days. When I'd thought I'd been bowled over by love, now I could see I had been constantly in a state of high alert; I hadn't had a chance to catch my breath, wonder if being with him was what I'd actually wanted since he wouldn't actually use my name. He had been constantly there, if not in my head, then on the phone, then in the house with me. If he had given me the chance to think, given me a moment's space, I would have seen him for who he was much sooner. I would have seen the ridiculous things I did to be with him: I still couldn't believe I used to sit in the dark for hours sometimes, waiting for him to come back. (He must have known he had me when I did that, because it was such an outrageous request to make of someone.) If, in the early days, I had had a chance to think, I might have hung on to my job, instead of giving it up because we were out so many nights that getting up was so hard. I might have found another job instead of listening to him when he'd said he liked me to be there when he got home and questioned me constantly about whether I really needed to work when he would look after me financially.

Out here, I was free; I had all the space in the world to think. I tugged my hat further down on my head, covering my ears. I was going to do something about my hair. I hadn't had a chance to wash it since I'd left, and it was becoming a mess. Todd had paid so much money for me to get it to what he'd deemed perfect, and I'd never really liked it. I'd grown it long to please him, having it straightened every eight weeks without fail. Once it was down past my shoulders, he'd wanted me to have my hair curled so it touched my shoulders. It'd meant going to the hairdresser's every week for her to do, and every time I'd come back, I'd look in the mirror and not recognise myself. It was Todd's favourite style; he'd asked me to just give it a try and when I'd admitted it looked good – not like me, or what I liked, but good – I'd somehow never managed to get it back to how I wanted. Admittedly, the longer style had become useful for hiding behind when the photographs started, but it still wasn't the hairstyle I would have chosen. Apart from the fact I'd never be able to afford its upkeep, this was my chance to change who I was. To make a choice about what I looked like after years of being controlled by Todd's idea of perfection.

I closed my eyes, the sounds of the night, of a city still in motion despite the hour, continued on around me. I was near to where people were, but also hidden, secreted away so I could sleep.

I can do this, I told myself. *I can do this.*

I wouldn't have chosen to live on the streets, even for a little while, but this was the best option I had. If I wanted even the smallest chance of being free, if I wanted to put all the flashbacks behind me, I had to do this. I had to make a move forwards, get over this little bit of my story written in the stars above, and see what the next bit held.

Brighton, 2016

On the little red mat outside my flat there is a bottle of wine, with an elaborate, shiny red bow tied around its neck. I pause for a second at the end of my corridor when I exit the stairway and see it. I glance around, checking if anyone is watching me because they have put it there. There is no one on the stairs as far as I can see; the lift doors are firmly closed, as are the doors to all the flats. There is no one. Just me and this mysterious bottle of wine with a bow. This is the sort of thing Todd would do, the kind of overblown, public romantic gesture I hadn't realised was actually controlling and creepy until I left him.

I pull the folds of my jacket around me as a layer of protection, clutch my bag a little closer to my body. It wouldn't be Todd, would it? My heart stops then painfully turns over to start beating again. *Have the other people, the people from Birmingham, found me? Is this what this is? None of them know my real name, but what if it is them? What if they've found me and are waiting to kill me?*

My footsteps seem to echo suddenly on the pale marble tiles of the corridor as I approach my front door. To hush my racing mind, I mentally scroll through the tunes on the music player that is my mind. I need something with a calm tune but a positive beat. Gwen Guthrie's beat to 'Ain't Nothin' Goin' On But the Rent' is suddenly running through my mind, being hummed out by my lips. I stand with the tips of my toes touching the edge of my mat, staring at the bottle. It is supermarket Prosecco. The bottle is cold, sweating slightly as it sits on my mat, its red bow screaming for it to be noticed. Maybe it's not for me, maybe someone's got the flats mixed up and their 'romantic' present isn't for me. Maybe I should just leave it there and let whoever left it realise their mistake. Mayb—

'Oh, good, you're back,' Eliza says right beside me.

I jump back, clutching my chest, and bite back the scream that was about to hurtle out of my mouth. 'What are you doing?' I ask her, backing away a couple of steps.

'Overreact much?' she says, tilting her accent to sound like an American teenager. I should have smelt her, her perfume being so potent today. It's so much more copiously applied than the other night that it is now officially offensive.

'Again, what are you doing?' I repeat.

'I came to see if you got my welcome-to-the-building present,' she says. Her face adds: *'Duh! What else would I be doing here?'*

'The bottle's from you?' I ask.

'Yes, of course. Who else did you think it'd be from?'

'No idea – there's no note.'

She giggles, and clearly has no idea how forced, false and unsettling that laugh is. 'Sorry, I totally forgot to write a note.' She takes a step towards me and I step back. Can't help it, that's the reaction I have to her. She stops and frowns a little at what I've done. In response I put my left foot behind me, and step back in a semicircle so it seems I am moving around anyway. 'I thought, well, it was all so rushed the other week, I thought you might need a friend if you've moved in recently. Marshall mentioned we should all get together, but I wanted first dibs on welcoming you properly. So, here goes.' Eliza reaches for the bottle and holds it like she is about to present me with an award. 'Welcome to our building, Nika Harper.'

Reluctantly, I take the bottle from her. She's going to invite herself inside in a minute, using this bottle as the excuse to cross my threshold.

'Thank you, that's really sweet of you,' I say.

'Come on then, get the glasses out, I'm gasping for a taste.'

'Ah, thing is, Eliza, I'm really tired. I did a double shift today and I'm really looking forward to a sit-down after a lengthy shower.'

'I totally get you,' she says. 'I won't stay long.'

'Seriously, Eliza, I would be no kind of company right now. How about we go out for a drink tomorrow night instead?'

'Oh, boo, you're no fun.' She pouts with her thin pink lips protruding oddly from her face.

'You've got that right,' I laugh. 'Tomorrow night, OK? I fancy that bar that's down on the seafront on the way to Brighton. How about we go there tomorrow, about eight o'clock? Maybe we can get something to eat afterwards?'

'OK then, spoilsport,' she pouts with her words now. 'But no excuses – tomorrow, definitely.'

'Definitely,' I echo.

Happy now, she turns to leave.

'Don't you want your bottle?' I call at her.

'No, no,' she replies over her shoulder. 'You keep it – we can drink it when we come in from our night out tomorrow.' With that, she happily sashays her way to the staircase, and hums to herself as she skips down, a potent trail of her perfume scenting the air in her wake.

Nika

Knock, knock, knock! at quarter to eight.

I've been hoping against hope that she'd call at the last minute and cancel. Well, actually, I was hoping she'd just cancel this morning, and then during the day I was holding on for a miracle that she would magically know my phone number and contact me to cancel. At about seven o'clock, when there was no sign of a cancellation, I had to peel myself off the sofa and go for a shower to get ready. (The absolute luxury of being able to leave soap and face wash and towels in the bathroom for use another time, knowing that no one else will touch them, still hasn't worn off.)

On the way to answer the door, I pick up my glasses, slip them on. When I'm alone I don't wear them, don't need to: I know who I am, what I really look like and I can see perfectly well. With anyone else, I need to hide my face. I've already got my coat on, and before I open the door, I slip on my shoes. I guessed she'd turn up early so she would have a legitimate reason – waiting for me to get ready – to come into my flat. I'm wary of inviting anyone into my personal space, it is a haven that is all mine, the first time I've had something that I don't have to share any aspect of with someone else, and I don't want anyone to breach that too soon – especially not someone like Eliza, who has issues with maintaining other people's boundaries and paying any attention to them saying 'no'.

183

'Hi,' I say to her when I have opened the door and she is standing there, coat over her arm, ready to step inside. 'I'm all good to go so I'm glad you arrived a bit early.'

She needs a second or two to rally and hide her disappointment. 'Oh, right, great,' she replies. Her gaze darts inquisitively over my shoulder before I step over the threshold and shut the door behind myself. She won't have seen anything because I have very little on show.

Outside, it is spring. The clocks will go forward in a couple of weeks and the evenings will become even lighter, the days warmer and less gruelling on those who spend most of their day outside.

'How was your day?' I ask her when we arrive on the pavement outside our building.

'Fine,' she mumbles. She's still sulking. She has sulked the entire journey down to ground level because I thwarted her plans to come inside my flat. Today her perfume isn't as heavily applied and I'm grateful. 'How was yours?' she adds grudgingly.

'Good. Actually, great.' I have great days now. Great days where nothing out of the ordinary happens, where I don't have to worry about where I'll sleep, if I'll eat, if I'll find one of my friends in a heap and will need to call an ambulance. I think about Reese and the others every day, they are there, haunting my thoughts, but not being able to do anything is oddly liberating, too. When I was there, I knew I couldn't do anything, but was always trying to work out how to. It was a madness I couldn't break myself free from: powerless to change anything, desperate to change everything.

A man in a long wool overcoat, a body-warmer and with his hat pulled down to cover his ears is coming towards us, and the desperate ache of missing Reese takes over me. So strong is the missing him, my insides feel squeezed and I want to gasp, to stop at the agony of it. I don't; I walk on, I stare at the man, wondering about his story, where he's been, where he'll go.

'You all right?' I say to him when we accidentally make eye contact.

He stares blankly at me, glances behind himself to see if I'm really talking to him, then glances back at me when he realises I am. I see him scouring his brain to see if he knows me from somewhere, if I am a woman from his former life who has recognised him. 'Yeah, yeah,' he mumbles.

'Did you know that man?' Eliza whispers when we are a few feet away from him.

'No,' I say to her. 'I was just being polite.'

'Got any spare change, darlin'?' the man calls after us in the gap before Eliza speaks again.

I stop and turn around. While looking right at him, I shake my head. 'No, sorry,' I say. 'But I can go to the supermarket café down the road and get you a coffee or a tea?'

He laughs, the grey-white of his teeth breaking up the griminess of his face. Still with a cheeky grin he replies, 'I'd rather have the money, to be honest.'

'I'm sure you would, but that's not what's on offer,' I joke back. 'Tea, coffee, hot chocolate – that's all I can stretch to.'

'Thanks, but you're all right.'

'Cool,' I reply. 'Next time, maybe?'

'Yeah, next time. Maybe.'

'Are you sure you don't know him?' Eliza asks as we resume our journey to the bar/restaurant near the centre of Brighton.

'Yeah, I'm sure.'

'But you were talking to him like you knew him,' she says.

'I'm talking to you like I know you,' I reply.

'Yeah, suppose so,' she says.

I don't add that out of the two of them, I know which one is probably the most honest about their intentions towards me.

Birmingham, 2004

'No chance of you going home, then?' Reese asked me.

We were in Bernie's at 1 a.m. We had an arrangement to meet every third night: if one of us didn't show up, the other one would go looking for them. I thought he'd set up the arrangement to look after me, but it was for his benefit, too, he'd confessed. 'Everyone's got their demons, Ace – mine's smack.' He'd been matter-of-fact about it, so matter-of-fact I thought he'd been joking at first. His eyes fixed on me the whole time, he'd shoved up the multiple sleeve layers on his left arm to show me. His forearm was a dappled mess of healing needle punctures and short, scabbed-over lines. I had almost been able to see him, holding his needle in place, his finger pushing the plunger down, filling his veins with the liquid that would take him away from his everyday life. *At least, that's maybe why he does it*, I'd thought as he'd tugged his sleeves back down, his face suddenly shy and his gaze avoiding mine. It had been an assumption. Maybe Reese didn't do drugs because he needed to escape, maybe he had other reasons. Whatever they were, he'd been very forthright and honest with me early on about being an addict.

Reese had cleared his throat, sipped from his coffee and let us sit in silence for a while. I sensed he felt emotional about admitting that to me; doing that had maybe hit him again in a part of him that wasn't ready to face up to what he was. 'At the moment, it's all good,' he'd said when he could face me again. 'Don't need it, don't miss it.' He took another sip of his coffee. 'Ain't going to lie to you, though, mate, don't know how long that'll last. But when I fall, it's a long way down and a long, long way to crawl back up. You look out for me, Ace, and I'll look out for you. That's how I've stayed safe out here – you hook up with someone who looks out for you. When I first ended up out here, cos of my stepdad beating the shit outta me every night, and my mum who looked the other way because he kept her in booze and fags, I had people who looked out for me. Some good, some bad, some really, really bad.'

'How old are you?' I'd asked. I wanted to know how long he'd been out here, if he'd come for a short while and ended up staying here. If, like the stuff he shot into his body, being out here was an escape from the world he used to live in.

'Twenty-seven,' he'd said.

'Twenty-seven?' He was only three years older than me. He spoke like a person at least ten years older than that; he looked like someone even older.

'Yeah, not much older than you, I know. I just look old, and I've been out here ten years or so, I forget how long, really. Just a long time, Ace. Meant to ask you, do you mind if I call you Ace, Grace?'

I'd shaken my head. I didn't, because he'd asked and would probably not do it if I'd said I did mind. 'Call me Ace if you like,' I'd said.

'So there's no chance of you going home?' He always asked me this. Usually I shook my head and changed the subject. But tonight, he'd given me a driver's licence with my new face and new name on it, and I felt I owed him a bit of an explanation, especially since he didn't want any money for the licence.

'No,' I said. 'I don't know where home is, for one. I left both of my last long-term "homes" under a cloud, shall we say. There really is nowhere to go back to.'

'So, who was it, dad, stepdad or uncle?' Reese asked.

'Who was what?'

'Who was fiddling with ya? That's why most girls end up out here – someone molesting them or someone knocking them about. You don't look like you were being knocked about, you've got a different kind of jumpiness – so I'm guessing it's the other thing.'

'You're Mr Sensitive sometimes, aren't you?'

'Yeah, no, sorry, mate. That was a bit out of order. I kinda forget sometimes cos talking to you is like talking to myself. Those are the things I say to myself. The beatings I could take, mostly, ya know, but when he started fiddling with me, I had to get out of there. Was cutting myself to get the pain out. Then got into smack and had to leave cos I could see what would happen: smack makes me crazy sometimes. I don't just pass out and everything is good; sometimes it makes me rage. I knew one day I'd probably get out of it and end up knifing the bastard, then spend my life in prison. The street is better than prison, believe me.'

'My dad wouldn't do something like that,' I said. I was staring at the photograph of myself, black and white and slightly out of focus from where it had been printed on to the pink, watermarked plastic of the driver's licence. I had cut off my hair to chin length, twisted it, and was going to leave it to turn into dreadlocks. Easier to care for, natural and, most importantly, how I wanted it to look. 'I don't have a stepdad. And I hardly ever saw my uncles,' I told Reese while still staring at the plastic picture of me.

'Family friend?'

In my head, the music for the 'Dance of the Sugar Plum Fairy' began to play. The up-down, up-down, up-down, up-down beat, the movements of the child's toy the dancer was meant to mimic, the way my body could never forget that dance. Other dances and routines may fade, but every time I heard the music, I would be back there and I would remember. 'Leave it, eh, Reese? Just leave it.'

'Sorry, mate. Forget sometimes what it's like for people who had it worse.'

'Where did you get the licence?' I asked him.

'Ask me no questions, I'll tell you no lies.' He grinned, flashing his grey teeth, some of them chipped, others stained brown over the grey. 'It's not stolen or nothing like that. And it won't stand up to proper scrutiny, but it'll help you get into hostels, maybe get a job.'

'Please tell me how much I owe you for it.'

'No, no, I've paid for it now. I don't want your money. I feel bad, see, that I didn't stop that arsehole quick enough.' He hung his head, staring at his clean hands with their ragged nails, dried-out cuticles. 'I wasn't paying attention. Was trying to score. I should have stopped him when he was making a move. Sorry, mate.'

'It's not your fault,' I said to him. Gently, so as not to spook him, because he was often jumpy, I put my hand over his. 'It was no one's fault but his. You saved me from ... well, you know. That doesn't mean I shouldn't pay you for this.'

'Yes it does. But listen, Ace, don't take anything from anyone else. No matter what's offered or how nicely it's offered. Not even from me after this. Not ever, mate, all right? Promise me.'

'I promise,' I said. I wasn't the type to take things without paying for them. That's why I wanted to pay him for the licence. It didn't feel right, not paying my way.

'Mate, I'm serious here. There are some bad people out there, they will do anything to get you hooked in then will do you serious harm to get you to pay them back. Don't take anything, ever. Not even from me, because after this, our debts are settled. If I fall down that hole again and you've taken something from me, I'll want it back. When I'm on that stuff, I have no friends, I owe no one and every single debt I'm owed I want paying back. Mate, when I'm down that hole, I'll do anything. And there are some bad, bad people out there who'll do anything, too. Just be careful, OK?'

'Yeah,' I said.

I should have told him to be careful back. I didn't think he'd need those words from me, though. I was the new girl on the streets, I had no idea what was out there. No idea at all.

Brighton, 2016

Marshall, Marshall, Marshall. Eliza has talked non-stop about Marshall since we sat down. His whole body must be aflame, never mind his ears. At her insistence, we have come here to a corner pub on Western Road on the way into the centre of Brighton instead of walking along the seafront to the place I'd mentioned yesterday. I thought it was for a quick drink, but we are now four drinks in – that I have paid for – and she is showing no sign of moving, and she has talked non-stop about Marshall since we sat down.

I stopped listening a while back, now I simply study her. She is about my age, maybe slightly older if she's the same age as Marshall. She's nervous, with anxious little movements where she moves her glass, she straightens up her drinks mat, she moves her drinks mat back, she shifts in her seat, she fiddles with her hair, she plays with the stem of her glass. All the while talking about Marshall and his life, his work, his marriage, his divorce, his son. I feel I know Marshall, have had a bird's eye view into his life, even though I have only met him the once. I wonder what it's like to be the object of someone's obsession when you haven't actually slept with them? At least with Todd I had slept with him, lived with him, which must have fuelled his obsession. This behaviour from Eliza is unsettling.

'Did you and Marshall have a thing?' I ask her, simply to confirm what I've already guessed about them: it has always been platonic.

Eliza, who has not sat still properly all evening, is suddenly motionless, except for her eyes, which narrow at me. 'Why do you ask? Are you interested in him or something?'

'Just curious. You've known him so long, as long as he was married, and before that, so I was just curious if your thing happened before or after that?'

'He's not interested in dating right now,' she says. 'There was a time when, you know, I thought... and I suppose he thought... but the timing was never right. We were never on the same page at the same time so it kind of never happened. Well, I say never, I mean it hasn't happened so far. You never know what the future might bring.'

'True,' I say to her.

'He's kind of special to me,' she says. Her voice is shy, hesitant when she says this while her demeanour tells me she will kill anyone who comes between the two of them. 'I wouldn't want to see him being messed about, not by anyone. I wouldn't take very kindly to anyone who upset him in any way.'

The pub's door opens and a group of people come in, laughing, joking, enjoying a Friday night in Brighton. Friday and Saturday nights were dangerous times for those of us who slept rough. Boozed-up people looking for a fight would often suddenly see us as easy targets, would goad people into fights, would sometimes even take a piss on those they saw sleeping in doorways, because they could. The people who have just arrived seem happy, relaxed; friends who enjoy each other's company, hopefully not the sort to pick fights with those they think are beneath them. I'm envious of the people who have just come in. I used to have that sort of relaxed camaraderie with Reese and a couple of others. I used to belong with them and we'd have moments of sitting around, talking, laughing, being friends. Our times together weren't all bleak and hard and scrabbling around for money to score or to eat or to afford to sleep indoors. Sometimes we were just like the people who've just walked in the door, and I miss those times. I miss those people, I miss the ability to fit in. I must have been crazy when I agreed to come out with Eliza because a tiny part of me was hoping that there was something about her that I could connect with. When she first spoke to me at the meeting she'd seemed nice. I thought that maybe there was more niceness about her, but no. It was the familiarity of bad behaviour. It was recognising bits of her that I'd been attracted to in others and wanting to make it work.

'Marshall must find it very comforting to know there's someone like you looking out for him,' I say. I drain my orange juice from my glass. I've bought the drinks all night – wine for her, orange juice for me. I stand up, pull on my coat. 'I have to go,' I say to her.

'What? I thought we were going to stay out for a bit, have something to eat? Maybe go back to yours and crack open that bottle I got you?'

'Eliza, do you know what Marshall is doing tonight?' I ask her.

'Erm, it's Friday, and his son isn't coming over this weekend so he's probably out with friends. Why do you want to know?' she asks.

'I was just double-checking,' I say. I hook my bag on to my shoulder. 'Thanks for the drink. Don't worry about rushing your drink to leave with me. On my way out I'll let Marshall know you're over here. I'm sure he'll be thrilled to see you.'

She spins in her seat, and feigns surprise when she sees him over at the bar, having just arrived with his group of friends. *Poor man. Poor, poor man.* Without another word to her, I walk over to him to let him know that his 'friend' is sitting over in the corner. I don't need to add that she's blatantly brought me along to stalk him on a night out.

Birmingham, 2006

My favourite place to wash and rest during the day became the library. I needed the day centre, and it was helpful being there, but being in the library made me feel normal. Every morning I would ring the three agencies I had signed up with from one of the pay-phones in Birmingham New Street station, would find out if I had any work that day. If I didn't have any cleaning work, I would walk down to the library, go into the toilets the moment it opened and have a wash. People rarely came into the library toilets first thing, so I had a few minutes of privacy to clean up as much as I could, to get changed. Then I would sit and read the newspapers and magazines, find out what was happening in the world.

I would read the local papers, see if there were any jobs suitable for me, then I would indulge myself, read a large chunk of whichever book I was working my way through. At midday I would ring the agencies again, find out if I had work. If I did, I would stay in a hostel that night so I could shower and be in work clean and on time. I rationed how much I ate, how much I spent on food. The reduced-price sandwiches in the supermarket, the squashier fruit on the market stalls, water bottles I could fill up from fountains.

It was an odd existence, but no more odd than the one I'd had before if I thought about it. At least, with this one, I had no one to answer to at the end of the day. Earlier, when I had gone into a newsagent's, I'd seen the news on the front of paper I'd been hoping to see: 'TODD CHAMBERS TO MARRY'.

It'd been two years. Two years it had taken for him to get over his 'broken heart' and move on with someone who had become a very dear friend to him in the light of Nikky Harper's disappearance from his life. I assumed it had taken him a year to stop looking for me. He'd given a couple of interviews – I'd never been able to read the full things because I was always turfed out of the newsagent's before I could reach the end, but the gist of what he'd been putting out there was that we'd been having problems, he'd suspected I was back on drugs, he'd wanted to support me, but I had rejected all help. He feared and suspected I was living in a hovel somewhere with someone who I could take drugs with. One of the stories had even heavily hinted that one of the reasons I'd split with him was because I'd tried and failed to get him into drugs, too.

It was all water off a duck's back. I was Grace Carter now. I didn't even know who Nikky Harper was, not really. The woman with her knickers on show, with her hair messily covering her face, with her large black sunglasses, was a stranger to me. It was hard to imagine what it was like to be in her skin, to see the world through her eyes.

All the while, of course, Todd would have been grooming someone else, finding another woman to fill the hole I had left in his perfectly constructed life. I couldn't be sure, of course, that he had stopped looking for me, but this headline had given me hope. He'd trashed my reputation, he was marrying someone else. Maybe I could go back to London and reclaim the life I'd had.

I thought this often as I worked, as I managed to spend more nights in hostels and off the streets. I was managing to save more money and I had a locker at Birmingham New Street where I stored stuff and kept some of my money rolled up inside a tampon box I'd resealed. If I kept on as I was, I would have the money to pay for at least three months in a house share soon. Or even a bedsit somewhere. Just a bit longer and I could make Birmingham my home.

I sat at Bernie's waiting for Reese. He was late. It was 1.30 a.m. and the only other times he'd been this late before, he'd been to score and had blown me off, had told me to do one when I'd gone to find him. I couldn't face that today. The news about Todd was what I wanted, was what I had been waiting for – although I'd thought it would have happened a lot earlier – but it had shaken me. I thought about him, the distance making me see him clearer. I had loved him so much. So much. I used to feel empty when he wasn't there, alive when he was. I'd hung on so long, I realised now, because I'd been convinced that I knew who he could be and I'd wanted that version of him back. I'd been certain that if I did what he wanted, made him realise he could rely on me, he would be the man I could trust with my secrets again.

From the moment he opened the café door, I knew Reese had been to score. He could barely stand up, his eyes were hooded, his reactions and movements slow. I reached into my pocket, pulled my headphones out and slipped them into my ears. I couldn't deal with this today. I couldn't hear the drug infecting his voice, wrapping up each word to leave his mouth in nasty, vicious spikes. I loved Reese – he had probably saved my life those first few nights and weeks up here – but when he got like this, it reminded me of the worst moments of my life. I would hear the 'Dance of the Sugar Plum Fairy' in my head, and all that came with it would tumble out into my mind. I loved Reese, but he was too damaged to be around at times like this.

When I'd first met him, he'd told me when he fell down the hole he had no friends and he hated everyone. I hadn't believed him until six months later when he did fall and he turned on me. Saying the most awful things, trying to get money off me, berating me for caring about him. When Reese fell down the hole of heroin, he knew it would be a long way back up and no one could help him climb.

'Ah, waiting for me, I see, just like the good little girl you are,' Reese said, sauntering over to the table. Gilly, a woman who worked at the day centre, would put songs on my player for me from her CD collection and she had recently loaded on a few more, but I didn't have time to look through them right then. I hit play, and Katrina and the Waves, singing about walking on sunshine, burst into life in my ears. That song took me back to the days I would walk to and from school, and it would sneak out of the open windows at the start of summer, the words bringing a smile to my face, the rhythm filling my body with pure joy.

Reese slumped in the chair opposite me, and my thumb moved over the jagged-edged dial of the music player, turning the volume right up so I couldn't hear him. He continued, though, his pale face creating ugly shapes as he spilled out the bile inside himself at me. He was saying to me what he wanted to say to himself, forcing out the things he kept inside – like he used to say, talking to me was like talking to himself sometimes. After a few seconds, I stopped watching, stared down into my coffee because I didn't need to hear his words or see them being formed.

In the moments between songs, I heard his voice, tried to ignore his words, my mind reaching forwards to grab the opening notes of the song that would drown out the pain of my best friend. 'Addicted to Love', the guitar chords played by Robert Palmer, started up. *I'm going to get a guitar*, I decided. *I will find some money and buy myself a guitar and teach myself to play.* It would be one more thing to carry with me, but I would probably keep it in my locker, and I would teach myself.

Movement beside our table made me glance up with my face still lowered. A man I had seen several times before in here and around the streets, coming out of pubs, driving past in a variety of expensive cars, was now standing beside our table. He was a bald, thickset, tall white man, who towered over us. Over Reese. With my head still down, I watched the exchange: Reese noticing him, staring at him for a few seconds, sizing him up, Reese suddenly remembering who he was, Reese pushing back his chair, getting to his feet.

The man who stood beside us wasn't like the other people I lived with on the streets. All his clothes were good quality, new, regularly washed, probably ironed by someone else. Not washed every two weeks in a laundrette and washed through every week in the sink of which-ever hostel I was staying at. He wore a lot of jewellery, chunky pieces that were there to make a statement. Rumour had it that he'd had a ruby embedded in one of his front teeth to look like a drop of blood, so that people would know his bite was worse than his bark. This man ate well, lived well – it was obvious from every movement he made.

Under the attention of this man, my thin, wiry, out-of-it friend lowered his gaze and closed his mouth. Reese smiled at me and I saw all the sadness, the betrayal that had blighted both our lives, sitting there on his shoulders. I wanted to reach out and hug him, but he didn't want me right now. He wanted to be someone else and that someone was a person I could not help, or love.

Reese stumbled out of the café and the man took his place in the seat opposite me. My thumb hovered over the volume dial, but didn't make contact to turn it down. If I didn't engage, kept my music turned up and my head lowered, this man, Judge, he was called, would leave me alone. Like most of the bad, bad people Reese had warned me about a couple of years ago, they didn't like to hassle

195

you into their fold, they wanted you to come to them. If I ignored him, he would go away, simple as that, until he found another way 'in'. I'd noticed him notice me a few times, but he had never approached me. Other bad, bad people had approached me before, and I had ignored them, just like I could do now.

I wanted, sometimes, only sometimes, what Reese had: escape. That was why he wasn't always on smack: he didn't need to be out of it all the time, only when it became too much and he needed to press the escape button. I wanted escape sometimes. When I was sleeping out and it was cold, it was wet, it was nearly Christmas, it was nearly New Year, it was nearly Valentine's Day, it was nearly Veronika Harper's birthday, I would want an escape. Sometimes, only sometimes, when I would look at Reese and how removed he was from everyday reality when he was drugged up, I would wonder about it. Often, very, very often, when the flashbacks and the insomnia were out of control, I would wish to be like Reese; I would long for a way to check out of the world and not have to deal with reality. The man in front of me, I was pretty sure, would offer me an escape in one way or another if I turned my music off and engaged with him.

I'd finally left Todd behind – it seemed like he had finally given up on me. It didn't change anything, really. I was still who I was, the person who had been taken in by him in the first place. The woman who now often went to sleep with the stench of whichever hidden sleeping location I'd chosen that night filling my nostrils. I washed in public toilets because more than anything I had to wash every day. I ate on-date food. I walked everywhere. I often couldn't speak to my best friend because he was out of his head on drugs. I was lonely. Especially in the day centre, when I would see people older than me and know that was what my future held. Especially when I saw women like me walking down the street, dressed in normal clothes, going to their normal jobs, sleeping in their normal beds. I saw them and I wanted some of that, or I wanted to not notice them.

If I turned off my music and talked to this man called Judge, that would all change. Maybe I would find a way to escape like Reese had. Maybe I would find my line in the sand and I would be forced to return to London and my old name. Or, I could carry on as I was. Maybe this man would be the reason my life changed again.

I clicked off the music player, took the headphones out of my ears, and watched the grin spread across Judge's face, while the ruby embedded into his tooth, that fake spot of blood, glinted at the centre of his smile.

Brighton, 2016
'Well, if it isn't my barista buddy,' the guy from earlier says as I approach him.

'Tea or coffee?' I say to him. In my hand I hold one of each in a paper cup.

'What if I want both?' he asks with a sideways grin.

'You can have both,' I say.

'Both it is, Barista Buddy.' He grins, and his laugh is chased up by a cough. It rattles through his body, shaking his thin form in violent ways. I almost reach out to steady him, and the need to help him is overwhelming. I want to ask him up to my flat, offer him a hot shower, some hot food, a place to sleep for the night. Of course I want to. Reese would be bawling me out about that right about now. He'd be reminding me that I care more about other people than myself, that what I would be doing would be dangerous. I know nothing about this man – why would I let him into my home just because he reminds me of someone? *'You've got a death wish, ain't ya?'* Reese snarled at me the last time I saw him. He had bawled me out, told me he'd had enough of me and didn't want to be around me any more because of that death wish.

I'd tried to argue with him, but I didn't have a leg to stand on – he was right. I did have a death wish. Since years before I left my parents' house I'd had a death wish, I had essentially wanted to end my life but not to die. It didn't make sense but it was basically what Reese had told me: I had a death wish that was playing itself out slowly, slowly, slowly, and was putting everyone I knew in danger.

I hand the man the two cups, bite my tongue to stop myself offering him more.

'Thanks, Barista Buddy,' he says. He turns away from me quickly, and sets off in the direction of the roads leading down to the seafront. I've walked down near there, and at night, homeless people hang around where there used to be arches but are now shops. He's moving quickly because, I know, he's going to try to sell them while they're hot. I saw Reese do that dozens of times. This guy is going to sell them to anyone who isn't desperate for a fix. A posh coffee would sometimes maybe make Reese 30p.

I let myself into my flat, missing Reese, and hating him as well. Why did he have to name it so baldly? Since he said that to me, the reasons why I have that death wish keep coming to me at night, waking me up with nightmares, snatching my thoughts at unexpected moments. I have a good few days, I feel happy and content; blessed to have such a simple life, then it will all come stampeding in again. Because of what Reese said, I know, some time soon, something is going to happen to make me address what I've been hiding from about my past.

8

Roni

'Miss? Miss?' The boy at the back of the class is bouncing up and down in his seat, his red curls jumping with him each time he makes contact with the seat.

This used to be my classroom. I am teaching at Chiselwick High School until a couple of weeks after the Easter holidays and I am here, in what used to be my and Nika's old form room. It takes me twenty minutes to walk from home – it used to take hours, literally, when I was the age of my students. Nika and I would stroll home on the nights we didn't have ballet practice, finding a way to make the journey home encompass Topshop and Warehouse and WH Smith and Waterstone's and Books etc. on the high street. Then we'd wander down to the café by the train station, where the owner would charge us for one hot chocolate split between two styrofoam cups, and throw in a biscuit free of charge. Those were the best days for walking home. Sometimes Uncle Warren would pick me up from school in his big car and Nika would have to walk or get the bus home alone and I never knew what she got up to on those days.

Every part of this school takes me back to yesteryear. Several times I have had to stop in the corridors, stand aside to watch Nika, tall with her black hair neatly folded into several long plaits, clutching her school books, and Roni, a fraction smaller, with her long brown hair swept back into a ponytail, also clutching her school books to

201

her chest, walking past me. I have watched them chatting, sometimes giggling, always pretending that their existence outside of school life isn't hard and complicated and full of horrifying secrets. Many times today I have wanted to reach out to them, to her, to me, to us, and place my hands on their shoulders and say, 'I believe you. I care about you. I will help you in any way I can.'

'Miss! Miss!'

It's been a whole fifteen minutes. I know exactly what he's going to ask. Every class I have covered this morning has had someone ask me it. Teenagers are as curious as adults, but not as shy.

I glance down at the seating sheet I have in front of me. 'Yes, Jeremy, is it? How can I help you?'

Now he has my attention, he is shy about asking the question that was burning on the tip of his tongue mere seconds ago. The room becomes a complete hush for the first time since they were told that I was to be their stand-in for the next few days.

'Erm... Miss...' His voice peters out.

I'm disappointed. I thought he, this class in general, had a bit more about them. They remind me of the people in my class at school, but maybe only because this used to be my classroom. They are completely different people, growing up in a completely different world. 'Come on, Jeremy, tell me what was so urgent you made me turn away from writing on the board.'

He positively curls into himself at that, terrified now of speaking. Maybe he thinks he'll be struck down by the Almighty if he asks.

'He wants to know if you used to be a nun,' another boy, Reg, asks. Jeremy turns and glares at him, shooting him an '*I was going to ask*' look.

'Yes, Reg,' I say, 'I was once a nun. And now I am a supply teacher.'

'But, Miss, Miss?' A girl now assumes the 'I have a question' bounce in her seat.

'Yes, Erin,' I reply, knowing what her question will be. It's always the second question.

'Miss, if you used to be a nun, does that mean you're a really old virgin?'

Titters break out around the class. It's incredible to me that no matter the age of the person – young, middle-aged or old – their minds immediately go to sex when they think of you being a nun. Despite everything that becoming a nun involves, it comes down to wanting to know how sex fitted in with that lifestyle. *If* sex fitted into that lifestyle. That is what the man at the recruitment agency who signed me up for supply work all those weeks ago was so desperate to ask but wouldn't – or couldn't, considering his job. That is what Cliff wanted to ask on our first – and last – date but hadn't the courage when he knew I was waiting for the question and wouldn't be tricked into answering it. Am I a nun and, if so, am I virgin? I'd love to see Nika's face whenever someone asks me that.

'What it means is, Erin, that I will pray for all of you tonight before bed, to put a good word in with God, so to speak.'

Above the groans and ahhhs that the thought I will pray for them elicits, a voice at the back says: 'Yeah, but why would He listen to you? Didn't you, like, diss Him by up and leaving Him?'

A smattering of nervous tittering rises up from the room, along with a couple of sharp intakes of breath.

My eyes scan over the class layout sheet, to see who it is that spoke and made what could be seen as a startlingly astute assessment of my situation. Gail. No one has said that sort of thing to me before in the last few weeks of teaching. She's slouched low in her chair, her fingers fiddling with a blue crystal biro, and she hasn't raised her gaze from the desk connected to her chair.

'God listens to everyone, loves everyone, no matter what they've done to Him,' I say.

'Yeah, *right*,' she scoffs, with her head lowered. Anger bubbles from her in each letter of those two words. She wants a row, someone to argue with, someone to win against. There was a time, not even that long ago, when I would feel like that: the anger would bubble up inside and I would need someone to vent to, vent *at*. It was never taken out on teachers, though. I would never dare.

'I think we should get back to what I am actually meant to be teaching you,' I say. 'If you want to debate about the existence and behaviours of God, you can always stay after school. That's a general invitation to everyone, of course. I would love to discuss God with any of you who are interested?' I say this to have the effect I know it will have – each of them lowers their head and finds what's going on in their books far more interesting than me. 'Well, you know where I am if you change your minds.'

Of course the only person who has now raised their head is Gail, at the back. She looks at me fully then, grins at me. *I've won,'* she is saying. The breath catches in my chest, and the shock of recognition reverberates through me. She's the girl I saw in the street the other week when I went out with Cliff, wrapped around a man old enough to be her father; she is the sixteen-year-old girl who reminded me of the me I was when I was younger. And, like me when I was behaving how she was, she is fourteen.

London, 1995

'Roni, let's just go, please.' Nika was tense, as always. She never joined in properly with the partying, she always came with me, but would never drink, never try anything, not even the smallest puff, and even when there was another man who might be interested in her, she wouldn't even think about kissing him, let alone anything else. I used to think she needed to escape like me but she didn't.

Earlier, we'd met at the bus stop where we met every morning to go to school. I'd asked her to come out because she'd been so quiet lately, and hadn't wanted to come out clubbing with me as much. If she didn't come, I didn't like to go because I didn't feel safe any more. When she was there, I felt safer.

I'd arrived at the bus stop after her. She'd been sitting on one of the fold-down seats, staring at the pavement with her arms wrapped around herself. I hadn't realised how cold it would be when I'd set off; it had been seeping in through my leather jacket, there had been

204

a mist in the air that felt like drizzle, and I'd suddenly realised what a bad idea this had been.

'I'm really cold,' I'd said to her.

'You're the one who wanted to meet here to talk.'

'I know, but I'm cold.'

A black car with blacked-out windows, which I'd seen drive past three times, had pulled up in front of the bus stop. The front passenger window had opened and the driver had leaned across, waving me over.

'Don't, Roni,' Nika had warned. 'It's Thursday night. Just don't.'

'I'm only going to talk to him,' I'd told her. He'd looked cute, younger than the guys I usually ended up with on a night out. He had really nice blue eyes, and his blond hair was lovely and floppy. He'd told me he had some really good gear back at his flat, and that he'd share it with us if we wanted. He also had some booze. Plus, it'd be a chance to get out of the cold. I'd swung towards Nika, beckoned her over. She'd shaken her head.

'Come on, he said he's got some really good gear,' I had told her, not that she'd have been interested. More than anything, I'd wanted to get out of the cold.

'No, Roni. *No.*'

She'd come with me if I went; I knew that about her. She wouldn't leave me alone. My hand had reached for the handle of the back door and the guy in the front had grinned at Nika. 'It won't take long,' I'd said, already half in the car, 'and it's a lot better than sitting out here in the cold.'

She'd got up, looking angry and frustrated, but had marched to the back of the car and got in after me.

We'd been here at his flat over an hour now and she wanted to go.

'Roni, let's just go,' she repeated.

'Just relax, will you? We'll be going soon,' I replied. Nika was sitting in a chair all on her own. Around the room, three friends of Big T, the driver, lay around like pieces of litter left on the beach, puffing too.

Big T sort of sneered at Nika, while the smoke from the spliff gripped tightly between his thumb and forefinger curled up and away.

He handed the spliff to me. I slipped it between my lips but before I could inhale, Nika stood up suddenly. I took it out again. 'I'm going,' she said. 'I'm not sitting here any more doing this crap, I'm going. Are you coming?'

Big T sat up suddenly. He was staring down Nika, his eyes hardened and mean. He'd seemed so chilled out a minute before, but his expression had changed and all of a sudden I was colder than I had been at the bus stop. The three other men, who had seemed comatose before, now all raised their heads and looked hard at Nika. 'I'm going,' she said again.

'Sit down,' Big T said. 'I said I'd drive you back and I will. You two just need to earn your ride home, that's all.'

For the first time, I saw it. It'd probably been there before, but it was such a fleeting thing, something so quick that I must have missed it before – terror. The terror I felt every time we went to a ballet lesson. The absolute fear that must have bolted through her every time I did this. Then it was gone, just as suddenly as it appeared.

Despite that momentary panic, Nika didn't sit down. She stared right back at Big T. 'No. I am not earning anything, neither is she. We're going.'

The men all sat up, staring at her. I couldn't breathe. I had got us into a bad situation, this was going horribly wrong, and we were going to get very badly hurt, probably even killed.

'Pretty big mouth on a little thing like you, eh?' Big T said.

'We are going. If you lay one finger on me or her, I will go to the police. We are both fifteen years old, just so you know. So if you want to shut me up, you'll have to kill me. Just so you know, there is CCTV at that bus stop that we were at, so there'll be videos of us getting into your car with your number plate for the police to see if you do anything to either of us.'

Big T looked at each one of his mates, trying to see if any of them knew if she was right about the CCTV, about whether the police could trace anything back to them. They all shrugged at him, not sure if we were worth the risk.

I felt Big T's hand on my shoulder and he shoved me off the sofa on to the floor. 'Just fuck off out of here.' He threw my jacket at me, and it half landed on my head. 'Wouldn't have wanted to do you anyway. You're rancid. You're both well rancid.' I stumbled to my feet and started to leave. 'I'd probably get knob rot if I went near you. Get out. Go on, fuck off out of it, you slags.'

We walked back to the bus stop in silence. I had tried to say sorry to her on the pavement outside the house, but she hadn't hung around to listen, she'd just walked off.

'I can't do this any more,' she told me when we stepped into the pool of light at the bus stop. I looked up, checked all around – no CCTV cameras. She'd bluffed Big T and his mates, probably saved us from getting killed or beaten up.

'I'm sorry about that,' I said. 'I didn't know that would happen. He seemed nice.'

'NO HE DIDN'T!' she shouted. 'He seemed horrible. They *all* seem horrible. They *are* all horrible. Do you know how many times you've done this? How many men there have been? How many times I've had to watch or listen?' She pointed to her head. 'The sounds stay in my head, I can't get them out. With everything else, it's driving me insane.' She stepped back and took deep breaths to calm down. 'I can't do this any more, Roni. I can't. I'm going to the police about Mr Daneaux.'

'What? No!'

'He's the reason you do what you do with all those men: being with horrible men is all you think you're worth,' she said to me. 'And he's the reason I can't feel anything any more except disgust. I hate myself so much – my body, my hair, the way I look in the mirror. I hate *everything* about myself . . . I can't take any more. I have to go to the police. I have to get it to stop. If I go to the police, my parents will have to believe me and they'll make him stop.'

I didn't know she hated herself. That she felt how I felt, because she didn't do the things I did, she didn't seem as broken as I was. I'd always thought she was strong, didn't need anything or anyone to make her feel better.

'You have to come with me, Roni. They'll believe me if there's two of us,' she said.

Going to the police was the last thing I wanted to do. I wanted to pretend everything was OK. I knew it wasn't, but if I didn't think about it, then I wouldn't have to deal with it or do as Nika wanted to do and go to the police. 'OK,' I said. 'I'll come with you.'

Nika

The problem with not giving people your phone number but having them live in the same building as you is that they tend to turn up.

The *knock-knock* on my front door early Saturday evening pulls me away from sitting on the sofa, staring at the television. I wasn't aware of what was on, I was staring at the screen, running my fingers through my hair and thinking about where to go next. Not physically, *physically*, I am signed up to live in this building for another eight months or so, but I am trying to work out if I need to get help. When I spent months and years going to Birmingham Library, I would read books about the reasons for my death wish. I would read and read and read, uncovering the theories, discovering the reasonings, identifying with the behaviours. Theory, though, has nothing on reality.

If I decide to get help, I will have to first work out if I want to crack open that little box that is my mind and delve inside. It may well be embracing my past so I can face my future, but whenever I think like that, another part of me sneers at me. I deride myself for even contemplating the idea. Why would I put myself through all that pain? Why would I dredge up everything when for the first time in a long time I am on an even keel? I am safe, I am warm, I do not need to worry about money, I have my own space.

I need to worry about Judge finding me, I need to worry about trying to fix my relationship with my parents. I do *not* need to make more problems for myself by thinking about unearthing my past.

I slip on my tortoiseshell glasses and open the door.

'Hi,' Marshall says with a smile.

Since the debacle with Eliza the other week, I have been very careful coming and going from the building so I can avoid the pair of them. That is a mess I do not need to step into then drag its entrails through my life. When I went over and told him that I was leaving but Eliza was sitting on the other side of the bar, he stared at me in surprise. He had been about to smile when he saw me, I think, but that was washed away on the realisation that he was being forced to spend a night out with Eliza.

The worst part is, I feel sorry for Eliza. *I* feel sorry for Eliza – she could do with some help, with a friend, someone to gently guide her away from this path she has clearly been careening down for a long while. But I can't do that. It wouldn't be fair on her, because I would be doing it for me, to feed that part of me that is addicted to helping others. Reese said it made me a *fucking liability*. He was probably right.

'Hello, Marshall,' I say coolly.

'I've been hoping to catch you this week, but you seem to have become expert at entering and exiting the building without being seen.'

'It's one of my superpowers.'

'What are your other ones?' he asks with a grin.

'How can I help you, Marshall?' I say. My frostiness isn't strictly necessary, but I don't want him to charm me into forgetting he has a mad friend who is targeting me because of him.

His grin fades and he lowers his head, abashed. 'I'm sorry about Eliza. She can be a bit full on. She has this habit of rabidly trying to befriend any women she thinks I might be interested in.'

'I don't think she tries to befriend them if the other night was anything to go by. More like warn them off. Apparently you're not in the right place for a relationship right now.'

'Jeez.' He rubs a hand over his eyes. 'It's hard to believe, I know, but she's a good person. She's got a heart of gold but she can be so intense. She does this sort of thing and it pisses me off, but when I get to the point of wanting to tell her to do one, I can't. She seems too fragile.'

'Fragile. Yeah.'

'Anyway, the point of my visit was to apologise and also to ask if you fancied going to dinner one night?'

'What about fragile Eliza?' I ask. Probably unnecessarily mean, but talk about a man in denial.

'What about her?'

'Aren't you worried about how she might react?'

'No. Yes. I don't know. Can we not talk about it?'

'Fine. When do you want to go to dinner?'

'What, you're actually going to go out with me?' he asks. He's one of those men who doesn't have a mirror, clearly. What is not to like about him? Tall, handsome, a moral compass that is directed towards the good side – expertly shown by him speaking up in the meeting. Admittedly, he has a Rottweiler friend who would savage anyone rather than let them near him, but that doesn't negate most of the good things about him. 'Most women who have had "the chat" with Eliza won't even give me the time of day, let alone go out with me. I usually get the chance to apologise and then things are awkward between us until we both pretend that we weren't interested in each other in the first place.'

'I like to live dangerously. When are you free?'

'Now?' he says, hopefully.

'I'm guessing you're worried I'll change my mind,' I state.

'Something like that.'

'Now's fine. Come in while I turn the telly off and stuff. It won't take me long to get ready.'

He steps inside, his gaze immediately examining the place, searching for clues as to my personality, what I like, what I've got on display, where things are placed. He'll be disappointed since I haven't had the mental quiet yet to think of what I want and where. I don't have much, either. A sofa that is the flat owners', TV, ditto, and coffee table, ditto. In fact, the only things in this place I own are my guitar, my clothes, my shoes and my toiletries. And my music player, of course. I've thought of buying a CD player or a laptop, but both seem to cost a *lot* of money, and both are things I would probably really miss if I lost them. My only real non-essential item I own is actually my guitar.

As he walks past it, Marshall strums his fingers across the neck of my guitar, propped up at the entrance to my living room area. 'Do you play?' he asks as the chord he's played filters away.

'A little,' I say. 'All self-taught so I'm still learning.'

A sudden coldness slips through my body: I've let him into my flat without thinking. I've simply invited him in without a second thought. He could be anybody, he *is* anybody, and I have just invited him in.

'I'm always impressed by people who can play instruments.' He holds up his hands. 'The owner of two left hands, that's me. Obviously ironic given my name and *Spinal Tap*, etc.'

I say nothing, but cross quickly to the television, switch it off. I was planning on changing, putting on jeans instead of these knee-length shorts, and another top instead of this double layer of vests, but since I've invited him in without thinking, it's best I get him out again as soon as possible.

I grab my cardigan from the sofa, slip it on, then make for the hallway, my heart pounding in my ears. I'm not scared of him – there is nothing about him that has set my radar going – but I am scared of myself. I am scared that I am still doing things that put me in danger without thinking. I push my feet into my battered white Converse shoes and pull on my jacket.

'See, ready in no time,' I say.

'That is seriously impressive,' he says with a laugh. He has a nice laugh, warm and genuine, just like him. He seems lovely, but still I leave a gap between us as he leaves to give myself enough room to slam the door shut if I decide to change my mind. I don't need to, of course, he's a perfectly pleasant person, we are off out for a perfectly pleasant early dinner. I don't need to worry about him. It's me I need to worry about. I really can be a liability sometimes.

Gloucester, 2006

'Are you sure you don't need anything, Ace?' Judge asked. 'It really will make things easier.'

I shook my head. Slowly I opened the clutch bag that Judge had given me money to buy, along with the gold cocktail dress I was wearing, and pulled out my music player. I unwound the headphones from around its black body, ready to shove each earpiece into its corresponding ear.

'Are you sure now?' Judge coaxed. The three other women sitting with us in the expensive, almost brand-new people carrier, who, like me, were all dressed up in clothes he'd bought and ready to attend one of his parties, were listening to him speak to me. When I attended these parties, he talked to me much more than them on the journey out to whichever country house he had hired, because they knew him, he knew them, they did as they were told because he was their supplier of money and drugs. I was just along for the ride, to make up numbers, and I was sure he saw me as a challenge. The conversation was always the same: 'I can sub you, if that's the problem?' he said. His voice was silky smooth, used to finding a way to lull you, calm you, make you so at ease you would always do what he wanted. I noticed sometimes, when I always gave the same answer – 'No, thank you, but no' – a little pink would creep up his neck, his fingers would knit themselves together and his expression would briefly betray his desire to have me closer: I was a challenge in that in the six months I'd been doing this, I had never once taken him up on his offer of 'something to make things easier'.

I sat on one of the backward-facing seats. Judge sat in the middle of the back seat, his legs wide open so the blonde to his left had to sit with her legs pressed tightly together, and the redhead to his right had squashed herself against the side of the car, her face almost flattened against the window. The brunette beside me sat very still, watching me from the corner of her eye. She was too scared to move her head to look at me in case Judge made eye contact with her and she wasn't immediately looking at him to respond.

'I wish you'd let me give you a pager or even a mobile phone,' he said to me. His navy-blue gaze stared directly at me when he spoke. He knew how to unnerve people. He was expert at it. 'It'd be so much easier for me to contact you when I knew one of my parties was coming up. I don't like leaving messages with Bernie – what if you miss one and miss out? Let me get you a pager at least.'

'It's OK, I'm fine as I am,' I said. Since he'd sat down opposite me that night at Bernie's, I had been entangled with him, but I was careful not to owe him anything. When he gave me money for dresses and shoes, I would always take their cost off the amount he paid me at the end of the night. I always refused his offer of drugs, mobiles, pagers, and even a place to sleep. I knew that owing Judge anything was a dangerous position to be in.

When we had first talked, he'd told me about his parties. Rich men paid a lot of money to come to Judge's parties, to be introduced to women, to spend the evening chatting to them – 'socially network-ing', Judge liked to call it. He was holding real-life dating parties, he'd explain to anyone who thought he was sailing a bit too close to the legal edge. He was paid to make introductions, to see if the people at the parties were compatible. If some of them sloped off upstairs to get better acquainted, that wasn't his fault since they were adults; if some of them decided they weren't that compatible even after becoming better acquainted, that wasn't his problem, either. He simply set up the parties, just like the legitimate dating agencies did, and he couldn't control what people did. He'd asked me if I was interested in coming to his parties, possibly earning some cash, and I had said I wasn't into that. Because I didn't owe him, he couldn't insist.

So, he allowed me to do what women like me, who weren't indebted to him, did – be part of the cover story. We mingled, we talked to people, we never went upstairs so if the police asked questions, we could honestly say we had never been paid to let anyone have sex on us, we weren't part of the people who helped Judge make money from immoral sources.

'Have you ever tried taking something to smooth out the edges?' he asked me. I had been about to scroll through the music player, to search for something that really would take the edge off, pour a soothing elixir through my mind and sensibilities, but I had to talk to him. He put up with a certain amount of disengagement from me, but he had his limits, I knew that.

'No,' I said to him. 'Never had any need or inclination.'

'You should try it,' he said. 'You might like it.'

'I might,' I admitted.

He liked that, and I was rewarded with a grin, with a flash of his ruby-embedded tooth. The atmosphere in the car jumped up a few notches: the other women were willing me from behind their extravagant make-up and overstyled hair not to do it, not to get myself to where they were. I'd agreed to go to his parties because I got paid. They got paid, but they also had a debt to him, the interest on which they could never hope to pay off.

'You know, a lot of the men who come to my get-togethers often ask if you're available for dates, Ace,' Judge said.

Cold sickness swept through my stomach. I knew where this was going. I should have seen it coming. 'Do they,' I stated flatly.

'Yes. Thinking about it, maybe we should give Gina here a night off the dating circuit.' He slapped his hand on the thigh of the red-headed woman, squeezed so hard I could see the agony in her eyes. 'Maybe you should give it a try.'

I said nothing, kept my gaze on the floor of the car. His feet were huge; his shoes were polished to a high shine, the laces perfectly tied.

'I know you said you weren't into that, but you might like it. You won't know how much until you try it. In fact, I insist you try it, tonight. You might find the world of dating fun.'

The brunette beside me, whose legs seemed to go on for ever, who injected between her toes – I'd seen her doing it at the last party – tensed. She was probably curling her toes inside her very high shoes and trying to forget what it was like the first time.

'I might,' I said to him, still with my gaze kept down.

'And you know, Ace, if you need a little something to help you through, just let me know, I'll help you out,' he said. 'Gladly. I'll even sub you it.'

I'd been stupid to think I could deal with Judge, that I could manage someone like him, get what I needed and come away. Men like him didn't get played or managed by women like me. All this time, he'd been humouring me, prodding around to find out my weak spot to see what could be exploited. If I had to do this, then I might need the other stuff from him and I would be hooked into him further. That's why I couldn't take any money for tonight. If I did, he'd say I owed him. I knew he paid the others more, so tonight, I could be going away with triple what I usually earned, but if I took a penny, I would owe him – he would tell me that I hadn't been good enough, I would have to earn again to pay him back for the refunds he'd had to give. (I'd heard him say that before.)

I thought I'd only have to do three or four more parties and then I'd have enough to self-finance a room at a homeless hostel for two years when my name got to the top of their waiting list. Self-financing meant I didn't have to sign on, claim benefits, answer any awkward questions about the name I'd left behind. I would have a permanent-ish address, access to an indoor phone, and I would hopefully be able to find a job.

I pushed play on the music player. 'Teardrops' by Womack and Womack began to play in my head and like I'd taken a drug, my body relaxed as the melody moved from the player into me. Roni always jumped into my memory when I heard this song. The song, explaining about *the tune, the words, the music not sounding the same without that person in your life*, all conjured her up in my mind. We'd been four-teen, bound together by something other than the same name and a love of ballet, and we'd gone to a club in central London together. This was one of the songs they'd played. I remembered it because we had gone outside for a few minutes, and this was the song blaring out from the open doorway as we'd begged and begged the large skinhead bouncer to let us back in to get our coats. We'd only been outside ten minutes, but in those ten minutes I'd found out what the other Veronica did when she needed to escape.

Brighton, 2016

'Do you want to go somewhere else?' Marshall asks quietly. He leans across the table, holding his menu against his chest, while his face is a picture of concern.

This restaurant is nice, not too posh, but comfortable, with booths and tables, funky decor, an interesting menu and friendly wait staff. I feel like a fraud, like everyone can see I do not belong here. Since leaving Todd, I could never have afforded to eat somewhere like this, even though it's not Michelin-starred. Normal becomes posh when you have lived as I have; and after the last few years, posh is not somewhere I fit in. The couple at the next table, they're well dressed and unruffled and they fit in. They have a bottle of wine on the go, are waiting for their main meals and constantly touch each other across the table – relaxed and happy to be out together. The parents in the booth to my right belong here: they sit with a child beside each of them, encouraging the younger ones to eat, while simultaneously trying to eat their own meals and hold an adult conversation. The people who I can see over Marshall's shoulder look like old friends catching up over expensive pints and posh pizza – they are obviously used to sitting in places like this. These people, those who are part of the early dinner crowd, are meant to sit in places like this, they belong here. Marshall belongs and so do I. So. Do. I.

'No, no, it's fine here. In fact, it's great here,' I say to him.

'You seem really uncomfortable,' he says, still with his voice lowered. 'We can honestly go elsewhere if you want.'

'I haven't been to a restaurant in a while,' I say with a smile. 'I think I've forgotten how to behave in one.' *I feel out of place. I feel like there is a neon sign above my head that points out that I was once a homeless person.* I glance down at the menu, see the words for the different types of meals. My heart rate starts to increase, the air around us feels very close, and I have to concentrate on drawing in breath. Slowly, carefully, I need to push that breath out again.

What will I order? How will I order? Will the waitress laugh at me if I order the wrong wine with my meal? Will she think I'm odd if I don't have a starter? If I do have a starter, will she look down on me because I've ordered the wrong type of main meal? Will everyone around me listen to me ordering and know that I don't belong, know what I used to be, how I used to live, what I did to make money, because I so obviously, blatantly don't belong?

I jump when Marshall's hand covers mine. 'Are you all right?' he asks. My wild eyes find his kind brown ones. 'You look absolutely terrified. We can honestly go elsewhere if you want.'

I do not want this to defeat me, but I can't do it. I can't sit here and pretend I fit in, that I am a normal person who has lived a normal life that involves eating *inside* restaurants. 'Actually, do you mind if we leave?' I say. 'I, erm, don't think I can stay here.'

'Of course, of course,' he says and calls the waitress over to get our bill for a jug of tap water and his half-drunk glass of beer.

A bag of chips, a wooden spork and too much salt and vinegar. That, *that* is what I know, what I like, what I feel comfortable with. We come out of the chippie opposite the burnt-out old pier, which stands forlorn and ominous against the navy-blue-grey sky, and we walk slowly to the traffic lights to cross to the sea side of the street.

Saturday night is gearing up in Brighton, swathes of people are moving towards the centre, towards the bars, the restaurants, the neon-lit clubs. We were lucky to get that table in the restaurant, and I feel bad that we gave it up. I couldn't stay, though. I thought I was ready, that I could restart my life as though nothing has changed. I'm disappointed in myself, thought I had more courage, but clearly not. Marshall hasn't mentioned it, hasn't asked what upset me so much, and I'm not sure I can explain it. He was enthusiastic when I suggested we walked down to the sea and got chips. Looking out along the coastline, the road stretches as far as I can see and street lamps on either side look more and more like fairy lights that have been strung up by a kind-hearted giant the further away they get. Brighton is vibrant, full of life, of people. I close my eyes and sniff, relax for a moment into the smell of Brighton, the scent of being by the sea. I used to do that sometimes in Birmingham. When I would be heading towards Bernie's for a coffee, I would close my eyes for just a moment and inhale the essence of my new city. Brighton smells of salt and vinegar; Birmingham smells of coffee and opportunity.

'Is it Eliza getting to you?' Marshall asks. We are slowly walking towards the pier, away from home. 'Are you maybe thinking you can't handle it after all?'

'It's definitely not Eliza,' I say. 'I'm not used to being in nice places any more, that's all. I'm not really dressed for it, and I felt really out of place. Like everyone was staring at me.'

'If they were staring at you, it's because you're beautiful,' he says.

I stop walking. It doesn't sound creepy or forced, like he is trying to flatter me or charm me – he sounds like he means it. Like he thinks I'm beautiful. That he's looked at me a few times and the thought has crossed his mind enough for him to say it out loud.

My stare makes him shy all of a sudden: he stops walking too and begins to stare very hard into his bag of chips, prodding around with his spork as though testing the chips for firmness. We stand there for a few moments, silent islands in the noisy seas of a Saturday night in a city centre. The sounds, the people, the blackness of the night flow around us, bending themselves around us so we are not touched in any way.

'Well, that was a conversation-killer,' he eventually says, raising his gaze to look at me.

In reply, I stand on my toes and press my lips on to his. Briefly, quickly, to see what it's like to kiss someone. To kiss a man I like, who thinks I'm beautiful. I have never done that – I have never kissed someone first. It has always been someone kissing me, touching me, deciding how they want things to go. Before he can react, I step back.

'I wanted to see if I could do that,' I explain to him. 'It's been a while since I kissed someone – I wanted to see if I could do it.'

'You can try out kissing me any time you want,' he says with a laugh.

I smile at him. I'm about to do it again, to lean in and kiss him, to this time relish and enjoy the feel of his lips under mine, when his mobile sounds in his inside jacket pocket. He pulls back, cursing under his breath. 'It's like she's got an alarm that goes off in her head whenever I do something she wouldn't like,' he says. 'Eliza. That's her ringtone.' He rubs his hand over his forehead, clearly pained and frustrated. 'I bet you anything you like she'll have been down and knocked on my door. Because I haven't answered, she will have knocked on a neighbour's door to find out if they've seen me.' The phone stops ringing during his outburst. He angrily spears his spork into a chip and it stands upright like a bare flagpole, while he reaches into his pocket with his free hand and retrieves his phone. 'Now she's ringing. And if I don't answer . . .' He pauses then nods his head at his phone as it trills into life again. 'She'll keep ringing until I do.' He rejects the call. Less than ten seconds later the phone rings again. He stares at the screen for a second or two, then rejects that call with a vicious stab of the finger. Then he turns his phone off. 'I hate turning my phone off in case my ex needs to get in touch with me about my son, but Eliza's driving me crazy at the moment. I've tried everything – ignoring her, talking to her, letting her down gently – and she won't leave me alone. I don't know what I can do about her short of going to the police. I don't know what her problem is but it's driving me insane.'

I know what Eliza's problem is, I suspected when I first met them, but the bottle of wine and her desperation to get into my flat confirmed it. I know what her problem is, but I'm not sure I can tell him. Firstly, he won't want to know and secondly, I probably shouldn't get any more involved than I already am. But then, maybe I could get away with not saying anything if I hadn't kissed him, hadn't brought myself closer to him.

'I know what her problem is,' I admit, 'but you're not going to like it. Actually, you're not going to like it or believe it.'

'What, she's obsessed with me to stalker proportions? Yes, I'd worked that out for myself.' He's angry, upset and feeling powerless. I know those feelings, how they slowly erode your confidence, force you to make your world small, and bland and unthreatening. Being told the truth of your situation is supposed to set you free, give you a chance to break out while placing you on the path to forging a new way of living in the world. Unfortunately, being told the truth can also keep you chained to the same point in history, can make you too scared to do anything because suddenly your existence is tainted by something ugly and terrifying and incomprehensible. And sometimes, sometimes the truth can make everything far worse than you thought was possible.

No matter how terrifying, though, the truth in this situation does need to be told.

'No,' I say, 'Eliza's problem is that she's a drug addict.'

Marshall laughs in my face, tells me I'm wrong and then stares at me with cold eyes. I shouldn't have expected anything less, really. Who wants to believe someone they know is a drug addict when they're relatively normal-looking and ordinary-acting? Who would believe it of a friend when that friend holds down a job and the most you've ever seen them out of it is when they've had a couple too many at Christmas? No, much easier to ask, 'Why would you say such a terrible thing?' to the virtual stranger who has told you this truth.

'Because she's a drug addict. I wouldn't say it if it wasn't true. Admittedly, I've only known her a short amount of time, but this is what she is. That's why she's obsessed with you: I bet you're the only person who hasn't cut her off, you probably still lend her money now and then, and you let her into your flat where she can still steal from you. Yes, she's obsessed with you, she wants to protect that relationship you have because you're the only person still helping to fund her habit.'

'She doesn't steal from me.'

'Of course she does. I bet you stuff has regularly gone missing from your flat but you've convinced yourself you've mislaid those things, or you tell yourself you had thirty quid instead of forty. I'm sure her other friends stopped lending her money an age ago when they weren't getting it back, stopped inviting her in when things were going missing. She's obsessed with you anyway, but you're also her lifeline to thinking she doesn't have a problem.'

'She's not a junkie.'

'Yes she is. I've known loads of drug users and drug addicts, and the addicts are all pretty much like Eliza, even if they don't have homes and jobs like she does.'

'I'd know if she was an addict,' he says sternly.

'You'd like to think you would,' I say to him. 'Look, Marshall...' I lay a hand on his forearm and speak gently, like I would to anyone who has just had a huge shock. He immediately steps away from me, stops me from touching him. 'Look, Marshall,' I say again. I try to keep my voice as gentle as before, but his rejection of me and what I am saying after the moment we shared, stings; is like a poison-tipped arrow stuck fast in my most tender, vulnerable part. Even after everything, I am still desperate for someone to believe me first time. 'I understand how much of a shock this must be for you. I'm not saying she's a bad person but she does need help and she's unlikely to get any lasting help if she doesn't acknowledge that she has a problem. And I think she's got a long, long way to go until she even recognises she's got a problem.' I scrunch up my bag of chips, my appetite gone. 'I'm going to head home. I'll see you around.'

'Nika,' Marshall calls at me when I am less than six feet away.

I rotate on the spot, knowing exactly what he's going to ask.

'What is it you think she's addicted to?'

I inhale. 'I can't be sure, but from the way she behaves and the deep paranoia, I think she's got a pretty serious coke habit, she does a huge amount of skunk – hence the heavy perfume to try to mask it – and she possibly does speed.'

He shakes his head. 'I really think you're wrong about this.'

I nod at him and turn for home.

'I really, really think you're wrong about this,' he calls again.

Yeah, I think as I walk, *that's what my parents said, too, the first time I told them the truth about something they didn't want to hear.*

Birmingham, 2010

Things got better. After that night that Judge had set up, which had been painful and degrading and humiliating, things got a lot better, for years.

I got a proper job and I worked set hours cleaning offices and I was happy. I met a man in a pub when I was out with some work friends and we started dating. It was almost like I was being paid back for all that had gone before. I moved in with him after three months. By the time I brought my rucksack and guitar to his house to move in, I'd been sleeping in a car I'd bought. I sold the car and saved the money for a rainy day. I moved in with Vinnie with my eyes wide open, I had my own life, my own money, my own control over my body.

We weren't the next great love affair, Vinnie and I, but we got on. If we went out it was to the local pub and our restaurant meals were takeaways. We mostly watched television together and I could sit on his sofa and look out at the rain teeming down, knowing I didn't have to be out in that, looking for shelter. Every night I thought of Reese, of all the others out there, and I said what I felt was a prayer for them: hoping they would be OK, that they would somehow stay dry, get some sleep, wake up to a better day in the morning.

Vinnie cheated on me in the end. I came home early one day due to a gas leak outside the building where I worked and sat quietly on the sofa, listening to him screwing her in the bedroom, sounding like he was having much more fun with her than he ever had with me. I knew I should either walk in there and confront him, screaming like a banshee, or walk away with my head held high and my dignity intact, but I was tired. I simply sat and waited for them to finish and

223

smiled at the woman when she nipped out to get a glass of water wearing nothing but a post-coital glow.

'We gave it a good go, didn't we, Ace?' Vinnie said after he'd shown his red-faced companion out.

'Yup, so we did,' I agreed. There was no malice there, no anger or hurt. Our relationship had never been that intense or that involved, if both of us were honest. We'd liked each other a hell of a lot at the start and it had sort of dwindled then limped along. Maybe because I knew what would happen when we stopped – I would be out on the street again. I would have to reapply for a long-term homeless hostel, the rain would be falling on me, I would be moving things from locker to locker at Birmingham New Street, I would be meeting Reese more often and sobbing inside for what he was going through. I would probably also see Judge, who was still smarting at me not taking his money. He had a long memory and all the time in the world to hold a grudge, I knew this. When it was over with Vinnie I knew where I would be again, and I accepted it.

It'd been a good three-and-a-half years. They were worth it. All those years of sleeping in a bed, eating regular meals, going to the dentist, not having to find a way to make tampons last for as long as possible because I wasn't sure if I could afford to buy another box. I'd had the good life with Vinnie, I couldn't hate him if I tried.

9

Roni

London, 2016

I am getting nowhere with finding Nika. Absolutely nowhere. I have searched the Internet as much as is possible. I have signed up for all those social media things that I had no need for before, and they have yielded no results. Even the electoral roll still has her living at her parents' address here in Chiselwick. I am torn over the thought of visiting them and asking if they've seen her. They were the main reason why she left. Them, and me and what I did.

I am starting to think it will take some kind of miracle to find her. Without the order of convent life, my insomnia is creeping back in, the noise in my head is slowly being edged up. I'm sure if I find Nika things will become quieter, there might even be a chance to find the silence.

It is Easter Sunday and I am at morning Mass. Yesterday, Mum said at dinner (I had made) that she was going to come with me as she missed Good Friday Mass. I knew she wouldn't. She said it as though she thought that was what I expected of her. Dad lowered his fork and stared long and hard at her. She pretended that she didn't know Dad was wondering if she'd had another knock on the head, and carried on eating slowly and deliberately. 'Shall I wait for you to come down ready to go or shall I meet you there if you're not ready?' I asked.

'I will be ready,' she replied tartly.

'Great. It'll be nice to have some company. I might go and talk to Father Emanuel after Mass. He was so helpful to me when I was considering becoming a nun. It will be nice to see him again.'

'Perfect.'

This morning I didn't bother to wait until the very last minute to leave – I knew she wasn't going to come. Mum likes to mess with me sometimes; I am never sure why, but she does. The church is at the top of a large hill, which is why I didn't want to wait for Mum. I wanted to arrive calm and ready, not puffed and out of breath. Churches have fallen out of favour in recent years, with people's busy, secular lives, with the scandals still attached to the Church, but I love Church buildings. I adore the smell, the pervading atmosphere, the constant move towards silence and serenity.

Father Emanuel stands to one side, smiling at the purple-and-gold-robed choir as they sing. Their voices fill the space; each word of the Latin version of 'Ave Maria' is perfectly delivered. I close my eyes as they reach for the second verse, unwrap it and offer it to the congregation, to the church, to the priest, to God.

With my eyes open again, I briefly cast my gaze around the church, searching for familiar faces. Nika might even be here. My eyes search a little harder, scanning the faces of those seated in the pews I can see from here. She may look different now. She probably will look different now. And maybe she is in here, has been in here since I arrived home all those weeks ago, and I missed her.

Fifth pew from the front on the opposite side of the church to me, I spot Gail Frost, my gentle nemesis from Chiselwick High. All the time I have worked there so far she has found ingenious ways to make digs at me about religion and God and my former life as a nun, all so quiet and understated that it is hard to get annoyed with her. I had to remind myself to tell her off, to threaten her with sanctions, to send her to the headteacher *every* time she crossed the line from funny to rude or nasty. It is difficult because she is so likeable.

She sits beside a woman who is the living image of her as a grown-up. Gail is a chameleon. On a night out, she is skimpily dressed with her swathes of black, natural hair, slicked into a side bun while she aims for the older-than-her-years sophistication. At school she is smartly dressed in full uniform with her tie worn low and top button open, while her hair is worn in large, childish Afro twists with coloured ties at the tops and ends. In church she is sober, almost sombre in a plain, navy-blue dress and her hair pulled back into a low ponytail. There are large hoops on nights out, tiny studs at school, pearl earrings at church.

I stare at her for too long, of course, and she moves her head in my direction to find the source of scrutiny. I offer her a smile of hello and in return she subtly rolls her eyes and turns back to the front, refocuses on the beautiful, ethereal sound the choir make.

London, 1997

I was searching for silence.

The noise in my head was raging all the time, I couldn't ever find peace. What I needed was silence so I could disappear from who I was meant to be for a while. Nika hadn't turned up for school five months ago, and the rumour was that she'd disappeared. Some (stupid) people were talking alien abduction. Other people said it was a kidnapping. Someone said they'd seen her walking towards the bus stop that went towards West Chiselwick Tube station with a bag and a suitcase.

I'd listened to them talking, speculating about how she'd gone, why she'd gone, where she'd gone, and I knew the why. It was because of me. Because of what I had done to her.

Everything had changed that day Nika simply didn't show up for school: my sleep, always erratic and broken, like the lines in a cracked ceramic plate, had fallen apart altogether and was full of jagged hours of nightmare-filled slumber while the loudness in my head got worse. I'd stopped the ballet lessons. Dad had wanted to know why, Mum hadn't wanted a fuss and they'd both told me I should go back after

229

a rest. When Mr Daneaux had turned up at our house – like he had at Nika's – they'd piled on the pressure. He'd offered free lessons, the lead role in every show, anything I wanted if I'd reconsider. He had told them he'd never had pupils as gifted as Nika and me, and it would be a crime for me to give up. I'd heard it all from them, many, many times, but Nika's disappearance had given me courage. I'd kept saying no, even when Mum had lost her cool for the first time ever, and had screamed that this was why she had never wanted a girl. Girls caused a fuss, they caused drama, and they didn't know a good thing when it was offered to them. Dad had stepped in then and said it was enough, to never speak to me like that again, and that while he was disappointed, if I didn't want to go they couldn't make me.

I'd thought the noise would stop, after that. That once I didn't see him every week, the silence would come and I would be free.

I wanted Nika back so desperately. I felt hideously sick, a very real pain in the middle of my stomach, whenever I thought about life without her. But those were childish wishes, a young mind's fancy. I couldn't have her back, that was the long and the short of it, the truth writ large in my mind. She was gone because of me and there was nothing I could do about it.

In the park, where we would sometimes walk on our convoluted route home from school, I sat on a bench. I did not know what to do. I'd silenced her with what I'd done and I'd basically silenced myself as well. Now she was gone, inside, in those tiny quiet cracks inside my mind, I knew she wouldn't ever come back. Under all the noise in my head, the raging in my chest, there was one voice, whispering. It spoke to me constantly, promised me all sorts of pain. I had taken to walking around at night – the noise in my head was particularly bad in night-time hours – and I would often find myself in the park, sitting on different benches for hours until I was too exhausted to do anything but sleep when I got home.

Sitting on this particular bench, in the middle of this particular night, I held in my hand a bottle of my mother's sleeping pills and I had beside me a screw-top bottle of wine. I knew I would find the silence at the bottom of those bottles. There was so much confusion, so little sleep, nothing that could make it stop. I didn't want to do it, not really, but it seemed the only way to make it all – the pain of missing Nika, the agony of being me who had done this terrible thing, the constant loudness in my head – stop.

'I don't know what to do.' I said those words out loud. They echoed in my ears. They danced around my heart. Nika had found her exit, her silence, and this was probably the only way to find mine. Wherever I went, the noise would follow me and I couldn't take it any more.

'You look so lost,' she said.

She was pretty, from what I could see of her. Most of her was draped in black robes, a strip of white across her forehead. She smiled at me and I stared at her, wondering if she was real and why she was there.

'I don't usually speak to people who don't speak to me first. But I was out ministering with some of the men who live in the park and you looked lost and I wanted to help.'

I was not lost. For the first time since I was eight years old I knew where I would find perfect silence.

'How about we swap?' she said. She held her hand out for the bottle in my hands; she wanted to replace it with a book.

No. I shook my head. I didn't want to swap. I wanted silence. I wanted escape. I wanted out but I wasn't like Nika, I couldn't simply walk away to try to start again somewhere else. It would be like this wherever I went. This was the only way to make it stop.

She smiled at me again. 'Please. Let's swap.' Her dark eyes never left their quiet vigil of my face. She was so still, quiet, sure. Silence. She was the silence. 'Please.'

I gave the silence, the bottle of tablets, and she handed me the book. 'I always read this when I feel like you do.'

'You feel like I do?' I asked her. How could she know what I felt like? Surely the only person who had any idea what it was like to be me had walked away and I was probably never going to see her again.

'Yes, I sometimes feel like you do. That's why I read this. Every word feels like a blessing. If you read it, you'll understand why I wanted you to make this swap. I will keep these and you, please, keep that.'

With one last smile, she got to her feet and walked into the night. I saw her heading towards a group of people who looked homeless, who hung about the swings in the park, with bottles and cigarettes, and the stench of people who lived on the street. She stood and talked to them, laughing and joking as though she knew them all by name. Once she was gone, I looked at the book properly, its pages browned by age, the edges curled from being frequently turned. Its cover had missing patches of colour, the ink having cracked and peeled off. She had given me her silence, her escape. I observed the book, wondering what its pages would hold for me.

'Will you be my silence?' I asked the book.

Now she had taken my small-bottle-shaped exit, I had no choice but to try it.

Carefully, I opened the book. There were too many words, the lettering too small. Even under this street lighting, it was too dark for me to read. I strained my eyes, trying to make them out, trying to find the blessings. I couldn't see it. I couldn't understand what she'd meant. I had given my silence for this book I could not read straight away. I'd have to go home. Was that her plan all along? To get me to go home, to get me to rethink what I was going to do?

Two days later, when I finally finished the book, I had found the blessings she spoke of and I knew what I had to do: I had to become a nun and see if I could find the silence in God.

London, 2016

After the service, I stand outside the church, waiting to speak to Father Emanuel. He is saying goodbye to his congregation, shaking their hands and speaking warmly to them. He is a well-liked priest, always has been. A couple who are waiting to speak to him look familiar. My heart leaps in my chest as I realise where I know them from: they are Nika's parents.

They are both dressed for a special church service, both look like the respectable parents who would bring up a person as vibrant and caring as my beautiful friend. I remember them from all our ballet performances, how they would sit up front, near my parents, looking so proud and receiving congratulations on Nika's behalf. All the while I knew that they hadn't believed her when she'd told them what Mr Daneaux was doing to her, that they had listened to him when he'd said she was overreacting and misunderstanding his touches, that the day after he'd come to her house, he . . . he turned the 'Dance of the Sugar Plum Fairy' up really, really loud during the session he had with Nika.

But they may have changed after all these years. Maybe now she's an adult, on an equal footing with them, and they don't expect unquestioning obedience at all times, they have fixed things with Nika. Maybe, after she left her celebrity footballer boyfriend, she came back and sorted things out with them and she is now living in another part of the country, with a new – married – name, maybe a couple of children, and that is why I can't find her. Maybe Nika is doing just fine and they are doting grandparents and she doesn't need me to come storming into her life, dragging up pieces of her past.

I shall speak to them. If they have fixed things, and they know where she is, then that will be no problem. They will tell me she is happy and I will not need to contact her. I will, but I'll have no need. If they have fixed things, I won't have to worry about speaking to them, reminding them of that time, imagining which one of them told her that if she wanted to keep on living in their house she would carry on with her ballet lessons and stop complaining.

The palms of my hands are damp, sticky at the thought of speaking to them. But I have to, if I want to find Nika.

While I wait for them to finish talking to Father Emanuel, I look around. Gail and her mother are standing a little way away, and Gail's mother is fussing over her, adjusting the collar on her dress, picking imaginary fluff out of her perfect hair. I would love to speak to them, to ingratiate myself into their world, but for what reason? They don't know me, and I would only be doing so because she reminds me of myself. After a few minutes, one of the choir members, still in his robes, approaches them. He slips an arm around Gail's mother's shoulders and kisses her lightly on the lips. Clearly he is Gail's step-father since he is an attractive, slightly older white man with a mixture of blond and silver hair. Gail rolls her eyes at her parents kissing and the eye roll lands her line of sight in my direction.

I offer another smile, another chance to connect. She glares at me this time and then slowly, very deliberately, turns her back on me.

Well, I think, *that's me told.*

'Hello,' I say politely to the other Mr and Mrs Harper as they reach the end of the path out of the churchyard. We are away from the main throng of Easter Sunday churchgoers and from where we stand, we can see out all over Chiselwick and the neighbouring towns. 'Are you Mr and Mrs Harper?'

They stop and look at me, sizing me up. Nika's mother frowns slightly, as though trying to place my face at some past point in her life. She is incredibly stylish: her hair is perfectly straightened under her black hat, and her make-up has been so carefully applied you wouldn't think she was wearing any. She has an expensive-looking black coat and a designer handbag. Beside her, Nika's father is also very well put together. He doesn't seem to recognise me, he simply looks at me with a pleasant, inquisitive expression on his face. 'Yes, we are,' Mr Harper says.

'I don't know if you'll remember me? My name is Veronica Harper. I was your daughter's friend at school.'

Their dual reaction, to hold themselves a little more rigidly, their faces a little more reserved, hints that they haven't resolved things with their youngest child.

'I've just moved back to Chiselwick, and I saw you and thought I'd ask you how Nika was doing? Does she still live around here?'

Mrs Harper swallows, slightly distressed at what I am asking. Mr Harper has softened a little, but not too much. For several seconds it seems neither of them are going to speak to me, and we'll have to stand here in front of this view of our home town, not speaking about the other Veronika Harper.

'No, she doesn't,' Mr Harper eventually says. 'Our daughter chose to estrange herself from us many years ago. She was a very troubled young woman.'

I shouldn't be surprised that this is the party line – that she chose to give up on them, that she was the one with the problems. I wonder, if I hadn't become a nun, what my story would have become. Would I have gone to university, got a job, got a husband, made babies? Or would my story have ended that night in the park, with a bottle of pills and a bottle of wine? I wonder what they would have said then? Would I have been exposed as a troubled young woman, who got drunk every weekend, had sex with older men in alleyways and cars, and who broke her parents' hearts by taking her own life?

'I see,' I say. 'I'm sorry to hear that.'

Mrs Harper suddenly grabs on to her husband and needs him to steady her, comfort her by putting his arm around her. If I didn't live with my mother, if I didn't know what they said to Nika, I would probably be completely taken in by this. I would be thinking Nika was a selfish child, that they were loving parents and I would be better off without her in my life.

'You haven't heard from her at all, then? Not since she left?'

'No,' her father replies sternly. 'As I told you, she chose to estrange herself from us many years ago.'

'She didn't even send a postcard or a change-of-address card?' I'm pushing my luck, I know that, but I won't speak to them again. 'I mean, you don't know even vaguely where she might be?'

Mrs Harper has a small sob that escapes from the back of her throat, and uncharitably, I think that she's a better actress than my mother. Mum can pull off a great performance of being a caring, involved mother whenever she needs to – but Nika's mum would beat mine hands down.

'Please, you are upsetting my wife. We haven't heard from our daughter in nearly twenty years. Do you have any idea how devastating that is to us? We gave her everything, all of the very best opportunities in life, and she threw them back in our faces. Our other daughter, Sasha, has been such a source of support and she has spent many years trying to make up for what Veronika did to us. She is also devastated by her behaviour. Thankfully our son had left home before Veronika's behaviour became out of control, but we have all been hurt and damaged by Veronika's actions. Now, please, we would like to stop talking about this.'

I lower my head. 'Of course,' I say quietly. 'I'm sorry.' Nika. My poor, poor friend. I didn't realise how cold they were. That all of her family had turned against her. That when she went to the police station she really had nothing else to lose because everyone in her family believed she was the problem, the one making a mountain out of a molehill. 'I won't bother you any longer.'

My poor Nika. No wonder what I did was the final straw. I was the only person she could rely upon and I...

The other Mr and Mrs Harper walk away and I feel it again: the swell of noise in my head, the crushing agony of knowing I have added to the pain of someone I so desperately loved.

I have to find her. I have to make things right.

Nika

Brighton, 2016

Nika, Have been trying to catch you but you've engaged that superpower of yours again and I didn't want to knock on your door in case you shut it in my face. I'm sorry about the other night. That I didn't believe you. I confronted Eliza about it and you were right. She's known for a while that she's developing a problem with the drugs she does and she wants to get help. It's a really good thing you brought it up. Thank you. I'm going to do all I can to support her in getting the right help, and she's going to pay me back for the things she's taken. If you ever want to try dinner again, let me know. My number's below. I live in number 207 if you ever fancy dropping by to try that kissing thing again. :)

Marshall

I know every word of Marshall's note, I've read it several times a day since he pushed it through my letterbox two days ago. Today, though, it's been playing on my mind a lot. I've been tempted to ring him, text him. Get in touch.

By the time I get halfway through my first floor at work, I am no wiser about what to do. It's an odd feeling to be believed after the initial anger, but he is in serious denial about Eliza. I'm not sure how much in denial Eliza is about herself and how much she admitted it in a desperate need to say whatever is necessary to keep Marshall in her life.

I push my trolley, loaded with towels, replacement toiletries, bedding and cleaning items, down the corridor to the next room. The person in 413 was actually very tidy and clean. I managed to get the whole room done in ten minutes. I'm always doing that, trying to grab an extra minute or two where I can so I can spend a bit of extra time on the really mucky rooms. These floors have bigger rooms, which take more time to remake.

The left wheel on my trolley squeaks sometimes as I push it, and I make a mental note to have it looked at by the maintenance guys. As I think this, Marshall's note scrolls through my mind like ticker tape on the bottom of a television screen.

I feel for him. He has no idea what is in store for him. Eliza seems like a good person, but she will do bad things. She probably already has done bad things but there are a plethora of bad things for her to do which she will work her way through. She will do those things and will be horrified that at the end of it people aren't there for her. That Marshall isn't there for her. At the moment, he thinks – truly believes – that by being supportive and caring, not calling her out for stealing from him, that it'll help her; that by being a shoulder to lean on, she will seek help for her problem. He thinks being her rock, the person she can turn to and will have her back when she's facing it head on, will be what keeps her fighting against her 'problem'. The reality is, it'll all be smoke and mirrors, it will all be lies, it will all come to nothing because she does not have a 'problem', she has an 'addiction'. Right now, she only wants her drugs, she only wants her life as it fits in with drugs, she only wants to get away with behaving like scum of the Earth.

Reese behaved like scum sometimes. Real, out-and-out scum. The only way I could stay friends with him, still love him like I did, was by being honest with myself about who he was and what he was willing to do to feed his habit. I did love him, too. I could love him because I saw exactly who he was. When I looked at him I didn't see the druggie who stole from me and Vinnie whenever I let him into Vinnie's house. I didn't even see the man who I had a coffee with after he stopped someone from attacking me. I saw the young boy who had to leave home because his mother didn't protect him. I'd never seen photos of him from the time before his life as Reese began, but I could picture him in my head. Under the grime, the needle-spackled skin, the dirty clothes, the grey-brown teeth and often his unkempt smell, I only ever saw the boy for whom home was so bad he had to run away. I saw him like that, but I knew what he was capable of.

Reese and I were bad for each other because he could do terrible things, he could screw me over, verbally abuse me, and I would still love him, would still look out for him, would still be his port of call when he needed someone to pretend his life was normal. Reese sometimes needed tough love. We both knew every time he went down into the hole of heroin that he hadn't fallen in, he had crawled in. He made the choice to do it. Yes, it was a choice made from the physical and psychological craving so strong he often couldn't stand the pain that came from living without it flowing through his veins, but it was still a choice. My choice wasn't so much physical, it was psychological, emotional, instinctive – I *had* to be there for him. I *had* to show him I believed him because no one else had. We both knew Reese needed tough love sometimes, Reese knew I needed tough love sometimes, but we neither of us were quite brave enough to bring it about.

Marshall has all of this to come: the relapses, the promises, the money, the emotional ringer he will be dragged through while Eliza pretends to him and herself that she wants to get clean. And, addict that I am, I want to be there for him. To help him while he helps her. To feed my habit with his need to help his friend.

I park my trolley outside 415. There is no 'do not disturb' sign hanging outside so I raise my hand.

Knock, knock! Wait ten seconds.

Knock, knock! 'Housekeeping!' I call. Wait another ten seconds.

Nothing, no response. That doesn't always mean the person is out, though – they could be in a deep sleep, they could be in the shower, they could have headphones on and can't hear me ... on average I scare the living daylights out of five different people a day.

I swipe the card attached to the loop on my maid's uniform, slowly open the door. When the door is open, I enter the room but stay by the door, then knock again, call 'Housekeeping!' again. No response. The room is darkened because the curtains are drawn, but it doesn't feel empty. The bathroom light is out, there are no shapes in the bed, but I am not alone in here. *Urgh.* On average, *this* happens at least twice a week – someone will 'accidentally' treat me to a full-frontal nudie show. I've seen far too many naked people – male and female – since I started working here, and none of them has the body that can make it worth my while.

Do I go or do I stay? I'm really not up for being flashed today. My eyes dart around the dimly lit room, taking in the mess, assessing how much time I'll need when I come back later. A man's suit jacket has been slung over the back of the chair by the window; on the low padded bench by the door a suitcase stands yawning open, but its contents don't contain clothes other than underwear, from what I can make out, so I'm guessing the person has hung them up. On the floor by the bed is a pair of trousers, one leg inside the other; a pair of men's tight underpants is on top of the trousers, and beside them is a white T-shirt. On the bedside table there is an expensive watch, a fancy silver lighter, loose change and keys – car and house. Not too messy – the bathroom may not need too much clearing up, either. *Do I go or do I stay?* The room is unnaturally silent even though I am not alone. *Do I stay or do I go?*

The bathroom light flicks on suddenly, and out of nowhere a form appears from the bathroom and pauses, leaning against the frame so their whole body takes up the entire doorway. The person is male, his doughy midsection topped by a toned, muscular chest. He's naked, of course, brandishing his body like it is necessary viewing for every person who walks the face of the Earth.

Immediately I avert my eyes, but I know he's probably switching his gaze between checking how embarrassed I am, and admiring himself in the full-length mirror I am standing beside.

'Oh, I'm sorry,' I say, averting my eyes. 'I thought you were out. Housekeeping. I'll come back later.'

I step back, ready to shut the door behind me. 'No, no, don't run away. You can still clean up around me. I *really* won't mind.'

His voice. His voice crawls into my ear, then spreads out through my memory, stroking every one of my nightmares awake, causing them to flash through my mind in an uncontrollable torrent.

'I-I'll come back,' I manage. I keep my head lowered, push my glasses back into place. 'Sorry.'

I step out of the room, swing the door shut. I can't luxuriate in a moment to steady myself, I have to move on, get into the next room, hide out and hope he didn't recognise me, hope he doesn't open his door, stick his head out and say—

'Nikky? Is that you?'

I keep walking, keep moving, because I am not Nikky. Nikky is a woman he made in his image.

'All right then, *Nika*. Nika Harper, you stop right there and talk to me.'

I don't even know why, but maybe I am, deep down, that twenty-one-year-old who did whatever he told me to do. Maybe I knew I'd always have to have this conversation, this confrontation, and there's no point trying to avoid it, and that is why I stop my trolley with its sometimes squeaky left wheel and I stop walking.

I can't keep running away from bits of my past. Some day, somehow, I'm going to have to deal with it.

I turn around to face him. It looks like the part I have to deal with now is the part involving Todd.

'I almost didn't recognise you with the hair and the glasses,' he says. 'You look really different.'

'So do you,' I reply. He's a little grey around the temples, the sun from his expensive holidays has weathered his skin and he's older, of course, but essentially he *looks* the same. But that's not what I mean when I say that. I used to be scared of him – more so after I left him. He was terrifying in my mind, scarier than the thought of sleeping rough. Maybe it was the thought of what he could make me do, how he got me to collude with him to treat me badly, that had sent me out there in the first place and had scared me most. Yet, standing in front of him, the flashbacks that moments ago came rampaging through my mind, trampling over all the good things in my memory when I realised who he was, don't seem to have been of him, the man leaning out of a doorway so he's not flashing the corridor. Those nightmares were of someone far more menacing. Someone charming and good-looking; cruel and cunning. That doesn't seem to be him. *He* looks completely different.

'Why don't you come back into my room so we can talk?' he says pleasantly.

I shake my head. 'No, I'd prefer to stay out here.'

'I haven't seen you in ten years and you want to talk out here?' He waves his hand around the corridor, which, as corridors go, is very pleasant. The lighting is low but not grungy, the carpets are clean, the wallpaper is fancy.

'Why not?' I ask. 'It's as good a place as any.'

'Come on, Nikky, just step inside for a moment.' He sounds jovial, like a man humouring his ex, like a controlling man who will turn on the thinnest of edges when the ex doesn't do what she's told.

'No, thank you,' I state. 'I can't talk for long, either, I have to get back to work.'

'Yeah, work,' he scoffs. At one point in my life, that scoff would have hurt. I would be hanging on, waiting for the other words that would cover the cut of those words and make me feel all right again. Right now, the smirk bounces off without even touching me. 'Hang on,' he says when I don't reply. He's gone a few moments, then re-emerges wrapped up in the white dressing gown from his room. 'I can't believe how low you've sunk, Nikky,' he says. 'There was a time when we used to laugh at people like maids in hotels, having to get down on their hands and knees for hours to make enough money for a packet of fags, remember?'

I shake my head. 'No, I don't remember because I've never laughed at anyone who has to work for a living, Todd. I don't think of people like that. Never have, never will.'

'Oh, come on, you know what I mean.'

'I don't, I genuinely don't, because I've always had respect for people, no matter what they do. It's not hard, you know, not thinking you're better than someone because they can't afford your lifestyle.'

'You've really changed,' he says sadly.

'Have I?' I reply. 'You haven't.'

'Look, this is silly, we can't talk properly like this. Let me take you to dinner tonight, we can talk and get to know each other again. Wouldn't you like that?'

I'm so appalled at that suggestion I have to stop myself screwing my face up like he has let off a very bad smell. I'm even more appalled when I realise he means it. 'I don't think so. Thank you, but no.'

'How can you say no to me?' he says. 'You owe me at least a little bit of your time, don't you? You walked out one day after a silly little spat. I had to deal with the aftermath of cancelling the wedding. Do you know what that was like for me? It was so humiliating. Some of my sponsors were down to come to the wedding, they were planning special celebration products, and you messed that all up for me. I've had to rebuild my life since then. Plus I've been going to see your family. Bet you didn't know about that, huh? Because you're *selfish*. Your parents said you left them in exactly the same way as you left me and that you'd always been a thoughtless child. I stuck up for you. I told them that the stories in the papers about you using drugs weren't true and that I had been taking care of you. I did all that even though you'd left me in the lurch.

'You owe me, Nikky, you owe me. Now, I'm willing to listen to what you have to say for yourself about why you did that to me, but not like this. We have to sit down properly, talk it all through. You need to understand that we can't pretend none of this has happened, but I'm willing to try.'

Todd has clearly had this moment, this conversation, mapped out in his head for years. He knows what I was meant to have said and when, what he was meant to have said and when, and how the whole thing would resolve itself. Todd speaks like that conversation has happened exactly how it was meant to in his mind, even though I have not said a word.

'Did Frank get his job back?' I ask.

'Frank? Who the hell is Frank?'

Frank is the man I still fretted over, who I felt so guilty about I often thought of breaking my exile to go and beg his employers to think again, who I almost returned to Todd for so he would tell them to re-employ him. 'Frank is the driver who you had sacked because he was nice to me.' This is clearly not part of the script he has in his head.

Almost visibly, a thousand thoughts run through his mind as he squints his way through his history. He's obviously done it since then, he's obviously had men removed from their positions for being too nice to one of his wives or fiancées. I'd wager he's had it done so many times he's genuinely forgotten who Frank is.

'Goodbye, Todd,' I say.

'Don't walk away from me, Nikky. You don't get to walk away again.'

Room 417 has a DND sign, so I push on, ignoring the braying man behind me, and stop outside room 419.

'Nikky, you come back here. Now. You come back here. I'm not finished talking to you.'

Knock, knock! Wait ten seconds.

'Do you hear me, Nikky? Nikky! *Nikky!*'

Knock, knock! 'Housekeeping.'

'NIKKY!'

I swipe my card, open the door and drag my trolley in with me when I'm sure the room is empty. I don't usually do that, but I need to shut him out. I need him to stop shouting. This is a nice hotel: the last thing they need is for some man to be stood in the corridor, screaming the name of a woman who does not exist.

Birmingham, 2015

'I thought you might like a hot chocolate?' I said to the girl.

I'd noticed her arrive a few days ago, walking into town from the direction of the coach station, and she was set apart from the other people who had arrived because she was shrouded in a new-girl fear that was like a thick, visible blanket. I'd noticed her walking and walking that night when I went to meet Reese. Now, she was sitting on the raised platform outside a closed shoe shop with her bag beside her and an air of hopelessness that had replaced the blanket of fear. That must have been what I'd looked like when I'd first arrived; it was certainly what I remembered feeling like.

I held out the styrofoam cup filled with a frothy hot chocolate to her. She seemed too young for coffee, would probably turn her nose up at tea, and I had no idea where to start with herbal stuff. Hot chocolate seemed a good compromise.

'If you're a social worker you can do one,' she practically spat at me with a slightly curled lip, and narrowed eyes.

'I'm not a social worker,' I said.

'Cop, whatever – I'm not interested.'

'I'm not a police officer, either. I'm a . . .' What was I? 'I'm like you. I'm homeless, too.'

'Yeah, right, you look it.'

I sat down beside her, without cleaning off a spot first, and she did a double-take because few 'normal' people did that. 'I don't sleep on the streets any more, no, but I live in a homeless bedsit-type thing.'

She turned her body, which seemed so fragile, like a bird with delicate wings, towards me, her face curious. 'You really slept on the streets?'

'Yeah, and if you're going to do it, I'll tell you what a good friend told me: you need to hide, sleep somewhere hidden so you'll feel a bit safer. But, if you sleep out a few nights in the open, there are

245

people who will help you. Get you a place in a shelter, get you the help you're entitled to.'

'They'd just make me go home. I can't go home.'

'They won't, you know. Maybe just—'

'*I can't go home!*' she screeched. I wasn't listening to her, and I should be. I had started this conversation – why bother talking to her if I wasn't going to listen? She wasn't ready to get help from someone who might want to talk her into going home.

'Sorry,' I said. I uncapped my drink and took a sip. Bought hot chocolate was a luxury I rarely indulged in. Its slightly too-hot temperature flashed over my tongue, leaving a temporary numbness in its wake. The girl hooked a lock of greasy hair behind her ear, revealing a crop of acne on the side of her face. She was probably younger than I thought. At first, from a distance, I'd been thinking sixteen, but now, more like fourteen.

'I'm Grace. What's your name?' I asked.

'Lori,' she mumbled. She held on to the hot chocolate, using it to warm her fingers. 'My name's Lori.'

'Nice to meet you, Lori.'

She nodded. 'I really can't go home. It's awful at home. I can't go home.'

'I understand,' I said. 'You know, during the day, there are centres open where you can get some food and can sit in the corner and sleep. And at night, like I say, just try to stay hidden. The library's a good place to visit. I used to try to stay in a youth hostel at least once a week so I could have a shower and wash my clothes. But that's hard if you don't have any money.'

She wasn't really listening to me, she was stuck back in the place where she had made the decision to run away rather than live with whatever was going on at home. 'Listen, if you change your mind about getting help, just ask a couple of the homeless guys to get a message to Grace, or Ace, as they call me, and I'll sleep out with you to make you feel less scared.'

'Why would you do that?'

'I know how scary it can be. But in your own time, when you're ready, you can get the extra help that's out there. In the meantime, though, it's really important that you stay away from people who offer you stuff.'

'How'd you mean?'

'I mean, yes, if I'm being strict about it, I shouldn't have given you that hot chocolate, but really, it's on me. But if you're going to live out here for a while, try not to owe anyone anything. You'll get offered stuff like drink or drugs and you'll think that person is being generous but really, they'll want paying back. And sometimes not just with money.'

She was looking at me, she was watching me speak, but she wasn't really hearing me. Lori was still in shock, probably. Reeling and unsteady from the fact she had escaped whatever was previously making her life hell. She wouldn't hear me this time, but if others told her and told her and told her and told her, maybe she would hear it. Maybe she wouldn't make the same mistakes most of us had made along the way. 'Lori, I'm really sorry that you've ended up out here,' I said to her. 'I know how awful it is when you feel like you can't go home.' I took another sip of my hot chocolate; this time it was the right temperature, the milky, cocoa sweetness of it slipping easily down my throat. 'If it's all right, I'll sit here with you for a bit. And if you want to talk about anything – *anything* – do so. I'll stay as long as you want me to.'

We sat there for most of the night and she didn't say another word to me.

Brighton, 2016

At the end of my shift, I am half expecting Mrs Nasir and one of the burly bellboys to be waiting for me, ready to search me and my trolley for something I have allegedly stolen from Todd. I am expecting him to do anything to discredit me, teach me a lesson for walking away from him for the second time. But nothing. I finish my shift, and leave the building without incident. I stand outside the service entrance, wondering what to do next.

247

That wasn't as scary as I always thought it would be. During an ordinary shift, I've discovered that Mind Todd is far scarier than Real Todd. Maybe my memory makes people scarier than they are. Maybe I should get another confrontation over with right now. It's not like I can go straight home anyway, because despite not being scared of him, I don't want Todd to follow me and find out where I live. So maybe the safest, sanest thing to do will be to go out of here, turn back off this seafront road and head back towards the centre of Brighton, get on a train and go and see my parents.

Birmingham, 2015

I arrived at Bernie's to meet Reese and he wasn't there. Lori was. She had her rucksack with her, and she looked dishevelled and tired. A tiredness swept through her body that you expected to see in those worn out by life. Her hair was pulled back into a greasy-looking ponytail, her clothes were grubby, she moved like a person who hadn't slept in weeks. She was weak now, emotionally exhausted, physically depleted enough to be doing what she was now – sitting opposite Judge.

My stomach turned over. I wanted to march over to their table and rip her away from him, remind her what I had told her, what I knew other people had told her, that you mustn't get involved with people like him, nor *with him*. *'You mustn't take anything from him!'* I wanted to scream. *'You must stay as far away from him as possible. Home is unbearable, and Judge will make here unbearable, too.'*

Pretending I didn't see them, I went to the counter and ordered a coffee, before I sat at the table I always sat at, facing the door, pushed my headphones into my ears and turned the music all the way up, drowning out the conversation he was having with her. I saw, though, how the conversation ended – with him passing her a small wrap she secreted away under her hands, him gently patting her hand with a verbal reassurance, her vigorous nod, her smile of gratitude.

Don't panic, I told myself. It wasn't too late. If I could speak to her, make her see that Judge wasn't the way to get through this, it would be OK. 'Living on a Prayer' continued to play in my ears and I counted down the seconds until he walked out the door.

Judge got up and moved to leave, but instead of simply walking out, he wanted to make his presence felt to me. 'Ace, nice to see you,' he said, standing too close to me. I could smell his aftershave, and it catapulted me, as always, back to the last night I had worked for him.

That night, when I had refused to take his money and the wrap of something he'd put on top to help me deal with what had gone before, he'd been quietly raging. I'd kept my eyes lowered and had simply repeated over and over that I didn't want the money, I wouldn't feel right about taking it because I wanted to call it quits. Eventually he'd accepted what I was saying and with a look that told me he wanted to grab me by the throat and snap my neck, had opened the car door to let me go. He'd wanted to hurt me, but couldn't. People like Judge managed to keep control by seeming to stick to a code of conduct. If I had taken something from him, he would be well within his rights, the code would say, to do whatever he liked to me. Because I never had, if word got out that he was hurting people who owed him nothing, people would turn on him, would find another supplier. He'd never be sure, either, when someone was going to talk to the police just to get rid of him. Judge had let me go that night, but it hadn't been the end of it. Over the years, he'd ignore me, and other times would come over to me, like now, and say how nice it was to see me.

I always kept my gaze lowered, and this time I took out my earphones and mumbled a hello, knowing which way this conversation was going to go.

'How you doing, Ace?'

'Fine,' I replied quietly.

I continued to stare down at my hands, examining the lines in my skin, the shapes of the wrinkles over my knuckles, the colour of my short, stubby nails. He leant in close to me, so near that his smell filled my senses; his breath moved gently over my skin when he spoke quietly and deliberately. 'Do you still think about that time, Ace?' he murmured. 'Fucked by six men in one night. They told me all about you, your body, the noises you made when they hurt you. It sounded so good, so special. And you did it for free.' He leant in so close his lips grazed my ear as he spoke. 'Never forget I did that to you. Never forget I can do that to you again whenever I want.'

He stood upright again, satisfied that he'd felt me flinch, pleased he'd got a reaction from me. 'Ace, if you ever want to come to another of my parties, let me know,' he said at normal volume. 'I'm sure there are lots of people who'd love to party with you again.'

'OK,' I muttered.

'Good girl,' he said. 'I'd certainly like to party with you again, if that makes any difference.' With one last grin at Lori, then me, he left.

I covered my mouth with my hand, inhaling and exhaling deeply to clear my nostrils of the smell of him, cleanse my mind of him, stop the flashbacks about that night rolling in and unspooling themselves.

'Do you know him?' Lori asked from across the café. 'Judge, do you know him?'

I nodded, not yet able to speak.

'He's been really good to me,' she said. 'He's been dead nice. I know you said not to take stuff from people, but he's been dead nice about everything. He even said he'd find me a place to stay if I wanted to stop sleeping out.'

'Lori,' I began, and then wondered what to say. She was in his thrall. Not so much that she'd agreed to stay in one of his houses, but it wouldn't be long. Not when he'd got her hooked enough to do anything he asked of her. 'Lori, just be careful of people like him, all right?' I had to be careful, too, that she didn't go mouthing off to him about what I'd said. There'd be repercussions if he heard I was slagging him off. 'Not everyone is who they seem to be, and it's not a good idea to take things from people you don't know. You don't know what they'll want in return.'

'But Judge's dead nice. He said not to worry about the stuff he's given me, that it was all part of the getting-to-know-each-other process.'

'Lori, I wish you would go and talk to the people who could help you. You're young enough to get all sorts of help and they won't make you go home. They really won't.'

She tutted at me, her nostrils flaring in disgust. Immediately she was on her feet, she snatched up her rucksack and sleeping bag and stormed out of the café without another look at me. Who could blame her? Really, who could?

I pushed the earphones back into place and reinserted the music into my head. I needed it to wipe out those two conversations, neither of which had done me any good.

Roni

'Hello. This is Edna Hyde, headteacher of Chiselwick High School, leaving a message for Veronica Harper. Ms Harper, I was wondering if you had had time to consider my offer of you coming to work at our school permanently? The children responded extremely well to you and we thought you fitted in at the school in a rather unique way. We will, of course, discuss with you updating your training, but I'd be grateful if you would please consider it. I look forward to hearing from you.'

I delete the message from the phone because I do not want to consider it. At any other time, I would of course consider the offer of a job at a school I loved teaching at, and I would love the regular income it would bring that would help me move out of my parents' house, but I haven't found Nika yet. It might sound ridiculous, but I do not want to be tied down too much until I have an idea of where she is, what I will do when I find her. I feel it is a 'when', not an 'if'. I have faith in that if nothing else.

The machine beeps, clicks through to the next message, also left this afternoon. Mum and Dad are not in, the house is in darkness and I am standing in the corridor, listening to the messages on the answerphone attached to the house phone. I really should get a mobile. I feel a lot freer without one, though. Not tied down to always speaking to people when they choose to speak to me.

252

'Hello, this is Cliff calling for Veronica. I hope this is the right number as I've left a couple of messages and I haven't heard back. Veronica, it would be nice to go out again? Well, it would be for me. I thought we had fun? Look, give me a call at the school—' I delete Cliff's message, like I have deleted his others. I like him, but I'm not looking for anything like that right now. I have to find Nika. That's the long and the short of it. I am being single-minded because until I find her, I cannot make any other plans for my life. I left the convent to do it, and that is what I need to do.

I am having trouble sleeping again. I am up for many hours in the night nowadays, and the fractured hours with their jagged night-mares are far too much to handle cooped up in my bedroom, trying hard not to make the bed frame creak with every move. I've taken to getting a bus up towards the centre of London and finding late-opening cafés to sit in to read.

I'm sitting in a bagel shop that is open most of the night, by the window, when the door tings open and I see her stumble in.

I watch her at the till, barely standing up and trying to order a coffee and bagel to go. The left shoulder of her coat, covered in an off-white fake fur, keeps falling off her shoulder, as does the spaghetti-thin strap of the black dress she is wearing underneath it. Gail.

After the third time of her looking over her shoulder through the glass front door of the bagel shop, I finally manage to catch a glimpse of him, the man she's with. He's another one who is at least three times her age, dashing in a salt-and-pepper way with a well-cut suit and an expensive-looking raincoat. His hands are buried in his pockets, but I know on the left hand there'll be a wedding ring, in his wallet there'll be a family photo with smiling faces of children, probably not much younger than the girl he's planning on having sex with at some point tonight.

Without really thinking about what I'm going to do next, I care-fully close my book with its bright pink cover and stand up, abandoning – briefly – my half-drunk coffee and untouched bagel, and head to the counter. 'Gail, how lovely to see you,' I say to her. She double-takes, is terrified for a moment when she realises it's really me, and then she shakes herself back to normal, back to that line of contempt she has for me.

'What are you doing here, Miss?' she asks. Her eyes dart to where I was sitting as though checking that none of the other teachers will be out in a café at 2 a.m.

'Catching up on my reading,' I say to her, raising my book so she can see.

Her eyes widen in surprise as she reads the title. Before she can say anything, I ask: 'Who's your friend waiting for you outside?'

'Erm…' She shrugs. 'Just some guy.'

'I'd like to meet him,' I state. I didn't mean to say that; I don't know what I meant to say, but not that, I don't think. But then, what was I meaning to do? I could have turned a blind eye, pretended I hadn't seen her and let her get on with it.

'Yeah, right,' she scoffs.

'Why not?'

'Who are you, my mother?'

'No, just someone who is interested. In you, your life, the "just some guy" you're hanging out with.'

What she's about to say is interrupted by the brief, loud knock of Just Some Guy rapping his knuckles impatiently on the window. When we turn towards him, he raises his hands at her in an aggressive 'what are you doing?/don't keep me waiting' gesture. She is momentarily worried, looks at me, scared, then she makes an 'I'm going as fast as I can' movement in reply. I smile at him, and raise my hand to wave at him. He shoots me a well-concealed snarl. I've seen that look from men like him so many times before. *Don't get involved*, that look is saying, *not if you know what's good for you*. Those looks were almost always directed at Nika when she wouldn't leave me with whichever man was pawing at me.

If I knew what was good for me, I would not have left the monastery, I would not have come out at this time of night to sit and stare at the pages of my book and wonder when I was going to get a proper night's sleep again. If I knew what was good for me, I would give up all ideas of finding Nika and would get on with my life. If I knew what was good for me, I might have taken the advice of the priest who now regularly hears my confession in north-west London and would have sat in that wooden box, found a way to tell all about what I did, and then accept absolution and move on.

I stride towards the door and open it, the jangling of the bell bringing the owner of the café from out back. He took Gail's money for her order then disappeared out back into his bakery area and had not reappeared since. I suspect he was stalling her, trying to stop her from doing what she was about to do because she is so young. If you ignore the clothes and hair, the make-up and the attitude, you can see she is so young.

The man straightens up as I approach. He takes his hands out of his pockets and confirms what I thought – wedding ring, thick and gold, sitting proudly on the ring finger of his left hand.

'Hello,' I say to him. 'My name is Sister Grace. I've just been talking to lovely Gail in there.'

He scowls at me, not sure what to think. I'm hardly dressed as a nun today, but his gaze does stray to the book in my hand and he's unsure.

'Did you know she was fourteen?' I say with what I call my 'nun voice and smile'. I only use it on particularly obnoxious people; that quiet, calm, patronising tone is so much more effective with the habit, but the name and the book in my hand should be enough for this deviant. 'Fourteen. And how old is your daughter?' I ask. It's a guess, of course. He suddenly stands up a little straighter, his arms fold themselves across his chest in a protective, defensive move.

'I-I-I-I don't have a daughter,' he says. By the end of the sentence, the end of the lie, he is quite confident about what he is saying. So confident, in fact, that he repeats it: 'I don't have a daughter.'

I hold out my Bible. It is pink and new. I bought it the other day when I reached for my usual Bible, much used and much loved, and couldn't make contact with it because guilt was spreading out through my fingers. I'd felt something every time I touched it, but hadn't been able to name it until that moment, and I realised. I felt guilty. That Bible had been a part of my life as a nun. As I regularly say to people, I'm not a nun any more. I needed to get myself a new one to match my new life. 'Swear on this that you haven't got a daughter,' I say to him. 'Swear on this that you haven't got a daughter and I'll believe you.'

He stares at the pink-covered book, his eyes full of fear.

'It's only a book,' I say to him. 'I'm sure someone like you doesn't even believe in all that God stuff. So just put your hand on this good book and swear that you haven't got a daughter.' *One who is probably the same age as Gail, which is probably the reason why you picked her*, I add silently. I don't care what anyone might think, someone his age going after someone her age is disgusting and perverted and if he has a daughter her age, then he is even more perverted.

The perverted 'ordinary bloke' in front of me stares at my pink Bible. The bell of the door tings and Gail steps out. 'What's going on?' she asks.

Just Some Guy looks up from the book at her. A thousand thoughts flit across his face as he takes her in, and I wonder if she can see them, understand them. He's older than me, probably from a generation where many, many people didn't necessarily believe in God but didn't actively disbelieve, either. They quietly ignored that part of life, hoping it would go away, and only went to church for the usual festivals of life, maybe even for Christmas. He's wondering, in that way a secular person who has memories of religion once being a large part of his life would, if Gail is worth it. If it is worth denying the existence of his daughter(s) so he can get to screw someone this young.

'I don't have to put up with this shit,' he says.

'No, you really, *really* don't,' I say.

'What's she been saying to you?' Gail demands.

'I asked him how old his daughter was,' I state, 'and he claimed he didn't have one. So I asked him to swear on my Bible that he didn't have a daughter and he was about to, I think?' I turn towards him, thrusting the book a little closer to him as I do so. 'You were about to, weren't you? I mean, knowing I'm a nun and all, you were going to swear on my Bible that you don't have a daughter.'

'She's not even a nun any more,' Gail tells him. 'You're not even a nun any more,' she reminds me. I think it's meant to reassure him, but it does the opposite. His eyes flash fear. Fear that I was once a nun, fear that I may actually know him and what his family situation is because his daughters go to a religious school or I've seen them all at church.

'Here,' Gail says stroppily and clasps his hand in hers. 'Just swear.' She pushes his hand towards my Bible. 'It doesn't matter, it doesn't mean anything. Just swear and we can get out of here.'

He snatches his hand away and takes a step back. 'Get off me,' he spits. Suddenly he's a lot less distinguished and attractive, now he's far more obviously the pathetic, cowardly pervert he clearly is.

Gail frowns at him, her face a tumbling mass of confusion. Under the make-up, the dress, the coat falling off one shoulder, is a confused, naïve girl. She's seen so much, she's experienced so much, but there are still moments like this that will trip her, throw her back into the world of being a teenager, barely more than a young girl. 'Why won't you swear?' she asks. 'If you don't have a daughter, why won't you swear?'

'Screw this,' he says. To Gail he adds: 'I bet you would have been crap, anyway, so screw you.' The most venomous tone he reserves for me, all his contempt and hatred, bundled together and thrown at me with: 'And screw *you* backwards.'

I'm surprised as well as relieved that he actually walks away. I'm even more surprised to find Gail has her face in her hands and is sobbing her heart out.

'How did you know?' Gail asks me. 'How did you know he had a daughter and that he was lying?'

She has both hands around a cup of coffee, and has pulled her coat up properly on to her hunched shoulders and stares into the drink's black depths as she speaks.

'How did I know that a man who wanted to have sex with a fourteen-year-old girl was probably a lying toad? I don't know, lucky guess?'

'He thought I was older. I told him I was nineteen.'

'Right, course you did, and you think he really believed that? He was mid-forties *at least*. And wearing a wedding ring. He has been around long enough to know you are not nineteen, no matter what he would have told everyone afterwards. He's old enough and experienced enough to know that girls – and that's what you are, sorry – always dress to look older. And if, by some miracle upon miracles, he was the one forty-something man in the world who didn't know that you were probably lying about your age, then I'd wager in his mind he would be *hoping* you were younger than nineteen so he'd have got away with having sex with a girl the same age as his daughter.'

She purses her lips together before raising her gaze. 'Are nuns even allowed to say "sex"?' she asks.

'I'm not a nun any more,' I reply.

'Yeah, right,' she says.

The man behind the counter, with his balding head and clean white apron, approaches with two fresh cups of coffee. When we came back in, I noticed that he had positioned himself on the other side of the counter, right near the exit, where he would have been able to dart out of the door and step in should things have turned nasty with Just Some Guy. When we returned to the table where I'd been sitting, he seemed to conjure from nowhere Gail's peanut butter and banana bagel, and coffee, gave me a nod of approval and murmured 'Good work' as he placed them in front of her. This time as he leaves our refills, he gives me a sad look – he's obviously seen girls like Gail in his place many, many times. He's probably glad that she isn't back out there with Just Some Guy, having who knows what done to her.

'How often do you go out like this, Gail?' I ask her.

Gail rests her head on one hand and stares at the table, shrugs. 'Dunno, once or twice?'

So that'll be three or four times, I immediately think. 'Do you get very drunk and take drugs every time?' I ask.

I remember the drugs headline scandals involving Nika before she disappeared from the magazines and papers. Her footballer boyfriend had been pictured with the coke he'd confiscated from her and the whole thing had blown up. He was the clean-living sportsman who was being brought down by his drink-loving, drug-fuelled girlfriend. But he vowed to stand by her while she went to rehab and got herself help. I had known it wasn't true. Nika, Nikky, whatever she was called, would never have taken drugs. Even after all these years, I knew Nika would rather suffer than give in to things like drugs.

'What's it to you? Why do you care what I do?' Gail asks.

'It's nothing to me, I suppose,' I tell her. 'But I care what you do because, well, you remind me of someone. And even if you didn't remind me of her, you're an interesting person, Gail. Despite the way you constantly have a go at me, I really like you.'

Her gaze flickers up at me for a moment, trying to gauge, probably, how serious I am. 'You think I'm interesting?' she mumbles.

'Yes. I genuinely find you interesting, and I truly believe you're important. Not like the men like Just Some Guy, who pretend to be interested in you so they can have s—' I'm not a nun any more, but having her question whether nuns can say 'sex' makes me falter on the word. Of course we can say it. Sex, sex, sex, sex, sex, sex, sex. We can say it as many times as we want. I'm self-conscious now she's brought it up. 'So they can have their way with you.' Now I sound like a prude, which a lot of people think nuns are but we're not. Not that I'm a nun any more.

Gail's lips turn upwards in a small smile. 'You're really weird,' she says.

'Wow, thank you, that's the nicest thing anyone's said to me all night.'

'Well, you are. I mean,' she looks around us, 'look where you're sitting at, like, three of the a.m. That's weird shit.'

'Where does your mother think you are?' I ask her. She isn't going to answer the drugs question, so I'll try another line of questioning.

'Dunno. At home, probably.'

'Does she work nights?' I ask.

'No, she goes out at night.'

'Where?'

'Dunno. She doesn't tell me. It's like, she's free to do what she wants now cos I'm old enough to be left alone and when I wasn't old enough she got herself a built-in babysitter.'

'I don't understand, sorry.'

'My stepdad.'

'Right. He stays in rather than go out with your mum?'

'He used to, but now they go out together sometimes, too.'

I know what she is telling me, even if she doesn't realise that's what she is saying. 'Do you get on with your stepfather?' I ask. I watch her answer. She doesn't reply straight away: she thinks about it, watches the still surface of her drink.

'Dunno,' she replies. 'Suppose.' A pause. 'Not like anything would change if I didn't get on with him, is it? So I make the best of it.'

'What do you mean?' I have teased information out of people before, but that was when they thought the way I dressed made me similar to a priest and everything I said was confidential until the day I die.

'He's a good bloke,' she says. 'Everyone says so. My real father, he's not around at all and that's cos he was a real bastard to my mum. Used to hit her and stuff, was really controlling and wouldn't let her go out, shouted at me and my brothers all the time. Then my mum met my stepdad and, you know, with his support she found the courage to leave. And everyone says how much of a good guy he is. He's got a good job so we can live in a really posh house, and he doesn't hit my mum, he lets her go out whenever she wants, gives her loads of money. Everyone says it all the time: "You've landed on your feet with him, Cecile. He's one of the good ones."'

'And what do you think?'

She shrugs at me, continues to stare into her drink, removed from what she is saying, set apart from who she is saying it to.

'Do your brothers like him?' I ask.

'I dunno, do I? I hardly ever see them.'

'So it's you and your stepfather alone in the house most of the time?' I ask. Is that a prod too far? Is she ready to admit anything?

Her gaze travels up from her cup, over my body until it hits my face. Her eyes are slightly narrowed, her lips a little twisted with scorn. 'If you've got something to ask me, just ask it,' she says. Right now, right this second, gone is the vulnerable girl who was going to drink some more and probably take drugs and let herself get screwed by a pervert, while pretending it was all her idea. In *that* girl's place is a defensive fourteen-year-old who has 'bitch' written all over her face.

'The thing is, Gail, I know that if I ask you, you're very likely to shout at me, or call me sick and twisted, and you're more than likely to leave. And then you'll have no one to talk to or – worse – you'll leave here and go find someone else to finish what you started with Just Some Guy earlier. So, no, I don't think I will ask you that question, actually.'

She sits back in her seat, shakes her head at me. 'Wouldn't God tell you to be brave and ask me anyway, no matter what the consequences are?' Gail has a real way about her, a way to make snarky things sound even snider, nastier. She is wrapped in a layer of so many prickles it would be impossible to get close to her without being hurt in many, many ways. She really is the younger version of me.

'No, God wouldn't tell me to do that or to do anything at all,' I tell her calmly. 'God doesn't actually speak to me directly. I thought you knew that? And even if He did actually speak to me directly, I have free will so I could do whatever I wanted no matter what He told me. We all have free will.'

Gail's hard face hasn't slackened at all.

'I mean, you have free will, Gail. You could choose to tell me what question you thought I was going to ask and you could answer it. That would be your choice.' I want to look away, to concede to the challenge her look is throwing at me, but that would lose her. She would think I am weak and can't handle it. That another person has entered her life, offered her something only to not deliver. 'I sense choice is important to you, Gail. And you can choose to tell me or you can choose not to tell me. That would be up to you. And if you do choose to tell me, I will believe you.'

We sit in silence for a few minutes. Neither of us is going to give in at this juncture, we both have too much face to lose.

'If I told you something,' she eventually says, still with 'the face' on her, 'you'd have to keep it a secret, wouldn't you? You wouldn't be allowed to tell anyone, would you?'

'I would, actually, because I'm not a nun any more. And even when I was a nun, I wasn't authorised to administer the sacrament of confession so whatever was said to me wouldn't have the sanctity of the confessional booth. But even though I *could* tell, I never did. I never would. If someone tells me something in confidence, I keep it. Always.' *I am excellent at keeping secrets.* Shamefully, I realise I have taken pride in that. Pride is a deadly sin.

'All right, I'll tell you,' she says. She drops 'the face' and stares at the table, gulping quickly but silently, obviously building herself up. Her eyes fly up to my face. 'And you won't tell anyone? You promise you'll keep it a secret for the rest of your life?'

'I promise.'

'This is really hard for me to say, you know?' she says, her face pensive and her hands knitted together as she plays with her thumbnails.

'I know,' I say gently.

Gail's large, brown, well-made-up eyes fill with tears as she continues to gather her courage.

I almost reach across the table to take her hand and reassure her, but decide against it. Any sudden movements may scare her, put her off.

After two more gulps, she looks directly at me, and I can see the agony and burden in every line of her features. She looks so much older and so much younger at the same time. 'When I was about nine or ten,' she says in a tone so low I have to lean forwards to hear her properly, 'I-I said "fuck" in church and I wasn't even sorry.'

Her grin is beatific, her brief 'got ya' eyebrow raise precisely delivered. Slowly I sit back in my seat and allow her to revel in getting one over on me. *This* is what is known as the fall after a moment of pride.

Nika

Of course I didn't see my parents.

Who was I trying to kid with *that* thought process? I was high on the fact I'd faced Todd and hadn't crumbled, so I thought I could do anything, take on anyone. I got right up to their door then reality came pouring into my head. These were the people who had let their seventeen-year-old daughter walk out instead of just considering if, for one moment, what she'd told them years ago and had kept telling them ever since was true – that there was a trusted person hurting her and she wanted them to make it stop.

The Todds of the world I could take on after ten years on the streets, but my parents? The people I'd always instinctively love no matter how badly they hurt me? No. Just no. I'd never be brave enough to do that. I almost ran back to the bus stop so I could get a Tube to Victoria and then a train back to Brighton. Now here I sit in the dark with my guitar on my lap, lightly running my fingers over the strings, touching them so gently they barely make a sound. I stare at the mantelpiece and decide to buy myself a small CD player to go just there so I can listen to music in the flat.

I wonder what Reese is doing, right now. Is he high? Is he still needing regular medical treatment? Is he clean after his stint in hospital? Is he having to take more beatings from Judge because he doesn't know where I am?

I think about Lori. Is she safe after everything that happened, after what I had to force her to do to get away from Judge?

I wonder about Mama Meachen, who came on to the streets five years ago and who cried and cried for her children. If I saw her, I would buy her coffee at Bernie's and would sit with her while she cried and told me her story as many times as I was willing to listen. She'd had no money, she hadn't wanted to be a benefits scrounger, she'd seen how people looked down on *them*. She'd only taken on that extra cleaning job but hadn't declared it to make ends meet and then she was being taken in for questioning, then the police were involved, then she was doing a little stretch of time. But during that 'time', her children had been taken into care, and she'd had a breakdown and she'd lost her flat. And now no one would listen to her, no one would help. She was only allowed to write to her children, and her world was so small and everything so bleak. She cried and talked and constantly retold her story because, I knew, she hoped that when she got to the end of that particular retelling everything would be different and she would be explaining how she was with her children again.

I think about Crazy Doug, who'd called himself that since university when he was at the top of his game. He said he used to work in the City, doing deals that would make your eyes water, until he'd started hearing voices one day and couldn't shut them out with the booze any more. He had started missing time at work, trying to shut out the voices. Everyone else had started to call him Crazy Doug, in mean, nasty ways, until he'd woken up one day and hadn't known which voice wasn't real and which was his own, and nothing had been the same since. I liked the stories Doug used to tell about the high-flying people he worked with and how utterly irredeemable they all seemed.

I wonder about Melvin, the wannabe street hustler who tried to act like Huggy Bear from *Starksy and Hutch*, but couldn't seem to get rid of his posh Etonian accent.

I think of Aimee, two e's no y, who would tell a different story to everyone she met about the life she'd had before the streets, and you could be sure each new tale was more plausible than the last.

I think of Tessa, who had fled an abusive relationship and had been diagnosed with anxiety and depression – diseases no one could see. She'd tried to keep going but it had all got too much, the tablets hadn't worked fast enough, the waiting list for therapy had been so long and when she hadn't been able to work, her landlord, unable to see her condition, how devastating it was to her life, had moved her on. Out on to the streets, out of his sight, out of his mind.

I think of how I used to be one of them. I used to fit right into that world. I loved it when they called me Ace, when they talked to me because I was their friend. When we'd sit and plot about taking over the world, or what we would do if the 'normals' recognised us as people.

I think of all those people I met over the years, who lived on the streets, who lived in the shelters, who would seem to appear one day and not be around the next, who were all part of that world where we would step through that divide that made us invisible. I think of them and I want to be back with them. I fitted there. I belonged there. I still feel sometimes that I'm playing at all this, that tomorrow I'm going to wake up and I'll be back in my room at the hostel, or I'll be round the back of the supermarket, and needing to go to the library for a wash and a wee.

That policeman had asked me if *that* was the life I was meant to live and I had thought no, I had thought that this – sleeping in a bed, eating in a small kitchen, having my days mapped out by the hours and rules of working life – was the life I was meant to live. What if it isn't like that after all? What if the life I am meant to live is not here, but out there, being Grace 'Ace' Carter with all those people I know, and all the people whose lives I heard about and can relate to? What if my life is meant to be lived as an invisible?

I reach over my guitar and pick up my mobile. I have two numbers programmed into it – Sasha's and the hotel. Maybe part of the problem of feeling like this life isn't my real life is that I have no connections, no real links to anyone. Maybe part of the problem is that Nika Harper needs to reach out and make as many connections as she can.

Hi Marshall. Do you fancy trying that kissing thing again? Nika

I press send before I change my mind, before I start to convince myself that I'd really like to live my life as Grace Carter again, forgetting all the people who'll be in danger if I go back to that life.

Absolutely. 15 mins? x

More like 5.

Your place or mine? M x

Yours. See you soon. N

Of course, his. I lay aside the guitar, pick up my keys, slip on my glasses. I might be trying to reach out, make connections, but I'm not ready to let him in completely.

Birmingham, 2015

Reese was waiting for me outside my workplace, which meant something serious had happened. He'd been sober and straight for a while now, he was daily going to the day centre and searching through options on what he could do next. He was looking much better, too. He'd taken to staying in a halfway house, so he had access to washing facilities, and his clothes were clean for longer periods, his face was clean, he'd even started to grow his hair in, and was flirting with the idea of shaving off his beard. He was often telling me while staring right into my eyes that he wanted to do something with his life, to maybe settle down with someone. When I saw him standing across the street, his manner tense, his face barely masking the terror, I knew it was serious.

'Who is it?' I asked him. I was expecting to hear of an accidental overdose, an arrest, a person who'd simply decided enough was

266

enough and whited out. (I was secretly shoring myself up for the day when Reese would decide that, when he fell into the hole again with no intention of waking up again after a huge hit.)

'Oh, God,' I replied when he told me. 'Oh, God, oh, God, oh, *God*!' This was probably the worst one. I'd actually forgotten. In four short weeks I'd turned my thoughts in on myself and I'd forgotten. 'You'd better show me.'

Lori sat on a torn piece of cardboard under the arches down by the canal. If she was in hiding it wasn't a very good place to hide, since everyone who lived on the street came down here at some point, but Reese probably took her there to make her feel safe. The solidity of the bricks, and the sheltering nature of the arches, made it feel secure. You could see light at either end, but you could have your back to the wall, use it to prop yourself up, and have the tranquil sound of water flowing beside you, too. I used to come here a lot, when I first lived outside. I never slept here because too many other people did, but I liked to be here when I needed to be alone and feel safe.

'I'm sorry I didn't listen to you,' she said when I sat down beside her. 'I'm sorry I thought I knew everything and it'd be different for me.'

'Tell me what's happened.'

'He says I've got to pay him back for everything he's subbed me. Everything, with interest. Judge. I thought he really meant it when he said he'd look out for me and everything seemed so much easier. And he was so, so nice to me. I didn't think he'd do this. I just want to go home. But I can't. He said if I don't pay him eight hundred pounds by Friday, I'm going to have to work for him. He said it'd only be for a little while, and he'd pick really nice men for me, but if he doesn't get his eight hundred then that's what I've got to do.'

Eight hundred. Judge was a bastard. I knew it, I'd always known it, but at moments like that, it was a stark reminder of exactly how evil he was. He knew she was little more than fourteen or fifteen, he knew this would break a person's soul, and he probably got off on it.

Breaking someone, making them his to use, was what he liked best, I think. Making money from that simply added to his pleasure.

Eight hundred pounds. My stomach turned over for her, I was suddenly hot and cold at the same time. There was no way she could raise even half of that. Running away was an option, but it'd have to be right away if he wasn't going to find her, and anyway, she'd just fall prey to the same thing in another town. Lori desperately wanted to be loved and wanted, for someone to take care of her. It was easy to see Judge was a bad man, but if life had been bad enough for her to run away, to stay away for this long, then she was going to overlook the obvious markers on someone like him until that moment came. If she stayed here and tried to reason with him, he'd have no worries about hurting her very badly – not so badly she couldn't 'work' but badly enough that she would know she was his.

'What are we going to do?' Reese asked. Apart from me, Reese didn't generally befriend new ones. He was nice to them, he looked out for them if it was his turn to in the shelters, but he was usually strictly arm's length – known to everyone, friend to few. He preferred it that way to protect against the times when he fell down the hole. He obviously saw something kindred in Lori because he had made it his problem, too.

'Fuck knows,' I whispered. I couldn't think, panic and flashbacks were stopping my mind from forming thoughts and hanging on to the ones that did come up. I didn't want her to end up like some of the other women I had seen working for Judge – not least because their usefulness had a short shelf life, and normals rarely noticed when they disappeared permanently. I didn't even want her to end up like me, and I was something of a homeless success story in that I'd been 'out here' on and off for over ten years and I was still alive and drug-free.

Right then, I needed music. I needed music to stroke its melodies over my mind, hush me and settle me enough that I could think. I needed to think.

'I'm so sorry, I'm so sorry,' Lori whimpered beside me. She wouldn't last very long at all.

Reese was wearing the hat I'd got him for Christmas last year. He still had his last one, but I was sure he put on the blue woolly one I made him whenever he saw me to make me happy. I remembered the driving licence he got me all those years ago. If Reese hadn't helped me, would I be the me I am today, or would I have been used up and spat out by Judge, or someone like him, a long time ago? 'How many people do you think you can get together to help us?' I asked Reese.

'Twelve, maybe fifteen.'

'It can't be anyone who's using at the moment,' I told him. He knew I was including him in that.

'I'm clean,' he said defensively. 'And if they're definitely not using, then maybe ten.'

'Right, OK. With us, that makes twelve. We've got four days to each get eighty quid. It doesn't matter how. We just need eighty each. When you explain to them what it's for, I'm sure they'll help. They just need to make eighty quid by Thursday.'

'Eighty?' Reese asked. 'But she said he wanted eight hundred.'

'Yeah, and no one has ever paid him back before. I bet you he wants a grand when we go to hand it over.'

'We? I ain't going to hand it over, Ace. Are you crazy? I'll help, I'll get everyone else to help, but I ain't going near him.'

'All right, I'll take her then,' I said. Judge's leering face as he reminded me of what he'd got me to do that night came into view, but I shoved it aside, dumped it on to the pile with all my other horrifying memories. 'We'll meet here on Thursday night.' I turned back to Lori. 'You can come stay at my place until then. You have to keep out of sight because I'll be chucked out if anyone finds out you're staying there, even for a little while. But we just need to keep you away from Judge until Friday.'

'Thank you,' she said between sobs. 'Thank you. Thank you. Thank you.'

I sat on the window ledge, the windows opened wide so I could smoke without the whole room smelling of cigarettes. I could be chucked

269

out for that, too. Time was when you could smoke in your room, but not any more. I had actually given up over fifteen years ago. These past four days I'd started again.

Lori was sleeping in my bed, her gentle snoring filling the room. I'd have to face the Devil tomorrow. And I couldn't sleep for thinking about it. I drew on my cigarette, felt that horror that seemed to live permanently at the bottom of my stomach rise up. More than anything I wished I could plug my music player into my ears, and play something to take me out of here for a while. I couldn't, though, I didn't have a music player any more. I wished I could plug my music player into my ears, and have something that would drown out the sound of the 'Dance of the Sugar Plum Fairy' playing over and over in my head.

'You have my money, Little One?' Judge asked. We'd found him in one of the booths in a pub on the other side of the city. There were several pubs that he 'owned' – in that he could walk in at any time and people would clear out of his booth, the bar staff would bring him his usual order and everyone knew well enough to stay away. While he spoke to her, he was focusing the strength of his navy-blue eyes on her, his non-physical way of terrifying her, ensuring that she would submit to all his demands. He was also pretending I wasn't there, for now.

'Yes,' she said quietly. She glanced sideways at me before she reached into her inside pocket and removed the white envelope and laid it on the table in front of him, next to his teacup. He was taking tea, a full white china tea set – down to the fancy sieve – was laid out in front of him. He wasn't a drinker. Everyone knew that. Judge always liked to be in control, which is why he never took drugs, never drank alcohol and was always trying to push them on to other people.

That envelope Lori had laid in front of him wasn't simply full of money: it was bulging with the things a group of people had done to help out a young girl; it was crammed with all of our dreams of a different life, our chance to rescue her from the life we were living.

Judge slowly took a sip of his tea, settled his cup back on to its saucer. He didn't pick up the envelope, or even acknowledge it, but instead he took his time to look up at her and then intensify his stare. She started to tremble as she stepped back so we were side by side again, in this together. 'I'm impressed. All eight hundred?' he asked.

'Yes,' she said quietly.

'Ah, Little One, I'm sorry, I really am, but it's actually a grand now. I was being kind, but it's a thousand I need from you, for the trouble and for being so patient. So,' he pushed the envelope back across the table in our direction, 'thank you, but no thank you, until you have it all.'

'Is it a grand, then, and the debt is all settled?' I asked through my dry mouth, my nervous, wobbly throat.

'Yes, Little One,' he said to Lori, while pointedly ignoring me, 'if you can get me another two hundred *pounds* in the next few hours the debt is settled.' He smiled sadly at her with his mouth closed, hiding his jewel that looked like a spot of blood on his front tooth. He pushed the envelope right to the edge of the table. 'Go on, take this, go off and have a good day. Report back to me here tomorrow morning and we'll get you started on paying back your debt.'

The next time I spoke I knew I'd be condemning myself. A part of me was terrified for what would happen to me, but most of me didn't care, really. I was doing this thing, it was going to go badly for me and I had found a way to be all right with that.

'All of it – the full thousand – is in the envelope. Count it and see. She got you the thousand.'

His hard stare shifted from Lori to the envelope, resting there. I could almost see him counting to ten in his head, reaching that, going to twenty... a hundred... a thousand... any number that would stop him going through the table as a shortcut to get to me.

'Well, ain't you the clever little psychic?' he said.

I said nothing and lowered my head, kept my gaze fixed on the red-carpeted floor.

'I presume this is all down to you, Ace?' he asked.

'Lori got the money herself. It's all her money, she's the one paying you back.' That had to be clear if Lori was to have a chance. After this, she had twenty-four hours at most to do what I said she had to do to get this money: she had to go and get help from social services. She was a child and they had to help her, it was the law. It might only be until she was sixteen, but those two years could make all the difference.

When we'd met last night at the arches to collect the money, everyone had told her what they had done to get it. They all spoke plainly, openly, about the crimes they had committed, the things they had sacrificed, the things they had endured, the repercussions they were going to experience, as they handed it to her.

We weren't simply going to give her that money: we wanted her to know what life was like out there, what she would go through if she stayed. She had to know that this wasn't only money we were giving her, it was the gift of a second chance. Something none of us had yet had.

I had sacrificed my music, had pawned my music player, knowing that it would be virtually impossible to get it back when I'd had to add some money from what I had stashed away to make up my eighty-quid share. She didn't realise how lost I was without my music, how it was the only thing that got me through the toughest times, that it was the place for me to hide. I'd wanted to explain that to her but couldn't. There were some things too private to share with anyone.

'Good for you, Little One. I guess you're free to go. But if you need any help, any time, come to me. My door will always be open to you.'

For the first time he looked at me. 'And you, Ace... I'll be catching up with you very soon.'

I nodded. I knew he would be. Over the years, when our paths had crossed, and he hadn't taunted me, he'd *always* given me the look that said he hadn't forgotten. He had a long memory, he didn't like the idea that he hadn't 'won' with me. It'd crossed my mind several times that there must have been other people who had turned him down, who had come close but had pulled away at the last minute. I'd never met any of them, though. It wasn't something to brag about, I suppose. I'd never told anyone about that last party I'd worked, about not taking his money so I would be free. Defying Judge wasn't something anyone would brag about if they wanted to stay healthy. Helping someone to escape Judge wasn't anything anyone did to stay healthy, either. My day 'catching up' with him was fast approaching, there were no two ways about it.

10

Nika

Kissing Marshall is so much fun.

We've been kissing for a week, and it's so much fun. I can't think of a word more appropriate. It is fun. With Vinnie, it was nice, but it wasn't like this. With Marshall, there is so much pleasure, so much to enjoy, so much to feel.

Eliza, who went away for the long Easter weekend visiting her parents and telling them everything (apparently), is still away, so we have no worries about her dropping by while we are kiss-kiss-kissing the evening away.

This evening, I haven't even bothered with going to my flat first or changing out of my grey maid's uniform. I have worked a double shift and have a lie-in tomorrow, so in my head, in my fantasies, this would be the time to see if I can move things forwards, strengthen that connection. *Knock-knock-knock* on his door and the varnished-wood door is suddenly thrown open and he is tugging me inside.

'I missed you,' he tells me with his lips against mine.

'Not as much as I missed you,' I reply. And the fun begins again. The kissing, his tongue gently exploring my mouth, my hands on his face, pulling him towards me until my back is against the wall and he is right up against my body. The fun shifts towards pleasure, sliding into desire. His kisses become firmer and he moves closer, presses himself against me a little harder. My fingers reach for his belt, unhook it, and then undo the top button of his trousers.

He pulls back a little. 'Are you sure about this, Nika?' he asks. 'There's no pressure to do this. Especially since I hardly know you and you hardly know me.'

'That's what makes it all the more fun,' I whisper back. 'We could be anybody.'

'Only if you're sure,' he says.

'Oh, yes, I'm sure.'

He steps away, takes my hand and pulls me down his wide hallway to the back of his flat. We pass the bathroom, the propped-open door of another bedroom, done up like the room of a young boy – obviously his son's room. On we go until we're in his bedroom. He shuts the door, and then we're on each other, he's slipping my jacket off my shoulders, I'm unzipping his trousers, unbuttoning his shirt, until my hands are on his chest feeling the short, curly chest hairs under my fingers. We fall on to the bed and move up, not kissing, partially undressing each other, until he reaches out for his bedside table, pulls open the drawer and takes out a condom. In the dark of the room, the heat of the moment, I feel safe enough to take off my glasses and leave them on the bedside table. His fingers are up the skirt of my uniform, pulling down my knickers. He kisses me again, deeper this time, harder, a promise of what is to come. He moans against my lips as I roll the condom on to him. Then the pause, the moment in the dark, where we stare into each other's eyes and I take him, guide him into me, causing us both to groan.

It all falls away, everything that I carry with me, that I've been clinging on to, falls and I am enjoying this. I am here. With someone. He is inside me and it is sublime, I am with him, and I am here. I am present. I have pleasure flowing through my veins. And I am here to witness it. He moves deeper into me and it's delicious, a thousand sparkles of an unnamed feeling swarming through every vein; I move against him and his moan fills every part of me with joy. We move together, groan together, hold each other, until we come together, the ecstasy of it reverberating around the room.

We haven't spoken since we came apart. We are side by side on his bed, both of us too spent to move, it seems. His body is wonderful next to mine. I am here. So often, during, but especially afterwards, I am not there, I do not feel, I try to scrub away every trace of it from my mind. I am here with Marshall and it feels . . . *good*. I haven't got a word for it because it's never happened in the past. *Good* is what this feels like, *good* is what this is.

Good that my body has been mine to do with as I please, good that I have felt pleasure from sex. Good that for the first time I have felt an equal in the act, in the initiating, in the participation, in the afterwards.

With Todd I didn't need to be there. My body was for him to dress up in the clothes he bought, and for him to have sex on when he wanted. And with Vinnie, it was something I did because we were in a relationship. Vinnie showed me that sex wasn't something to endure or to hate. It wasn't hideous, and he always showed me respect, but I was absent then, too, coming back afterwards and not feeling sick like I *always* did with Todd.

This is the first time I've had sex in my body. This is the first time I've realised I can experience pleasure from sex.

'Are you OK?' Marshall asks out of the blue. He pulls me into his arms, holds me close, kisses me on the forehead. He sounds concerned; his hold seems more comforting than post-coital closeness. 'Was doing that what you wanted?'

'Yes, of course,' I reply.

'I hope you didn't feel pressured or anything like that,' he says gently. 'I didn't mean for you to feel like we had to do that. I'd have been happy to wait, especially since we don't know each other very well.'

'I didn't feel pressured.' I'm confused now. This is the first time in so many years that I've wanted to have sex with someone and the first time *ever* that I've been present enough to enjoy it. Why would he think otherwise? 'That was what I wanted, and I really, *really* enjoyed it. Couldn't you tell?'

'Well, yeah, but you're crying.'

279

I'm crying? I touch my face, touch the tears that have escaped my eyes, tears I didn't even know had been shed. I wick them away, reach out and grab my glasses from the bedside table and fix them into place to hide any more of that. 'I'm sorry,' I say to him. 'It's not you, it's me and my mixed-up mind.' I sit up, safe enough to face him now I have my glasses on and my face obscured. He has a little frown crinkling his forehead as he stares up at me. 'It was amazing.' He reaches up and brushes a lock of hair away from my forehead, clearly not convinced. 'I was a little overcome. Haven't... Haven't done that in a very long time and, like I say, mixed-up mind up here.' Ostentatiously I lean forwards and press my lips on to his. 'I'm sorry if I've freaked you out, that was all good.'

'I just want to make sure that this is what you want.'

'Well, I guess there is one way I can prove to you that it's what I want.'

'Oh, yes?'

I climb on top of him and start to unzip my uniform. 'We could do it all over again but with far fewer clothes.'

'I like that idea. I like it a lot.'

Birmingham, 2016

I rubbed my aching fingers over my red, tired eyes as I left work, wandered down from the quiet side street where I'd just finished my cleaning shift and on to one of the larger main roads towards home.

I was tired, bordering on exhausted, but I'd been working every shift I could to make enough money to get my music player back, which I had, last week. I also needed to save as much as I could to get enough to cover my rent and bills when the inevitable happened with Judge and I would be out of work for a while. I didn't think he'd kill me, but he was going to hurt me very badly. I had, for the most part, squared that in my head. Accepted it as an inevitable consequence to getting involved with someone like him in the first place.

I'd thought about running away, of course, but his reputation meant he'd have to hurt someone else in my place. I had done this. I would have to take it. As far as I knew, Lori was as safe as she could be. That night we'd given him his money, I'd taken my sleeping bag and we'd both slept out on the streets, not hidden like usual, but out in the open. I'd slept across the road from her, so I could see her, but she was on her own and when the charity officials who worked with the most vulnerable homeless people had seen how young she was, they had approached her. I'd seen them before, knew they were genuine, so when she had gone with them, I knew this was the best chance for help she was going to get.

She'd waved at me as they'd walked away, and I had looked through her. I'd wanted to wave, I'd wanted to run up to her, hug her, tell her I hoped she went on to better things, but I couldn't. She had to know there was no option of her coming back here, that we wouldn't – couldn't – help her out again. If she came back, she'd be on her own, she'd owe the people who had given her money, she would be in real trouble and I wouldn't be able to help her. I wasn't sure I'd be in any position to help anyone, least of all myself.

I turned on to the main road, started down towards home, and as I hit the road, a play of light on the buildings opposite reminded me of the other Veronica.

Roni. Everything about her was vivid in my mind: her features, our friendship, her betrayal, the relentlessness of missing her . . . all moved through me in one gush, like a ghost passing through a solid object.

I stopped, almost winded by the thought of her. Why now? Why so powerfully? Had she died? Was this her coming through to me before she went on to wherever the dead go? Was this a warning that something awful was about to happen? On shaky legs I continued towards home, the fear of what that moment of Roni had meant spreading through me with each step.

I didn't notice the car at first. When I did notice it – black and shiny with blacked-out windows – I thought it was another kerb-crawler, mistaking me for a working girl. It kept pace with me a little too long to tell me it wasn't a kerb-crawler, then when it had my attention, it drove on a little before stopping. The back door popped open, sat gaping wide, like the mouth of a monster, ready to gobble me up in one gulp.

281

This was it, then. This was why Roni had come to mind. It wasn't she who was about to die – it was me. Then there would be only one Veronica Harper who grew up in Chiselwick, whose talent meant she could have been a real ballerina, whose life had been for ever changed by that love of dance. Slowly, I went towards the waiting mouth, stooped a little to look in. Judge's spot of ruby blood glinted at me as he grinned. 'Hello, Ace,' he said. 'Let's go for a little ride.'

Brighton, 2016

Marshall watches me getting dressed in the dark and doesn't say anything. I know he wants to ask me to stay. But that would be silly when I've got my own bed, five floors up, and we really don't know much about each other at all. Once I have everything on, I lean over the bed and kiss him. He doesn't say anything when I pull away, and neither do I. He carefully brushes my hair away from my forehead and looks sad for a moment. If he asks me to stay, I probably will, but I hope he doesn't. I hope he lets this thing develop naturally, slowly. I hope I do, too. Marshall lifts his hand in a wave and then rolls over, closes his eyes and pretends to go to sleep. And I let myself out of the flat, knowing that I'll be back again tomorrow.

Birmingham, 2016

Toto's 'Africa' played in my mind, over and over, as we drove out towards the derelict industrial area. They were redeveloping the area – it had been so barren and bleak most of the time I had lived here, but now it was being regenerated. The beauty that was always there, that was so clear and apparent in the city centre, was being remade out here. It would take years to complete, but when it was done, it would look spectacular.

I tried not to worry about what Judge would do, if he would leave me alive, if it would be so hideous I wouldn't be able to cope in the aftermath. Judge did not become who he was and did not control what he did without having the capability of doing things most people wouldn't dream of. I could not try to second-guess what he had in store for me, that would add to my torture. Instead, I composed a letter in my head to my parents.

Dear Mummy and Daddy,
I'm writing to you because I am at a time in my life when I probably won't see you again. I want to say I am sorry we never got to speak again. I wish things had been different. And I wish… I wish you had believed me. I know it was hard to hear, but I wish… But no matter, I suppose now. Please can you tell Marlon and Sasha that I wish I'd had the chance to get to know them properly.

As I mentally wrote the goodbye letter, something that would never been seen by anyone, my words became mingled with the words to 'Africa' ringing in my ears: *The need to hurry, how difficult it would be to keep the true loves apart, the feel of rain—*

The car came to a stop inside the shell of an old factory that had fallen out of use a long time ago. The roof was still on, but was punctuated by huge chunks of sky; the walls seemed strong and sturdy. No one would find me out here, of course. Not for a long while. I thought of Reese. He hadn't turned up for coffee last night or the night before and no one had seen him when I went looking. I wouldn't see him again. He would go to meet me for coffee and I wouldn't show up. And he would know that Judge had probably got me and that no one would find my body.

I unclipped my seatbelt, as did Judge. The futility and sheer oddness that came from securing my seatbelt when I'd got into a car to be driven off to be killed almost made me smile. I'd made sure I was in good condition for what I was about to be subjected to.

Judge had been staring at me the whole of the drive. We were the only people in the back of the car and his eyes, that intimidating blue gaze, had never left me the whole time. He probably expected me to try to talk him out of it, beg him, maybe. I hadn't. I wouldn't give him the additional pleasure of my begging then him hurting me anyway.

283

Judge's thick fingers ran carefully over his left eyebrow and he looked pained, genuinely agonised at having to do this. He had always seemed to me to be someone who liked the quiet control of the threat of violence, the power never having to carry out the threat brought him.

'I could never work you out, Ace,' he said. 'Right in the beginning, I noticed you, but could never work out who you were. You weren't a user, you didn't drink, didn't seem to want much of anything. You can't get involved with someone who doesn't want anything,' he said.

He was wrong, of course. I wanted lots of things, but those things I couldn't buy, couldn't trade for, couldn't have. I wanted lots of things all the time, but they were things no one could give to me.

'Part of the problem was that I could tell that you didn't care about yourself enough.' He opened his car door and got out. Slowly I did the same, for all the inevitability of this, I didn't want to rush towards it.

Once outside the car, I saw him: *Reese.*

I swung towards Judge, then back to Reese. My friend was standing a few feet away, flanked by two men bigger than him, stronger than him. My stomach lurched, and I suddenly knew what it was to be afraid. I thought I had been afraid before, I thought I had been scared on the drive out here, but now I was terrified – for Reese. My whole body was burning with terror.

Reese's thick woolly jumper, his long winter coat and the padded body warmer over it did nothing to hide how thin and fragile he was. When I'd first met him, he'd been wiry-looking; over the past few years he'd just become thin and ravaged by his habit, by the way he lived. He was clean right now, had been slowly putting on weight and looking normal, but sandwiched between the two men he seemed slight, delicate.

When he hadn't turned up for coffee the last two nights I'd thought he'd fallen down the hole again, after being clean for so long I thought he'd given in and was back where he had started.

'Do you know the day I knew I had you, Ace?' Judge said. 'When this one here came at you in the café, shouting and all sorts, and you just sat there and took it. Anyone else would have told him to fuck off, but not you, you sat there and took it because you cared about him. Caring about people is an admirable quality. Stupid, too. I knew I had you, then. All I had to do was talk to you when you were so shaken up by someone you cared about and you'd be working for me in no time.'

Reese's eyes were fixed on me, mine were fixed on him.

'*I'm sorry,*' I mouthed at Reese.

'You thought you were too good to work for me though, didn't you, Ace?' Judge continued. 'I made sure you were fucked by six men in one night, really hurt by a couple of them, too, and *still* it didn't turn you because you thought you were better than that. I let that slide. And then you take away Lori, my beautiful Little One. Do you know how many men I had lined up for her? How much someone so young could have made me? Punters pay through the nose for the virginal types. I had it all planned, laid all that groundwork, and you get involved with that.'

'*I'm so sorry,*' I mouthed again at my best friend.

'And then I realised: hurting you won't teach you a lesson in staying away from my stuff, will it, Ace? It might be momentarily satisfying, but you won't learn anything from it, will you?' He raised his whole arm to point his thick finger at Reese. 'But I reckon making sure he can never eat solid food again, or walk without a limp again, and a few other things, will make sure you *never play with my stuff again.*' He laughed; the sound was serrated, had a cutting edge that sliced through me like a buzz saw. 'What do you reckon?'

'I'm sorry,' I said to Judge. 'I'm sorry, Judge. Please don't do this. I'm sorry. I'm so, so sorry. I'll do anything, *anything.* You want me to work for you? I'll do it, I'll work for you and I'll never complain. You don't even have to pay me, I'll do whatever you want, but please don't do this. Please. Please.'

That was what he wanted. What Todd had wanted. Todd had never been happier than when I was begging him to love me again, saying sorry for upsetting him, trying to appease him by doing whatever unreasonable thing he wanted; all of it showing him that I knew my place and he was in absolute control. That was what Judge wanted, fundamentally. To know that he was in ultimate control, that no one thought they could go against him. If I had to do that – beg, lower myself, sleep with whoever he wanted – to save Reese I would. I absolutely would.

'It's good to see you finally know your place, Ace,' Judge said. 'But it's come a little too late. I can't let you get away with this. It'd make others think they can, too.' He nodded at me. 'Do you see? You've done this. You. You've done this to your friend, here. Not me, you.'

'Oh please, oh please, oh please,' I begged desperately. 'Oh plea—' The sound that came from Reese made me clamp my hands over my ears as it ripped though every fibre in my body. It kept coming, the sound, the agony, the sight of what was happening. Over it all were Judge's words: '*You've done this. You. You. You. You.*'

Roni

There's something pleasant and unpleasant about Tube journeys. I am on my way back from confession at the north-west London church that has started to feel a bit like my parish church and the train is packed with shoppers on their way home, and partygoers on their way out. Between stations, while the train hurtles from one stop to another, I shut my eyes, try to find a state of mind where I won't have the noise and voices of my past constantly screaming at me. I try to find some semblance of silence, try to remember why it was a good idea to leave the convent.

I remember how much fun it was being among the Sisters. Every day was different, we would find so many things to laugh and joke about. At recreation, we would all be doing different things, sewing, knitting, reading, drawing, simply chatting, and it would be like how I imagined boarding school would be. We'd be all together, friends, spending time together, getting to know each other, chatting about our day and what was going on in the outside world. Those of us who actually went out – ministering with the homeless, women's shelters, working in the hospitals attached to convents or, like me, teaching at convent schools – would sometimes share our observations with our Sisters, but we had to be careful not to bring outside burdens and miseries and frivolities with us. If something happened that added to our understanding of Scripture or prayer, or there were people we would like to pray for, we would share it, but nothing else.

Recently, yes, it'd been harder to find the silence in the monastery, even in prayer, and the Great Silence was sometimes the start of the most difficult part of my day, but should I have left? Really?

Yes, I wanted to find Nika, to quell the feeling inside that I am Judas, but really, what was it that stopped me from simply revealing all in confession and then moving on, having been absolved? The priest in the north London church said it the first time I spoke to him: I have been punishing myself all this time. Was it really necessary to do so?

The train lurches to a noisy stop, jerking people forwards then back as it does so. The doors open, announcements fill the air, there is a burst of noise as people enter and exit the carriage. The closer we get to Chiselwick, the more people leave and the fewer people get on to take their places. My carriage is practically empty now, no one is standing, I am alone on this bank of seats and only a couple of people occupy the seats opposite me in this section. The doors bleep then shut firmly together. I am about to close my eyes when I realise the person opposite is studiously staring away along the carriage, obviously trying to avoid being noticed by me.

'Well, this is awkward,' I say to him.

He grins before he reluctantly looks in my direction. 'Who for? Me, who has left more than a couple of messages for you, or you, who hasn't returned any of them?'

'Not sure, really,' I say. Who knew London was so small you'd constantly be running into the same people? I pick up my bag and cross the aisle to sit next to Cliff. 'I guess awkward kind of covers both of us in that scenario.'

He smiles again. 'Am I allowed to ask why you haven't returned my calls, apart from the obvious?'

'What's the obvious?'

'That you want nothing to do with me.'

'Oh, no, it's not that.'

'You do want something to do with me?'

'I think so.'

'But you haven't returned any of my calls because...?'

'Truthfully, because there's something I have to do and I don't want to get distracted by anything while I try to do it.'

'Ahhh, I see ... so you're on a mission from God.'

We both laugh. He's nice when he laughs – he's nice when he doesn't laugh, too. He seems genuine. I have seen so many sides of people over the years. They reveal themselves in so many different and seemingly insignificant ways, and most of the time, they don't even realise they are doing it. Do they double-park? Do they spit in the street? Do they interrupt other people? Do they say thank you to someone who lets them go in their car even if the other person won't hear? All little indicators of the soul of a person. Cliff seems to have a sincere soul, there have been no little tells so far with him that he isn't who he seems to be. 'No, I'm not a Blues Brother, thank you, Clifford.'

'Hey, you're the one who made it sound like that's what it was.'

'I suppose I did.'

The train rolls into the station, slower this time. Maybe because there are longer pauses between stations the further away from central London we move, the driver doesn't feel the need to speed up quickly and then brake as though trying to avoid hitting an animal on the track.

'What was it like, being a nun?' Cliff asks. 'Did you have to sit and talk about God all the time?'

'No, not really. We didn't talk much, we spent a lot of time in silence, but when we weren't in silence we had a lot of fun. We're just normal people, who happen to devote our lives to God and doing His work.'

'That's just it: do normal people do that?'

'I like to think I'm normal,' I say. 'All the nuns and Sisters I ever met were normal. We simply have God at the heart of everything we do. We try to be kind, to show the love and beauty of God to others if we meet them, but also to pray for the love of our Lord to surround and protect the people of the world. Being a nun or a Sister isn't like a job, it's a vocation, it's part of who you are. You don't simply switch it off at the end of the day, you don't ever stop trying to put God at the centre of everything you do, just like you don't switch off being married at the end of the day. You are a normal person when you're married, and you're a normal person when you devote your life to God.'

'I suppose I have issues with the awful things that people do in God's name,' Cliff replies.

'Me, too,' I admit. 'I also have issues with the atrocities committed by elected officials in my name, your name, and the names of everyone who did and didn't vote for them.'

Cliff looks me over like he is impressed by me, his gaze lingering on my lips. He's attracted to me but he also seems quite taken by who I am as a person as well.

'Why did you stop being a nun?' he asks and eventually draws his gaze up from my mouth to my eyes.

'I told you, I have something to do and I couldn't do it while being a nun. I couldn't do it and put God at the heart of everything I do. At the heart of most of it, but not everything.'

'It's not because you missed things, like, say, physical contact?' Cliff is trying hard not to look at my mouth; I think he's trying hard not to imagine what it'd be like to kiss me.

I am finding it hard not to think about what it'd be like to kiss him. I can't remember the last time I kissed someone, or someone kissed me. During my wild time there wasn't very much kissing at all. The last person I can remember kissing with any clarity is Big T when I was fifteen, just before Nika asked me to go to the police with her. That was over twenty years ago. After that, it is hazy because I stopped going out as much. And the men from the clubs rarely wanted to kiss when they realised that they didn't need to. When they gathered by how drunk and compliant I was that simply getting me alone was enough to get what they wanted, they rarely bothered with much of anything except the stuff that got them to orgasm.

'I sometimes missed physical contact,' I say. Sometimes I would have liked to have curled up in someone's arms, been held by them, felt safe and protected. Emotionally, I felt like that with God, but not physically. Sometimes I missed the physicality of sex, the closeness it brought between two people. Only sometimes, though. Mostly sex had been complicated and muddled and sullied by what else had been going on at the same time, so I didn't miss it, I simply missed what it represented, how close it brought me sometimes to the silence and how far away it took me from the screeching inside my head. 'I really missed being hugged.'

'Right,' Cliff says. 'Being hugged.'

He stares into my eyes, his gaze unwavering.

'Is there something you'd like to ask me, Cliff?' I query.

He's wondering if he'd dare. The train pulls into the next station – I must be nearly there at West Chiselwick, the closest Tube station to my parents' house. I don't want to look away, though, to check, to break eye contact when Cliff and I have got to this point.

'Yes,' he replies, still gazing directly into my eyes.

'Ask away.'

'Can I kiss you?' His voice is barely above a whisper, even though we are the only ones in this part of the carriage. There are only three other people at the far end of the carriage, too. We are practically alone, but he is still whispering.

I shake my head. 'Not until you ask me that question you've been dying to ask since we first met,' I respond in the same low voice.

From the corner of my eye I spot the station we are pulling into: West Chiselwick.

'This is my stop, Cliff, sorry.' I gather my bag and stand up. 'I'll see you.' I make for the door and he sits, stunned that he's been thwarted at such a crucial moment.

'I'll call you,' he shouts after me as I step out of the doors.

I stand on the platform while the doors beep shut. I raise my hand and wave. He makes the 'call me' sign in between waving at me. I'm not going to call him. I want to, I'd love to, but I can't. Not until I've done this thing that I need to do.

Nika

Brighton, 2016

Most of the time, we don't make it to the bedroom. I barely make it through Marshall's front door and he is all over me, I am all over him: we're tugging at each other's clothes; kissing each other's lips, necks, faces, any bare skin; we're touching each other, pulling each other near, he's entering me, I'm holding him as close as I can; we're orgasming; and then we're laughing at ourselves for being so needy and craven and desperate.

This evening has been intense: he was loud as he orgasmed with his face against my neck; I had to close my eyes tight to stop myself dissolving into uncontrollable tears as the waves of what felt like ecstasy flowed through my body. We did it again on the sofa, screwing instead of him cooking me noodle stir-fry like he'd promised. Now it's late and a lazy fug has settled over us. We sit on the sofa, me in my vest top and knickers, him topless with his jeans undone. This is what it was meant to feel like with Todd, but it never did. Whenever we cuddled up, there was always the sense that it was fake, forced; I was always on edge, waiting for that moment when he'd let me know I'd upset him, that I'd cracked one of those eggshells I constantly walked on and I would need to spend the evening apologising and trying to make things right.

'These are good noodles,' I say to Marshall.

'I have to agree with you that they are indeed fine noodles.'

I dig my toe in his bare side and he laughs while twisting away. 'Nothing like a spot of modesty to keep you on an even keel, eh, Mr Marshall?'

'What? Why deny it if you're good at something?'

'I suppose so.'

'Come on then, Ms Nika, we really should at least attempt to get to know each other. If only so we've got something to talk about between sessions.'

'I suppose you're right. How long have you been divorced?'

'Three years, four months and ... um ... five days.'

'You know the exact amount of time?'

'Yeah. Not really my choice – she didn't love me any more and wanted out. So, I moved over here from Worthing way and we worked hard not to get bitter about splitting up and we're sort of friends now and we are almost always on the same page when it comes to parenting our child.'

'How old's your son?'

'Nine. Nearly nine. I miss him, a lot. That's the hardest bit about being divorced; everything else I can deal with, but being away from him is not easy. I see him every other weekend, and sometimes during the week if he wants to because he has all these after-school activities I'd never get in the way of. He calls me when he wants to come over. He's got his room here and sometimes he comes to stay for a couple of weeks. But it's hard. And, don't get offended, but I don't ever involve anyone in my relationship with him. It has to be a long-term thing before I think about introducing him to anyone.'

'That's very sensible,' I say.

'Me, sensible. Wow, that's something I never thought I'd hear. Your turn: when was your last significant relationship?'

'Erm ... the last person I called a boyfriend and lived with was about five years ago? I think? Yeah, five years ago. Wow, I keep forgetting how old I am now. Five years. OK, now you: what's your favourite flavour jelly bean?'

'Whoa, what is this, an interrogation? That's a very personal question. I'll have to get back to you on that one. Your turn: why did you freak out in the restaurant the first night we went out?'

I sigh. It is easy to be honest with Marshall, but how much honesty can he take before he starts to wonder if being connected to me is actually a good idea? 'Because I often feel I don't fit in and I don't belong in nice places. I panicked that night that everyone would see that I was a fraud and they'd laugh at me, or worse, I'd be asked to leave. I know, I know it's irrational, but I can't help it sometimes.'

'You're no fraud, Nika.'

'Why, thank you. Your turn: what is the one song that you're most embarrassed about listening to over and over and over?'

'I don't get embarrassed about my musical tastes. I'm a rap man at heart, but I like a bit soul, a bit of Motown, tiny bit of rare groove. Nothing to be embarrassed about there.'

'Don't believe you. Everyone has that one song they're embarrassed about – what's yours? Be honest.'

'Right, well, you must tell no one this: Paul McCartney's "No More Lonely Nights".'

I was not expecting that. I smirk at him, almost spitting noodles as I do so.

'Hey, come on, not fair. You mustn't do that. I was being honest, you told me to be honest.'

I smirk again. 'There is such a thing as too much honesty. And don't worry, I will *never, ever* tell anyone about that.'

'Right, what's yours?'

'I have loads. A few years back, I didn't have a computer but I had a music player and this woman I knew would put her music on it for me. Loads of stuff from the 1980s. And, intellectually, I know most of it is pretty terrible, but you know, I loved all that music. Apart from that "No More Lonely Nights" mess you were talking about right there... So there's loads of stuff that should be embarrassing that I've listened to over and over, but I'm kinda not. However, if I was to choose one, it'd be Toto's "Africa". I love the music, the relentlessness of the beat, but some of the lyrics... No matter how hard I try, I can't square the way they've managed to crowbar the word "Serengeti" into a song. I just can't. So it's that one.'

'Serengeti? As in the wide open space?'

'Yes, Serengeti. I mean, I can almost overlook how the song suggests that Africa is a country and not a continent, just, but the whole Serengeti—'

Knock-knock, ring-ring.

Marshall's fork stops on its journey to his mouth and the happy fug we've been chatting in starts to leak out of the room, chased away by the return of the person we haven't really talked about at all in the last three weeks. When she extended her trip by a week, then another, I guessed that she had probably lost her job and was at her parents' trying to hit them up for money, while she told Marshall she was trying to get help. (No one can extend their annual leave for that long so last-minute, but I kept my counsel in case I was wrong.)

'I'd forgotten she'd be back,' he murmurs. 'I mean, she rings me several times a day, but I'd kind of put her to the back of my mind. I thought we had a few more days at least.'

Knock-knock, ring-ring.

'I'm guessing she's not going to take finding out about us very well,' I say to him.

'No, she will not take this very well,' he says. 'She's sounded so together on the phone – what if it derails her recovery? I kept wondering if I should tell her on the phone before she came back. Now I'm convinced I should have.'

Knock-knock, ring-ring.

'Do you want me to go hide in the bedroom?'

Marshall inhales, steels his nerve. 'No. She's going to find out at some point, this is as good a time as any.'

He puts down his plate on the low coffee table in front of us, then gets up slowly, like a man approaching his execution. After leaving the room, he comes back, snatches up his T-shirt and puts it on, does up his trousers. I put down my plate, too. Pick up my shorts and struggle into them. Quickly, I roll on my socks, wrap my scarf around my neck, pull on my cardigan. I'm about to settle back when I notice my bra is on the floor, and I snatch it up. In the background I can hear the door opening, I can hear Eliza's hellos, the warmth of Marshall's reply. I don't have time to put it back on; if I hide it behind a cushion, she's bound to find it. I stare at the black lace bra like the time bomb it is, then shove it down the sleeve of my cardigan, fold my arms across my chest to hide the bulge it makes and to obscure the fact I'm not wearing the thing up my sleeve.

'Come in, stay for a drink,' he says loudly to warn me. 'Nika's here, we're having noodle stir-fry for dinner. I didn't know you'd be back today, otherwise I'd have made some for you, too.'

'Hi,' I say to her brightly when they appear in the doorway. 'Marshall mentioned you'd been away. Did you have a nice time?'

Eliza stares at me. She does not speak for thirty very long seconds, she simply stares, probably running through how she'd had 'the talk' with me, wondering why it didn't work as well as it had on the others. 'Nika,' she states. 'Fancy seeing you here.'

Marshall moves across to the kitchen area of his living room, glugs white wine into a large glass for Eliza and brings it to her. She sits on the armchair opposite where I am sitting on the sofa, holding the wine glass in one hand, the other hand gripped tightly on to the arm of the chair. When she is settled into place, she stares at me.

'You all right?' Marshall asks, tapping her on the shoulder, before he moves across the room. 'You're giving Nika some pretty heavy-duty death stares there.'

'Was I?' she says, and glances affectionately at him as he comes to sit on the sofa. 'Sorry, didn't mean to. My mind was elsewhere.' A few seconds later the green glare is back on me.

Marshall glances at me, before saying, 'Actually, Nika—'

'Was just leaving.' I edge forwards on my seat, and stand up without uncrossing my arms. 'I'm just leaving. It looks like you've got a lot to talk about, and I've got some stuff to do, so I'll see you both. I'll see you both soon.'

'Stay,' Marshall implores. 'Finish your noodles at least. You were just saying how good they were.'

'They are good, but I really should be going.'

'*Bye. Then,*' Eliza says.

I can't help but smile at her: she thinks a glare has intimidated me, that in my life I have been so sheltered something as simple as a glare from her will send me out of Marshall's life. It doesn't occur to her that I might be doing it for Marshall. He can't see it, but there is a new level of instability to her that makes her unpredictable and dangerous. How dangerous is something I can't yet gauge so better to withdraw until I can be prepared for her.

'Good to see you, Eliza, hope to see you again soon.'

'I'll see you out, Nika,' Marshall says.

When I am in the corridor, hidden from the main flat by the door, I run my fingers across my throat and shake my head at him. *Don't tell her,* I mouth at him.

He opens his hands. *Why?*

I shake my head. *Just don't.*

Open hands again. *Why?*

I wave my hands and shake my head. *Trust me, just don't do it.*

He shrugs. *OK.*

I press my fingers to my lips, loading them up with a kiss, then move my hands to him. He does the same to me.

I like him *so* much. It's not simply the sex, and the intensity, it's being connected to him. Being connected to him makes me feel like I'm connected to the world, that I can speak to people and I can try to sleep the whole night through. Being connected helps me believe there is more good than bad in the world, and that I will find my way through somehow. For the first time in so long, I have more than momentary, fleeting wisps of hope floating around me. I have a way to be connected to the world; I have the hope that, through this, I can *stay* connected.

'Do you hate me?' I asked Reese four days after Judge had him hurt. He'd been out cold for two of those days, drifting in out of consciousness for the other two. He'd had surgery on his left knee, had needed almost every finger to be set in splints ready for a cast in a few days, and his torso was wrapped up in bandages to help support his cracked ribs and bruised internal organs. The bruising on his face was minimal – they had wanted to hurt him, to make him scream, and he did that more when they hurt his body, not so much on his face. He was a mess, would probably be in hospital for a while because his injuries were severe and he had nowhere suitable to stay outside of hospital. I asked him if he hated me because since I had arrived today he had said nothing, absolutely nothing, to me. I had talked a little, but he had just stared at me as though he didn't know who I was, and I wasn't sure if he was pretending for the audience of the other patients in here, or if he genuinely didn't know who I was. Or, as was most likely, if he hated me.

In reply to my question, he glared at me for a moment, allowed his anger and disgust to find their target at the centre of my chest, then slowly moved his head away, looking out of the window on the small ward he was on. There were seven other beds in there, each spaced equidistant to each other, each with a side table, a chair for visitors and a long green curtain. I got up, pulled the curtain around the bed, sealing us in a little so we could talk a bit more freely. The other patients were focused on themselves, not us, but you couldn't be sure who was listening and what they would learn.

'I'm so sorry,' I said to him as I sat down, tucking my chair closer to the bed. I'd been saying that since he'd arrived here, before and after his surgery. Even though he'd been asleep, I'd been whispering it to him, hoping it would filter into his consciousness and he would know that I was here, and that he had someone to come back to. Someone who was so sorry for what had happened to him. 'I'm so, so sorry. I didn't know he'd do that.'

'You didn't have to go with her,' he said quietly. 'You could have let her go and give him the money on her own, so he'd never have known we were involved.'

'I couldn't have done that. You know that. He would never have just accepted that. He would have told her all sorts, hooked her back in. He couldn't do that with a witness who would tell everyone how he went back on his word. And he doesn't think you or anyone else was involved. Just me.'

'Just you?' he said, still looking away. They'd shaved his hair to put stitches in at the back of his head where it'd been kicked a couple of times. 'Look at me, Ace. Look what he's done to me because you wanted to help out some silly bint who wouldn't listen. Everyone had told her not to take stuff from him, not just you. Everyone told her and she wouldn't listen. You help her and look what happens to me.'

He'd wanted to help her out, too, he'd seen that thing in her that he'd seen in me and he'd wanted to help. The others had too. We'd all got involved because we were trying to turn back time, stop another person becoming us and erasing themselves from 'normal' life. He'd forgotten that desperate need to help he'd felt because he was in pain. He'd been hurt. His world had been turned upside down. He was right, too, he had been hurt because of me, he'd been a casualty because I'd got on the wrong side of a hideous person. He was like Frank the driver who lost his job all those years ago. Collateral damage. Frank and Reese were both collateral damage, victims of the choices I had made.

'You've got a death wish, ain't ya?' Reese said quietly but viciously, his words full of venom and anger. 'All that stuff he was saying, he was right – you don't care about yourself enough not to be reckless. That's why he hurt someone else, cos that *does* make you care, doesn't it? In all the time I've known you, Ace, you only ever get upset or show fear when someone else is in trouble. You're a fucking liability and downright dangerous to anyone who knows you when someone like Judge is involved because he can read people and a situation like that.'

'That's not true,' I protested even though it probably was true. Was something to do with the numbness that surrounded my emotions. It sounded like how my ability to blot out feeling much of anything would probably come across to other people.

Moving swiftly but carefully, trying not to dislodge or further damage anything, Reese turned back to me, his disgust becoming a quiet, low-burning anger as he stared at me. 'The fuck it isn't. The way you were begging him, promising him anything, would you have done that if he'd been about to do that to you?'

No. The answer was no.

'I would. The whole drive out there I was begging him for my life, promising all sorts, but I bet you didn't say a word until you saw me. *Then* no one could shut you up. It ain't on to have friends when you're so reckless about your own safety, Ace. It just ain't.'

'I'm sorry,' I said to him. 'I'll go. Leave you alone. I'm sorry. That's all I should have said, really – I'm sorry that I got you into this.' I rose from my seat.

'Nah, nah, don't go,' he said, softly. 'Sit down. Stay.'

'No, you're right, I shouldn't have friends when I am the way I am.'

'Oh, sit down, you silly cow. You know I don't mean half of it, I'm just mouthing off, ain't I?' Pain shot across his face as he tried to move his hand to tell me to sit. 'Sit down. You owe me, so sit down.'

I did as I was told. I remembered how that first night I met him he had said that when he was down the hole he collected every debt owed to him. I'd never owed him anything until now.

'Did he really make you fuck six men in one night?' Reese asked.

Their hands, their faces, their bodies, the sounds they made, what they did to me all came rushing back at me in a barrage of images, crawling through my mind, slithering over my body. I was immediately stiff and immobile, locked into that night. I forgot, most of the time; even when Judge mentioned it and tried to humiliate me it never had this effect. I was feeling low, though. I hadn't felt this low, defeated, fragile in a long time. My usual defences were down and I couldn't stop this particular flashback playing itself out in my head, in my body.

A tear that had formed in my eyes when Reese had been 'mouthing off' spilled over and began moving down my face. I raised my hand to wipe it away, to hide my hurt from Reese, and that seemed to break the hold the flashback had. I could move again, I could shove that night, those acts, to the back of my head where they belonged. 'It was four, actually. He thinks six but two of them didn't want to, loved their wives, found the whole thing repulsive but had got into business with him and this was a condition of it. We just sat and talked for a bit, but they made me promise not to tell him or anyone.'

Reese shook his head slightly in what I assumed was despair. 'Why'd you even get involved with him in the first place? I thought you knew better. You *did* know better.'

'He caught me when I was really low.' I shrugged. 'It all seemed so hopeless there for a while, Reese, and he just happened to sit down opposite me when I was at probably the lowest point.'

My friend's gaze stopped being so rage-filled, and he connected the dots of what Judge had said to what I said, and the realisation of when I got involved, what his role had been in it, seemed to jerk across his brain.

I needed to speak before the memory took root and he started to blame himself for something that was not his fault. 'And I liked the money,' I admitted. 'I liked being able to sleep in a hostel or a B&B for weeks on end.' I rubbed my hands over my face. 'And getting dressed up, having a couple of drinks... I felt almost normal for a while. I feel awful about it now, I felt awful about it then, even before I had to let those men screw me. I know that's awful that I felt like that and I do feel ashamed, but that's what it was like.'

'There's no shame in that.'

'I don't want you to hate me, Reese,' I confessed. I could put up with a lot, but not him hating me. It sounded juvenile and young, but he was my best friend. Since Veronica, I hadn't had many friends, people who I could rely on and spend time with without any expectations. 'I don't think I could stand it. You think I don't feel anything for myself but I do. I would feel so . . . lost, terrified and, I don't know, suicidal probably if you weren't my friend any more.'

Reese inhaled deeply as he stared at me, his eyes seemed to be microscopically examining me.

What does he see? I wondered.

I would stare into a mirror and see eyes, nose, mouth, cheeks, forehead, chin, long dreadlocked hair wound up into a bun at the back of a head. I would not see the way those features were arranged, the blemishes adding depth and shade to the skin. I never noticed if that combination was pretty or handsome or stunning or plain. I would stare into a mirror and see nothing beyond a set of features.

'What did you want to be when you were little?' Reese asked.

'Way to reassure me there, buddy,' I said. 'I, who you think feels nothing, have just spilled my guts out and you're changing the subject.'

'I'm serious: what did you want to be when you were little?'

'A ballet dancer,' I admitted. 'Not a ballerina in pink with the tutus and tiaras and stuff. I wanted to be a real ballet dancer, to actually dance for a living. I didn't have to have the lead roles all the time, I didn't want to be a star or anything like that, I just wanted to be a dancer. If I got to be the star, that would be the icing on top of the amazing cake that was being able to dance ballet all my life.'

'Why didn't it happen? Weren't you good enough or something?'

'I was good enough. Apparently I was naturally gifted. Me and another girl, we were set for great things. But I had to stop, and then I left home and never really danced again.'

Ah, I saw him think. *Ah*. It clicked into place for him: he'd been waiting more than ten years to find out who and now he thought he knew. I glanced down at my hands. I'd managed to keep them relatively soft and in good condition over the years. No more £20 tubes of hand cream, but they were all right, they would do. In my shoes, though, my feet were ugly. They were ugly, with almost deformed, twisted toes, and hard, almost permanently calloused soles because I'd wanted to be a ballet dancer. I'd trained so hard, punished my feet more than any other part of my body so that I could do it. Even if I could forget that dream, my feet would never let me.

'Do you think you'd have even met me if you'd become that ballet dancer?' Reese asked. *Urgh.* Being given the shove by a friend, by *this* friend, was like having something hard and solid and heavy slammed into the centre of my body. It had even more pain attached because he had used my confession about what I used to dream of against me.

'Yes,' I said. 'Absolutely yes.'

'Nah, mate, you wouldn't. You know that. When are you going to stop living this life and go back to where you should be?'

'This is my life, Reese. In case you didn't realise, it's not easy to get off the streets. And don't give me any of that "if you work hard, keep your head down, you can be a valued member of society" crap, nor that "you live on the streets because you choose to" bollocks. The truth is I had no choice when I turned up ten years ago. Everyone might have thought I did, that I could have gone to the authorities, but no one would have listened to me. So I know you and a lot of the others think I'm not like you and not a proper homeless person, but I am. I have been for ten years and I probably will be for another ten years, maybe even twenty years. This is who I am and the life I'm living. And that's why I know you, that's why you're my friend.'

'What's your real name, Grace Carter? If we're such great mates, tell me your real name.'

It was my turn to shoot a look of disgust while I sat back in my chair. 'I keep forgetting, you're not only a bastard when you're using, are you?'

'Thing of it is, mate, you and me, we're bad for each other. We keep each other here. Stuck. I should have OD'd a long time ago, that was my destiny. You should have found another Vinnie and gone to live somewhere else an age ago. But you keep me here, you give me a reason to live. Sometimes I don't want to be here, you know? And you get in the way of that. I'm grateful, don't get me wrong, but some mornings, when I look up and see that hole I need to crawl out of, I just can't, but I have to, because the thought of you sitting there, waiting for me and then going round the streets looking for me . . . I can't let go.'

'That's good. It's good that you've got a reason to hold on. That's good.'

'Look at me, Ace. The people I deal with on a daily basis did this to me because they could. This is my life. But you shouldn't be here. When you got with Vinnie, that should have been your chance to move away, leave me and everyone behind. But you didn't cos you've got this weird loyalty thing, because you care about me more than you care about yourself . . . In the nicest way possible, Ace, you need to fuck off and stay fucked off. Go live the life you were meant to.'

'This *is* my life.'

'And you think Judge is going to stop now? You think this is it and he's finished with you? You really think he won't be using everyone you've ever even looked at to teach you more lessons? When he's having a pop at the rest of us to get at you, what are we supposed to do?'

'It will be fine because I'm going to go to the police.'

He closed his eyes, scrunched up his face as though vicious fingers of pain had strummed across his nerve endings. 'Fucking hell. You don't know when to quit, do ya? The rozzers? Are you out of your mind?'

'No, it's the only way to stop him.'

'I've already told them I don't remember anything, was out of it and it could have been anyone. What, you're going to go back and tell them otherwise?'

'I'm just going to tell them what I saw, what happened.'

'You were gone before the ambulance arrived and left your mobile phone behind so they could find me – you're going to go in and confess all now? Even if they believe you, what good do you think it'll do?'

'I didn't want to leave, you made me. I would have stayed and told them everything then. And it's not just about what happened to you, is it? I went to loads of his "parties", I talked to people, I listened to them talking. All those "contacts" of his who loved nothing more than to talk business and brag in front of the women because we weren't really there to them – I heard it all. It's all stored up in my head. I know it's years ago, but he won't have changed, he'll still be doing the same old things because he's got away with it for so long.'

'Ace, look at me. *Look at me.*'

I did as he asked, really looked at him. His bruising, the bandages, the damage left by someone who wanted to teach me a lesson. 'This will be you or you will be dead, if he gets even a hint that you're talking to the rozzers. He'll kill me, too. This guy doesn't mess about, you know that. He took us out to the middle of nowhere because he didn't think I'd live long enough for the ambulance to arrive. People like us don't matter to him. Going to the rozzers will do no good and lots of harm.'

'I have to, Reese. For once the bad guy has to get punished. Just for once.'

'The world don't work like that, not for the likes of you and me.'

'Yeah, well, maybe this time it will. Maybe this time, we get justice and the bad guys get to go to prison.'

Reese frowned at me, looking at me as though I was speaking a foreign language. Maybe I was, maybe I was being idealistic and stupid in the wake of all that I'd seen of the world, but for once it had to happen. For once I was owed the right thing happening to someone who was wrong; for once, someone who went through life hurting others would get what was coming to them instead of con-tinuing on as though protected in a special non-stick coating that let them get away with crimes against others time after time, year after year.

'There's no point talking to you. You're just going to do this and fuck the consequences. Look what that attitude did to me, really look, and then tell me it's worth it to get "justice", like "justice" isn't just for those that other people actually care about.'

I said nothing.

'If you do this, mate, that's it, me and you over. I won't see you again, speak to you, I'll probably go off and OD first chance I get, cos I'll have no one to live for, cos you'll be fucking dead. In fact, yeah, go on, do it. Give us both a way out of this world.'

I wished I could make him understand why I had to do this. 'Reese, you deserve to have someone care about what happened to you the other day. And what happened to you all those years ago that brought you out on to the streets. You're a human being, you're just as important as anyone else who's been attacked. You deserve to have someone – lots of someones, actually – care about it. I want to make someone care about what happened to you.'

Back and forth, back and forth he moved his head, and with every move his eyes grew colder, more distant, until he could have been looking at a stranger, he could have been staring at nothing. 'I'll see ya, Ace,' he eventually said. He shifted, his movements full of agony, until he was turned away from me and could pretend I wasn't there.

That was it: over. It had been since before I'd sat down, if I was honest with myself. Probably since he'd wanted me to leave him back at that derelict warehouse. I had thought he'd changed his mind, but no, my lack of interest in myself apparently was always going to make me a liability to someone like him. Being around me was dangerous. If I didn't report it to the police he might possibly still speak to me, would keep me around to have a go at when he was out of it and the drug was fuelling his vicious thoughts and loosening his usually friendly tongue, but it wouldn't be the same again. He wouldn't meet me for coffee at Bernie's. We wouldn't walk down by the canal, watching the leaves drift away on the water. We wouldn't sit in shop doorways looking at the stars and pretending how we lived was how we wanted it. He wouldn't look at me sometimes as though he wanted to tell me something and couldn't quite find the words. Judge had known what he was doing when he chose to hurt Reese instead of me. He'd known it would mean the end of our friendship *and* it would make everyone else – the network of people we all relied on in various ways – be wary of me. He'd isolated me and that would mean, when he wanted a tiny bit more revenge, I'd have no one to help me.

'I love you, Reese,' I said. I had to say it – it'd probably be the last time he would be this close to speak to me. He had to know that no matter what he thought about what I was going to do, this was the bald, unvarnished truth of the situation. He did matter; someone did feel that much about him.

I wanted to hear it back, I desperately wanted to know he felt the same, but I would be waiting until the end of time if I thought Reese would say it, especially now I had decided to do this thing. 'I'll see ya,' I mumbled to his silence, before I began my long journey to the police station.

11

Nika

I'm impressed. Eliza's managed to leave it a whole seven days before she arrives at my doorstep. Marshall and I haven't seen each other since her return because she's been waiting for him to go to work together, somehow managing to leave work at the exact same time as him, and staying all evening to talk about her recovery – basically doing everything she can to keep us apart.

'Can I have a word?' she asks.

'Sure,' I say, trying my best to be pleasant. Eliza moves forward to come in and is surprised when I don't oblige. Instead, I stand my ground. I'm not going to let her in, she doesn't get to do that. 'Is it a long word with lots of letters?'

She frowns at me, unimpressed by my wit and my not letting her in.

'What I mean is, will it take a long time, this word you want to have? If it will, we can go for a walk. If it won't, then we can talk here.'

'I don't think you want to talk out here. The walls are quite thin and I'm sure you won't want anyone to hear what I've got to say. I think we should go inside.'

'A walk it is, then,' I reply without moving. 'Or we could go to your place.'

Her face draws in on itself, her green eyes wary, her features tense. There isn't enough perfume and room scent in the world to cover the smell of skunk in her flat. She might get away with giving people

311

the impression she's just too heavy-handed with whichever perfume she's wearing that day, but there's no way she can hide it on her belongings. And if I go into her flat, smell it, I will tell Marshall, she can be sure of it. 'OK, let's go for a walk.'

'I'll meet you outside,' I say to her, then step back and shut the door, gather my phone, my keys, coat, shoes. It's not cold outside, I don't think, but I may need to walk around after Eliza's 'word' to clear my head or to get rid of her.

She's still there, standing guard at my door. I smile again: it's amusing that she thinks I'm scared of her, that she thinks of all the things that have happened to me in my life that she features anywhere near the top ten. I was talking to Sasha earlier. She told me that she'd told Mum and Dad that she'd seen me and the first thing they had asked was if Todd knew. First question. Not how was I, where was I, would I come and see them? No: first thought Todd. Sasha is moving out soon and can't wait: *'I feel so ungrateful, but I don't want Tracy-Dee ever thinking this kind of behaviour is normal.'*

Outside, the heat of the promised summer rises up to greet us. About a week after we'd started sleeping together, Marshall asked me if I minded that we never did anything – that all we'd do is screw, eat, and then I'd go back to my flat. *'Do you mind that we don't go out and wine and dine and do stuff?'*

'No,' I replied. *'Should I?'*

'Most people do when they're dating,' he said.

'Maybe we should do that when we get bored of having so much sex, then?' I replied.

'Good plan, that woman, good plan.'

'I know you and Marshall have been spending a lot of time together,' Eliza says to cut into my thoughts. 'As soon as my back was turned you moved in on him.'

'When I first met you, you seemed so nice,' I say to her. 'I genuinely thought we could be friends.'

'When I first met you, I didn't think you were a back-stabbing whore who'd go sniffing around my mate the second my back was turned.'

Wow, that came from nowhere, I think. There is no reasoning with her, not that I want to, or need to. Not really. 'Fair enough. Is that the word you wanted to have?'

'I want you to stay away from him.' Her voice vibrates with the strain of keeping herself in check. 'Stay *away* from him. He doesn't need someone like you hanging around him.'

'Someone like me?'

She stops walking. 'I've been on the Internet trying to find out about you. But you know what's odd? There is nothing about you. It's like you don't exist.' She's trembling as she speaks; colour is rising up her neck, spreading up towards her cheeks. Her agitation, the need for something to calm her down, is almost painful to watch. From her back pocket she retrieves her fancy phone, with a touchscreen and sleek body. I'm surprised she hasn't already sold it, although it's probably only a matter of time. Unless she's managed to scam cash from her parents on her recent visit. 'But then, the other day, I was scrolling through Facebook and this comes up.' She shows me her phone. I am looking at a picture of a woman in her thirties. She has long dreadlocks, loose around her face, but there's enough of her face on show to see her features. She has cheekbones that are prominent from the way she smiles, brown eyes that look tired and don't quite hit the centre of the camera. Below the slightly blurry picture of this woman I vaguely recognise are words. I read them several times before I actually take in what they are saying.

Have you seen this woman?

Grace 'Ace' Carter is in her thirties and went missing from her homeless hostel bedsit in the Birmingham area in January 2016. Grace is vulnerable and is thought to have been suffering from depression, and her family and friends are very worried about her. If you or anyone know where she might be, contact her uncle on the email below. Please share.

'OK, it's very sad she's missing, but I don't know what it's got to do with me,' I say. My voice does not waver, my expression does not falter. I do not give anything away.

'That's what I thought first of all, but then I looked properly and I thought, "She looks like Nika." And then I looked a bit closer, and I realised, that *is* Nika. That is you. Cut off the hair, add glasses and this Grace Carter person doesn't just look like you, she *is* you.'

If Eliza is looking for a reaction, she doesn't get one. What am I supposed to do? Break down and confess all to this woman who means me nothing but harm?

'It all fits,' she says. 'This homeless woman called Grace Carter disappears in January and not long afterwards you turn up here with a new name, new look and not very much of a backstory. Marshall doesn't know very much about your background, I don't, anyone I've asked in the building doesn't. So, what did you do, steal someone's identity and then take over her life?'

It's Judge, of course. He's trying to find me, trying to shut me up. I've been keeping an eye on the news, but there's been nothing at all about him being arrested or even investigated. I've assumed that the policeman, DS Brennan, was working for Judge when he persuaded me to leave, that all the stuff he told me in the car about how Judge would go through every single one of my friends until I shut up, how I shouldn't worry because he – DS Brennan – would take care of Reese whilst he was in hospital and would keep an eye out for him when he was released, had all been lies to stop me testifying against Judge. But this thing on the Internet, when Judge is using people's willingness to help others to try to find me, I assume to silence me, means the policeman might have been genuine. And the fact Judge is looking for me at all means he must think there's a real possibility that he might be charged with something. It also means he might have killed Reese to shut him up.

'You watch too much telly,' I say to Eliza.

'You aren't getting around it by trying to make out I'm crazy,' she says. 'That *is* you.'

'If you really believe that, then you should pass on whatever information you have to the police.'

'What?' She wasn't expecting *that* response.

'That's what I would do. I don't believe everything I read on the Internet. I don't know who it is that is looking for anyone who appears to be missing, so if I genuinely thought someone was committing a crime or someone was vulnerable and missing and I knew where they were, I'd report it to the police so they could decide what needed to be done. But that's me.'

Eliza's lips scrunch together like screwed-up tissue paper, her nostrils flare like a bull about to charge. 'Stay away from Marshall. Stay away from both of us,' she says. 'I've noticed you, Nika, always skulking around, won't let anyone into your flat, keeping yourself to yourself. Well, I'm pretty sure you won't want Marshall to see this, so stay away from him or else.'

'Or else?'

She fronts up to me, right in my face. Her perfume is overwhelming this close, but I catch the scent of what she is trying to hide – cannabis in its strongest form, skunk. When you know what it smells like, no perfume can disguise it. 'Or else I will show him this and then you'll have to tell him all your little secrets or lose him.'

He was never mine in the first place, I should point that out to her. No matter how much you may love someone, you never possess them. You can only ever borrow the right to spend time with them. I was only ever borrowing the right to spend time with Marshall because it was what he wanted, too. Yes, I thought when this began it was going to work out, he was my first connection to the world and through him, through learning from being with him, I would form more connections, more and more of them until I was properly hooked into life, into the world. It turns out I was only borrowing that time with him. It was never going to be anything more permanent than that.

I can't make connections to the world. Not when I am who I am. Not when I opened a letter my sister forwarded to me today and I

315

found that once again the past has chased me down. Once again, I've been reminded that I am not normal, I am not like anyone else, and I am not allowed to have nice things like my dalliance with Marshall. I am broken, and no matter how hard I try, how hard I pretend, nothing is going to fix me.

'Does Marshall know you've lost your job, Eliza?'

Unlike me, Eliza isn't very good at disguising moments when she is caught off guard: her eyes widen in that moment of shock, then the horror ensnares her face and she takes a step back. Too late she remembers that she is meant to have the upper hand, she is the one who is meant to be in control here, and she rallies, pretends I haven't guessed another of her little secrets.

'Just remember what I said. Stay away or I show Marshall this picture, all right?'

Her dramatic walk away is wasted on me. I don't care about Eliza. I don't care about anyone right now. Right now, all I care about is how to fall off the face of the Earth again.

Roni

On my bed, Mum has left a pile of my post and a message written on the notepaper she uses to write her shopping lists: *'Veronica. Kindly return the many calls to Cliff. It is rude to not return calls and I do not like having to speak to him. Kind regards. Mum.'*

It *is* rude not to return Cliff's calls. But I'm a bit concerned that he hasn't got the message yet that I will not be pursuing that element of dating for the time being.

I open my payslip, my bank statement, the other pieces of junk mail that have somehow managed to only find me now that I am back living here. Maybe I should contact the junk mail senders – I'm sure they'd find Nika no worries. The final envelope is bigger than normal and with a thick, expensive texture to it. It's obviously an invite, but it is postmarked Brighton. I'm not sure what it could be, or who I know in Brighton. Once open, I have to read it over and over again. Revulsion has worked its way through my body several times, squeezing out my capacity to breathe. I stare at the words that are gold-embossed onto the thick cream card in my hand.

This could be called divine intervention. A fulfilment of the desperate, life-limiting need I have to find Nika. But is there really no other way? If she is alive she will show up and I will be able to find her. But really, is there no other way? The invitation falls from my numb fingers and I sit back on the bed. I move back as far as possible, to the very furthest corner, and bring my knees to my chest as I stare at the invite. I really, really wish there was another way.

Daneaux Dance Studios

cordially invite you and a guest to our

40th anniversary celebrations

on Saturday, 21 May 2016

at our brand-new Brighton Studios

From 7.30 p.m. until late

Cocktail attire preferred

Please RSVP number of attendees to the email address below
We look forward to sharing good food, company and memories with you.

12

Nika

The brass plaque on the wall beside the red door reads:

Daneaux School of Dance
Est. 1975
Paris. London. Brighton

At the centre of the red door there is huge silver 40, above two white balloons also branded with the number 40.

Inside I can hear the sounds of a party, a hubbub of people talking, glasses clinking, low music and frequent bursts of laughter. I stand on the steep stone steps leading up to the dance studio and close my eyes. I can imagine who is in there. All the girls from when I was taking ballet, when I wanted to be a dancer. All the women from before I was even born. All the women and girls who came after me. So many of them, all of them with different stories, different life experiences, all here to celebrate the life and times and enduring success of the man who abused me for six years, nearly eight if you count the two years he spent before that grooming Roni and me to be so enamoured with him that we would question ourselves before we questioned or spoke out against him.

I don't know why I've come here. When I opened the letter, forwarded by Sasha with a Brighton postmark, I hadn't been expecting to see his

321

name, see his wife's name, to be confronted with the fact they lived so near to me now. The generic letter inserted with the invite was appealing with me to come and mark another important anniversary in the life of a great man. His dance school had produced dancers who had gone on to secure prestigious scholarships at prominent dance schools across the world; he had personally tutored women who had danced for all of the best ballet companies across the globe. And he had been responsible for young girls who had found a way to express themselves through dance, who had enjoyed the freedom that dancing gave them.

A great man, respected by so many.

I have not come to celebrate him. I suppose I wanted to come along and see if anyone would show up. I was hoping as I walked here that he and his wife, possibly his son, would be sitting alone, having to think back over all the things he had done and realise that no one would pretend now, when the girls didn't have to go because their parents compelled them to, they would vote with their feet, they would stay away. They would not flock into his place of business and his home address, and share drink, food, time and stories with him.

I arrived and discovered he is not alone. He is surrounded by people, the party on all floors of the house sounds full, burgeoning with people who think the world of him and his dance school.

I did not understand why they sent me an invite to my parents' address. Was it all so easily forgotten that I was the one who spoke out, who went to the police, who ran away as soon as she could? Or was I so unimportant, was what I accused him of so ludicrous to everyone, including my parents, that they thought I'd laugh it off as a childish misunderstanding to be set aside now I was an adult and understood the ways of the world? Or, as is most likely, did they send an invite to me, thinking it would get to the other Veronica?

When I was sixteen and a half, it stopped, *he* stopped. I had been to the police a year before and nothing had changed. If anything, it got worse. But then, when I was sixteen and a half, the lessons became about dancing, about teaching me new techniques instead of punishing me for repeatedly speaking out.

I remember the day it stopped clearly. I heard his breathing change, and the familiar dread of knowing what would come next began to creep through me because the sound of his breathing was always the warning. The next thing he said would be the start of it and I braced myself for that, for my body to become rigid with fear, for my mind to try to blank out, when the studio door suddenly banged open. It was Mrs Daneaux. She seemed to be all smiles, but still had that cold look in her eye she'd reserved for me since I'd told her what he'd been doing and he had convinced her I was lying.

He went to greet her, tried to shoo her out again, but she was having none of it. She decided to stay and watch the progress of one of their star pupils. After that, she regularly showed up unannounced, which stopped him from touching me again.

So for the last six months of living in Chiselwick, I learnt to dance again without fear lining the pit of my stomach like cement, and without bile foaming like lava in my throat. I never remembered what it was like to dance for the love of it and I still had disgust crawling over every part of my body, and the memories of what had happened were like scorch marks in my mind, but I could dance.

I know, even now, if I told people about it, they would question why I put up with it when I was fifteen, when I was sixteen, when I was nearly seventeen. Surely by then I was older and taller and stronger. I could have stopped it if I'd wanted to. I know people wouldn't understand, whatever age I was, whenever I saw him, whenever he came near me, whenever anyone did something that triggered the memory of him, I would become eleven years old again – horrified that someone I adored would do something that felt so awful; I would be thirteen again – stupefied because what he did to me was so distressing I'd spent the whole night throwing up. When I was older and apparently able to stop it if I wanted to, I was actually still thirteen, stuck back in that moment of terror, frozen with shock.

When I was sixteen and a half it all stopped, but I never quite managed to stop the feelings of hating myself that made me want to disappear.

I shouldn't have come to this place, I realise. I should have stayed at home and told myself that everyone had abandoned him, instead of coming here to see the reality is that no one cares what he was accused of, everyone still considers him a great man.

'I wondered if you'd show up,' she says. Her voice hasn't changed at all. I remember it as clearly as though I only heard it yesterday. Standing beside me, waiting for our turn on the stage, shouting into my ear that this club was rubbish and we should try somewhere else, begging me to speak to her and repeating that she was sorry. I remember her voice clearly, even though nearly twenty years have stacked themselves neatly between us. It won't really matter how she looks, because she sounds the same. 'I should say, I hoped you would turn up. You're the only reason why I came here,' she adds.

That's the real reason I came here, of course. I wanted to see the other Veronica Harper.

Roni

Brighton, 2016

I have been keeping watch across the street since six o'clock so I can see who comes to the party and I will not miss her. As time went by and she did not show up, I started to think she wouldn't. That she would do the sensible thing and stay away from a part of her past she wants to forget. That would be it for me if she did stay away, though, I realised, there would be no way of finding her.

When I saw her approach, walk up to the red door, and pause, staring up at the building in front of her as though deciding whether to ring or not, I was almost sick with anticipation and dread. She had the same gait as she had when we were seventeen. She was the same height, and although her hair was straight and short and she looked like she was wearing glasses, I knew instantly it was her.

I approached slowly, my heart ricocheting in my ears, my breathing as loud as that of a long-distance runner.

'I wondered if you'd show up,' I say to her. She doesn't move, but she has heard me because her entire body becomes rigid where she stands. 'I should say, I hoped you would turn up. You're the only reason why I came here.'

She doesn't move at all. She stands rictus-still and lets me talk. When I finish what I have said, she still does not immediately move or talk.

'That sounds like you're blaming me for the poor choice you made this evening,' she eventually says.

'I hope it doesn't. It was my roundabout way of saying I wanted to see you desperately, and if it meant coming here to do it, then that was what I had to do.'

The other Veronika Harper, the one who has a 'k' instead of a 'c', slowly turns around to face me. I've imagined this moment a million times in my head. We would see each other, our eyes would meet and we would throw our arms around each other, bury our faces in each other's necks and cry. We would cry away the years we've been apart, we would sob aside our separate lives and we would find a way to come back together. To be true friends again. I have recreated this scene so many times in my head, I can almost feel my arms around her, her tears on my neck, my cry-punctuated confessions.

As it is, the best either of us can do is offer a small, uncomfortable smile, try but fail to make eye contact, move down the steps to the pavement and stand near each other, seeming awkward and out of place.

'I don't even know why I'm here,' she admits. 'It was such a shock, I guess, getting the invite and to find that they were here . . . living so close to where I live. It never even occurred to me to search for them, you know? That part of my life was over so I didn't expect to hear from them again . . . And then they're in Brighton. And life is carrying on as always for them. I don't know, maybe I came to look people in the eye and see if they remember.'

Oh. I thought she might be here to see me. I thought that might have featured in her reasons for allowing herself to be pulled into such a painful segment of her past. And she lives here, in Brighton.

'It's good to see you,' I offer. 'Like I said, I only came to see you. I came to say I'm sorry. That's the reason I wanted to find you. I've wanted to say it for years and years. I'm so very, very sorry.'

In the silence after my apology, I have been staring at her shoes, too cowardly to face her properly. She is wearing white Converse trainers that have seen many, many better days. I wonder if, like me, she avoids ballet shoes like the plague. The mere thought of fitting them on my feet turns every part of my stomach. I wonder if it's the same for her. Because, even though what we went through seemed the same, sometimes felt like carbon copies of the other's experiences, it was different. Every experience couldn't be swept away or minimised by lumping us together to become faceless 'survivors' of a horrific man's perversions. Maybe, after all these years, Nika has found a way to dance again.

Her white Converse shoes have musical notes written in black marker along the bottom rim. 'Are those notes to a song?' I ask.

'Yes,' she replies. That confirms it: she isn't going to accept my apology; she is probably going to avoid talking about anything that might lead to an apology. As part of my conceit that there is a way to put this right, I thought it would be easy. Not easy, simple. I thought I would be able to say the words, mean the words, and all would be forgiven. In my arrogance, I thought forgiveness would only entail finding Nika, the act of seeing her, the moment of reunion, the utterance of those golden words. I should have made my confession when I had the chance, I should have allowed myself to be absolved. It is hubris to believe you can achieve forgiveness without any help from God.

'I used to see you in the papers and magazines,' I offer as a way to make her talk. It will probably outrage her, encourage her to engage.

'That was never me,' she states quite plainly. 'That was someone who looked remarkably like me and had a similar name. What about you, what have you been doing?'

'You wouldn't believe me if I told you,' I say. Out of everyone, she is the one who, having been there, probably won't believe the transformation in me.

'Right, OK,' is her reply before she shuts her mouth and keeps her gaze lowered.

'What, you're not even going to ask?' I'm affronted. More of my vanity, my need to have people as interested in me as I am in them. Actually, no, it is my need to have *Nika* as interested in me as I am in her.

327

'No, I am not even going to ask. I'm sure you have your reasons for not telling me and I respect those reasons, even if I don't know them.'

'I became a nun,' I say.

'See? If you didn't want to tell me, why bother bringing it up? And then take the piss out of me. What was the point? Did that moment of piss-take really give you such a lift that it was worth it?'

'I'm not... taking the you-know-what. I became a nun. Honest to God.'

That does it, that makes her look at me again. '*You* became a nun?'

I grin at her, take the chance to look over her face, note her wrinkles, her blemishes, the shaping of her look through her glasses. 'I received a calling of sorts and followed it.'

'I thought your calling was to be a dancer? All either of us ever wanted to be was a dancer. That was why we became friends. That was all we ever talked about.'

'Things change.'

Nika

Veronica Harper, a nun. I suppose stranger things have happened. But a nun? I never would have guessed.

I've missed her. I'm ashamed to admit that to anyone, especially myself. But I've missed Roni. Even when I couldn't talk to her, when I refused to hold her hand, she was special to me. Our friendship lived at the very core of who I was. Without Roni, for a very long time, I did not feel alive, real or part of normal life. That is why it hurt so much, of course. Why I couldn't simply brush it off and be understanding as I had been in the past. Roni was a part of me and when she let me down, I lost that part in the most painful separation I'd ever experienced.

Roni

'Where are you staying tonight?' Nika asks me.

'How do you know I don't live in Brighton?' I ask. I bristle at the implication that it's obvious I am not quite 'Brighton cool'. This dress I am wearing, it may not be the skimpy garbs from yesteryear, but it can pass muster. The same with my coat. I could be 'Brighton' if I wanted.

'You don't live in Brighton,' she tells me. 'I was going to ask you if you wanted to stay at my flat, but if you live in Brighton, you go right ahead and go home. We can always do a girly catch-up tomorrow.'

'I don't live in Brighton, you're right. I would love to stay if that is still on offer?'

'Yes, sure, why not.'

I'm not thinking when I breach the gap between us and curl my hand around hers. I do it because it's instinctive. I love the feel of her skin against mine. Her skin has a special code, one that only I can read. When I touch her, I am transformed. I remember all the good things about her. I want to lean over and press my lips against hers. Not in a sexual way; it would be the quickest way to connect with her, to let her know how much I missed her, how incomplete I was without her. I've prayed for her every night since I last saw her, even before I decided to become a nun I would ask God to keep her

330

safe, to protect her from harm. Now I know, after all those years of not seeing anything about her after she left her famous boyfriend, that she's alive and well, and I want to kiss her. I want to express in the most physical way possible that I love her. She's my name twin and my reflection.

'I really missed you,' I say.

Carefully, without drama or venom, she tugs her hand out of mine. I am cold now we're not touching. 'I didn't miss you,' she says.

'Wow, thanks.'

'I didn't. I simply kept finding other fucked-up humans to take your place.'

13

Roni

'I only have one duvet because I don't have visitors to stay,' she says. The walk back to her flat has been silent. It reminds me of the time we walked back to the bus stop from Big T's house and the silent disappointment that Nika seemed to be carrying with her. As we have walked her body language has changed, cooled. She seemed to be regretting the decision to let me into her life so soon, possibly worried that I will believe it is all forgiven. *I* certainly don't believe that. I realised how puny, insignificant and inadequate the word 'sorry' was when it left my mouth earlier. I do not think I am forgiven at all.

'I'll use my coat, it's fine.'

'If you want, you can sleep in my bed.'

I can tell this is one of the first times she's let someone in here. The flat is barely decorated. It has stuff – sofa, TV, armchair – fully equipped kitchen area off the living room, but nothing personal. She could be a nun, her surroundings are so sparse. She has CDs lined up along the mantelpiece, lots of brightly coloured spines on either side of a portable CD player and radio. The alcove on the far side of the fireplace has a few novels stacked up, most of them old and well read. There is no rug on the floor, the curtains look like they come with the flat. She has a guitar propped up by the armchair, a newspaper discarded on the sofa, a neat stack of mail on the bar that separates the kitchen from the living room.

Everything is orderly.

'You live like a nun,' I say. 'Actually, it's like you don't live here at all.'

Nika rubs her hand over her eyes. 'You can always leave. If you want to be insulting and rude, I will happily point you in the direction of the door and we can wait another twenty-odd years to catch up, yes?'

'No. Sorry. Sorry. That came out really, really wrong. I'm a little overwhelmed with seeing you. Almost seeing *them*. Can I hug you?'

She shakes her head, and takes a definite step away from me. 'No, no you can't.' She takes another step away, until she is at the entrance to the kitchen area. 'Do you want a cup of tea or coffee? I have milk and sugar and everything so I can make it properly.'

'I'm sorry,' I tell her.

'You said that already. Look, I'm going to make a cup of coffee. It'll probably keep me up all night but I don't care.' Nika is nervous, I think. Her movements are agitated, she can't keep still: while she waits for the kettle to boil, while she lines up two mugs, heaps coffee into both, takes out the milk, she jiggles, moves. It reminds me of the conversation with Mother Superior and the way my leg would not stop jiggling. It reminds me of the way her leg jiggled when she told me *he'd* come to her house and had charmed her parents into sending her back to him.

I hear a short, electronic buzz and seconds later she reaches into her back pocket and takes out her phone. She stares at it, obviously reading the message. Rather than reply, she tosses the phone on to the side, shaking her head in what looks like despair. Boyfriend? Lover? Fiancé? Husband? Which one has sent her even further into a spin? The rolling boil of the kettle fills the room and then the steam billows out of the spout and she turns it off before it automatically shuts out.

'I was scared,' I try again. I think of Judas, of *what* he did, *why* he did. Why I think he might have done what he did. 'No, that's not right. I was terrified. I was—'

'Can we not do this now?' Nika interrupts. She almost throws the kettle back on to its stand. 'I thought I could talk to you and listen and stuff like that, but I can't. I can't. It's as simple as that.' Nika tosses the teaspoon she is stirring the coffee with on to the side. 'You can sleep in my bed, we can even go and sit in there right now with our coffees and chat about our lives, but let's not do that other bit now. Not tonight.'

When? I want to ask. *This truth is burning a hole in my soul, it needs to be let out. When? When will I be allowed to do that?*

'No boyfriend or anything on the scene then?' I ask her.

Her bedroom is just as empty and devoid of any love or emotion as the living room. It is functional, like my cell in the monastery and my rooms in the various convents I lived in. She is choosing to live like this. I wonder why. Is that what happens when you are like me, when you are like her: you strip yourself of nice things, you shed all the shackles of 'stuff'? The side lamp is on, and we are at opposite ends of the bed, our knees drawn up, and coffee mugs in our hands.

She glances briefly at the phone that now sits on the bedside table. 'No. Nothing like that.' She's lying. It's so obvious there's someone, but it's not viable. 'What about you?'

'Yes, well, I used to wear a wedding ring, of course, since I was a bride of Christ. Not any more, obviously.'

'Why did you leave?'

'You don't want to know.'

'What, were you caught shagging one of the priests?'

'No! The very idea!'

'Why then?'

'Because of you. I wanted to make things right with you. I didn't know how I was going to do that, or where to find you, but I did know I couldn't do that and be a Sister or a nun. I was a nun in training, then became a Sister and then went back to being a nun. Either way, I couldn't do it if I wanted to make things right.'

Light from the side lamp doesn't radiate very far, but her discomfort at the idea I did something because of her is clear. She stares down into the depths of her cup, strokes a lock of her hair behind her ear. 'Why did you become a nun in the first place?' she asks. She is still staring into her cup as a distraction from the woman sitting at the foot of her bed, as a way to avoid looking at me.

'That's a long story.' She probably doesn't want to know how she features in it so I decide to cut that bit out. 'I met a nun. I don't know what she was doing in a park late at night, but there she was.'

'What were *you* doing in a park late at night?'

I hesitate. Will she think less of me for knowing I was chasing the silence, the escape from the raging in my head? Probably. I still judge myself for it. I have been taught over the years to have compassion, for myself as much as anyone else, but that is one of the things I struggle with. That and what I did to Nika. Honesty, though, is necessary if I'm going to tell the story properly. 'I'd stolen my mother's bottle of sleeping pills and I had a bottle of wine and I was going to kill myself. I was sitting in the park contemplating it.' It seems such a long time ago that I had those feelings swirling through me. I was so desperate. The need in me to stop the noise, find the silence, was like nothing I'd ever felt before.

She doesn't seem to react to what I have said, except for the wince of what looks like remembered pain. Was she there, too? Did she get to the edge like I had? 'The nun – and she was dressed like a nun with the robes, the tabard and the wimple, not a Sister – sat down beside me and asked me to swap my bottle of pills for her book. Two days later when I finished the book I wanted to become a nun.'

'You read the Bible in two days? Impressive.'

'She didn't give me the Bible. She actually gave me *To Kill a Mockingbird*, said every word was a blessing and she read it whenever she felt like I did.'

'*To Kill a Mockingbird* made you want to become a nun? Bloody hell, I never got that when I read it! Not sure I want to read it again now.'

'No, it wasn't specifically the book. Well, it was, but it wasn't. It was the power of the book. There was something inside it that felt so real, like I could be anyone in the book, I could be anyone I wanted to be ever. And it was so silent in my head when I was reading. There was this bit where the pretty-much atheist character in it said it was a sin to kill a mockingbird and I realised what the nun meant when she gave me the book about every word being a blessing. I had another option because I would be killing a mockingbird if I killed myself. Then I thought of the woman who gave me the book. She knew what was going on in my head and being a nun gave her the confidence to speak to me at such a desperate time. If an ordinary person had given me that book I would have told them where to go, I think. I listened to her because of who she was, what she was dressed like. I wanted to explore what it was like to be like that.

'It wasn't completely out of the blue, I've always believed in God, I've always been interested in what was "out there" and there seemed to be so much beauty and peace in God. The nun and the book reminded me of that.' And it was another way to chase the silence. After reading the book, I knew that God and the silence would find me. I would also be able to atone for what I had done to Nika while living the simple life and chasing the silence.

'It's safe to read *To Kill a Mockingbird*, then? It won't make me want to give up my life to God or anything like that?' Nika says. I know she's said it to break up the atmosphere of seriousness and solemnity that's built up in this room, but still, it makes me bridle a little that she seems to be mocking me slightly.

'I have just told you some of my innermost thoughts and motivations for taking one of the biggest steps in my life and all you can do is make a quip about being able to read a book?' Maybe more than bridle a little, actually. It hurts. That is my pride talking, though. My ego. Since I left my life of holy orders I have noticed how hard it is sometimes to live in and with humility.

'What else do you want me to say?' Her laugh is gentle and lights up her face. She isn't mocking me, she is trying to deal with what I have said. 'What am I supposed to say? I asked you a question and you answered, that's how conversations work.'

'All right then, Miss Conversation, where did you disappear to when you left that man you were going to marry? Todd, that was his name, wasn't it? One minute you were all over the magazines, being snapped going into wedding boutiques, and the next you'd dropped off the face of the Earth. What happened?' I'm not going to tell her that I used to keep track of her because I liked being able to watch her life without intruding – she might take it the wrong way. She might think I relished in any way that she seemed to behave like I had a few years earlier.

She smirks, but not nastily. She smirks as though I won't believe her if she tells me. 'I slept rough for a few years. Bought a car and lived in that for a while. Met a guy, lived with him for about three-and-a-half years, probably about three years longer than I should have because it was nice sleeping inside night after night. After that ended I started sleeping rough again and in another car, and in various hostels before I was finally able to get a room in a homeless hostel. Then I moved to Brighton and came to this flat after a very short stint lodging in a person's house.'

I look around the room again: I understand now the bare surfaces, the lack of 'stuff', the functionality of everything. She had nothing for many years and that is a hard habit to break. At my parents' house, in my temporary room, I have nothing that isn't essential, either. Poverty was one of our vows and that is another habit that is hard to break.

'You were homeless?' I ask.

'I was homeless,' she confirms.

I ministered with homeless people over the years: worked in soup kitchens, sometimes carrying out late-night meal runs where we went around giving food and hot drinks to the people who were sleeping out. Some years, when the temperatures dropped particularly low, we would open up the local church hall so people could sleep inside. There were so many sad stories that I heard, so many damaged people who ended up alone and frightened with nowhere to go. I hate to think of Nika living like that. She must have been in so much pain, she must have been so scared half the time. Maybe that is why there's a hard edge to her. I can't imagine you'd survive very long being homeless if you were as giving and generous as she used to be. Anything could have happened to her and it probably did. The things I saw... the young girls who fell into prostitution, the men whose mental illness drove them out of their family homes, the women who had lost their children after leaving an abusive relationship, the young women with anxiety and depression unable to get recognition for their silent, hidden conditions. The physical, mental and emotional toll it took on the people I met was overwhelming and difficult to observe. No matter how long I did it for, how experienced I became at helping the home-less, I would go back to my cell and sob with the pain I had witnessed. I would pray for peace for the people who I had been with. I would ask the Lord to watch over them, to ease their suffering. I would pray for her, too: every night Nika was in my prayers and I had no idea she was one of the homeless people I cried for. She was out there.

'What are you crying for?' she asks me while rubbing her eyes with her forefinger and thumb.

'I'm so sorry, I'm so sorry,' I tell her. I don't want to keep crying in front of her. I don't want to make this all about me. 'I'm so sorry. I'm so sorry.'

'Please stop saying that. You didn't make me homeless.'

We both know that's not true. If we retrace our steps, skittle back-wards along the winding, rocky path of our lives, I know the point where the most significant fork in the road is. Where our lives diverged, and where she probably began on that path to meeting Todd, leaving him, becoming homeless. Spending years and years out in the cold, all alone, doing all sorts to get herself through. She probably took drugs. She probably prostituted herself. All because of what I did.

I can't stop sobbing and because I'm shaking so much, I'm spilling coffee all over her one duvet. I wanted to make it right, but how can I? How can I atone for what I did when this was the consequence of my actions?

'Urgh! Stop it!' Angrily, she flings back the duvet, slams her coffee cup on to the bedside table and slips out of the bed. 'Stop it. I didn't let you in here for this. I don't need or want any of this.'

She doesn't manage to leave the room, which is what I think she was meaning to do. I think she was removing herself from me so she could compose herself, she could put away all that she has told me and all I have reminded her of, like folding away clothes into a suitcase, then slamming shut the lid and putting that suitcase of memories far away out of reach. Instead, I watch her make it to the door, where she stops and rests her head against it. Slowly she bashes her head against the white many-panelled door. There's no sound so I know she's not hitting her head hard, but she does it all the same. *Bash, bash, bash, bash,* until her legs give way and she is a heap on the floor, her face is in her hands and she is sobbing. I want to go over and comfort her by putting my arms around her but I'm frozen by my own sobs.

And anyway, why would she want me to comfort her when I was the one who did it to her in the first place?

London, 1995

The policeman stared at us like the stupid, fanciful little schoolgirls we were. We sat in front of him in the small, dark room with a tape recorder on the table between us. He was angry-looking: red in the face, a nose like a bumpy, funny-shaped potato, and small, mean blue eyes. I was scared of him, more scared of him than I was of why we were there.

Nika looked scared, she was trembling, but she was still talking, she was telling him everything. He wasn't taking notes even though he had a pad of paper and black biro in front of him.

'You know what you're saying, don't you?' the policeman asked when she stopped talking.

She nodded.

'You could ruin a man's life by making up something like this.' His voice was stern, angry even. I was quivering on the inside, shaking on the outside. He would scream at me if I told him the truth.

'I'm not making it up,' Nika said. 'I'm not, I'm really not.'

'Now you listen.' The policeman slammed his finger down on to the notepad in front of him. 'Good men's lives are ruined because of silly little girls like you making up terrible lies like this. Come on, what's the real reason you're here? What did he do? Did he tell you off, let you know you weren't as good a ballerina as you thought, so you've cooked up this little plan to get back at him?'

'No. I wouldn't do that,' Nika said. 'He does it to her, too, doesn't he, Roni?'

His small, mean eyes were glaring through me all of a sudden. He was going to shout at me, he was going to tell my parents and then everything would come out. They would have to know about the drinking, the drugs, the unsafe sex with all those different, nameless men. If I told the truth, everyone would know the truth about me and they would all hate me. They would all think I was a slag and dirty.

'Well?' His voice was harsh, rough.

I glanced at Nika, she was holding my hand, willing me to do it, to tell the truth. She'd already told her parents and they hadn't believed her. She'd said they would if she got the police involved. They would believe us and then it would all stop.

'Does he "do it to you too"?' The policeman was being nasty. That was nothing, I knew, compared to what everyone else was going to be like when they found out.

I shook my head. 'No. No, he doesn't.'

I felt her hand slip away from mine as she broke our connection. I couldn't look at her, couldn't see what her face was saying.

'Roni?' she asked, desperately.

'We made it all up,' I said.

'Roni, just tell him the truth. It'll be all right if you tell the truth.' She didn't know about the other stuff so how could she know it'd be all right? She thought because she was often there when some guy was fucking me, or when I smoked pot or snorted cocaine or was falling down drunk, that she knew everything. She didn't know the half of it.

For the first time since Nika had started talking, the policeman looked happy. He sat back and nodded his head, all the while sneering at Nika. That was how other people were going to look at me if they knew: like I was dirt, like I was a piece of crap he'd bin his shoe if he stepped in.

'You girls, you're all the same. Can't take a little banter, make small things into something more than they are. A good man's life could have been ruined tonight.'

'I'm not lying,' Nika said quietly.

'Now you wait there, I'm going to call your parents. I think they need to know what you've done.'

'Please don't call our parents,' I said in desperation. They couldn't know about this. 'We're sorry, we're really sorry. We won't do it again.'

'I'm not lying,' Nika said again. 'And I don't care if you call my parents because I'm not lying.'

'Please, please. Don't call our parents. We honestly won't do it again.'

'You're lucky I don't fingerprint you and arrest you for wasting police time,' the policeman stated. 'Now get out of here before I change my mind.'

'I'm not lying,' Nika said. 'Why won't anyone believe me? I'm not lying.'

'Get out of here. *Now.*'

'I'm sorry, Nika. I just couldn't tell him the truth. I couldn't.'

She stared at me as though I wasn't there. Her eyes had glazed over and she looked like she wasn't here any more. Her body was still in this world but whatever essence there was inside that made her Nika was gone. She looked how I felt most of the time – my body was always there but the person I was inside was mostly elsewhere.

'They won't let me stop. They think he's so wonderful and that he's doing so much for me to make my dream come true. And for free, too.' She was talking to the air. 'While I'm under their roof, I have to do what they tell me. I have nowhere to go, and no one believes me. I have to get out of this place. I have to leave.'

344

'I'm sorry, Nika. I'm sure the policeman will go and speak to him anyway, and he'll tell him that they know. And I'm sure he'll stop.'

She didn't speak to me. Not another word after that. We carried on sitting next to each other at school until our exams were finished. Every ballet lesson after that we would sit next to each other and not speak. I would hold her hand and she would act as if I wasn't there. She hardly spoke to anyone – she kept herself to herself. She came to school and did her work. I found out that she had two jobs (three if you counted the paper round she did first thing in the morning), and I saw her at ballet twice a week – for the class lessons and then for the individual lessons. She barely spoke and I knew what she was doing. She was making herself invisible. Because when she did what she did next, when she finally left, she wanted no one to really notice.

Nika

Brighton, 2016

I'm not even sure why I'm crying. I'm not a crier. Crying gets you nowhere.

I learnt that at an early age, when Mummy used to shout at me to stop being a baby.

Crying gets you nowhere, I know that. Except to be told you're making the man you love feel guilty after you have finally seen his true form.

Crying gets you nowhere, I know that. Except to let out some of the horror that lives inside.

I'm not even sure why I'm crying. I wasn't meant to. I was meant to exit the room, compose myself, come back and tell her to stop it or to leave. To let her know that she is the first person I have willingly invited into my home – *my home* – and I don't need her acting out like this. No one needs her to be acting out like this. Now, I'm scrunched up on the floor, sobbing and not knowing if I'm ever going to be able to stop.

14

Roni

'Town Called Malice' is bouncing out from Nika's portable CD player.

We're on the duvet on the floor in her living room, with the tops of our heads touching, staring at the ceiling. I should be at church. It's Sunday and I should be at church, but I haven't been able to leave this place. *We* can't physically leave this place. She's called in sick and we've lain on this floor for hours, listening to music and talking every now and again about stuff like our favourite jelly bean flavours and when we last tried to count all the stars in the sky.

It's almost like last night never happened. That we didn't sit and cry in her bedroom, then she didn't get back into her bed and the two of us didn't lie at opposite ends, crying ourselves to sleep. Almost, but not quite, because we don't talk about anything to do with our lives before now. We have found stuff, by which I mean safe stuff, to talk about, but not the other stuff, the real stuff. That stuff we shy away from like it's a tiger that will overpower and devour us.

'What's the song you've written the notes to on your trainers?' I ask her. That seems a safe question, nowhere near the tiger.

It isn't – safe, that is. She sits bolt upright suddenly. I roll over to look at what she's up to and find her staring at the opposite wall. I don't need to see her face to know she has that vacant look back. To

349

know that she has suddenly checked out. 'I'm going to the loo,' she says and is up and away before I can properly react.

Knock-knock! Comes from her front door and I'm not sure what to do. Answer it? Pretend there's no one in? The quite loud music won't let us get away with that, I don't think. Maybe that's why they've come round – the music might be too loud. I turn it down a couple of notches and hope they go away.

Knock-knock! Comes again. I go to the corridor, look in the direction of the bathroom, which has its door firmly closed, then at the front door. I have to answer it, don't I? Don't I? What else can I do?

A tall, well-built man with the most beautiful dark brown skin and large dark eyes stands on the other side of it. He's shocked for a second and does a double-take before his rather handsome face settles into a frown. 'You're not Nika.'

'No, I'm not. I'm the other Veronica Harper.'

'I don't know what that means, sorry.'

'I went to school with Nika, or Veronika with a k, as she was called, and I'm Veronica with a c, as I was called. We have the same first name and surname. So she became Nika and I was Roni.'

'That was about as clear as mud, to be honest. Sorry, that sounded rude and I didn't mean to be. I think I'm easily confused. Is Nika in?'

'Yes, she's in the bathroom at the moment. Would you like to come in and wait?'

'I'm not sure I should. I'm not sure she wants to speak to me, really.'

'Why, what have you done?'

'I'm not sure.'

'Are you her boyfriend?'

'No, he's not,' Nika says from behind me. The frostiness in her voice tells me that I've done the wrong thing by quizzing him in the way I have. I've most likely done the wrong thing by even answering the door when it's not my home.

'Hi, Marshall,' she says. 'What can I do for you?'

350

He stares at her like he wants to grab her and kiss her, like he wants to hold her and never let her go. I look down at my bare feet because the depth of emotion and desire between them is so barely concealed it's practically naked. It's exposed, virtually tangible.

'You want to do this here, on the doorstep and in front of your friend?' he asks.

She inhales slowly, exhales even more slowly. 'Come in,' she says.

'Sure?'

'Yes. Come in.'

We all end up in the living room and I dash to pick up the duvet and return the cushions to the sofa, while picking up the coffee cups we've left on the floor, too. I return the cups to the kitchen area and lurk about for a few seconds. I don't know what to do. Do I stay here? Do I go into the bedroom out of the way? Do I leave?

He's clearly comfortable talking in front of me, because he begins: 'I thought we had a really good thing going and then you've given me the brush-off and I haven't seen you in over three weeks, you're not answering my texts. What's going on?'

And she's clearly comfortable talking in front of me, too, because she replies: 'It wasn't exactly love's young dream, was it? Both of us knew it wasn't going to last long.'

'I didn't know that at all! Yes, it was mainly physical, but I genuinely thought it was more as well.'

I turn my back to them to try to pretend I'm not there. This is mortifying. I don't want to listen to this stuff. On public transport, people would often talk about this stuff when I was sitting right in front of them because I was invisible in my nun's habit. They thought I wasn't listening, or they believed if I was listening, anything I heard would be kept secret until the day I die. This man, this Marshall, has no idea that I used to be a nun, and he's having this frank conversation with me there.

'Marshall, it was good sex, but I thought we both knew it was just that.'

He remembers I'm there then, and glances in my direction. Even though I have my back to them, I know this because Nika says: 'Oh, don't mind her, she used to be a nun. Or a Sister. Or a nun. Both, I think. She won't tell anyone what we're talking about.'

'All right then. It wasn't good sex, it was *fantastic* sex. You enjoyed it, I enjoyed it – a lot. And I don't understand why you've backed off without even an explanation. Is it Eliza?'

Who's Eliza?

'No. Well, a little, actually. She's served me up another couple of dollops of crazy, but even without her, my life is too complicated. So much has happened I...' Nika's voice wavers and then stops. I know what she wants to say and it isn't what she will say.

'She doesn't think she deserves nice things, or nice people, in your case,' I say. I still have my back turned so I'm not sure if they're looking at me or not. 'Nika doesn't think she has a right to good things happening to her or being around good people.'

'I don't need you to speak for me,' she gently reminds me, probably with a smile pulled tightly across her incredulous face.

'Yes, you do,' I tell her. 'You need someone to speak for you right now because Marshall seems a nice man and you have no right to bin him off to punish yourself. If he wasn't a nice man or if you didn't like him any more or even if you did like him but you didn't want to go out with him, they'd all be legitimate reasons to give him the elbow, but not if it's to hurt yourself. Doing that is like jabbing huge chunks of glass into your forearm to release the pain, when all you're actually doing is causing yourself even more pain.'

'What would you know about it, being a nun? And where does a nun learn expressions like "bin him off"?' Nika says.

'I know stuff. And I know how people talk.' Mainly from watching the relationships of other people developing around me; often from sometimes thinking what I would like from a relationship and accepting how I would do everything I could to sabotage it because I would not feel worthy, I would not be deserving. Like not pursuing things with Cliff, who I actually quite like. Everything that I have come from tells me I cannot have nice things.

'Well, this is awkward,' Marshall says to the quiet in the room. 'I'm not sure what I'm meant to do now, really.'

'You can sit down and we can play card games, if you want?' Nika says. 'If you want. I've, erm, got a pack of cards somewhere, and we can put some music on. I think I've even got "No More Lonely Nights" somewhere.'

'Hey!' Marshall exclaims.

'Sorry, only kidding. You can stay and play card games, if you want. I mean, if you want.'

'Yes, I do want,' Marshall says.

'And you, Nun Face, you can stay too. As long as you stop speaking for me.'

'OK.' I didn't realise me staying wasn't a given, but I don't say that. That would come across as very entitled when I owe her so much. 'Thank you. Can I stop facing the wall now?'

'If you want,' Nika says.

I haven't been to church. Nika is saying goodbye to Marshall at the front door and I haven't been to church today. I haven't prayed at all today. I'm a bit jittery, unsettled and uncomfortable in my skin. Like I've forgotten to brush my teeth.

I didn't want to leave, though. Not even for a moment – I kept hanging on and hanging on to go to the loo because I was fearful that if I left the room, the atmosphere would shatter and all the good feeling would dribble out, leaving us as three strangers pretending we have anything in common while sitting around listening to music from nearly three decades ago.

Really, I should be going home. Now Marshall has gone, I should go and leave Nika in peace. I don't want to, though. I want to stay.

'I haven't been to church today,' I tell her after she has made me a final cup of tea. Someone should know this, I think.

'Is that good or bad?' she asks.

'I don't know, to be honest.'

'As a woman of the cloth, I'd hope you were always honest.'

Is that a dig about what I did all those years ago, or is it her having a laugh?
'I am honest. I don't know how to feel about not going to church on a Sunday for the first time in over twenty years.'

'It must be strange.'

'Really strange.'

'Thank you for what you said to Marshall. You shouldn't have got involved, but thank you.' She whispers this, like a young girl sharing secrets with her sister in the dead of night. She wants no one to hear, not even me.

'Are you going to start seeing him again?' I ask her.

'I've got work at six o'clock tomorrow morning. If you want to stay, you have to be ready to leave by five-thirty. I don't imagine that's hard for you since you must have been getting up at that time for years.'

I'll take that as a 'Mind your own business', then, I think while she gets up and leaves the room. At least I have another night, though, to try to say sorry and try to heal the hole that is slowly eating away at my soul.

Roni

I had to ask Nika four times before she would give me her phone number. The first three times she outright ignored me and got on with whatever it was she was doing, the fourth time I stood in front of her as she loaded her packed lunch and music player into her coat pocket, and asked her.

After a giving me a long, hard stare, as though assessing whether to say no or not, then sighing in resignation, she wrote the number down on a piece of paper and handed it to me without looking in my direction. What we had yesterday was gone, we were back to being strangers.

'Can I call you?' I asked her when we got to the road where we parted ways – her onwards to the hotel she told me she worked at, me left and up the hill to the station.

'If you must,' she replied. She wasn't looking at me and that hurt. My pride again, or simply my feelings? I had hoped we'd slightly broken the barrier that time and my betrayal had erected between us, but no – she'd withdrawn from me, maybe even further than before.

'I must.' I hoped I'd sounded funny when I said that. 'I really must. I found you again; I don't want to lose you. Not when I have to say sorry properly.'

Her gaze found mine then and we stared at each other. I suddenly saw her as she was the day we spotted each other across the ballet studio. She had pigtails on either side, with pink ribbons on the ends, and she had that look that said she was going to be a dancer, that being a ballerina was the only thing she ever wanted to be. It was best friend and soul mate at that sight, for me. For her, too, from what she had said to me over the years. I wanted to kiss her again. To connect to her without words, just like we used to when we were young. After staring at me for a few more seconds this morning, she shook her head as though exasperated by me. 'Bye, Roni.'

'Just to be clear, you don't want the knickers and bra you lent me back, do you?' I was trying to hold on to her a little while longer. If I couldn't hold her hand, couldn't hug her, couldn't kiss her, I wanted her to be near me just that bit longer.

'No, I really do not want them back. Bye.'

'Bye,' I said. Disappointment washed through me. I didn't realise it until I'd seen her on the steps – Nika was where the silence was. Being with her gave me peace. Maybe because she could understand, she was the other half of me, the missing part that quelled the raging inside. If I could find a way to tell her I was sorry, then maybe the silence would be there all the time, and I would be able to let her go. She'd be able to choose to be my friend or not and I would be able to accept that.

She walked away quickly, before I could say anything else to prolong our time together and I had to reluctantly turn towards home.

The second I walk through my parents' door, the oppressive nature of being there and having the secret history of that house bearing down on me is almost too much. I can't breathe properly; I have to squint my eyes a few times because the noise in my head has jumped up a few notches.

By the telephone there is a notepad and pen and even from the front door I see Mum's passive aggression waiting to pounce on me. She has used red ink, and large writing with several instances of underlining, to write messages that cover the whole of the front page of the notepad. I approach it with trepidation. I bet Cliff has called again and that has sent her over the edge. In my defence, I did return his call(s) but he didn't answer when I rang, so I had left a message saying basically, yes, OK, I understood he was ready to ask me *that* question, but as I had explained, I wasn't up for dating at the moment but I would be in touch at some point when I had done what I needed to do. It is not my fault if he didn't understand that as 'stop ringing me'.

I pick up the pad when I see there are four pages of messages. Four pages in red ink, each more aggressively written and underlined and exclamation marked than the last. I didn't know someone would actually take the time to fill half a line with !!!!!!!!!!!!!!!!!!!!!!!!!!!!s, but there it was, another facet of my mother I had been introduced to.

I flip to the last message to see when she took the last one, since I have been gone less than forty-eight hours. At the bottom, she has written in capitals and underlined six times:

GET YOURSELF A MOBILE PHONE!!!!!!!!!!!!

I was going to anyway. I have it all worked out: I will get myself a mobile and I will use it to forge links with Nika. I will send her text messages, I will call her once a week, I will slowly build up contact so we can be friends again. Once we are friends again, I will apologise. I will explain everything, about why I lied to the police, and she will hopefully understand. Not even forgive me, just understand how sorry I was. How sorry I am. How sorry I will always be.

I flip back to the first page of messages, start to read. With each message I read faster and faster, flipping the pages as quickly as I can until I get to the final message. They are all calls from one person. I rip off my coat, throw it down where I stand and take the stairs two at a time. I have to get showered, get changed and get out.

The messages are from Mrs Cecile Frost: Gail has tried to kill herself.

Nika

Brighton, 2016

Seeing Roni has wrecked my head. More than I thought possible. That she wanted my mobile number was a normal request from someone you want to keep in touch with. But do I want to keep in touch with her? I think sometimes I hate her for lying to the policeman. It wasn't only that, though. It was all of it, really. I was sucked into her orbit, made to live out what she did. The sounds of her being screwed by horrible men from the various clubs and bars never went away. They smeared themselves into the shells of my ears, immediately sliming across my memory. I would relive the sounds, the experiences, and it would be like whichever man it was would be grunting in my ear, not hers, and I would be powerless to stop it. I would have to lie in bed at night, listening to it all over again until the memory had played itself out and another, a worse one, would rush in to take its place.

And because I loved her so much, I could never simply walk away and leave her. Not until she lied to the police officer. She had backed away from ending the pain so many times over the years, but that was the final straw for me. I couldn't take any more. I had no way to make it better after the visit to the police station. I stood on the pavement outside and she was talking to me, and I realised I had to leave. Unless I wanted to sleep on the streets, I would have to be single-minded, save up, leave home – basically take my parents up on their offer to allow me to stop the lessons when I stopped living under their roof.

I thought I was ready to see Roni, that I'd know how to deal with her if she was right in front of me. But I couldn't.

After work, I am going to get drunk. It'll be the first time in over ten years, but I am going to get drunk and I am going to put my music on really loud. I am going to let go for once and try to claw back the time I had before life in Brighton started to be about my past again. After work, I am going to start again, *again*. And this time, it is going to stick.

15

Roni

London, 2016

When you're a Sister or a nun, people don't see you. They see what you wear and they see what it symbolises in their minds and memories, but they don't see you, the person. I am still adjusting to walking down the road and people smiling at me and men giving me a once-over to see if they think I am 'hot', as the girls I teach say. I also am still getting used to walking through a hospital, say, and people *not* noticing me. There is no veil, no large cross, no plain blue uniform of skirt, blouse and cardigan, so they do not see me as there to offer spiritual aid and comfort in someone's time of need. Without the items that usually made me blend into the background everywhere else, in a hospital I am just another visitor, seeing a loved one who isn't very well.

I find Gail in a bed on the children's ward of the hospital she has been taken to. There are four other beds in there, the two opposite are occupied, and it is as pleasant as a hospital ward can be – cream-painted walls and brightly coloured pictures of animals and familiar TV characters stencilled and stuck up around the room. The curtains around the beds are cream with tiny blue flowers and each little bed bay has a television hanging down over the bed and a padded easy chair. She is sitting up in bed, staring at the television, remote control in hand, but she doesn't seem to be using it. Instead her eyes are wide, wide open and her body is rigid as though she's been petrified by something that she has just seen.

'Took your time,' she says when she sees me. Slowly I pull the curtain around us and stand by her bed on the opposite side to the chair.

'I was visiting a friend in Brighton,' I said. 'I only just got the messages and came straight here. And by the way, hello to you too.'

'You've got a friend? I doubt it,' she says.

'Did you ask to see me because I'm the only person you feel comfortable insulting?' I ask her.

'Probably,' she says. Her body has relaxed a little since I've been beside her bed, the muscles that stood out, the probably hyper-vigilant nerve endings, all seem slightly soothed for the moment. She smiles shyly at me from under her lowered eyelids. 'Thanks for coming.'

'How could I stay away when I knew the welcome would be this warm?' I say. 'And it's no problem at all. I wish I'd been able to get here sooner.'

'My mum's freaking out,' she states. 'Everyone else is calling it a cry for help.'

'Was it?' I open my mouth to ask. In the nick of time I hold my tongue – she needs to admit it to me so she can admit it to herself. Me asking won't make her question herself; it will make her give me the answer she thinks I want to hear. If I wait, she might tell me the truth.

I sometimes wonder, after all I know about life now, all that I have prayed about, if it would have been a cry for help if I had taken my mother's sleeping tablets all those years ago. Or would it have been what I truly wanted? I remember very clearly, as though it is something I experienced merely seconds ago, the agony that was the inside of my head. Every thought scraped a fresh line of unmitigated pain across my mind. If I reached up, I would have been able to feel the pulsating pain as it throbbed all rational thoughts out of my head. When I was where Gail is, I know that I was chasing the silence and relief from the agony within. Taking the tablets might not have been a cry for help at all.

'It wasn't a cry for help,' Gail says. 'Who would help me? Who would even listen to me, let alone help me? I was so tired. I wanted to sleep for, like, a thousand forevers and wake up to find all the stuff making me tired had gone away. Do you understand?'

'Yes, I understand. I really do.'

'Aren't you going to tell me off? Tell me I was being selfish and that it's a mortal sin and all that other nun stuff?'

'I'm not a nun any more. And even if I was... I couldn't tell you off for something I almost did myself.'

'You almost killed yourself? Why?'

I sit down on the bed and stare down at the blue waffle blanket she has on her bed, the large strip of folded-over white sheet. It reminds me of the veil I used to wear. 'My life was rubbish. I shouldn't say that because I truly believe all life is valuable and precious, but at the time, it felt like my life was rubbish. I had stuff going on at home, my parents barely noticed me, my best friend hadn't spoken to me in eighteen months and then she ran away. I felt so alone.'

'Why didn't you do it?' she asks.

'You wouldn't believe me if I told you. But the fundamental reason is that I didn't want to die. I wanted to live, and just wanted everything that was awful about my life to go away. It didn't really, but I managed to focus my attention on the new goal I had, which was becoming a nun.'

Gail raises her eyes (ironically) to the heavens and drifts away from me like a cloud blown away by a sudden gust of wind. She thinks I'm trying to convert her, to bring her into the fold that I have left, instead of simply relaying to her a part of my story.

'You need to tell someone what he's doing to you,' I tell her. 'Even if you don't think it's that bad because it hasn't gone beyond brushing up against you, you need to tell. He has no right to touch you, to say stuff to you, to show you inappropriate pictures. None of it. He has no right to make you feel like this. It doesn't matter who he is, he has no right to do this.'

Her face twists in pain and terror. 'What if she doesn't believe me?' Gail says inside a sob. I am being turned inside out, violently eviscerated by the memory of feeling like this. Poor Gail. I remember what it was like. To have the smell of another person all over you mingled in with the scent of your own fear, to be constantly on edge waiting for it to happen, to be terrified that you will be blamed. I hate that another person is going through this. I hate that Gail is going through this. At moments like this, I remember the other reason for leaving. It was there, and I did not want to face it, did not want to examine it in any detail because I would be behaving like Judas again – I would be betraying another love. At moments like this, I question why fragile, lost souls like Gail have to go through what I did, what Nika did, what thousands and millions do. Free will is the answer, of course. Humans have free will, and we often seem to use that freedom to harm others.

It *almost* broke Nika that her parents didn't believe her, what *did* break her, though, was me lying to the police officer and ensuring that he didn't believe her, either. She was relying on me, she had been my rock in so many ways for so many years, and when I was called upon to stand up for her, I behaved like two of Jesus's most beloved apostles on the night before the crucifixion: I became Judas first of all and betrayed her; then I became like Peter and turned away when asked to confirm the truth of what she was saying. I betrayed her; I lied about her. I did it because of free will. My free choice to behave in that way directly harmed another. I had my reasons, but as time has gone on, I know those reasons weren't good enough. Nika's already-nightmarish life became a living hell because of my free will. I know, because Mr Daneaux told me.

'I can't promise she'll believe you,' I tell Gail. I take her hand. 'I *will* promise that I will be with you for as long as you need me to be. I will support you, I will speak for you and with you. And I will help you keep on telling until someone believes you.'

'Really?' she asks, sniffling back the tears.

'Yes, absolutely, yes. And if you're not ready to tell, I will still support you. But Gail, I think you should tell. If it's the choice between your life and believing that staying silent will protect your mum, your life and safety come first every time. *Every time.*'

The curtain is whipped back suddenly and we're confronted by two perplexed and quite angry-looking people: Gail's mother, who up close really is the older version of her daughter, and her step-father from the choir, who holds himself like a man who is used to being in charge.

'Who are you?' Cecile Frost demands. 'What are you doing with my daughter with the curtain closed?'

I stand up and release Gail's hand. Gail's mother's eyes dart to where my hands were, then she rapidly, critically, checks me over again. She thinks that danger comes from the outside, from perverts who hang around street corners, trying to snatch children off the street. She doesn't realise that perverts can also live in your home, sleep in your bed, make love to your body, stand beside you in hospitals. '*I said*, who are you?'

'My name is Veronica Harper, I was a supply teacher at your daughter's school. You got my number from Gail's school and called me? It's me you've been leaving messages for the last couple of days, saying Gail wanted to see me?'

'Oh, right, you're the nun, yes?'

'*I'm not a nun any more,*' I almost say but don't. There are some points that need to be laboured upon but not this one and not at this time. 'That's right.'

'Why did she want me to call you? I mean, who are you to my daughter?'

The man beside Gail's mother is switching his gaze between Gail and me. He's trying to work out what Gail has told me and if he needs to start damage limitation by painting her character as bad, as troublemaking and untrustworthy, while simultaneously implying someone has been planting false memories into her mind. Do to Gail what Mr Daneaux did to Nika.

'Because of my former vocation, I think Gail felt able to confide in me some personal things that she might not want to share at the moment.' I leave it to Cecile to infer from what I have said that I am bound by the absolute rule of the confidentiality of the confessional.

'What personal things?' Cecile's attention flies towards her daughter. She moves to Gail, takes her hand and lowers herself to her level. 'Are you pregnant?' she asks her daughter. 'Is that what this is all about? Because I don't care about that, I couldn't stand to lose you over that.'

'I'm not pregnant,' Gail whispers.

'Oh, Gaily, what is it then? Because I'm running out of clues here, and you haven't said a word to anyone in nearly three days about why you did it. I mean, have you told this woman why? Because I need to know, too. Whatever it is, I'll still love you; nothing will change how much I love you. You and your brothers, you are the most important things in my life. You can tell me anything, *anything*, I thought you knew that. *Anything, any time.*'

'Come on, Cecile, give the girl some space. She'll tell you in her own time,' Gail's stepfather says. Panic. What his wife is saying is not what he wants to hear, it is not what he wants Gail to hear. To carry on getting away with what he has been doing, he needs Gail to believe that her mother is like my mother, like my father, like Nika's mother, like Nika's father – unengaged, disinterested, more likely to believe the adult than the child. He needs to show Gail that no one will believe her, no one cares that much about her, that she is isolated and alone.

'Mr Frost, I think we should leave Gail and her mother alone for a while. It can't be easy for Gail, talking with an audience. How about we step into the corridor for a little while so they can have a chance to speak?' *And I can decide if I'm willing to be arrested for assaulting you or not.*

'No, no, I'll stay. Cecile and Gail both need me to be here.'

'It's all right, babe, you go,' Cecile replies. 'I think this woman's right, we've been crowding her. I need to talk to her one on one to find out what's going on. That's what's important right now. You can support me afterwards like you always do.'

He glowers at me, glares menacingly at Gail, tries to tell her to keep her mouth shut. Gail is staring at me and can't see the looks he's giving her. I smile at her, nod my head slightly. This could be her only chance to do this for a while. I was telling the truth – I will be there with her every step of the way if she wants me to be. All she has to do is speak. But I can't do that part for her. And if she isn't ready, she isn't ready and I'll wait until she is.

In the corridor, Gail's stepfather paces up and down, a caged man trying to get out and back into the arena where he can control what lions of truth are set free. 'That Gail, she's a little minx sometimes,' he says to me. 'I could throttle her for what she's putting her mother through.' He shakes his head, paces a little more, back and forth, back and forth, in front of me. 'All she does is cause her mother worry. Out all the time, drinking, smoking, taking drugs, probably. I'm sure she's always running around with boys.' He stops to gauge how well his character-smearing is going, if I'm buying it. All those things are shocking to anyone, but particularly to a nun. He probably thinks I'm bound to turn against her now, to not believe a word that comes out of her slutty little mouth.

In response, I say nothing.

'I-I-I-I mean, I know I should be more understanding of her situation, growing up without a father figure, but I believe young people need discipline. They need firm boundaries, someone who is going to keep them on a good moral path. Don't you think?'

He begins to pace a bit harder, faster, more frantically when I say nothing at all again. 'I think it's good that she's got someone like you, a woman of God, to guide her back to a purposeful path. I'm an active member of my local church, too. A lot of people have turned away from the Church in recent years but I think it's an important part of family life. Gail is not that keen on attending with us, but we think it's important. Maybe you can help advise her on the importance of having God in her life. It will help her to cut down on the lying, the drinking and running around. I think it'll really help her to have you around.' He stops, frowns at me approvingly.

I'm not sure why he thinks I am on his side or why I would be bothered by his approval or lack thereof, but he conveys it to me with his nod and expression. I stand very still and watch him. He is valiantly battling with my silence, the uncertainty of not knowing if his wooing exercise is working or not.

Will Gail be able to do it? I wonder as the man who has created a hell on Earth for a fourteen-year-old girl, paces back and forth in front of me.

It is plain what he is doing: with each word, he is prodding at me to try to find a weak spot, something that will move me from where I am – an unknown quantity in this dynamic – to firmly on his side. He desperately needs me to shout down Gail's mother and Gail when the truth starts to leak out.

'Not much of a talker, are you?' he says to me.

I shake my head.

His face creases into an understanding smile. He is calming down, reassessing this new piece of information and thinking of a new way to access my support. Next tactic: charm. If someone doesn't talk much, they are more likely to respond to someone calmer, quieter, more self-effacing; I'm more likely to be a support if I like him, see elements of myself in him. He stops the pacing, and leans against the wall opposite, mirroring my pose – legs slightly extended, hands resting between the middle of my lower back and the wall.

Right on cue: 'Sorry about before,' he says, quietly. 'All that stuff isn't like me at all. I'm so worried about Gail, and, of course, what all this is doing to her mother. It makes me a little crazy. Sorry.'

I listen to him talk and wonder what will come after the charm, what tactic he'll try next. Unfortunately, I'll never know: Gail's mother is a blur as she shoots past me towards her husband. He only has time to stand a little way away from the wall before she punches him so hard I'm sure I hear her hand or his jaw or both, crack. I'm so taken aback I can't respond. He staggers back against the wall, cowering while he clutches his jaw, confusion and shock on his face. He's shocked because he thought he'd groomed Gail enough not to tell, had groomed her mother enough not to react, had perfected his image enough for no one to believe he is capable of it. Gail's mother moves in on him again, grabbing his shoulders and bringing her knee up between his legs. This time I do react: I grab her away from him, hold her back while he keels over, a tree felled by one swift chop where it counts.

370

She is spitting venom, her body poised to attack again, and I'm finding it hard to grapple with her, to stop her from inflicting more damage. 'You bastard,' she hisses. I'm assuming she doesn't want to disturb and upset the other young patients by screaming at him, although how she manages to restrain herself vocally when she is a fighting bundle of anger, I don't know. 'You're lucky I don't cut it off. I've called the police; they're on their way. I just wanted to kick the living daylights out of you before they get here. You bastard! She's my baby, she's my baby.

'The police better lock you up for a long time because if I get my hands on you again, I will not stop until you are dead. Do you hear me?'

'No, Mrs Frost,' I say. It's taking all my strength to hold her back. Part of me doesn't want to, of course. Part of me wants to let her go, to let her at him to give him everything he deserves. But Gail doesn't deserve to have her mother in prison, or even taken away from her no matter for how short a time. 'Stop. Go back to Gail, please. She's the important one right now. Really, she's the one who you should be worried about. Go back to her, please. *Please.*'

That seems to sink in and she calms down enough to wrench herself away from me. 'And you,' she snarls at me. She closes in on me, her face right up against mine. I shrink back. 'You call yourself a woman of God – she is a child. She. Is. A. Child. You should have told me the second you found out.'

'I was trying to support Gail, let her decide what to do.'

'*She's a child,*' she replies with contempt. 'You don't let children make those decisions. You tell someone. You tell me, you tell the police. You don't just let her walk back into a house where a pervert is abusing her. She could have died. If you had done something, this wouldn't have happened. We wouldn't be here now. She could have permanent liver damage from taking those pills. She could have died, all because you were too cowardly to speak up. You're a disgrace as a human being. I don't know which God you think you work for, but it isn't mine.'

371

Every word, every syllable, every letter of her contempt is justified and I hang my head in shame. I did wrong, trying to do right. I should have gone straight to Gail's mother, to the school or to the police. I should have done something. Doing nothing meant that Gail was pushed to this. Her mother, who has snarled at me again, goes back to her daughter. Around me nurses and doctors and orderlies and patients are staring. They have heard every word and are probably judging me, too. I know only God is meant to judge, but how can I not judge myself in this situation? How can I turn it over to the Lord and find forgiveness and understanding in Him? What I did – *nothing* – is unforgivable.

The noise in my head is suddenly so loud. So loud. I can barely think, it is so loud. When she has gone, I slam my hands over my ears, even though I know the noise is inside my head. Maybe if I can stop any more noise coming in from the outside, it won't be as bad on the inside. But no, the noise keeps on coming. I start to walk quickly towards the exit, the noise so loud it's blinding me as well as deafening me. I need silence. I need to find the silence. I need anything that will make this noise and pain stop.

I need Nika.

16

Roni

Nika isn't answering her door. I've been buzzing and buzzing and buzzing her and she won't answer the door. I am desperate now. From the moment I left the hospital I have had this feeling inside, a desperate, urgent need to speak to her. It has only got worse with time. Trapped inside my chest is a bag of wild, agitated cats fighting each other, fighting to be released. I need to see Nika so I can set everything inside my chest free.

And she isn't answering. I came straight here from the hospital and it is late afternoon. I thought she would be here by now and I would be able to see her. I push the buzzer again, knowing that it is buzzing into an empty flat. Or it is buzzing into a flat where the resident is sitting on the sofa, ignoring the desperate, slightly crazed woman standing on the doorstep.

I swing away from the large doorway, wondering what to do. Should I walk down towards her hotel? What if she takes a different route home from work and I miss her? I'll have all these emotions, this bag of crazed cats in my chest, for much longer, far longer than I think I can bear. A blonde woman wearing a raincoat approaches the front door and in my desperation, I go towards her. I calm myself, though, don't want to appear too erratic and unstable for her to speak with.

'Excuse me, do you know Nika?' I ask her. I even manage a normal smile.

'Yes, why, who are you?' she asks. I want to take a step back from her: she wears far too much perfume – if I get too close I'll end up doused in it, too. She also wears far too much make-up, and I wonder for a moment what she has to hide.

'Erm, I'm an old friend. I've trying to reach her for a while but she doesn't seem to be in. I've been wondering if you've seen her today?'

This seems to tweak her interest and she moves from being slightly scornful and irritated to all ears. 'An old friend? Is this about Grace? Grace Carter?'

I shake my head. 'Who's Grace Carter?' I ask, even more confused. The noise in my head is up near the levels of deafening me from the inside out. I don't have time for games and talking about Grace Carter, whoever she may be.

'No one, I thought... Never mind,' the blonde woman says, disappointed and then back to being uninterested in me again. 'You say Nika isn't in? Well, sorry, then, I can't help you really.'

'I thought she'd be home from work by now as she was out so early this morning...'

'Sorry, can't help you.'

The woman shoves her key into the lock of the outer door. If she'll let me in, I can wait outside Nika's door. Then it occurs to me – of course! Of course! *Marshall*. Maybe she's with him. 'Do you know Marshall?' I ask.

The woman stops pushing open the door and turns to me. 'Yes, I know Marshall,' she replies, looking at me suspiciously. 'I know most of the people in the building.'

'Do you know what number he lives in?'

'Yes, but why?'

'I thought Nika might be there.'

'Why would Nika be in his flat?'

'Because he's her...' *Eliza*. I am probably talking to Eliza. *Of course* I'm talking to Eliza. Neither Nika nor Marshall had said anything about her again after mentioning her briefly during their initial conversation, but I know without a doubt that this is her and I should not say anything

376

more, not when I know she is capable of dropping a couple of dollops of crazy on Nika and interfering with their relationship.

'He's her what?' she asks.

'Friend? He's her friend. She mentioned he was her friend the other day.'

'Right. And you think she might be in his flat, since she's his friend?'

'It was just a thought,' I say. 'She also mentioned someone called Eliza, do you know her? She's another of her friends. If you could tell me where she lives, maybe Nika's there?'

She regards me with contempt, her green eyes hard and unconvinced: she has not been fooled *at all* by my cover-up attempt. 'I'm Eliza. But obviously she's not in my flat since I'm out here.' Eliza stares down her nose at me. 'But you're right, she might be in Marshall's flat. Why don't we go and check?'

She is terrifying. In the moments when she realised that I was about to say Marshall was Nika's boyfriend, a transformation has taken place, moving her from wary stranger to violently jealous ex. Although, I can't imagine Marshall with her. She seems too... there's a word for her, it's there at the back of my mind, on the tip of my tongue to describe the many facets of instability she is displaying but I can't put my finger on it. She simply does not seem like Marshall's type. But who is anyone's type? If you knew me between the ages of twelve and sixteen you would not have thought I was God's type. Although, God does want sinners to turn to him, so maybe I was always God's type, I simply didn't realise it until the nun gave me her book.

'No, it's OK, I think I'm just going to wait for her here.'

'Good idea, I'll go up and check on my own.' The fake smile she treats me to before she steps in through the doorway is sinister and quietly ferocious. She seems to be already dismembering Nika in her head.

This is why I should have a MOBILE PHONE!!!!!!!!!!!!!!!!! I could warn Nika about the trainee serial killer heading her way. And this Eliza hasn't told me which flat Marshall lives in so I can't buzz up to him to alert him to her approach. It sounded, from their conversation the other day, that Marshall and Nika mainly had sex. Which would make it a safe bet that if they're together, they're more than likely engaged in *that* right now. If Eliza knocks on his door and they're *in flagrante delicto*, she's bound to find out. I suspect when *that* happens Eliza's going to go absolutely—

'I thought you'd gone home?' Nika says to me. I have been so busy fretting in the wake of Eliza's exit that I haven't been watching the comings and goings on the street.

'I did,' I say. I have to stop myself from throwing my arms around her. I am so relieved to see her. Now the noise in my head will stop, and Eliza won't find her in some state of undress in Marshall's flat and start dismembering people. 'I came back. I had to see you. I need to explain.'

'Roni, not tonight. I am exhausted in every way possible, this is not the time for this conversation.'

'I have to tell you why. It's not an excuse, and I don't want you to forgive me or even to understand, but I want to be honest. Please. Afterwards I'll do my best to leave you alone. It'll be hard, but I'll try.'

I wonder what she is seeing when she stands very still, watching me like she does from behind her glasses. I wonder if she sees me with pigtails with pink ribbons at the ends, wearing the same expression as her – someone who has also decided she wants to be a dancer. I wonder if she is looking back through time to the moment when she knew we were going to be the best of friends, the closest of soulmates.

Possibly, probably, because eventually she says: 'Fine. I'm too tired to argue with you right now. I'm too tired for much of anything.' Her keys jangle as she moves to unlock the front door.

'Oh, by the way, I think I might have dropped you in it with Eliza?' I figure I should mention that now, before we start to talk about the other stuff.

Nika rolls her eyes. 'Why, what did you d— Actually, to be honest, I don't want to know. I don't care. I'll deal with her when I have to. Just come in and tell me what you want to tell me and then you can get the last train back to London.'

*

She doesn't make me get the train back to London. She sits and she listens and I find myself telling her everything. I was going to tell her a portion of it and explain why I did what I did, but then I can't stop. I talk and talk and talk. I even tell her about Gail, about what Gail's mother said to me and how I knew it was true. As I talk, the noise in my head eases, it lowers and lowers and lowers until I can't hear it. Until there's barely a sound in my head.

When I had made my decision to become a nun, I started to go to weekly confession. I used to seal myself into the wooden box and tell everything to the priest of a church three train stops away. I did not want to speak to anyone who might know me or who might recognise my voice. I wanted the freedom to speak freely. The priest would listen and he would absolve me. When I left the confessional, for a time, the noise in my head would be gone, banished by speaking my truth. I would have the silence I craved. That was how I knew becoming a nun was the right thing to do: where God was, I could find the silence, God was in and with the silence.

That effect, anaesthetising and cleansing as it was, had started to fade in recent years. Most acutely in recent months when thoughts of Judas started to encroach on all my prayers and all my thoughts away from prayers. That was when I accepted that I had betrayed Nika in a way that I could not ask anyone but her for forgiveness. I accepted, too, that I had betrayed God by not being honest about what I had done in any of my confessions. I was a betrayer, a coward, and this was my chance to put things right.

'Will you pray with me?' I ask her when I have finished talking. We are sitting in her bed again, the warmest place in the flat, it seems, unless we sit directly in front of the lit oven.

Nika shakes her head. 'That's not for me. But feel free to do it if you want.'

I ask her another question then, and she stares at me. She stares at me and stares at me and stares at me. 'Yes,' she eventually says.

And she doesn't say another word to me all night.

Nika

I'm doing it for Reese. He's probably dead because of me and I need something good to have come out of the death wish he said I have that most likely got him killed.

I'm also doing it for a fifteen-year-old girl whose best friend betrayed her when she needed her most.

I'm doing it for me, for Nika, the girl that no one would ever believe.

17

Roni

'What's this, brought another nun to try and convert us all, have you?' Uncle Warren says with a laugh.

My uncle's laugh – actually, his voice – grates on me today. He sits on the sofa beside my mother, wearing Dad's slippers, with the top button of his shirt open. It's obvious he slept here last night. I'm grateful I wasn't here: he would have tried to speak to me, probably would have made a few of his unfunny quips then expected me to accept his apology. I would have, as well. It's hard not to when someone is telling you they are sorry and you're almost trained to make allowances for them.

'Nika isn't a nun,' I say to Mum and Dad.

'Nika? What sort of a name is that? Sounds Eastern European. And no offence, love, but you don't look Eastern European,' my uncle says to my friend who is standing beside the living room door.

I ignore my uncle. I can't allow myself to be sidetracked by thinking about his nastiness and the effect it has on me. I have to do this. 'Mum and Dad, do you remember Nika? The other Veronika Harper?'

They are having tea and coffee in the living room and it is all very civilised and genteel, the epitome of what my mother wanted for her life. I often think she only had children because that was what she, a white, middle-class woman with a respectable husband who had a good job and drove a nice car, was expected to do. She never really

383

engaged with any of us, but by the time she reached the task of bringing me up, she acted as if she was literally going through the motions because she couldn't be bothered any more. I was 'a fuss' personified and that was draining for her. That's why we children adored my uncle – he was engaged with us, he didn't mind the fuss, the mess, the effort required to spend time with us. My uncle gave us attention, the type we rarely received unbidden from my mother, and we loved him for it.

'Oh, yes!' Mum says. She gets up and bustles out of the room to retrieve more cups, more side plates for pieces of cake. While she is gone, Dad puts aside his paper and stands up. He holds out his hand to warmly shake Nika's hand.

'I remember you, Veronika,' he says. 'You danced so beautifully as the Sugar Plum Fairy in *The Nutcracker* one Christmas. We originally hoped our Veronica would get the part but you did an excellent job. And Veronica had her chance the next year with her role in *Swan Lake*. You were fantastic, though.'

'Thank you,' Nika says. She can't take her hand back from Dad quick enough. All the time she is watching him warily. She has been wary and anxious, has pretty much permanently had her headphones from her music player installed in her ears, zoning out while the music plays, since we left Brighton for here this morning. I have been chasing silence all this time; Nika has been using music as her drug of choice. I know she is itching to put her earphones in right now, to escape from this.

When Mum has returned with two cups, Nika shakes her hand, too. Uncle Warren hasn't moved from his seat so if Nika intends to shake his hand she will have to go to him. It's obvious she doesn't want to be here and that even walking into the living room has been enough of an ordeal; there is no way she is moving from where she stands by the door, ready, it seems, to make a run for it.

It is a sunny Tuesday afternoon in May. I want to remember that. Remember this feeling, what the world felt like before I unpack these coming moments of honesty and truth.

'It's so nice of you to visit us, Veronika. The other Veronika,' Mum says with a laugh. 'I always found it so strange that two people could be from completely different families but have the same last name and would then call their daughters the same thing.'

I have to do this now, before I chicken out and let my mother slide into being the perfect hostess and it becomes a nightmare trying to get her to listen. I turn to Nika, then swing back to my family. I wish my brothers were here. No more secrets, no more lies. I want all of them to know. It's time. Trembling, almost violently shaking, I hold my hand out for Nika. When she doesn't take it, I turn to her again. She is standing frozen, petrified by what I'm about to do. I keep my hand out for her because I need her to do this with me, I need her to hold my hand so I can say it out loud.

'*I need you,*' I say to her in my head.

She steps forward and slips her hand into mine; our fingers intertwine and I am brave. I have courage. She is standing beside me and there is near silence in my head. This is the right thing to do.

'Bloody hell! You're not about to tell us you're one of *them*, are you?' Uncle Warren says. 'I always did think you were a bit odd, and wanting to be around other women all day... Well, you know how that's gonna turn you. It's not—'

'Mum and Dad, when I was fifteen I went with Nika to the police.' My uncle stops moving and speaking, as do my parents. They obviously do not know about this. 'Our ballet teacher had been molesting us since we were eleven, and he progressively got worse until at thirteen it got as bad as it can get. Nika went to the police...' I have to stop. I can't do this. I remember the emptiness of her eyes as we stood outside the station, the way she had disappeared into blankness because she knew no one would believe her now and she had to go back to him again and again. 'Nika went to the police and I... I lied and said it wasn't true. I had to lie because... because Uncle Warren had been molesting me since I was eight years old and I was scared what he would do to Brian and Damian if I had to tell the police about it.'

In my parents' living room, five people react in different ways to what I have said: *I* feel the tears that have been sitting at the rim of my eyes start to fall; *Nika* does not move and I suspect she doesn't breathe; *my uncle* turns white and looks from one parent to another to see who is going to react first; *my father* stares at me like I have just appeared in front of him in a puff of smoke; and *my mother . . . my mother* glares at me as though I have betrayed her by telling this secret that was not so secret to her.

'He stopped because Mum walked in on him . . . she walked in on him forcing . . .' I have to say the word, I have to say that hideous word to not minimise it any longer, to make it clear how horrific it was. 'Mum walked in on him . . . r-r— *raping* me in the kitchen when he was meant to be watching me after school.'

'*Veronica!*' Mum breathes in a shocked voice.

'I saw you, Mum. I saw you in the reflection of the kitchen window. I saw you walk into the kitchen with the shopping, and then walk out again, and come back making lots of noise so he would know you were there.' Nika's hand is tight against mine, so tight we are both probably in pain because every one of her finger bones seems to dig into me. 'You saw what he was doing to me, how he was hurting me, and rather than shout at him or get rid of him or call the police, you just walked out again.'

I saw her outline in the kitchen window, and I thought I was saved, that what was happening was over and now she knew, she'd stop him, she'd get rid of him. But instead, she stepped backwards, and pulled the door almost shut behind her. I started to choke and cry, not only because he was hurting me, but because my mum had seen what he was doing to me and she had gone away. And she wasn't coming back. The minutes between the realisation that she was never coming back and her loud slamming of the front door followed by her excessively loud 'I'm home' call were the longest I'd ever experienced. He'd let me go, hissed at me to put my knickers back on, fix myself up, and to remember that if I ever said a word to anyone he'd kill my brothers and make it look like an accident.

386

'I couldn't tell the police officers the truth because he'd always told me he would kill Brian and Damian and I knew he'd do it. He was always here and I knew he'd do it during one of the times he took them out on their bikes and everyone would think it was an accident, except I would know the truth and it would be my fault they were dead because I didn't keep quiet.'

After that day that Mum saw him raping me, my uncle never touched me again, but he was always around, regularly leering at me, constantly in my face. He never touched me again, but the threat of it was always as clear and present as daylight; the knowledge that my mum knew and would do nothing so as to avoid causing a fuss was always there, too.

After that day, my mother never looked me in the eye again; she acted as though I was invisible.

My father is on his feet. 'Is this true?' he asks my mother, his voice quivering. He's confused and angry and shocked and scared, all at the same time, each emotion vying with the others to be the one let out first.

'It wasn't like that, Geoffrey.' Mum is shaking and white, her hands moving frantically as she tries to explain, but she hasn't moved from her seat. 'He said it was only that one time, that he'd got caught up and confused about how he felt about her, and it had gone too far. I told him. I told him not to go near her again. I made sure he didn't touch her again. I let her go out as much as she wanted so she could be out of the house if he was here.'

'STOP TALKING, MARGARET! STOP TALKING RIGHT NOW!' Dad screams at her. Dad turns to me and opens his arms to me. Nika releases my hand and I go to him. He takes me in his arms, holds me so I am close, I am protected. 'My poor baby girl,' he whispers against my hair. 'My poor, poor baby girl. I'm so sorry, I should have known. I should have known. I am so very, very sorry that I didn't. I'm so very sorry I didn't protect you.'

The noise in my head is gone. Probably not for ever, but I can think at last. I can think and I can stop thinking. I can be. I can find the silence, even for this tiniest moment of time. My father rocks and hushes me and there is silence for once.

'And Nika, I'm so sorry for what you went through, too,' my father says, releasing me from his hold to bring her in, too. He wants to comfort her, to show her that he believes her. That she matters, too.

We turn to where she was standing, but she's gone. My uncle has gone, too, probably running while he has the chance. But Nika is the one I care about. She deserves to have someone comfort her, to tell her they believe her, to hold her and tell her they're sorry. She deserves that, more than I do.

I tear out of the living room, out of the front door and on to the street. I look up and down the road, my eyes wildly searching for her, but there's no sign of her. No lone figures walking away in either direction. Just houses and cars. No people. No Nika.

'NIKA!' I call out because she can't have gone that far. 'Nika, come back. NIKA! PLEASE! *Please, come back.*' I stand in the street and shout for long enough for curtains to start to twitch, people to start to take notice. I keep on screaming, though, shouting for her to come back. Eventually, my dad comes and places a hand on my shoulder.

'She's gone, Veronica. She's gone. Come back inside. Come back and tell me everything.'

'But I couldn't have done it without her,' I explain. 'Her parents never believed her and now she's gone and she doesn't think anyone cares about her. It's not fair, Dad.'

'I know, Veronica, I know.' He gently brings me back into the house and takes me in his arms again to try to hug me better.

Nika

London, 2016

I hear her calling my name, telling me to come back.

I can't go back. How can I? Her father believed her. She didn't need me to be there, all she needed was to say the words and he believed her. No one has ever believed me first time. How could I go back and watch her have what I needed all along?

'NIKA!' I hear her screaming.

But I don't move from sitting here behind a parked car. I'm not going to move until she goes inside and I can go away from this place, this town, and never come back.

18

Nika

I want to go back to my flat, crawl into a hole and disappear again.

I am tempted, in such a visceral, animalistic way, to ditch this life and go back to being Grace Carter. That is dangerous thinking, precarious fantasising, not only for me but for everyone I knew back then, too.

Instead, I walk slowly back from Brighton station, keeping my head lowered in case I see anyone I know. When I arrive home, I let myself into the communal hall, then walk up the three flights of stairs to the second floor, walk along the corridor that is identical to my floor and stop outside 207.

Marshall won't be back from work yet, but I need to not be on my own. I need to be with someone I feel safe with and who knows me as someone undamaged and untainted by life. I have had to switch off my phone, because Roni has been calling it non-stop since I disappeared from her house and she stopped shouting for me in the street. I know she'll turn up at some point, maybe even today, so I need to be not there right now. I sit down, pull my knees up to my chest, slowly push a black earbud into each ear. I push the play button on the music player. INXS's 'Need You Tonight' starts to play in my ears and I smile to myself. Sometimes my music player seems to know what I'm going through and throws up a song accordingly. I haven't heard this song in an age. I rest my forehead on my knees, curl up into the music and allow myself to drift away.

'Talk about your dream come true,' Marshall says.

One of my earphones has slipped out of my ear, so his voice wakes me up. I lift my head – sleeping sitting up has etched many kinks into my muscles and moving even slightly has fired up several of my pain centres. It aches again to lower my legs, to turn to face the man who has spoken to me. His face crinkles up with such an affectionate smile that it takes my breath away. No one has ever smiled at me like that.

'How do you mean?' I ask him.

'I've been thinking about you all day, and I come home and there you are waiting for me. I didn't think I'd ever get that far into your life where you'd sit and wait for me.'

Instead of replying, I take the other earbud out, cut off Boyz II Men's 'I Swear' mid-chorus and slowly wind the wires around the music player.

'Ahh, another of my famous conversation-killers.'

'It's been a long day,' I say to him. 'I wanted to see you, that's all. If it's not convenient...?'

'At what point did you get "not convenient" from what I said?' he jokes. 'I wanted to see you, was wondering how long I'd have to leave it after spending so much time with you and the other Veronica, and now you're here. All very convenient for me.'

'And it's not a bit creepy for you, especially since you've got someone else who's always turning up?'

'No, it feels nothing like that.'

'I'm not really up for... you know. I was hoping we could maybe talk?'

'That's cool. Totally cool. I have some stuff to tell you, anyway.' Marshall lets go of his laptop bag and stands up. Once fully upright, he holds his hands out to me. My fingers slip easily, neatly, familiarly between his as he draws me upwards. I think of holding Roni's hand while she told her parents the absolute truth about her life. Who she

394

was, what she had to put up with, why she did some of the things she did. I remember the pain there was from holding her so tight. I could feel her slipping as she spoke and I had to cling on to her, hold her there so she didn't stop speaking. I remember the moment of release, when her dad opened his arms to her and she went to him. I'm jealous. Why was she believed and me not? What is it about me that I have to carry this secret shame alone, no matter what I do?

Marshall holds on to my fingers a while longer, as though he knows I'm about to fall. What happened has tripped me up, made me fall when I didn't think there was much that could do that now. I think of Reese's hole and how I have my own one, how I am teetering so close to the edge of it, I need to cling on to the outer edge and stop myself slipping. If I fall back into wanting to be Grace Carter, I will not haul myself out of there again.

'You want noodles?' Marshall asks. He still has hold of my hands, staring into my eyes – he probably doesn't realise he is keeping me from falling backwards.

'Yeah, I can eat noodles.' Yes, I can eat noodles. And I can pretend everything is normal for now.

'Eliza fell of the wagon,' Marshall tells me while he chops up vegetables in his kitchen area.

I am standing right beside him (I need to keep him close) while I roll a dirt-covered leek back and forth across the counter, listening to the *fhap, fhap, fhap* of his knife at work. It has a rhythm that is tranquillising, almost soporific. Every time I try to hook into its beat, though, he stops chopping and starts another vegetable. 'Oh,' I reply.

'You don't believe she was ever on the wagon, do you?'

I shake my head. 'Not really, no.'

He stops what he's doing and stands very still, his head to one side as he stares at the stainless-steel cooker hood. 'Neither do I, if I'm honest.' *Fhap, fhap, fhap* starts up again. 'I was being pretty arrogant, telling myself I could help her and that one conversation would do it. She came over the other day and stole the new tablet I bought for my son's birthday. This weekend he's meant to be coming to stay for the week, and now I can't give him his birthday present because she's stolen it. Just took it right from under my nose. I couldn't believe it. She denied and denied and denied it. Even tried to blame you by hinting I didn't know you very well but I was letting you into my flat. It was only when I threatened to tell her parents and the police that she admitted it. Cried and cried, promised she'd pay me back because she'd sold it.'

'When was this?'

'Sunday night. She came over after I came back from yours, and by Monday night when I confronted her, she'd sold it. Then she tries to tell me she's sold it because she's lost her job. I mean, what the *hell*…?' Marshall slams the knife down in frustration. 'How did she even know where to sell it so quickly? It defies belief.' He starts chopping again. 'I can't even think about her, let alone look at her. I've had my phone off all day. I actually thought she'd be sitting outside, not you.'

'Did she tell you when she lost her job?'

'No, although I should have guessed as she never had her pass to get into the building the last few times she's come to work with me. I suppose it must have been before she went to visit her parents. This is so not what my life has been about so far. I don't know how to deal with all of this.'

'It's hard when someone you care about is in that particular hole.'

'Which leads me to ask how you knew? I meant to ask before but we're not exactly known for talking.'

'Well, Marshall, I know because one of the absolute loves of my life – not a boyfriend or anything like that – a friend who I adored was a smackhead. I call him that and it sounds disrespectful, and I should say heroin addict, but if I do that, I minimise what he was. I make it sound like he didn't behave in some pretty appalling ways to get money to feed his habit.' Marshall's *fhap, fhap, fhap* stops again. I have been staring at the white tiles of his kitchen floor while I speak and now I look up to see him staring at me. He has shock on his face. No, not shock, shock is only fleetingly expressed. He has horror on his face. 'But I loved him so much, you know. So I put up with it. I learnt to stop enabling him when it came to giving him money, but I couldn't cut him off. He told me himself that me not cutting him off was probably one of the worst things I could do for him. I couldn't, though, not until I had to.' I couldn't cut him off. Reese was my drug of choice. People who need me are my drug of choice. That's what's different about Marshall: he doesn't need me in the same way that Roni always needed me, in the way that Reese needed me, in the way that Lori needed me.

Marshall puts down his knife, his cooking forgotten as he finds out more about me than he imagined. 'Is he OK now?' he asks.

The torment of that question claws through me and I have to close my eyes, centre myself before I can answer. 'He's probably dead.' I say this out loud and it rips through me again. 'I have no way of knowing for sure, but for various reasons, I think he's gone.'

'Jesus, that's horrible. Can't you find out?'

I shake my head. 'No, I can't. The thing of it is, Marshall, not so long ago, I used to be homeless. Reese, my friend, was someone I met when I was homeless and I can't contact anyone from that life.'

'I had no idea,' Marshall says. 'You always seem so unruffled; calm and together. I think that's what unnerves Eliza – she can't get to you like she has other women . . .' He winces suddenly. 'And you had to sit there and listen to Sebastian spouting on and on about homeless people and how unwanted they are. Jeez, I'm surprised you didn't get up and lamp him one. I wanted to and I wasn't even "out there". I had no idea.' He draws me into his arms. Roni was hugged like this by her father – she was held close by him when she needed him to. Marshall kisses the top of my head, holds me even closer.

'You know what this means?' Marshall says, after he has held me for a while.

'No, what?'

'We're definitely more than just good sex now.'

'I thought it was fantastic sex?' I say to him. 'Don't be downgrading it.'

'Just checking you were paying attention,' he says. And if possible, tries to hold me even closer.

At 2 a.m. I creep out of Marshall's flat. I'm not ready yet to stay over all night. He did ask me to stay, but I said I'd think about it. When he fell asleep I'd thought about it enough and I decided to go home, give myself some space to process what has happened in the last twelve hours: Roni has finally told me everything and I completely understand now why she lied to the police. Roni's father has believed her without question and she is finally getting the support she needs.

And I have made love for the first time in my life. Marshall and I didn't just have sex, we made love, we revealed our vulnerabilities to each other, were slow and considered; I've never felt myself in my body as I did tonight. I felt every caress, every kiss, every touch, every sigh, every moan, every stroke inside me. It scared me a little, how easy it was to let go with Marshall because none of it reminded me of anything else. Everything with him was new, respectful, equal and overloaded with pleasure. That was why he wanted me to stay, I think, he wanted to recreate that closeness and intimacy in the morning.

I need time away to process. To examine how tonight, I could step away from my past for a while and be with him without holding back. Those reservations and fears and terrors and reminders will return, I know that without a doubt. But tonight I was free of all that.

I almost scream at the figure sitting in the corridor opposite Marshall's front door. I stand on Marshall's welcome mat and stare at her, amazed that she can do this sort of thing and not see how crazy it is. She glares at the bra that is peeking out from the bundle of clothes and shoes in my arms.

'Don't say I didn't warn you,' she whispers.

'Eliza, this is crazy.'

'*Don't say I didn't warn you,*' she hisses.

'OK,' I say with a shrug. 'I won't.' Well, really, what else am I going to say to someone as unstable as her?

19

Roni

I have been thinking. I have been thinking and thinking and thinking.

I have not been praying. Because I cannot pray about what I have been thinking. I have been thinking about revenge on Mr Daneaux. None of it seems very fair, none of it seems right. My uncle has disappeared. Dad has said he thinks he's run off to Spain, but is determined to catch up with him if that is what I want. What I want is revenge on Mr Daneaux.

I should pray about it, I should turn these thoughts over to the Lord so that He can guide me, He can show me the way. But I am too angry for that. I am too angry for much of anything. I am angry and I am confused. Both emotions flow through me like co-running rivers; every so often the banks of one river will break and the breach will see wave after wave after wave of that emotion coursing through me, battering and flattening all other emotions and all other types of rational thought. Anger is the river that bursts most often.

Out of everyone, Dad is the person who has taken the brunt of most of my anger because, I suppose, I can talk to him. He will listen, he will hold me, he will tell me over and over again how sorry he is. He accepts what I have said to him: that he didn't pay enough attention to my brothers and me. Damian and Brian have now both confessed how terrified they were of Uncle Warren, and have revealed the things he subjected them to when they were alone with him. Never anything like he did to me, but always stuff that was designed to 'toughen them up', to 'teach 'em how to be a man'. A lot of the time they hid their injuries because they knew Mum would do nothing, she would more likely tell them off for causing a fuss than patch them up or berate our uncle. Dad struggles with the reality of what being married to a person like Mum has done to his children. He knew, he has admitted, that she was at times ambivalent towards us, and would sometimes step in to stop her, but he never dreamt this was what the result of being the 'working' parent would mean. Three days ago he told Mum he is divorcing her and that he is going to cite her failure to protect me in the list of unreasonable behaviours. He has also started searching for a new place to live because he cannot stand the thought of staying in this house with all that went on in it any longer.

I am angry with Mum, of course I am. But there doesn't seem to be much point because everything, *everything* is all about her. In this whole thing, she is the victim, apparently. As she says: she did the best she could at the time for all of us and can we all stop making such a fuss about it now? She constantly demands to know what I am going to do about Mr Daneaux because if I go to the police, it'll likely be in the papers and she can't stand to be the mother of a girl in the papers who is accusing such a well-respected man of child abuse. What would people think of her? What would they think of the nice middle-class family that we were? If anyone brings up my uncle, she pretends they are not talking, she pretends that she doesn't understand what they mean. She pretends away a fundamental part of my life and my anger seems to bounce off the shield she has erected around herself.

Nika is not answering the phone. I haven't the energy to get down to Brighton to see her and from the fact her phone is almost permanently turned off, I know she is not interested in speaking to me anyway. She did what she promised to do – come with me – and now that promise has been fulfilled, she is not engaging with me any longer. I can't blame her for that. It must have been so painful for her to see my father immediately believe me, immediately take me in his arms. She never had that. She has never had anyone stand up for her.

Which is why I am so angry with Mr Daneaux. Why I am thinking about revenge. He has hurt her and he has got away with it. He has hurt her and nothing is going to be done.

At least, with my uncle, his life as he knew it is over. He cannot come back here and carry on as normal. He lives with the threat of police over his head and he will never know when there will be a knock on the door coming to drag him back to face his crimes.

Uncle Warren causes the banks of my confusion river to regularly burst, too. He was nice to me in the midst of his abuse. He would buy me things, he would give me money, he would listen when I talked. And then he would do those awful things to me and I would be in pain, I would be scared, and then I would be confused about what to feel. He messed so much with my mind, made sure I adored him before he started to do what he did. Even then, it started off so slowly and carefully, half the time I wasn't sure if what he was doing was wrong. Then when I knew it was wrong, I grew to hate him but I still liked him as well. He would often apologise afterwards, say he was sorry and didn't mean it, and I would not know what to do. I almost told, so many times, but the thought of Damian's bike, the blood I'd tried to clean up from his knee, his pale face as he'd tried to endure the pain, would appear in my mind and I would remember that Uncle Warren could and probably would hurt my brothers. I was so confused all the time, and I'm often confused now. As time goes on I'm less confused, more angry, more hateful of him.

And more hateful of Mr Daneaux.

I have been thinking about Mr Daneaux. And how I would like to get my revenge.

Nika

'Nika, I know you don't want to talk to me, and I'm so sorry for everything. I have to put things right. I hope you listen to this message when you find out what I have done, and I hope you understand. I have to do this. It's not fair that you don't get justice, and you don't get to have people believe you. If I do this, they'll know what he was like and they'll believe you. I have to do this. I . . . I love you. You're the best friend I ever had. And I'm so sorry again for how I let you down.'

She won't do it. No one actually does it. No one normal, anyway. We talk about it, we think about it, we tell ourselves about it, but we never actually do it. No matter how much we want to, we never actually do it.

I hit '1' on the small keyboard of my phone to listen again to the message she left about an hour ago.

There is something . . . something in the inflection of her voice, the melody of her words. If this were a song, I would be listening for how the words are arranged, how they flow with the harmony of her voice, what is missing as well as what is there. She speaks again in my ear and I listen to her.

'1', I press. What is it? What is it that is missing? Something is needling me, is stopping me believing that she will not do it. Something is missing from this arrangement of lyrics and tune, something vital that makes me more and more uneasy as the minutes

404

pass by. God. What is missing is God. Every time I have spoken to her, there has been a mention of God, her faith, her belief in a higher power. She might think about doing this, but God would hold her back, her faith would hold her back. She speaks of justice, but not forgiveness.

She's going to do it. Roni is actually going to do it.

Nika

'Do you ever wonder if you've lived the life you were meant to?' I ask her.

She is at the top of the stone steps. They are etched with the filth of their years, could probably use a good hosing down and going over with a scrubbing brush. Roni is facing the red front door, and looks poised to press the bell, to start this process.

'No,' she says.

'I don't believe you,' I reply. 'Come on, tell me, do you ever wonder if you've lived the life you were meant to?'

She sighs, and dips her head. I bet she has screwed up her lips, has closed her eyes, is trying hard not to pray for the right answer. 'Even if I do, what difference will it make?'

'I used to think I hadn't. I used to think that there was a life I should have lived and when I stopped being someone else, I could recapture it, restart it, whatever. Thing is, this is who I am. This is the life I was meant to live simply because it's the one I have lived. When people used to tell me that being homeless wasn't the life for me, I used to defend myself and say that it *was*. I never believed it, though. I kept thinking if I could scroll back a few years things would be different. To before I left London, before I met Todd, before I left Chiselwick, before I went to the police, before I told my parents. I kept "before-ing" myself, and what was the point? Truly, I have lived

406

this life. It is mine, and mine alone. I am who I am because of every single thing that has happened to me. I can't pretend I'm happy all the time, I can't pretend I haven't thought about ending it all more than once. But I am who I am. This is who I am. I don't need justice.'

She turns to look at me then. She is struggling: she wants to break down in tears, but she is fighting herself. 'What if *I* want justice? My uncle has disappeared, probably gone to Spain, and I want justice. I want this man to pay. Not just for me, but for you, too.'

'I don't need justice,' I repeat.

'Well, I do,' she says, so full of determination she grits her teeth before she spins on the spot and pushes the doorbell.

'You won't be able to do it,' I tell her. 'You saw your uncle for years and you didn't do it – what makes you think you'll be able to do this?'

'Because it's for you.'

'I don't need justice.'

'You don't understand!' she cries. 'It was—'

She's cut short by the door being opened. The tall, sophisticated-looking woman on the other side is immaculately dressed. She's a classic beauty, always has been. I remember the first time I saw her, how beautiful I thought she was. She was poised, almost regal, and I wanted to be like her. I wanted to be *exactly* like her. Her hair is now a grey-streaked bun, her face has a few more lines, but she is essentially that goddess I saw that day as an eight-year-old who decided she wanted to be a ballerina.

'Hello?' she says, smiling at Roni first, then me. 'Can I help you?'

I take the steps as fast as I can, put my hand on Roni. 'No, no, wrong address,' I say. 'Sorry to have wasted your time.' I tug at Roni, try to get her to move.

'Don't I know you?' she says when Roni does not move, will not move. Instead Roni stares at the woman as though she is an incarnation of the Devil.

'No, no,' I say quickly. 'Come on, Roni, let's go.'

'Roni?' Mrs Daneaux says. 'Wait a minute... *Roni?*' She moves her gaze to me. '*Nika?*'

407

'Yes,' Roni replies. 'That's us. And I've come to give something to your husband.' I don't know who is more surprised when Roni suddenly barges past the woman in the very expensive cashmere twinset – Mrs Daneaux or me. I didn't know Roni had it in her. She marches straight into the building, her eyes wildly searching for where her quarry might be. 'Darling, who is it?' His voice. I am eleven again, horrified by what he has just done for the first time. I am thirteen again, hearing the click as he pushes play on the CD player and the 'Dance of the Sugar Plum Fairy' fills the room and I am almost broken by what he does next. I am fifteen again, seeing his face as he tells me the police have been to talk to him and he is going to punish me for continuing to tell people our secret.

I inhale, inhale, inhale, inhale. My heart feels like it is hurtling through time, attempting to escape the past in the present-future. I need to get away from here, I need to turn and run.

'What is going on?' Mrs Daneaux demands of Roni, who is racing up the stairs, to where the voice has come from.

Calm, Nika, calm, I tell myself. *You have to stop Roni. Forget about him – think about her and what will happen to both of you if she does it.*

I barge my way in too, nowhere near calm. But I have to stop her. I don't want justice, I don't want any of this.

In their living room at the top of the house, Roni is standing by the dining table. From the look of the table, the smell in the room, they have had their dinner, drunk their wine, now they are on to fine port and a cheeseboard with various types of crackers, and fruit. I might have guessed, if I thought about them for any longer than was necessary, that they were people who turned dinner into an evening-long indulgence. Roni's hand is precariously close to the knife placed on the table to slice fruit. It is small, sharp, dangerous. There are two other people in the room – a man and a younger man – and I try not to look at them. I focus instead on Roni, who is staring at the couple in front of the fireplace while her hand moves closer to the wooden-handled knife on the table.

'Who *are* you people?' Mr Daneaux says and the torment of all the years sweeps through me again. I try not to petrify, but I am fighting a pitched, losing battle with my terrified younger selves.

'I'd like you to leave before I call the police,' Mrs Daneaux states, coming up behind us.

'Call the police,' Roni says. 'I really think they should be here for this.' Her voice has changed. She sounds detached, she sounds cold. She is stepping outside of herself so she can do this. The other two people in the room are not speaking – they are probably as focused on the weapon that is millimetres away from this stranger's hand as I am.

'Roni, please don't do this.' I am speaking to her slowly, calmly. Her breathing is quiet but erratic, which tells me she is not quite ready. She is working herself up to it, and when her breathing, the sound of what she is thinking, finally slows and normalises, she will have completely detached. That's when she's most likely to do it. That's when she will use that knife on that man and there will be no going back for either of us.

'The thing is, Nika, I have to do this,' she says.

'You really don't.'

'I do. You don't know how terrible I've felt every day, *every* day since I lied to that policeman.'

'I do know. I've felt it too. We both went through it, remember, so I do understand how you felt.'

'No, you don't. It wasn't the same.' She turns to me, briefly, shakes her head in what I think is regret and turns back to her prey. 'I'm sorry, I'm so sorry.' She shakes her head again, as though trying to dislodge a memory, trying to rid herself of a truth she does not want to tell. 'After you went to the police, and they came to have a "friendly" chat with him, he never touched me again.' It's my breathing that is slow and measured now, almost at the point of being deadly. 'He said I had shown great loyalty but you ... you had to be punished. That was why you always went first after you told the police. He would tell me afterwards what he had done to you, while I had to dance for him.'

From the corner of my eye, I see the younger man, possibly his son, raise his hand to his mouth while looking at the older man. Beside me Mrs Daneaux keeps making small little gasping sounds, and I think she is crying but I can't think about her, I can't think about anyone else.

The only person I am truly focused on is Roni. And what she has just confessed. 'That was nearly a year before it stopped because his wife kept dropping by,' I say to her.

'He said you deserved everything he did to you. *Didn't you?*' She spits the words at him, her breathing slowing some more. She's approaching that point when she's going to do it. 'I'm so sorry, Nika. I'm so sorry. But it was me who made his wife turn up. I knew she was like my mother, only worried about herself, so I wrote an anonymous letter saying that her husband was planning to leave her for his *Nutcracker* pupil.'

'That was *you?*' Mrs Daneaux says.

'Yes, that was me. I had to do something. The things he told me he was doing to Nika…'

Roni stops crying, fretting. She's calm now; still; ready. Ready to take his life and make him pay for what he did to her, to us, probably to countless others.

I focus on his son, just a bit older than us – his eyes are wide, horrified. He used to come to group classes, but he always sat to the side with a book and never once joined in. He doesn't deserve to see this happen.

'It's not your fault,' I say to Roni. 'You are not to blame, for any of it. Not even lying to the police is your fault. And it's not down to you to get justice. Let's just go.'

'He has to pay for what he did,' she replies. 'He has to pay. And once I've done this, I'll be able to sleep at night and I'll stop hating myself and I'll feel normal.'

'Oh, Roni,' I say teasingly while I move towards her. 'You really are the queen of magical thinking, aren't you? That's not what will happen. What will happen is every day for the rest of your life, you will remember his face, you will remember the sensation, and you will likely never sleep again. You know that, don't you? Deep down.' I am close enough that our bodies almost touch. I feel the heat from her bare arms, even though they are covered in goosebumps. Carefully, I cover her hand with mine, wrap my fingers around hers, and slowly I move her away from the table, away from the knife, away from making one of the biggest mistakes of her life.

I am trying not to look at *him* because every time I catch a glimpse of him the memories flash through my mind, reverberate through my body. Every time I can hear his frequency and how it resonates in the world, I feel pain, I experience fear, I remember what it's like to want to stop existing.

Slowly, carefully, I pull Roni back until she is by me, by the door, ready for us to leave. The three other people in the room exhale, but the breath I can hear loudest, most clearly, is *his*. He was scared. Actually, properly scared.

I want him to feel that again. I want him to know what it is like to feel small and weak and terrified of what will happen to you next. I want him to experience for even the shortest of seconds, what it is to be truly scared. My gaze is drawn to the knife. To what it could possibly do. To the one thing that has ever made him feel what it's like to be the victim.

Roni

She's quick, so quick I can barely register what is happening. She moves at lightning speed, and the knife is in her hand before I can say stop, don't do that, it really isn't worth losing your immortal soul for. *He* isn't worth losing your freedom and soul for.

I imagined it would take more force than she uses, it would be harder than that to do what she does. His face is a mask of shock, his eyes twin beacons of pain, his mouth a small 'o' of surprise before he slumps, falls to the floor in one move.

The four of us left standing are suddenly petrified; all horrified immobile by what has been done. But it is Mrs Daneaux who recovers enough to move first: she throws down the knife in her hand. It clatters loudly on the polished wood floor. My gaze moves from the man on the ground to the fruit knife his wife has just wielded. I take a step backwards, pushing distance between me and the wooden-handled weapon. I can't believe I thought for even a moment that I could do what she has just done. I can't believe I thought myself capable of it.

'What have you done?' Nika says quietly. Her shock runs like a network of veins through every syllable. 'What have you done?'

Without warning, Mrs Daneaux explodes. The beautiful, poised shell of a woman that she was, the one who I wanted to be like, who wears cashmere and pearls, and has her hair swept up in the most

412

elegant of styles, disappears and a screaming monster takes her place. 'YOU TOLD ME IT WAS ALL LIES!' she screams at her husband. *'That they didn't like how much you pushed them, so she had made it all up! You told me that once you offered her the role in* The Nutcracker *she would back off and it'd be clear that she had made the whole thing up to manipulate me, control you! And it wasn't lies, you were doing that to her! To them! You were doing that to them and all the others who have accused you!'* Her eyes are wild, her body is murderous, everything about her now is incensed.

In the background, I see her son, the carbon cut-out looks-wise of his father, calmly remove his mobile from his pocket and begin to dial. Press, press, press goes the index finger of his right hand. 'Ambulance, please. And police,' he says in an undisturbed, even tone. All the while, his mother continues to scream.

'You forced me to move here from London because those new girls didn't understand your methods, they were going to lie about you, too, and in this new climate a good man's reputation could be ruined by the simple allegation, you said! I left *everything* behind because of you and now I find out it was all true! You abused those girls! You raped them! And I believed you every time!'

The son's eyes seem glazed over as he speaks into the phone, as though he is in another world, one where the horror of what he is hearing is wiped away as soon as it reaches his ears in order for him to quietly, sedately call an ambulance, tell them his father has been stabbed by his mother. *That his mother is hysterical. No, he isn't in danger. Yes, he would like the police. Yes, he knows CPR and he will be administering it as soon as he puts down the phone if he needs it but his father doesn't seem that bad right now. No, he's fine, he really is, he doesn't need them to hold on the line until the ambulance arrives.* 'Yes, please hurry,' he says to end the call.

When his son hangs up the phone, he doesn't move to his father, to comfort him, to administer CPR, to even acknowledge him. He stands still, his eyes still wide, his face now a deathly white oval against his thick black hair. He looks from Nika to me to Nika again.

I can't look at Nika because I do not know how to face her after what I have just revealed. I can't look for too long at the man bleeding on the floor in front of me. He is oddly, eerily silent but his eyes are open, sweat is pouring from him, and he has his hand over the knife wound, so I know he isn't dead. Every time I glance briefly in his direction, I see his eyes are unfocused, as though seeing something that isn't there. I suspect I know what he is looking at, what it is he is probably seeing as his life force drains away. Which is why I can't look at him for too long because I know what I should be doing: offering comfort. I should be holding his hand, offering him the only version of Last Rites I can perform as a former nun – being a comfort to him in what could be his final minutes. But that is not in me. I simply can't do it.

Suddenly, the son seems to snap back into himself, the shock of what has happened gone. He moves towards his mother and I expect him to open his arms, to draw her close, to comfort her and tell her, in whispers we aren't privy to, that he understands and would have done the same if it was him. Instead, he reaches around his mother, snatches up the cloth napkins from the table, and suddenly, he is on his knees, beside his father. He carefully takes away his father's hand, briefly examines his wound before he pushes the napkin over it to stem the flow of blood. He is so tender with him, so caring and worried, I'm stopped short. *Where is my humanity, my forgiveness, my compassion as a woman who once devoted her whole life to the Lord?* I ask myself. *Where is my compassion as a human being?*

This is why I could never have stayed in the monastery, I remind myself. *I could never have this amount of forgiveness in my heart. And forgiveness, true forgiveness, is about this ability to move beyond your personal hurt and do the right thing, even if it does not directly benefit you. This moment, all the moments leading up to it, have shown me that.*

'You need to live,' he says to his father, calmly. 'You need to live so you can face this. You don't deserve to die without facing up to what you have done.' He then looks at his mother, who has finally stopped shouting and ranting and is staring at her son. 'And I hope there's a special place in hell for you for looking the other way all

414

these years.' After his quiet, damning words, he seems to glaze over again while he stems the flow of blood from his father's wound and waits with the rest of us for help to arrive.

The sirens arrive first, then the heavy, hurried footsteps of people trying to help. There is shouting and there are orders, the house is intermittently lit with the flashes of the blue-light-topped vehicles outside, we are moved aside, then moved apart; many people are talking at once. I finally look at Nika, try to see what she is thinking, feeling, what she wants us to do from now on. Whatever she wants I will do, whatever she needs I will provide for her. My whole life will be about her and how to make it up to her now.

She stares through me, does not seem to notice I am there. She seems to not notice anyone is there. She moves where she is prodded to, but doesn't respond to even the simplest questions.

Is this it? Is it all over now, or is it just beginning?

20

Nika

London, 2016

My parents' house is in chaos when I arrive.

The front door stands wide open. Outside, there is a parked white van with its side door open, and it is partially stacked with brown cardboard boxes. Boxes line the corridor, leading to the back room. Some boxes sit at the bottom of the stairs. All sealed up and ready to be stacked into the van. I bet Sasha and Ralph had no idea they had so much stuff crammed into my parents' house.

I go up to the front door, and walk in. I probably should knock – I am a stranger after all – but it'd also feel odd to do that. This was my home, the place I should have been able to come to when I was homeless, after all. That was what was so odd about being known as 'homeless'. It was as though being called that means you are merely without a roof over your head. What if you're without all the other things that make up a home: love, acceptance, attention and caring? A sense of belonging? Aren't you homeless then? Aren't you without a home? What I had with Todd wasn't a home. What I had on the street was all of those things.

'Nika! Oh my God!' Sasha says when I enter the back room.

She steps around the items littering the floor and comes to me, throws her arms around my neck. It's still a little jolting to see how much my sister loves me, how pleased she is to see me after so many

419

years of feeling she didn't notice me at all. 'I'm so glad to see you. How did you know we were moving today?'

'I didn't,' I reply, hugging her back. I cling to her for a few seconds: she probably won't be hugging me again when she hears what I have to say. She'll probably want me nowhere near her when she hears me speak. I have to do this, though. No matter who it hurts, I have to do this and lay it to rest. Roni would have wanted to come with me, but the police kept her for longer because they were talking to her about her uncle.

Besides, how can I trust her ever again? She lied to me. Even that night in my flat in Brighton, when she acted as though she had told me everything, she was still lying, still holding something back.

Both my parents are sitting in the chairs they've always sat in. I'm glad, in a way, that they're in this back room, the room for everyday use, which is right next to the kitchen. Even before I left I avoided the front room, which was mainly for posh visitors. I always associate that room with the day Mr Daneaux came to convince my parents that the way he was touching me, the things he was making me do to him, were perfectly normal and I had got it wrong. Every part of that room reminds me of him drinking tea, eating biscuits and telling my parents I had the lead role in *The Nutcracker*. He fully raped me for the first time the very next day and told me he could do whatever he wanted to me because he now knew no one would ever believe a word I said.

'Ralph! Babe!' Sasha screams, most of the sound travelling straight down my ear. 'Babe! Nika's here!'

'Nika?' Ralph says. I hear him moving around upstairs, then he picks his way across the room and comes hurtling down the stairs. He moves quickly down the hall and comes to me, scoops me up into a hug. 'Nika! My God, how wonderful to see you!' he exclaims. 'Sash has been over the moon since you got back in touch. Over the moon. And I am, too, obviously. Tracy-Dee can't wait to meet you. She's at school now, obviously, but later, you know?'

I don't remember Ralph being so talkative, ever. *Ever*. Or ever being so pleased that I'm around. I try to scroll through my memory like I would with my music player, trying to locate a time when Sasha and Ralph cared so much about me. But Sasha was hardly ever around. She was out a lot with Ralph because she was mainly trying to avoid being home in the atmosphere we lived with.

'Now if that doesn't tell you how excited we are to see you, nothing will,' Sasha says. 'In case you'd forgotten, Ralph hardly ever speaks so much.'

My parents haven't spoken. They're probably in shock, to be honest. I'm still in shock, being back here, seeing this place, seeing them. Nothing has changed in all the time I've been away. Nothing fundamental, anyway. The carpets look newer but they're a similar pattern to the old ones, the wallpaper is newer but it has the same flock look as before. The furniture is tired, and old, but it still reminds me of the furniture they had when I lived here, when this was 'home'.

They look the same. My mother is perfect, as she has always been: she is very poised, her clothes always pristine, make-up carefully applied. I think Mrs Daneaux reminded me of her, when I first met her – a beautiful woman who held herself well, and always looked good no matter what. My father is comfortable, as he has always been: whenever he came through the door from work, he would change out of his suit into casual slacks and long-sleeved T-shirt. I guess for my father to be here he must have retired. I haven't asked Sasha much about them; I haven't had the heart.

'You do realise the van is wide open out there, don't you?' I say to Sasha and Ralph.

'What?' Ralph says, trying to look at Sasha and out the door to where the van is parked at the same time. '*Sasha!*'

'Don't blame me, you're the one filling the thing,' she snipes back. 'Well, don't just stand there, let's go and see if anything's missing. Pillock.'

'You're the pillock!'

'No, *you* are.'

'No, *you* are!'

They squabble all the way out of the house and leave me alone with my silent, wary parents.

'Veronika,' my father says first.

'Hello, Daddy,' I reply. 'Hello, Mummy.'

She remains silent, removed and aloof. I imagine I hurt her very badly when I left. She would have had to explain my absences at family gatherings; she would have had to explain away why I was all over the print media, famous for taking drugs and flashing my knickers, calling myself Nikky and doing nothing good with my life. My father would have found it easy to rise above it all, to ignore it – after all, he had a son who was important and worked in the City. No, the daughter was the mother's responsibility. It was the mother who was meant to show her what it was like to be a woman, how to be good at what she does, by modelling modesty and dignity, decorum and intelligence. The younger daughter should be married with children by now. If she wasn't, that was down to the mother. My mother. Everything I ever did was a reflection on her mothering abilities. I understand that now. I understand why she couldn't accept what I was saying about Mr Daneaux – that would have meant she had failed. If what I was saying was true, then she had raised a daughter who didn't know how to say no, she was raising a slut. It didn't matter that he was forcing me; she didn't want to be the mother of a daughter that anyone – and there would be more than one – who would question the girl's role in the dynamic of her being repeatedly raped by a man who taught her ballet. All those years of going to the library in Birmingham taught me a lot. I read and reread every book I could find on what had happened to me, first as a child, as a teenager, then as a woman living with a man who slowly took her soul apart.

I read the different theories, the various thoughts, the myriad explanations. I know those theories so well and I can see why they are right and true, and how they could sometimes fit neatly over my life and experience like a snug cover. But after the thoughts, the intellectual understanding, there is this: my parents didn't believe me. They believed a man who was working up to raping their daughter instead of listening to that very daughter they had brought up to tell the truth. They were convinced that it was a problem they could ignore away.

My parents didn't believe me.

My mother returns to looking at my father. 'As I was saying, I don't think they will fit all those things into that one van. But, ah, what do I know? No one wants to listen to me about anything.'

I'm here for my mum's sake, more than mine.

'Why are you here, Veronika?' my father asks.

In the background, I hear Sasha and Ralph's footsteps as they approach. Good, good. I can tell them all in one go and they can all then take a moment to digest the news and then all decide how much I have disgraced the family name – again.

'I'm here because I have something to tell you,' I say. I suddenly, almost violently, wish that Roni was here, so I could reach out and take her hand, find the strength in her physical presence to do this. 'I don't know if you remember the other Veronica Harper? Well, last night she went to the home of our former ballet teacher, Mr Daneaux, ready to harm him for r-r—' I still can't say the word. I can barely think it, and I can't say it. 'She wanted to kill him for abusing her and me all those years ago.'

'What?' Sasha says. She moves into the room, stares at me through a deep, confused crinkle of a horrified frown. 'What are you talking about?'

'I know you didn't believe me at the time, but after last night he is now being investigated for historic child sexual abuse crimes. The police say he's likely to have abused quite a few other young girls as well as me and Veronica, so it's probably going to be all over the papers. They won't print our names, but I wanted to tell you before that happened because they will print his name. You can have a chance to get your story straight or to decide to pretend that you vaguely remember the ballet teacher and don't remember anything untoward going on with your daughter. Whatever. I thought you deserved to know.'

'What is she talking about?' Sasha says to my parents. When they remain silent, she turns back to me. 'What are you talking about?'

'I can't say it again, Sasha. I've talked and talked to the police about it for most of the night and I can't say it again. I just thought you should all know because it's going to be public and I'm going to go on record, I'll probably have to go to court if it comes to that. And most people will know he lived and taught around here and that he mainly did those things to his star pupils, of which I was one.'

Sasha's face starts to tremble – she looks like she might start crying. 'Did you ... did you tell them that you'd been abused by this man and they did nothing about it?' she asks.

Todd, too, I want to say. Todd spent years sexually abusing and raping me but in a different, quieter way. In all my reading I found out that if it happened to you as a child, especially if you didn't tell or no one believed you, you are likely to fall into a similar relationship as an adult. You are likely to end up with another person who will abuse you, too. It is the familiarity, being used to someone trampling over your boundaries, being used to always doing what others want, never expecting to be treated well, always being grateful when you are.

My sister spins towards my parents. 'YOU DID NOTHING?' she bellows at them. Her rage is so unexpected, I take a step back. I didn't think someone would respond like that on my behalf.

Ralph puts a hand on my shoulder and I nearly leap out of my skin. 'I'm so sorry, Nika,' he whispers. 'I had no idea. This shouldn't have happened to you.'

Sasha comes to me, grabs me into a hug and clings to me. 'Why didn't you tell me, Nika? Why didn't you tell me?'

We were never that close; we were never really how people tell you sisters are meant to be. And anyway, 'I couldn't handle you not believing me, either. Mummy and Daddy didn't believe me – I couldn't stand to share a room with you and have you not believe me.'

'This is so horrible,' she says. 'It all makes sense now, why you just disappeared into yourself for all those years. I was so caught up in trying to escape the hideous atmosphere in the house I didn't even notice properly. I never understood why you left and wouldn't even think about coming back. That's why I kept sending your letters on to you – I just wanted to keep in touch with you, let you know you had a link somewhere. I didn't understand why you wouldn't talk, why ... I can't believe they did nothing.'

Sasha believes me. Ralph believes me. Two people I know believe me the first time they hear what I have to say.

Sasha lets me go, turns to my parents. 'I can't believe I lived here all this time and let you look after Tracy-Dee when all along you protected someone who had raped your daughter. Well, no more. Ralph,' she says over her shoulder, 'pack up everything, every single thing you can because we're not coming back here. I don't care if we have to throw stuff in the bin, we're doing this in one run.'

She slips her hand into mine. 'Come on, Nika, you're staying with us.'

'No, no, I'm fine. I've got a life and a job and everything back in Brighton,' I tell her. The world feels floaty right now, nothing feels real or touchable. I am like a helium-filled balloon – light and ready to drift away. If I close my eyes and let go of her hand, I will float away. Everything is a bit surreal because for once I have been believed straight away.

'No, Nika. I'm overruling you on this. You need someone to take care of you for a while. She's staying with us, isn't she, Ralph?'

'Yes,' he calls from the corridor. He is moving quickly; the packing that was being done at a leisurely, almost languid pace, from what I picked up from the atmosphere when I walked in, is now being done almost frantically.

Sasha leads me out of the house and puts me in the front seat of the van, then returns to the house to join her husband in the frantic packing.

Mummy didn't speak to me once, I think as I sit on the bench seat of the van, tethered there like Sasha has tied down an over-inflated balloon.

Even after all these years, my mother's doubt about me can't be put aside. I am not the daughter she wanted, I am not the girl she wanted to bring up. I wonder if she would have liked me, preferred me, if I had just shut up and put up all those years. Or is it that my mother has been there, too?

I remember that look in her eyes sometimes, the way she would glare at me as though she couldn't understand what the big deal was. When I wasn't eating, when I would sit and stare into space, when I would vomit before my ballet classes, I would sometimes see my mother looking at me as though I was making a mountain out of a molehill. *Every girl has this happen to them,* she seemed to be saying with that expression, *why are you making such a big deal about it?*

Quickly, decisively, I wipe that thought away. No one who had been through that would let someone else go through that, *would they?*

'We're going to look after you,' Sasha says to me as she climbs into the van some time later. 'Stay as long as you want, because for the next little while, this is going to be all about you.'

Roni

They believe us. They believe Veronika Harper and Veronica Harper. They believe what he did to us; they have opened up an investigation into him and will be contacting all his current and former students to see if any of them will speak to them.

They believe us. And one of the police officers even apologised to me and to Nika (separately) for not believing her all those years ago. I don't know what Nika said, or what she felt when they told her that, but I hope, hope, hope that being believed this time helps her. It can't erase the past, but it can make the future a little better. At least I hope it can. She left the police station before me. I had to stay longer to tell them all about my uncle. They want to open up an investigation into him as well. Not only for what he did to me, but also the crimes against my brothers. They will talk to Brian and Damian to see what they want to do.

Mrs Daneaux will probably be charged with attempted manslaughter; her husband is expected to make a full recovery from what we heard and saw last night. I said to the police officer who questioned me that is a good thing, but part of me wishes it were different. I admitted that because I was confessing to everything. *Everything.*

I have finally confessed to everything. Everything that is inside me has been told and retold to another person. Not anyone who can tell me to say a number of Hail Marys, who will listen to my act of contrition, who will then absolve me of my sins, but someone else. I will go to confession, tell a priest everything at some point, reveal the true contents of my heart, my lapse in being able to put aside the vengeful thoughts, the unforgiving thoughts, and my inability to comfort a man who may have been dying. Yes, I might not be a nun any more, but as I explained to Cliff, being a nun is part of who you are, not a job. I still feel like a nun, I know that I should, for the most part, behave like one. But for now, what seems most important is that I have confessed.

I am unburdened and burdened at the same time.

Since I am here in Brighton, I have thought about visiting Nika's flat, trying to see her so I can tell her again I am sorry. But that would be for me, not her. That would be another attempt by me to make her OK when she has every right to not be. I hope she has called Marshall, that she is curled up in his arms, basking in the adoration he so obviously feels for her. I hope she is not alone and she has someone to take care of her.

I hope this is the beginning of the next phase of her life. It's certainly the start of mine.

I'm sitting here in the police station foyer waiting for Dad to come and pick me up. I pull my knees up to my chest, rest my head on my knees. I hope he doesn't take too long.

21

Nika

I have been away for nearly three weeks.

Sasha would not let me leave, and once she made that decision, I found that I couldn't leave because I didn't want to.

I slept in their tiny box room, which had nothing but the bed, a circular rug on the floor and a lamp that sat on the floor beside the bed. I slept a lot, would often miss whole chunks of the day from simply rolling over and going back to sleep. At night, I was often plagued by the past: worry would creep in with the darkness, crawling its way through my mind and keeping me awake with its half-formed remembrances and body-tremoring flashbacks.

My big sister called my work and told them. Just like that. I should have been angry at her for not checking with me first what I wanted them to know, but she thought I had nothing to be ashamed of, that I had done nothing wrong and she was going to fight anyone who dared to question if I had. Mrs Nasir was very understanding, apparently, and turned down Sasha's kind offer to go and work in my place to make sure I kept my job.

I often heard Sasha and Ralph talking in the night, and I knew she blamed herself for not noticing. For being out of the house, for us not being close enough for me to tell her. *It's not your fault,* I wanted to say to her. *It's no one's fault but his.*

431

She also went to see Roni's dad. To tell him that Roni had to stay away for now and to stop ringing me. 'I felt so sorry for him,' she explained afterwards. 'Most of the time we just sat there in silence cos we didn't know what to say. He looks like someone's taken him apart, piece by piece. He seems so broken but trying to keep it together for Roni's sake.' *'Like I am with you,'* she silently added.

I sent Marshall a text telling him I was away for a couple of weeks and I would get in touch with him when I got back. Which is now. I am back now. I am back at work, I have plans to meet Marshall, talk to him properly about all that he has read in the papers recently. He knows I knew Mr Daneaux, and that the story has completely shaken me, but he doesn't know the full extent.

Planning to tell Marshall, I think, has brought Todd to mind a lot. Maybe because of how he used what I told him about my abuse to hurt me. He got some kind of sick pleasure from it, I think, and I was in a place where being treated like that was all I knew. I read all about it at the library, and I can look back and see it, but it's only now I can feel it. Roni engaged in drinking, drug-taking and reckless sex with older men to treat herself in the only way she knew how. Todd did that for me.

Thinking about Todd always leads into thinking about Roni. We're so intertwined, our stories curling and curving around each other like two trees growing from one root – even after years apart, the stems of our stories are twisted together. We are like music on a song sheet: right-hand notes and left-hand notes, both played together, both necessary for the song to be complete.

I haven't seen her. She has done as Sasha asked and has kept away, which is the best thing for both of us. It's given me a chance to want to talk to her. If she was in my face all the time, I would want her far away. I need to talk to her. Now that we've been believed, now that other people have come forward to tell about Mr Daneaux, our worlds are different.

I step outside the service entrance at the back of the hotel, into the wide alley-cum-side street that runs along the back of the hotel.

I'm always amazed that this wide space exists out here, when every-where around this part of Brighton is narrow and close, as though hunched up together to keep warm against the strong breezes that roll in from the sea. Usually there are three or four members of hotel staff standing here, smoking or drinking cups of coffee, or having a good old gossip about someone else who works in the building. Today, it's empty. The light is fading and soon the sky will turn a light pewter, signalling the start of evening and then night.

Roni. The thought of her rushes through me, like it did all those months ago when Judge decided to get payback. I have to stop – the thought of her is so powerful as it sweeps through my body and mind, a strong wave that almost knocks me over. *Roni.* I take a deep breath in, hold it. When I feel the panic coming on, I know to remember to breathe. Breathe. It's what the books all told me over the years to do, to breathe. It quells the panic, soothes my mind. I reach into my pocket, take out my music player. I don't usually wear headphones when walking around, I don't feel safe if I can't hear what is going on, but after the breathing, music is what helps me.

A scuffling noise to my left doesn't do enough to distract me from unwinding my headphones. I need to breathe. Breathe. More scut-tling, and then footsteps, and then a hand around my throat, shoving me back against the wall.

'Hello, Ace.' Judge's voice is against my ear, his body is keeping my body against the wall, his hand is slowly crushing my throat. 'Long time no see.'

I close my eyes but I can still hear his breathing, I can feel his scent filling my senses.

I don't have a death wish any more. Reese would be proud of me. I now have a reason to not want to die. All those thoughts, all those feelings have gone now that I have connections, that I have a home, that I have people who believe me.

'Aren't you pleased to see me, Ace?' he whispers into my ear. 'I've spent so long looking for you. I knew it'd only be a matter of time

433

before you pissed off someone enough for me to catch up with you. Really nice young lady who tipped me off from my social media posts. Said you had a new hairstyle, new glasses, new name. She even told me where you worked – isn't that nice of her?' He moves his hand up and down, trying to make me nod. 'Yes, it was, Judge,' he says for me.

I open my eyes and he takes my glasses off and tosses them to one side so, I presume, he can see directly into my eyes.

I wonder if he can see in my eyes this one thought: *I don't want to die. I don't want to die and I don't want to die like this.*

'I made a mistake all those years ago,' he says. 'Should have put you down there and then when you wouldn't do as you were told. But you have to be careful, don't you? If them on the street think you're not being fair, they don't play by the rules and you end up with lots of unnecessary losses and having to work harder to find replacements.' He presses his lips even closer to my ear, probably gets his usual thrill when I flinch. He loves that moment when a person recoils, shows him that they know he's in charge. 'That was my mistake. I don't make many but I should have put you down all those months ago, not your smackhead mate. I thought it would keep you in line, maybe even get you dealing and tomming for me, but instead it gave him ideas. Ideas that he could take me down.' He pushes his body even closer to me. 'I've lost everything cos of you, Ace. The previously loyal have turned against me, only worried about their own skins. I've stayed out of the way so far, until I found you. It won't be worth it, to do you, but it'll be a start.'

I used to be Grace 'Ace' Carter, invisible and unnoticed. No one would care if I died alone in an alleyway, killed by a drug-dealing pimp I was once stupid enough to be involved with. I am Veronika Harper now, though. And I was stupid to think that this doesn't happen to all sorts of people, visible or not.

'Don't do this, Judge,' I say. Someone is going to come soon. I know they will. This place is behind a busy hotel, a shortcut to part of the Lanes from the seafront. Someone will come and they will stop this. If I keep him talking for long enough, someone will come. 'I didn't know Reese would go to the police,' I say. 'I honestly didn't. He was completely against it. He completely cut me off when I suggested it. I didn't know. Please, please don't do this.' Whatever this is. Because I have no idea. Would he really do something here? When anyone could walk by at any second?

He is suddenly in my face, his face so close to mine I can count the open pores of his skin. He looks tired, and desperate; all his luxuries have been stripped away and he is like the people he used to prey on. 'Ah, Ace, it's good to hear you beg again. I could live on hearing you begging and pleading.' His red jewel embedded in his front tooth glints every time his lips part. He has nothing to lose, it's obvious. Someone with nothing to lose will do anything.

But someone is going to come along any second now. Someone is going to come and save me from this. I thought I'd given up on the idea of rescue, but I haven't. Not now that I know there are people who will believe me, there are people who will take care of me, will love me. I want to be rescued from this. I want someone to come around that corner, to step out from the hotel and see this and help me.

'Please? *Please.*'

'Oh, Ace, yes, that's exactly how I like it.'

Someone is going to save me. I know it.

He stands back suddenly, and I can breathe for a moment. He uses the distance he has put between us to draw back his fist then drive it deep into my stomach. The punch doubles me over, and I clutch the place of impact.

'Bye, Ace. Never forget me, eh, baby?'

His footsteps hurry away, not running, simply walking quickly, a man in a rush to get from here to there. A man who doesn't even look back at the woman he's just assaulted. At least it was just that, at least he decided to punch me and let me go. Maybe he isn't as bad as I thought he was. Maybe, like with Todd, the reality of Judge is much smaller, much more diminished than the thought of him. I try to stand upright, but I'm too winded from the punch, so instead

I step forwards. *Walk it off, Nika. The sooner you get moving, the sooner you'll be able to walk it off.* I manage one step, force myself to make another, then stop. I have to stop. This punch... it was so hard. It was so hard I can barely breathe. And my hand, it's wet. It's sticky and it's wet.

I take my hand from my stomach, stare at it: a shock of sticky redness covers my fingers and the palm of my hand. My mouth fills with saline and the tang of blood-red iron; a swirl of light whirls around my head and then drains away. I'm stumbling... staggering... falling...

No one's going to come, are they? No one is going to rescue me. This is it. This is where I stop being Veronika Harper, Nikky Harper, Grace 'Ace' Carter, Nika Harper. This is where it all ends. I will stop being invisible because I think everyone will see me now. Everyone will see me when I am...

Roni

London, 2016

I've been praying for Nika. I used to pray for her every night when I didn't know where she was. When I began my journey to becoming a nun, she was in my prayers. When I became a nun and then a Sister and then a nun again, Nika featured in every one of my prayers.

I miss her.

Missing her is like an ache I cannot soothe. So I pray for her, I pray for her to be OK, wherever she is, for her to know how much I loved her, how much I love her still. The world doesn't feel the same without her in my life. I had her for such a short amount of time, there was so much I wanted to say. And now I won't get the chance. I've lost the best friend I ever had.

Is this the life I'm supposed to live? Without her? I don't know. I don't know. I pray for her, even though I am angry with God. I can say that now, I can say it because I know He doesn't mind if we question Him. I love Him, I always will. Because my God loves me, has given me free will, I am allowed to be angry with Him, to not understand Him, to question Him. I know His plan will be revealed in time, but in that meantime, I am angry and I am hurt and I can still love Him with all my heart.

My anger towards Dad has all but gone away. I still feel flashes of it, but no way like before. He is still accepting, still trying to navigate the way forward when Mum is refusing to engage in the divorce

437

process. Not only that, she has been – apparently – revictimised because what Mr Daneaux did has been all over the papers and she now has people questioning her mothering skills because she had no idea what he was doing to the students he classed as special.

My uncle is still being hunted by the police and I hope he can feel their approach like I used to feel his approach when we were alone in the house; I hope he feels sick and powerless and absolutely terrified.

I am waiting for God's plan for me to be revealed. In the meantime I am still supply-teaching at Chiselwick High, and praying for Nika every chance I get. Because that is all I can do.

I'll never forget the first time I saw Nika when I moved to her school. And then seeing her again in the ballet studio, her face amongst the others saying exactly what I was thinking: *I want to be a ballet dancer. I want to be one of the special ones who can go all the way.*

I miss her so much. And all I can do is pray for her, and hope I'll see her again some day.

22

Roni

'Miss! Miss! Miss Harper!'

I am in another world and only hear my name after a fair few shouts, I imagine. I stop on the pavement outside Chiselwick High. It's late and I am about to begin the journey home. I stay here late to avoid going home to my parents and the craziness in the house. I would move out but I don't want to leave Dad. He is looking for a place for us to live and said last night he thought he might have found one.

Slowly I turn to the source of the shouting and see Gail running towards me, waving her hand to get my attention. Behind her, with her arms folded across her chest and a face that tells me she would slap me silly if she could, is Gail's mother. *She* is how I always imagined mothers would behave in the wake of the news of their daughter or son being abused. Not how my mother is behaving.

'Hello, Gail,' I say. I am so happy to see her. She and her family moved away from Chiselwick after the investigation into her stepfather began, so I didn't see her before the summer holidays or now after them, when I've been teaching here.

'I've been waiting for you,' she says when she arrives in front of me. 'Emma said you were back working here but you'd probably be moving on soon? I wanted to thank you.'

441

'Thank me? I let you down in a pretty spectacular way, Gail,' I remind her. To receive confirmation of this, I glance over her shoulder and her mother glares at me in return.

Gail also looks over her shoulder at her stern, unmoved mother. 'Is that what Mum told you?' She shrugs. 'Suppose she's right in one way. But when I needed a friend, you were there for me. Even though you are weird and a teacher. And sort of a nun. Not that I've got anything against all that. I told Mum that if you'd gone to the police or told her I would have denied it. And that would have been worse because then I'd never have been able to tell her the truth. I told her that you did what I needed – you listened and you believed me and you said you'd be there for me and you encouraged me to tell. I told Mum all that.'

'And she still hates me, right?'

Gail shrugs. 'Yeah. She's kinda stubborn like that.'

'You seem so much better, Gail, I'm very pleased.'

'I'm pretending, Miss. Not all the time. Sometimes I feel OK about everything but when I don't... I pretend.'

'Don't pretend too much, OK? Your mum needs to know when you're feeling bad so she can support you. She can't take the pain away, but she loves you so much, she can do her best to be there for you.' I don't know if what I'm saying is right, but it sounds like good advice and maybe it will help Gail to not isolate herself and to give her mother the chance to help her.

'I'd better go,' she says. 'Mum only let me out because I said I'd go whether she let me or not. She was not happy when I said it was you I wanted to see. She'll get over it.' Rather than taking a step backwards, she steps forwards. 'Can I hug you?' she asks.

'Only if your mother says it's OK,' I tell her.

Gail rotates on her heels. '*MUM!*' she bellows. '*Can I hug Miss?*'

Glaring at me the whole time, her mother nods slowly. Gail throws herself into my arms, almost winding me as her body connects with mine. 'Thanks, Miss,' she says. Then she's gone, waving at me, skipping back to her mother. Her mother winds her arm around her daughter's shoulder and starts to walk away. I smile at her, try to connect, attempt to show I understand how she feels. She cuts her eyes at me and walks away. I don't blame her, not really. How can I blame her when she is behaving exactly how I wanted my mother to behave all these years?

six months later

Nika

I should be dead.

That is the long and the short of it.

I was there for at least ten minutes, they said. Ten minutes and not a single person came out for a cigarette, a coffee, to leave work, to cut through to get to the other side of the Lanes.

I should be dead.

And no one really knows why I'm not. I had extensive blood loss, his weapon nicked a major organ, my health isn't the best after years of living an impoverished lifestyle.

I suspect I know why I am still here, and I can't really tell anyone about it. They'll think I'm crazy. *I* think I'm crazy and I was there.

I kept phasing in and out. The blackness clearing for a moment, giving way to bright white agony, followed by the weightless sensation of drifting away. The thing that kept me anchored, tethered to this world, was someone whispering the words to Toto's 'Africa' in my ear. Every time I phased in, I would hear the words being whispered to me, as clear as anything, and I would cling to 'the Serengeti' and how it didn't fit. How it was a stupid word to insert into a song, as I'd told Marshall all those months ago. I believe that is what kept me here, but I can't tell anyone that.

I am healed now. Stitched up inside, sewn up outside, the wound scabbed over, the scar still in the process of scoring itself into my skin. Everyone knows I am healed. And it still hurts. I tell no one this, I want no one to know that it still hurts. Constantly. A reminder, I suppose, of how close I came.

They caught Keith Iain Junn, also known as Judge, a couple of days after he tried to kill me. DS Brennan from Birmingham explained how they finally caught up to him, but I didn't really take it in. It was something other to me, at the time, and by the time I was aware enough to ask, I didn't dare, in case anyone thought I was dwelling on the negative instead of focusing on the positive.

I saw Keith Iain Junn in the papers, suddenly a rather pathetic-looking man, and I was still scared. I shouldn't have been, I was safe, but I couldn't tell anyone that I was scared of everything now. Now that I knew how much I wanted to live, how much I wanted to be here, everything scared me because anything could harm me. It was a good thing, in a way, because it now meant I was able to feel, care about myself. I had come to see myself as someone important and worthy of being loved.

As it was, Judge, master criminal, drug dealer and pimp, decided to end his life in prison after three nights. DS Brennan from Birmingham came back to see me and to tell me he believed Judge had been helped out on that score, he was in deep with some pretty nasty people, but no one could prove anything, so nothing could be done.

When I saw DS Brennan that second time, my heart lifted because I thought he was going to tell me about Reese. When I asked, he was uncomfortable. Then he admitted everything. 'It was Reese who wanted you to leave,' he explained. 'I went to see him that night you came to the station and he told me if I persuaded you to leave for good, to go and live the life you were meant to, he would testify against Judge and he had an army of people who would testify, too. We had to move him to protect him – new name, new life.' I knew instantly why Reese had done it: no debts. He knew that his actions had originally pushed me to get involved with Judge and he wanted in some way to make it right. The policeman added: 'I asked Reese if he wanted me to pass on a message if I saw you again, and he said, "Tell her: me too." I don't know if you know what that means? But because he's in the protection scheme, you won't see him again.'

I'd secretly been harbouring the fantasy that at some point I would find Reese again, we would see each other and everything would be all right. That dream was gone. Reese, as I knew him, was dead. But he did love me. Just like I did love him. I cling to that.

My parents made the journey to see me in hospital because they had to – it was all over the papers, they couldn't avoid me *and* avoid explaining to their friends why they had disowned me. They sat on the visitors' chairs and said nothing for an hour then left again, that box ticked, that duty fulfilled.

Sasha, on the other hand, was all for moving down here to take care of me, but I managed to convince her that her husband and daughter needed her in London and to just stay with me for a little while.

Marshall takes my hand and helps me out of his car. 'Are you sure about this?' he asks. Since I came out of hospital and I forced Sasha to leave, he has been taking care of me and our entanglement has become more intense. We spend time together, listen to music and talk and laugh. We laugh so much I've almost forgotten what life was like without so much laughter. Occasionally we even have sex and make love. He knows everything about me, because it was all detailed there in the papers. I was grateful to them. After all those years of running from the limelight, of hiding my face and hiding my truth, I don't mind the press attention now. The papers say what I struggle to say, they help to find more people whose lives were shaped by the man who taught me ballet, they tell Marshall what happened so I don't need to. He knows almost everything about me now and he doesn't treat me any differently, he still wants to spend most of his free time with me.

'Am I sure about this? Yes. No. But I have to do it.'

I can walk, I am fine, I am healed but it hurts. I think I know how to stop it hurting so much.

Eliza is gone. Her flat sold, her belongings packed up and disappeared from the building almost overnight. She's gone into rehab, allegedly, but I think Marshall tells himself that to make himself feel better for calling her parents and telling them everything. She confessed to calling Judge about me to protect Marshall. She was horrified that it'd almost got me killed, but it was the straw that broke the camel's back, apparently. Marshall's rock bottom; the moment when he became all about the tough love.

Slowly, slowly I ease myself down on to the top of the stone steps outside this building in Hove, not far from Brighton. I don't need to move so gingerly, but like I said, it hurts. It truly hurts. This road is quiet and tranquil, this house seems beautiful and calm. The blue door is shut so I sit on the top step, and wait.

'Call me when you're ready to go,' Marshall says. He presses his lips on to mine, closes his eyes, rests his forehead on mine for a moment. When he pulls away, he stares into my eyes and grins at me, another way of him telling me how much he adores me. 'I... well, you know.'

He's been trying to say it to me for a while but he knows I'm not ready to hear it out loud. I'm certainly not ready to say it out loud. But I do, and he does, and we both know it.

I smile at him, hope my adoration of him is clear. 'Me, too.'

Eventually there is the creaking of the front door opening, and the footsteps of a person leaving. I haven't seen her in seven months. I couldn't. She tried to come to the hospital, she tried to come to my flat, she called and called me. And I couldn't. I simply couldn't engage with her.

Six... seven... eight and she is lowering herself to sit beside me.

'How long have you been waiting out here?' she asks.

'Long enough. I don't exactly have anywhere to be right now.'

'I thought I'd never see you again,' she says.

'And yet, you moved all the way to Hove to make sure of that,' I reply.

'It's not all about you, you know. I like it here, I feel like I fit in. And it's silent here. I've finally been able to get a glimpse at God's plan for me and this is part of it. This is where the silence is. And I've got a great job, working at a homeless shelter, and I've got a sort-of boyfriend in London. I also get to see more of my brothers because now I'm here with my dad and not my mum, they come to visit regularly.'

I close my eyes. Think of all the things I want to say to her. I would have understood if she had told me that Mr Daneaux didn't touch her again. It was bad enough it happened to me, I'd never have wanted her to go through it as well. She didn't need to lie.

'What is the one song that you're most embarrassed about listening to over and over and over?' I ask her.

'Urgh, I don't even have to think about it: Toto's "Africa". Stupid song, which makes it sound like Africa is a country. And then they manage to crowbar "Serengeti" into it. But I love it and I could listen to it again and again.'

I smile to myself.

'I'm sorry, Nika,' she states.

'You must never lie to me again,' I say to her.

'I won't. I absolutely won't. And I am so, so sorry.'

'I know.'

'No, no,' she says. 'Nika, look at me, please.'

Easing myself so as not to jar the centre of my pain, I turn towards her. She stares at me, her blue eyes are clear, open and unburdened. She seems freer. She says she has found her silence. I did not know that was what she was chasing, but she has found it and her burdens are falling away.

That part of my journey is just beginning, but I have people who unconditionally believe me. The police officer dealing with the Daneaux investigation is like a rabid dog – she is constantly on the phone, updating me, reassuring me that she will do everything she can to have him locked up. I have been referred for specialist counselling so I can start processing what I've been through. I am nowhere near where Roni is, but I'll get there.

I did not break when I was forced, every week for over eight years, to be with the man who groomed me to adore him then abused me. I did not crack when I lived with a nightmare of a boyfriend who tried to make me his dress-up sex doll. I did not shatter when I spent more than ten years without a home. I did not end when I lay in an alleyway slowly bleeding to death. I am here at the start of my recovery, and I will get there. I know I will.

Gently and carefully, as though terrified I will come apart if she presses too hard, Roni puts her hand on my face. 'I am sorry,' she states.

As carefully as she touched me, I take her hand from my face, slip my fingers between hers and hold her hand, like she's always wanted me to.

'Trust me,' I say gently, 'I know.'

THE END